For Derek,
   Who knows
Lincolnshire so well .
                Sarah Hogg

KATHERINE'S

HOUSE

KATHERINE'S HOUSE

Kettlethorpe, a modest little group of buildings deep in the English countryside, has housed many lives woven of great events and private joys and griefs. It was the home of Katherine Swynford, perhaps the most romantic figure of medieval times, but before and after her of knights and farmers, soldiers and lawyers, maids and maidservants, whose footsteps echo through the house's history. From the Viking raids of the ninth century to the bomber raids of the twentieth, through civil war and social revolution, this book is a story of life, love and loss – and a small piece of gold – over the span of eleven hundred years.

KATHERINE'S HOUSE

A NOVEL

SARAH HOGG

The Book Guild Ltd

First published in Great Britain in 2019 by
The Book Guild Ltd
9 Priory Business Park
Wistow Road, Kibworth
Leicestershire, LE8 0RX
Freephone: 0800 999 2982
www.bookguild.co.uk
Email: info@bookguild.co.uk
Twitter: @bookguild

Typeset in Sabon MT

Printed and bound in the UK by TJ International, Padstow, Cornwall

ISBN 978 1912881 499

British Library Cataloguing in Publication Data.
A catalogue record for this book is available from the British Library.

For Douglas, Charlotte, Quintin, Steve, Elizabeth, Steph, Alex, Eleanor and Cicely, who make these stones live.

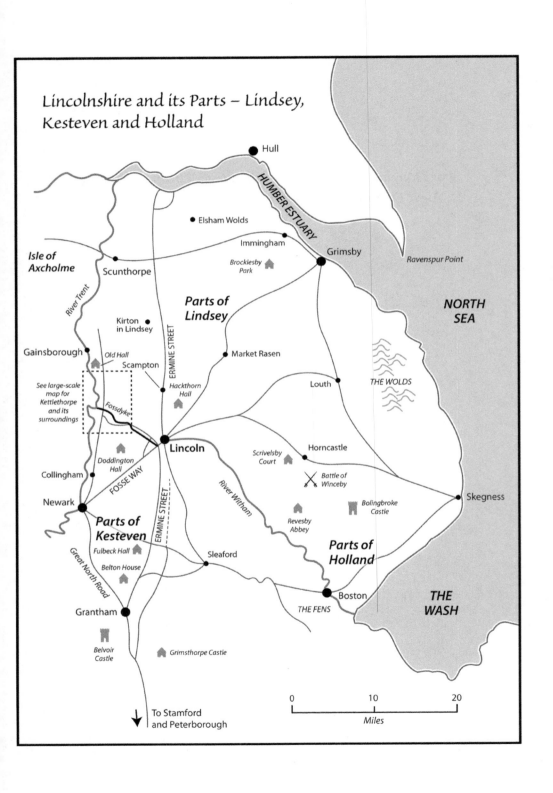

Lincolnshire and its Parts – Lindsey, Kesteven and Holland

Hull

Elsham Wolds

Immingham

HUMBER ESTUARY

Grimsby

Ravenspur Point

Brocklesby Park

Isle of Axcholme

Scunthorpe

Parts of Lindsey

NORTH SEA

River Trent

Kirton in Lindsey

ERMINE STREET

Market Rasen

Gainsborough

Old Hall

Scampton

Louth

THE WOLDS

See large-scale map for Kettlethorpe and its surroundings

Hackthorn Hall

Fossdyke

Lincoln

Scrivelsby Court

Horncastle

Doddington Hall

Battle of Winceby

Skegness

Collingham

FOSSE WAY

Bolingbroke Castle

Newark

ERMINE STREET

River Witham

Revesby Abbey

Parts of Kesteven

Parts of Holland

Great North Road

Fulbeck Hall

Belton House

Sleaford

Grantham

Boston

THE FENS

THE WASH

Belvoir Castle

Grimsthorpe Castle

0   10   20

Miles

To Stamford and Peterborough

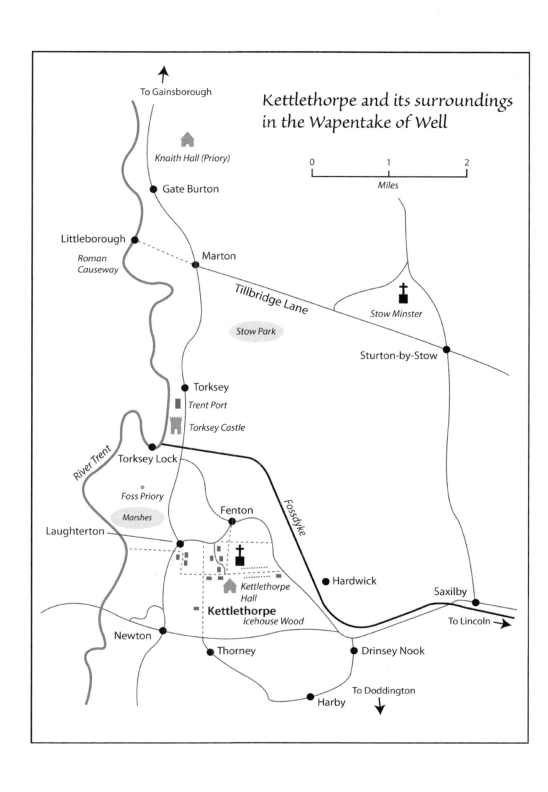

To Gainsborough

Kettlethorpe and its surroundings
in the Wapentake of Well

0   1   2

Miles

Knaith Hall (Priory)

Gate Burton

Littleborough

*Roman
Causeway*

Marton

Tillbridge Lane

Stow Minster

Stow Park

Sturton-by-Stow

Torksey

Trent Port

Torksey Castle

Torksey Lock

River Trent

Foss Priory

Marshes

Fenton

Fossdyke

Laughterton

Hardwick

Saxilby

Kettlethorpe
Hall

Kettlethorpe
Icehouse Wood

To Lincoln →

Newton

Thorney

Drinsey Nook

To Doddington

Harby

CONTENTS

THE MIDDLING SORT

GRAND DESIGNS

LITTLE WILLIE

HOMECOMING

THE GOLDEN STONE

When we had lived at Kettlethorpe for a few years, a lady wrote from Florida, asking to visit. That wasn't unusual. Kettlethorpe isn't beautiful: the size of your average Victorian parsonage, it has a lopsided front, further unbalanced by a pair of blocked windows, with a porch stuck awkwardly on the front. But it was the home of Katherine Swynford, possibly the most romantic figure of the Middle Ages.

An orphan of modest means, she became the mistress of the greatest and richest of the sons of Edward III. In his twilight years, the great Duke of Lancaster shocked the court by marrying her. The Beaufort bloodline legitimised by their union crowded on to the fifteenth-century political stage and provided the Tudors with a claim to the throne.

No wonder Katherine's story has retained a hold on the imagination of so many, and has spawned accounts, both fictional and non-fictional, of her life. On me it cast even more of a spell: when, house-hunting in the area, I found a small and unprepossessing ad for Kettlethorpe, I dragged my husband to take a look.

It was cheap, with reason. It was reassuringly unpretentious, but in pretty poor repair. Still, the sun was shining on the ruins of a medieval arch, and a boy was skating on a ditch full of frozen water to the west of the house. We were lost.

Katherine's disciples continued to call, stimulated by further books about her, notably Alison Weir's admirable biography. When the parish put on a pageant, two thousand Katherine fans came. So, on another occasion, did the lady from Florida, who unwittingly started me on this writing adventure.

She was exceptionally nice and polite, but as she left she flummoxed us. She asked if she might take a pebble from under "Katherine's arch". Should we tell her that we'd just had half a tonne of gravel delivered, to make good our muddy paths? We didn't. And then she wrote to tell us she'd had it encased in gold.

I felt glad as well as guilty. All right, Katherine's foot had never trodden that stone. But it carried history, and memories, for one pilgrim at least. That left me thinking about time and place, and the memory baked into physical objects. And so I began to find out more about the people who had, over the centuries, trodden Kettlethorpe's paths.

Of course it was Katherine's footsteps that rang loudest in my imagination. But the more I listened, the more I began to pick up the echoes of those who lived here before and after her; whose lives, if not as famous or fairy-tale, seemed to be as full of events as hers.

John de Ken, who survived the turbulence of the early thirteenth century, culminating in the Battle of Lincoln Fair.

Katherine's children, whose lives were transformed when, in 1399, their step-brother Henry of Bolingbroke landed in the Humber estuary.

Isabel Hall, daughter of Charles, who was the Parliamentarian owner of Kettlethorpe when a Civil War skirmish outside the house left half a dozen dead.

Sir Wharton Emerson Amcotts, aspiring baronet, who gave Kettlethorpe a brief moment of eighteenth-century grandeur.

The North American bomber aircrew who came to earth in Kettlethorpe in 1944.

It was these stories, and more, that gave me the idea behind this book: to write about the long sweep of history as seen through the prism of a single house. That was the link between them; but I would use another to forge the chain. A small piece of gold.

HISTORICAL NOTE

Kettlethorpe was never a stately home, and only briefly a substantial building. But from invaluable research carried out by an Edwardian clergyman-scholar, living nearby in beautiful Doddington, I could trace its owners back to the shadowy, probably ninth-century, figure of Ketil, through to the early twentieth century, when village memory (and the Lincolnshire archives) could take up the story. And I soon began to realise something these ghosts had in common: that the house had given them ringside seats at some of the greatest events in England's history.

At first I thought it was because of Kettlethorpe's proximity to historic Lincoln. The city's strategically important Roman fortifications were built at the junction of Ermine Street and the Fosse Way; part of those walls still stands. What is probably England's most beautiful cathedral still dominates the skyline for miles around. Game-changing battles were fought in Lincoln in the twelfth and thirteenth centuries. The city was on every Royal Progress planner's to-do list, and on Cromwell's to-capture list. So to live near Lincoln was, perhaps, to live at the gate of history.

But Lincoln was in decline even in Katherine Swynford's time, when it had lost the wool staple, and it has been out of the way ever since. Engineering gave it a day or two of glory in the early twentieth century, but Dr Beeching severed most of its railway connections in the 1960s. It wasn't until the 1990s, when it finally founded a university, that the city began a renaissance.

Something closer to home was of much greater significance to Kettlethorpe's history – the River Trent.

From the Viking raids, and the Norman colonisation, through the Civil War, history has swept through the Humber estuary, up the Trent into the heart of England. And Kettlethorpe's stretch of the Trent was strategically important.

To get north from London, up the main eastern route through England via York to Scotland, you needed to cross the Trent or the Humber. Ermine Street ran north from London, through Lincoln, and on Roman-straight to the Humber – but then you needed a ferry, for a tricky crossing.

So the Romans had constructed an offshoot of Ermine Street from north of Lincoln to the Trent, and a causeway across it at Marton (only four miles north of Kettlethorpe), roughly where the river becomes tidal. Harold Godwinson used that route, on his hasty march north to deal with brother Tostig, before doubling back to fight Duke William. William Marshal used the same road, to march to battle with the French.

But when the Great North Road superseded Ermine Street, the marching armies crossed the Trent nearly twenty miles further south. Only if one side held Newark, as the Royalists did throughout the first Civil War, was the other again forced to look for crossing points farther north. (Cromwell built a bridge of boats, at Gainsborough.)

All these links were vital to conquerors and defenders alike – the more so because just a mile from Kettlethorpe, at Torksey, the Romans had dug the Fossdyke, to connect the Trent through Lincoln via the Witham to Boston and the east coast. The little outcrop of Lincolnshire that includes Kettlethorpe, in the old Danish district, the wapentake of Well, has frequently been a war zone.

The more I learnt about the people who lived in it, the more they wrote their own stories. But my account – dialogue, emotions, actions, even some of the protagonists – is of course fiction. A bastard or two here, a brother or lover there – they were needed for the thread of my story.

Because Kettlethorpe's inhabitants were so often of the "middling sort" – soldiers of fortune, farmers, at most minor gentry – it was easy to give them walk-on parts at great events without betraying history. But after each chapter, I have added a confessional – distinguishing between real and imagined characters, or real characters to whom I have given imagined roles.

A wonderful array of relevant documents was brought to Lincoln in 2017, at the instigation of Lord Cormack, Chairman of the Historic Lincoln Trust. The *Battles and Dynasties* exhibition contained priceless material from as far away as the De Morgan Library in New York.

Lincolnshire is a county in which roots run deep. A remarkable number of the names that appear in the story survive in the county, even in the local villages, today: Dymoke, Willoughby, Fane, Heneage, Monson, Thorold, Pelham, Wells, Cole, Turgoose, Arden. If I have traduced their ancestors, I can only apologise. I am deeply grateful to those who helped: particularly the Eleys at Hackthorn, whose office manager miraculously produced for me the Kettlethorpe rent roll for 1645. And my particular thanks go to Air Vice-Marshal Paul Robinson and Dr Nicholas Bennett, for reading parts of my manuscript and making such helpful suggestions.

As my thanks do above all to my family, and especially my grandson and editor, Alex. They have put up with my growing obsession, and the increasing amount of time I have spent living with ghosts, trying to give colour to shadows, hoping to touch these stones with gold.

THE SAXON GIRL

FOSSDYKE MARSHES: 873

I n the sharp spring sunshine it looked a good place. The pasture in the clearing, Ketil noticed, was already a rich green – boggy ground in places, no doubt, but lighter in others, and fine for beasts if it were to be ditched well.

He'd found the little cluster of huts by sheer chance. They were hidden from the track alongside the old silted-up Fossdyke by a slight drop in the land. He and his men had been trampling their way along the dyke's overgrown banks, in hopes of finding it was still a passable route from the Trent to the big trading post at Lincylene.

They'd found it blocked beyond hope where its course swung east. Frustrated, he and his men had struck inland to find a shortcut back to the river.

The river! So much of Ketil's life had been spent on the water, from the North Sea through the Humber estuary to the Trent, up which the longships had sailed and rowed into the heart of Saxon England. It was tricky to navigate, tidal from just about here, with the strong current that gave the river its ancient name. But he had plundered along its shores since he was a youngster, and now he had his own longship and crew to provide for, and the pickings were getting leaner.

Raids had turned into a fight for land, and had driven deeper into the countryside: the settlement at Stow, with its great Anglo-Saxon church, had been burnt to the ground just three years ago. Viking settlements had spread along the Trent. Torchesey – Turc's island, at the junction of the Trent and Fossdyke – had been turned into a military stronghold: Ketil had spent last winter encamped there with the Great Danish Army, before it moved north to Jorvik.

If he was going to settle anywhere, Ketil thought, this would make as much sense as most. It was close enough to the river for security, far enough to be out of its flood plain. There'd be marsh fever here, of course, but so there always was in the lower ground west of the ridge that ran south from Jorvik through Lincylene to Ancastre. Horseflies and mosquitoes in summer, but rich hay, fine crops. Yes, a good place.

They had seen the raiders too late, these Saxon churls, and had struggled to close the gate to their flimsy palisade. They'd escaped previous raids, hidden as they were: Ketil could see none of the telltale signs of blackened ruins and scorched ground. Plenty of livestock, too.

They had plainly grown careless of their good fortune. A proper ditch around the compound would have quickly filled with water, greatly strengthening its defences. As it was, the men were no match for Ketil and his crew, who simply struck them aside, bludgeoning a couple to pulp to cow the others. The women, children and livestock had been chased into their huts, which made things simple. Set fire to the hut, and people or beasts would run out soon enough, while his men stood ready.

Ketil thought about his men. There was his brother, Erik; he could sail back home with a skeleton crew and bring his wife, children and the old man – if he would come, rheumatic and cross-grained as he was now. The rest of them must stay here, meanwhile, to guard the settlement.

Ketil had no wife, though he had got a child by one of their Saxon captives, the twelve-year-old son now by his side. The girl had died giving birth to this boy, a baby endowed with Ketil's big bones. She'd been too young, Ketil's mother said, and scolded him for wasting chattels.

He'd take a woman here, to warm his bed. He wouldn't burn this hamlet: he'd put the men to work for him, hand out the women, farm the land, put down roots. Pity about the Fossdyke. But there was always the Trent. And plenty of good, mature timber to build a longhouse.

Emboldened by the long silence, a head peeped out of the big hut in the centre of the compound, before being jerked abruptly back inside. A girl, dark blond, with startling blue eyes. Young, but not too young. That one, he thought.

873–1066

"*Thorps*" – *small hamlets* – *with Danish names sprang up throughout Lincolnshire and Yorkshire. Ketil's survived long enough to acquire his name; I chose the Danish encampment at Torchesey in the early 870s as a likely-enough genesis of this settlement, but, like everything else in this prelude to my story, it can only be a guess.*

Five years later, after Guthrum's defeat by Alfred at the Battle of Edington, peace was brokered between Wessex and the Danes, who settled down to imitate the wealth-creating farming methods of the Anglo-Saxons. Sheep grazed the Lincolnshire wolds and flatlands, as well as the South Downs.

Peace negotiations took eight years, and it took still longer for England to become a single, Christian realm, with Danish rulers resurgent in the eleventh century. Under Cnut, England was briefly part of a North Sea empire embracing Denmark, Norway and part of Sweden. For this, the Humber remained a vital artery of rule, with the Scandinavian army based at Gainsborough.

But by the second half of the eleventh century, intermarriage had blurred the difference between Dane and Saxon. So, too, it had between the "English" combination of the two, and another tribe of Scandinavians in Normandy, whose ruler now laid claim to the English throne.

And as King Harold Godwinson discovered, cousins and even siblings could fight each other quite as enthusiastically as Saxon had once fought Dane. In 1066, he found himself threatened from both the Humber and the Channel. He took himself north first.

And in Lincolnshire, Sheriff Marleswein raised the fyrd to support him.

THE FALLING SPARROW

KETIL'S THORP: 1066–76

Erik Ketilson rolled over on to his back with a satisfied sigh. No hurry. No one could see them here: the top of the stack of hay sank in the middle, making a sheltered, invisible nest. The sun, sliding down to the west through an almost cloudless sky, was still wonderfully warm for late September.

Harvest was safe in the byres, but there was still no chill in the air, only a soft breeze from the south-west. It was a last precious summer afternoon. He dozed.

Albertha lay in the crook of his arm. Waking, he squeezed her little round breast, feeling aroused again. But she woke with a start, and sat up, pushing him off. "I must be home, before I'm missed." She gave him a sly smile, conscious of his desire, but reached for her blue gown.

Erik waited until she was entangled in it, then shoved her back down, pulling up her skirt and using it to trap her arms and muffle her protests. He parted her thighs and her protests turned into little moans of pleasure as he fondled her, before entering her again. She arched her back and then wrapped her legs around him. They came together, pleasurably, easily, naturally, as young creatures do.

He sank on to her breast, pulled the skirt back to let her breathe, and gently bit her neck. "Some men," he muttered provocatively, "say you should tie a wife's hands when you bed her, to stop her hindering your pleasure." His father had quoted that old pot-house advice to him, after a few horns of mead, to provoke his mother – a Jarl's daughter, who considered she had married well beneath her.

They had all known it was a boorish tease, to get a reaction from her. But she had run to the priests at Stow, and secured him a half-hearted reproof from Father Petroc. Ketil knew he had donated too much to the rebuilding of the great Minster at Stow for most of the other canons to worry about a little ill-use of a woman. Hardly a crime: a wife was property, after all. And even Father Petroc, who had advanced ideas about women's souls, found it hard to see Ketil's formidable wife as a victim.

Albertha turned her head away. "But I am not your wife." Another secret smile. "And it's my pleasure, too."

He let her up, and helped her to dress, lacing up the back of her gown. She gartered her short hose, slapping his hand away as it slid up her leg, and made a rueful face at her crumpled cap, pulling it over her dark curls and tying it tightly under her chin.

"You shall be my wife." And why not? She was weddable as well as beddable. He was a good, even a very good, match for her: her father's lands, between Leugttricdun and Neutone, were not as good as at Ketil's Thorp: they were flooded by the Trent one year in three. Her father was always having to beg pasture for his beasts. But they and the lands would come with her, as she had no brothers, and march well with those Erik would inherit.

She looked at him, not smiling now. "I am hand-fasted."

He knew it. They had been meeting like this all through the summer, and he had not dared to ask her for certain. But gossip in the pot-house he frequented at Neutone had already put fabulous sums on the bride-price Jehann Comberlayn was paying for her. He was rich enough for the stories to be true. The money came from dues exacted at his grain store, by the causeway across the Trent between Martone and Littelburg.

"I will fight for you," Erik said, with more bravado than he felt. Comberlayn was old, and fat, but wealthy enough to hire a champion. And Erik, truth be told, had never faced anything more challenging than a bout at staves with the best of his father's men, who weren't hired to kill him.

He had mustered with his father early in the year, riding south when the saintly King Edward died, after a twenty-four-year reign, and Harold Godwinson called up the fyrd to support his succession. But the storm had passed, Harold's rebel brother had fled, and the fyrd had been sent home without any fighting.

Still, Erik was eighteen now, and had nearly succeeded in growing a warrior's moustaches. He was inordinately proud of them. His mother laughed, dismissively, but his little sister admired them. He was a fine-looking young man, with the golden hair of Norse heroes, bright blue eyes, and long limbs.

"I will fight for you," he said again, trying to sound confident. Perhaps Comberlayn would back away.

Albertha looked at Erik, thoughtfully. She always seemed to know what he was thinking: perhaps she was a seer. He had suggested that, once, to his parents, in the hope of raising Albertha's status in their eyes.

His mother had been caustic. "Every fool wench knows what a fool boy is thinking." And his father had said shortly that he wanted to hear no more of the girl. When the time came for Erik to wed, they would find him a worthy bride, one they were ready to pay a price for.

Erik shrugged on his tunic and jumped down, to lift Albertha to the ground. Holding her close, he toyed with the idea of tumbling her again, for the fun of disordering the gown she had striven to make neat. But the light was fading and she spoke true: she should get back. And he was hungry.

"Maybe Father Petroc at Stow will wed us, if he knows we have lain together," he said, hopefully. "He has always had a kindness for me, since a child." Would that kindness extend to provoking his father's wrath? Unlikely. Ah well, it would be worth a try: no use looking to the sorry little Ketil's Thorp priest, who was under his father's thumb. "Come, I'll take you home."

She shook her head, alarmed at the idea. "My father will kill you if he sees you with me. Talk to your father first."

"I will," he promised. "This very evening. And he will find a bride-price." He felt a glow of happy assurance, though he knew it was misplaced. His mother would sniff, his father would jib at the price. And he would not want to make an enemy of Comberlayn.

In the mellow evening they walked hand in hand to the Sallie Bank, the ridge of earth thrown up to mark his father's boundary. He watched her run lightly along the track home. The hay that still stuck to the embroidered hem of her gown made him grin, wondering how she'd explain that away to her father. But he was doting fond, her mother was dead and her nurse no tale-teller. Albertha would talk her way out of trouble; she always did.

He turned and loped back across the moor, giving the shepherd boy a friendly wave. But as his home came in sight, before the haystack and fish pond, he checked in surprise. It was like an ant's nest. Men were pouring through the gate, or clustering outside it, and there were sounds of horses and harnesses, excited hounds, tramping boots and shouts of command.

Erik broke into a run, jumped the ditch, or most of it, scrambled up the ramparts and squeezed through a smaller wicket gate in the palisade to avoid the scrum. He burst into the farmyard just as his father came out of the house.

"In Odin's name, boy," his father started, then looked round guiltily to see if Father Petroc had heard him. The Norse gods came more easily to his lips than the name of Christ. But he had of course been christened: with a Bishop as his overlord, that went without saying, and he tried not to offend the church's sensibilities, reverting to the old ways only when out of its reach.

On winter evenings, when not abusing his stuck-up wife, he would bawl out the old songs of rape and pillage from the longships, though he himself had never been farther to sea than the mouth of the Humber. It had sounded, Erik thought, as if the Vikings did much more rutting than raiding: but he guessed his father's choice of songs was calculated to annoy his mother.

She would sit at her loom, lips pressed, jerking the weft in her irritation. His sister had once been foolish enough to point out that she was pulling it much too tight, and had got slapped for her pains.

This evening, it seemed, Father Petroc had come as a messenger. From his fleeting grin, he had certainly heard Ketil's pagan oath, but he was not foolish enough to rebuke a warrior, not in times of war. And war, Erik realised with a quickening of his pulse, was the message that had been brought.

Ketil swung back to his son. "Get your arse over to the armoury before I stick a spear up it, and collect what you need. Then go find your mother, she's packed your saddlebags, no doubt with rubbish. Find those thick boots I gave you and a padded tunic, you'll need them. And take something to eat on the way, I can't wait for you to fill your belly."

"What's happened?" Erik asked.

Ketil swore again. "That whoreson Tostig has come back up the Humber with an army, that's what's happened. I knew he would."

He turned away, to get the milling men into marching order. But his frustration went on spilling out of him, in a tirade against the folly of the Godwin family.

"Harold should have put Tostig's eyes out before he took the throne, brother or no, not let the bastard slip away to Norway. I said at the time, he'd never be safe on his throne with Tostig at large. And now Tostig's brought Hardarda down on us. They say he's fought and won one battle already. Hurry, boy. We need all the light left to get to Litelburg tonight."

"Litelburg?" Erik was bemused, his mind still full of Comberlayn, and his big grain store on the way there, close by the causeway across the Trent, selling to travellers at prices they could not afford to refuse. "Why?"

Ketil stared at him. "Has your brain dropped between your legs? We'll meet the army there, of course, when it crosses the river. King Harold's at Lincoln, and Marleswein's raising the fyrd for him across the shire. Word is, Tostig and Hardrarda have taken Jorvik. We're marching north to drive them out. So hurry, you fool. Hurry."

Erik cast a quick look round the yard. His father was one of the chief men of the wapentake of Well, this western district of Lindsey in a loop of the Trent. Most of his neighbours seemed to have answered his hasty summons. Sheriff Marleswein should be pleased; it was a strong contingent. He could see Albertha's father, with a knot of his men from Neutone; the brawny blacksmith from Fenton, with his sons; and a small group of ruffians from Drinsey.

Few were mounted: the fyrd fought on foot, behind a shield wall. Only the wealthier ones, like his father, rode to the battlefield, and even then they would dismount to fight. A shiver ran up Erik's spine at the thought of the shield wall, where every man depended on the courage of his neighbour.

But at least all these men would be well equipped: his father had seen to that. A train of pack animals was being loaded with mail shirts too heavy to march in, helmets and shields, as well as sacks of meal and dried meat.

Leofric, his father's servant, was bringing Erik's own horse, his mail shirt strapped behind the saddle. Erik's little sister was weaving her way across the yard towards them, bursting with self-importance but struggling under the weight of his saddlebags, followed by a wench with his boots and some food. Erik hastened to relieve them of their burdens. Typical of his mother, that she wouldn't carry anything out herself.

His father was already mounted, and was now leading off. Erik hurriedly buckled on the bags, pulled on his boots, grabbed the food and vaulted on to his own mount, scrambling to catch up.

On the right, just outside the gate in the palisade, the Ketil's Thorp priest feebly squeaked a blessing, shaking holy water at them. Erik saw Ketil touch his amulet, in response. He grinned. Trust his father. Pagan to the heart. Well, as for Erik, he'd take a blessing, whichever God it came from.

But as he made a clumsy sign of the cross with half a loaf in his hand, his horse took exception to the priest's waving Aspergillum, shying to the left. And as Erik steadied the beast, his eye was caught by a small figure in a blue gown and white cap. She was running towards them, through the dusk, along the track by the fish pond, a larger woman lumbering behind.

He stood up in his stirrups and waved, laughing with the thrill of war, wanting to wait, just to tell her the news. But his father raised his arm in command, and when he swung the column ahead past the little church, Erik's own horse bounded after its stablemates.

And they were gone.

*

Jehann Comberlayn was dead. He had been skewered by one of King Harold's men, when he asked too much for the grain in his store, the day the army arrived on the Lindsey side of the river. It had happened just a day after the men joining the fyrd had left Ketil's Thorp. Albertha said a Mass for him, ashamed at how her heart had lifted at the news.

It sang with hope at the more momentous news that followed, of King Harold's great victory in the North. At Stamford Bridge – won, they said, without much loss in the local fyrd. Could her dream possibly come true? Might Erik return and ask for her, with his battle honours, brushing his parents' doubts aside? She had hugged the thought to herself. And waited for him to come home.

She knew, soon enough, that it could be a long wait. For next they learnt that Harold's army had gone south again. Or rather, that the part of it had gone which still had mounts fit to carry them. There was need of speed: word had come that William of Normandy had landed.

Sheriff Marleswein was left to govern the North, and the Lincolnshire contribution to this forced march south was small. But Ketil stayed with the King, and Erik with him. Ever the opportunist, Albertha's father followed, though well in the rear: he stopped off at home with news, and the usual string of fussy instructions, on his way.

Erik did not stop. But a small cloth package came secretly to Albertha as the army passed, confirmation that he was safe and loved her. It held a heavy ring of rough gold, with a red gem sunk into it. No doubt it had been plundered from the battlefield; it was a warrior's ring, far too big for her. She hung it on a wool strand around her neck, hidden beneath her gown.

No news came from the south for a time, but they had expected that. Hope survived even the first accounts of the battle that had taken place near Hastings. King Harold's forces, Abertha and her household learnt, had had the advantage of the ground, dug in up on a hillside. Duke William had sent wave after wave of warriors up against the shield wall, but it had not broken, and the Normans had suffered much loss.

Then the stories got a little worse. The Normans had not been defeated: it had been a slaughter on both sides. Still, the fyrd was fighting on. Soon after that, however, came the news that King Harold was dead. He had died on the battlefield, it was said, amongst his men.

All was not lost, even so. A pedlar from the south, seeking business in less troubled regions, had it on good authority that Edgar the Atheling, the fifteen-year-old great-nephew of King Edward, had been named by the Witan as Harold's successor. He was said to be continuing the fight. But then came the dispossessed from Winchester: Duke William, they reported, had taken the ancient capital – and the royal Treasury.

Albertha went to seek enlightenment of Father Petroc. If true, he had explained gently, that meant Duke William could now pay his mercenaries to complete his conquest, and send them far and wide to secure territory for themselves. It was a bad sign that Archbishop Stigand had abandoned Edgar, transferring his allegiance to the Duke. William's way was clear to London, where resistance was fading. And, Father Petroc said gently, if those dear to Albertha did not come home soon, maybe it was because they could not come.

London! Few in Lindsey had been there, and certainly not Albertha. She knew more of Winchester, the old royal borough of the Saxon Kings, though she had not been there, either. But London had been made more important by King Edward, Father Petroc said – "Saint Edward, rather, for though he has yet been canonised, he surely will be!" The King had built a new palace just to the west of London, on Thorney, an island in the Thames.

Then, Father Petroc had explained, very willing to distract Albertha from her troubles, the Saint had begun his life's work. It was the creation of a new West Minster to rival what was now called the East Minster, the greatest church in the old city. The new church had sadly been ready for consecration only last December, when King Edward was already in his last illness. But at least the Saint could be buried there, and rest in peace inside his glorious gift to God.

"Is it bigger than the minster here?" Albertha had asked timidly. Stow's was a great church, the biggest she had ever seen. Father Petroc had smiled, a little abashed. "Daughter, to tell truth, I have not been to London, nor seen the West Minster. But I believe so. And they say Duke William plans to be crowned there, not in Winchester, to take the oath by King Edward's tomb."

That, Father Petroc thought privately, would be the masterstroke: it would crown victory with legitimacy, in some English eyes at least. Peace would not come quickly, but it was time to put aside hopes of William of Normandy's defeat.

Yet Albertha's own private hopes had not quite been extinguished. She had not heard from Erik, but she had not heard ill of him, either. All the same, the waiting became harder as she began to suspect she had another secret. In the end she had found she could not carry the burden on her own.

Wary of telling her local priest, she again sought the counsel of Father Petroc.

He heard her confession; poor child, he thought, there would be plenty with the same grief, both widowed and unwed. Armies always scattered their seed as they passed. There would be much hardship this winter.

A kindly man, he tried to offer comfort as well as absolution. "The Lord will hold you in His hand," he assured Albertha: "God is mindful even of the sparrow, which does not fall to the ground without Him knowing, and putting out his hand. Wait, and have faith."

She waited, and clung to faith, or at least to hope. But now she had to let that go. Father Petroc had been wrong. All, she now knew, was lost: her faith, her love, her hopes, her own and her child's future, all had died on Senlac Hill.

Her father had come home, and told her plainly what had happened, all the long way down south.

"They died bravely," he said, a little grudgingly. "Senlac Hill, the place is called. It was a long battle – God save us, it went on for hours. Ketil Ketilson fell late in the day, so they say, close up with the housecarls around Godwinson's body. His young fool of a son stepped out of the shield wall to try to protect him. One of M'Duke's horsemen cut him down."

He saw no need to dwell on the fact that many of the bodies had been so despoiled and mutilated that their mothers would have had difficulty in recognising them. What had been done to King Harold's corpse, however, was news that was spreading fast, so he hastened to tell Albertha that the Conqueror had been deeply shocked, and showed his anger.

"M'Duke has banished Godwinson's butcher from his army," he said, approvingly.

Shocked? Or thought it politic to seem so, Albertha guessed; how gullible men are, when they want to believe something. And she wondered when, for her father, "The King" and "William the Bastard" had become "Godwinson" and "Monsieur le Duc".

Before the battle, she thought: her father had clearly not been part of the last stand on Senlac Hill. Nor, like some of their neighbours, had he come back to collect his possessions and flee to the Fens, where resistance to William was rumoured to be gathering. Her father had always had an eye for the winning side.

And he had not come home alone.

"I am in the train of Sieur Jean de Caen," he said proudly. De Caen was, it seemed, one of three knights sent with a small force to this strategic wapentake on the Trent. They were to act as a foreguard for a new Bishop of Dorchester, its overlord, whose diocese included Lindsey and indeed Lincoln itself.

It was rumoured, Albertha's father told her importantly, that the warrior-cleric Remigius de Fecamp, kin to the Duke, would be appointed, in recompense for his support. These were his men: three of the warriors that Remigius had supplied to King William, Albertha was told, in support of his rightful claim to the English throne.

Sieur Odo de la Croix would take lands further north along the Trent, beyond the Fossdyke, to protect the causeway; Sieur Guy de la Haye would take most of the troop to Lincoln itself, where a new Sheriff would surely be appointed, given how close Marleswein had been to Harold Godwinson.

Numbed by despair, Albertha scarcely heard this long recital of shire business. Eventually her father stopped, and looked at her more closely. "Forgive me, girl, I had forgot you lost your swain. But you need not grieve for Comberlayn any longer, I have a better match for you than that old miser."

Her father was still talking. "So go and make yourself fine, my girl, and do me proud. Your best gown, those brooches of your mother's, God rest her soul. Pinch your cheeks, you're very pale. Where's your distaff? He should not see you idle, you'll have a household to run. And chaste. I've sworn to him you're chaste: where's Pora? Get her to leave her tasks and sit with you."

She looked at him blankly. He checked his impatience, but his anxiety showed. "Sieur Jean is coming, girl, I came on ahead to see all's ready. If he finds you to his liking, he'll wed you. And make me steward of all his lands. I've done well for you, as I said."

There was indignation in his voice, that she had not shown gratitude. But there was pleading in his eyes. He needed her, she realised, to win the trust and favour of his new master. And she realised, at the same moment, that she needed to win this Norman stranger, too.

She would not wear the blue gown. But otherwise she would do her best. Pora brushed her curls, spit-and-polished her brooches and clipped them on the warm red gown that heightened Albertha's pallor but also enhanced her dignity. She sat docilely twirling her distaff, Pora at her side. When Jean de Caen came, she raised her wide grey eyes to him. She gave him her smile that lit up her face. And hid all her secrets.

*

Father Petroc, it turned out, had not been so wrong after all.

Sieur Jean wed Albertha within days, before the cringing Ketil's Thorp priest. She wore the same red gown, veiled her hair, and hid her ring: later, she would take it to a goldsmith in Lincoln, and have it beaten into an ornament she could wear without question. Jean bedded her with a brisk brutality that touched no memories, and departed to "pacify" the countryside, on his way south again for Duke William's coronation.

It was not how Albertha had hoped to come to marriage and motherhood, but it was a chance. Enchantment was broken, summer was over. Now, for the sake of the life she carried, as well as her own, she must contrive to survive the harsh winter of reality.

The longhouse at Ketil's Thorp had been abandoned. Erik's mother had taken her daughter to sanctuary in Stow, fearing further reprisals against what were now called rebels.

Albertha and her father celebrated Christmas alone, learning later that King William had been crowned in the Abbey that very day. Jean came back in the new year. She told him she thought she was with child: it should be born at Lammastide. He was pleased with her, assigned three of his most trusted men-at-arms to watch over her, and left again with all the rest.

Jean and his men were hunting rebels in the North when, during haymaking, the baby came. As her pains started, Pora helped her drag herself to a cott in the woods, where she and the baby could cry out unheard. It was a long, agonising night, but as dawn broke she was delivered of a healthy child.

Pora cared for the baby in secret while Albertha walked abroad with a pillow under her gown, so Jean's men could see she was coming close to her time. At Lammas she retired into her chamber, and next day sent one of his men with news of the birth of a fine boy to Jean. He came home six weeks later to find a well-grown child at his mother's breast, christened John.

He had bright blue eyes and a fuzz of dark gold hair, much fairer than Jean's or Albertha's. Her father, however, swore the child was the image of his grandmother. Jean nodded, took John in his arms, and gave him the kiss.

God had stretched out his hand, and caught the falling sparrow.

*

So now she had a life. A new life – a better life, Albertha knew, than most. Not what she had known before: love, and laughter, and the careless confidence of youth in its own invulnerability. Those were gone, along with the peace and plenty of her childhood. All our memories of childhood are filled with the sunny days: but to Albertha it seemed as if she had lived in the Garden of Eden, before the serpent found his way there.

All her life, until last Christmas, England had been ruled by one King, Edward. It was his death, and a quarrel between brothers, that had opened the chink in England's armour through which Duke William had forced his way. Irony of ironies, it was the rich pickings, the produce of peace, that had drawn him: the prosperous farms with their cattle and grain, the fat sheep grazing the southern hills.

Now the Norman hand lay heavy on the land. For all he claimed right of inheritance, and swore to rule by the old ways, Duke William made his own, brutal laws. More and more of the north of the country was "pacified"; the smell of burning homesteads wafted up the Trent. And year by year, Albertha noted, even the collaborators found their privileges and lands given to Norman incomers.

It went hard with the thegns, with their role in the governance of the country so deep-rooted, to find themselves vassals without rights, exiles in their own country. There was no choice of ruler for them now; the Witan had become King William's servants. He would tell them what to do, not the other way round.

A high rate of geld was levied. Those who struggled to pay found their property transferred to any Norman who offered to find the money instead: and so Albertha's husband built up his holdings amongst the properties of the dispossessed. There were only a few native-born who managed to play the same game and keep the Conqueror sweet: men like Colsuen, who became one of the greatest landowners in Lincolnshire. Jean hated him, and so did the dispossessed.

It went hard even with the clergy, who – with the Pope's blessing on Duke William – had turned swiftly to the winning side. How desperately they tried to preserve the wealth of their churches and abbeys, scuttling to make friends with the Conqueror! How confounded they were to find their friendship unvalued, and themselves briskly replaced by Normans.

But few dared speak against it. An extraordinary exception was Guitmond of La Croix-St Leuffroy – one of Duke William's own, a monk from Normandy. Astonishingly, he refused all offers of preferment: *I deem all England to be the spoils of robbery, and shrink from it and its treasures as a consuming fire.*

So Father Petroc quoted admiringly to Albertha, when she came to visit him at Stow. He was frail, now, but his mind was as good as ever, and word came to him from all over England and beyond. He trusted Albertha, as she trusted him, and shared dangerous news of resistance and rebellion with her, while knowing neither of them ever could – or, to be honest, ever would – take part. Still, they enjoyed exchanging rumours, of the Earls in the North, or Hereward in the Fens, refusing to accept Norman rule three, five, eight years after William landed.

There were moments of excitement, as when Edgar the Atheling surfaced again, here in Lindsey, with Danish troops. But these moments never lasted long. And while her heart stayed in rebellion, slowly, inexorably, Albertha found her mind tugged to the Norman side of the argument, by her marriage, by her family, by her longing for peace.

For conquest went hardest of all, Albertha reflected, with women. They were not people, to be accepted or outlawed, but simply chattels, the spoils of conquest, expected to yield value commensurate to the risks taken to win their possession.

Her husband was, she realised, better than most of the motley crew of adventurers, soldiers of fortune with little to lose, who had been attracted to William the Bastard's gamble. Jean did not ill-treat her, even when she failed to breed any more boys; he and John seemed quite content with each other, and with her girl babies, who thrived.

His was not an easy life, she soon realised. It had begun harshly, as a waif clinging to life in the gutters of Caen. "A bastard, like Duke William himself," Jean would tell Albertha. He had had to fight hard for survival, harder still for his advancement in William's service, of which he was immensely proud.

But even now, it all had to be earned. Jean was not left to enjoy the spoils of conquest, to manage his lands and bully his new tenants. He was called to arms by Bishop Remigius, whenever resistance flared in the region.

As it frequently did, in those early years of the Conqueror's reign. Lindsey was border country, between the settled south and the wild north. It was bounded by forests to the west, across the Trent, and marshland to the south-east, around the Wash. These were both good hiding places for the dispossessed, the *silvatici*, the wild men of the woods. They were hunted, and killed, but always there were more.

Stories grew up around them that would last hundreds of years. They gave rise to myths that were the solace of a people who had become an underclass. Later, they would be romanticised by those who had survived and prospered, the very people who had outlawed the *silvatici* and breathed easier when they were gone.

Duke William brought his army to deal with the rebels cornered in the Isle of Axholme, up in the north-western corner of Lindsey, in the most serious confrontation between Conqueror and conquered to take place in the early years of Norman rule. But he left Remigius to deal with the further unrest along the Trent, which eventually provoked the deliberate destruction of much of Torchesey, just along the road from Albertha's home.

It was a fearful slaughter, and outlying hamlets like Ketil's Thorp were razed to the ground. That was a bad time for Albertha. Though her home at Neutone was untouched, among the destitute refugees struggling south were many known to her from childhood. She struggled through the sorrow, with the smell of burning in her nostrils and hatred rekindled in her soul.

A castle, of course, had been swiftly constructed in the old Roman fortress of Lindum, presided over by the new Norman sheriff. Marleswein had fled north again. Here in Lincoln as elsewhere, castle-building – and the raising of geld to finance it – had been the Normans' first stamp of authority.

Remigius, by the time the castle was completed, had moved the headquarters of his bishopric from Dorchester, on the Thames, all the way north to frontier country – to Lincolnshire. He rebuilt the nave of Stow Minster, but it was to Lincoln he was bound, on King

William's orders. He was planning a new cathedral there. If he built on top of Lincoln hill, alongside the castle, it would dominate the skyline from far and wide – unlike Stow Minster, which sat in low ground, and could be seen only from the villages around.

A cathedral at the top of Lincoln would be a reminder of God's power, and of the Bishop's authority. Or so Father Petroc told Albertha, wryly, as Stow Minster lost its status and servants. He was too old to move, he said; and what use would he be in the new Bishop's household?

She visited Father Petroc as often as she could. To begin with she would always pay her respects to Erik's mother, too; but those dutiful visits were never a success. The widow sat in her cell surrounded by the household treasures she had taken with her from Ketil's Thorp, burning up with bitterness at her fate.

With a sad, twisted logic, she blamed her dead husband for her misfortune, complaining again and again that Ketil should have had the good sense to ignore Marleswein and support Duke William, and building fantasies about what her position might have been if he had. Yet at the same time she upbraided Albertha as a traitor, scorning her for stooping to marry a Norman adventurer. Just, she said, what could have been expected of a Saxon wench.

Albertha made these purgatorial visits largely for the sake of Erik's sister, that lively and lovely child. She had grown into a pale and awkward young woman, oppressed by her mother's anger. Once, she managed to slip out in time to walk with Albertha around the minster, and whispered fiercely that she would escape as soon as she could, to the new priory at the Fosse: they had salvaged enough for her to take a good dowry, and she would steal it from her mother if she had to.

Albertha promised to help. But she did not tell Jean any of this, least of all about the treasures hidden at Stow: he was inclined, when feeling irritable, to complain about how he had been robbed of his rightful gains from Ketil's Thorp.

She had taken her own little treasure to Lincoln, to the goldsmith's on the steep and narrow street in the Romans' old walled town, above the Stonebow Gate. He had made a fine job of moulding the soft gold of the ring into a cross, flattening the four ends into little trefoils, and placing the red gem at the centre. An honest man, he showed her the small piece of gold he had kept, as payment for his work.

In those years she had freedom to visit Stow or Lincoln, because Jean was called up, often, to assist in the subjugation of a turbulent region. He had been part of the force sent to harry the North, a progress of thorough and systematic destruction from which, some feared, it might never fully recover. He was part of another confrontation that finally drove Hereward out of the Fens down south of the shire, the last serious challenge to Norman rule.

This warrior-service took its toll; he stayed fit, and aged well, but still he aged, his lean body crisscrossed with battle scars. He found the marshy lands along the Trent unhealthy, after the Normandy climate, and missed the oil and fruit and wines of his native land; but there was a future for him here, and none where he came from, so he endured the ague, grumbled at the pottage, and took pride in his lands.

Over time, Jean and Albertha built a relationship of mutual grudging respect. It was her he trusted to run the manor in his absence, not her father, and to oversee its rebuilding. When, early on, she had clashed with one of his men-at-arms – a lazy, truculent fellow from Fecamp who saw no reason to obey an Englishwoman – Jean had sided with her, and thrashed the man for insolence. Her lot had become much easier after that.

It was harder for her when his compatriots came, his fellow adventurers from Normandy – Odo de la Croix, Guy de la Haye, and Ivo Taillebois. With the last, of whom he was somewhat in awe, Jean was constrained, even guarded. Ivo had wedded the daughter of Thorold, the former Sheriff of Lincoln, and soon became Sheriff himself. But with Odo and Guy, his *compains*, Jean would drink deep draughts of the rough red wine brought from his homeland, and they would relive their feats of arms together, bragging as soldiers do.

About Senlac Hill, however they did not brag. It was enough to recall the hell of it, from the cruel bright dawn to late afternoon. Again and again, they had clambered over their dead and dying friends to batter themselves against the English shield wall: even encircling cavalry charges had not broken it. The attack had gone so ill that when rumour came the Duke was killed, they were ready to believe it.

"But do you remember," Jean always said at this point, "how M'Duke pulled off his helm to show himself to us, and we all took heart?" So on they went, up a hill now slippy with blood, never giving up, but never breaking through. Until, that is, the moment when one of their humiliating retreats had enticed the English into pursuit.

It was a feint, Guy always insisted, a *ruse de guerre* devised by the great Duke himself, but Jean and Odo only laughed. They had the same argument each time the story was told, for Guy alone believed it was anything other than another retreat, or that anything more than luck had turned defeat into success. Well, luck or cunning, it had certainly given the Normans their chance.

"You know full well," Guy would shout, unwilling to concede his point, "how we drew the damned English on, how they ran screaming after us down the hill? The fools left a gap in their line big enough to let an army through!" Scrambling through that gap, the depleted Norman troops had surrounded Harold's best men. And that gave them the opportunity, Guy insisted, hammering the point home with his clenched fist, to teach those English rebels a lesson. A lesson? A slaughter, Albertha reflected in silent fury, a butchery so savage that it still haunted Jean's dreams.

It was hard for her to listen, harder still to watch John, once he was old enough to understand, hanging on Jean's every word, his eyes shining with hero-worship. Part of her could be glad that her son had a hero, a sponsor, a father – for all they both knew – able to give him privileged access to this frightening new Norman world. Another part of her – the cowardly part, she told herself –

could even be glad that she and her ageing father, now fading into foolishness, also had Jean's protection in that world.

But still there was heart-sickness, the bitterness of loss, not just of Erik but of all her old world, leaving her an alien in her own home. From those evenings she would retire as soon as she could, and in the early years the pregnancies came so regularly that she seldom lacked excuse.

There was, all the same, one point on which these bloody soldiers' tales gave her comfort. Since her father had come home and given her his account of the battle, she had borne an unreasoning conviction that Erik's death had been her fault: that he had tried too hard for glory, because he had something to prove. He had wanted so much to show that he was a man, who could make his own decisions, choose who he would, to share his bed. It had made him foolhardy: she had made him foolhardy, she feared. The guilt had lain heavier than Erik's child in her belly.

But the stories Jean and Odo and Guy told had banished, or at least lightened, that burden of guilt. Caution could not have saved Erik. They told of a killing field in which coward and brave died without distinction, and from which no one escaped – except those like her father, who had never quite been there. It did not make her happy, but it did bring her relief.

And, alien or chattel as she might feel herself to be, Albertha learned to find riches in her life. There was plenty to keep her busy, to stop her dwelling on the past: her children, her manor, the miracles of new life, the gathering-in of harvest. Jean asked little but obedience, and Albertha gave it. Her only small woman's gesture of defiance was, in Jean's absence, to give succour to rebels fleeing from Norman vengeance.

Word spread along the Trent that round the back of the hall, at the entrance to the undercroft, if you came at dusk, you could always count on help. Help from the Lady Albertha, with no questions asked. And those who knew did not betray her to the Normans in her household. Those poor souls were only beggars, the men-at-arms were told; it was an old custom, for the lady of the manor to feed and clothe them, a duty blessed by our Saviour, and the Lady Albertha was a good daughter of the Church.

One bright but chancy summer day, on her way back from the newly rebuilt church in Neutone, whither the Ketil's Thorp priest had fled from the ruins of his own, she rounded the end of the hall to see two men sitting on the bench in the patchy afternoon sun. They were eating what they had plainly just been given, a loaf and some goat's cheese. They were also plainly, too plainly, fugitives – *silvatici*, who had been living rough for a long time.

Nothing exceptional in that, except that this pair had not had the sense to wait until twilight before coming for food. At least they had hidden their weapons. But Jean's men-at-arms might well decide to lay hands on men so obviously able-bodied, and equally obviously outlaws. Albertha looked round, quickly. Praise be, there was no sign of trouble: the men-at-arms were lazing in the meadow the other side of the manor, out of sight, and in any case the woods were close enough on this side of the manor for *silvatici* to vanish at need.

One of the two was a small weather-beaten fellow, who wore only animal hides; the other – bigger, younger – had a leather jerkin over the remains of a good cloth tunic of Lincoln green. Pora was with them, holding a pitcher, and when she saw her mistress she made an awkward little protective movement, as if to try to hide the two men.

But then the younger one got to his feet, and turned his face towards Albertha. As he tossed back his shaggy, tarnished lion's mane, she saw the long scar, running deep from hairline to bearded chin. And his bright blue eyes. With just a hint of mockery, he made his obeisance.

And of course she knew him.

Much passed between them, without a word spoken. *I thought you dead; you never sent word. You left me to suffer, without you.*

I was sore wounded; then I was hunted; then I learnt you were wed. I suffered, too.

For all that has passed, her eyes said, *I would still follow you, away from here, but I cannot. I am tied. You must leave before the men-at-arms see you, but first* – checking him when he would have spoken, she tugged at the thin chain about her neck, and pulled out the cross.

His eyes widened: she saw he had understood. Then, with a little graceful sweep of her hand, she invited him to follow her. Just as far as a clearing in the woodland, beyond the line of the buildings.

A boy was there, a boy perhaps ten years old, with a thick shock of red-gold hair. A fine boy, well grown and vigorous, but playing gently, with two excited little dark-haired girls, who clung to him in delight. A nursemaid sat on the grass, with a swaddled baby on her lap. A young Saxon churl, all they needed for protection so close to home, lent sleepily on his stave.

And Albertha turned to the stranger, her eyes blurred, but with the smile that lit up her face.

*

John was growing up wholly Norman, in thought and speech, she told Father Petroc wistfully, when she brought the old man – lonely now, with Stow near-deserted – some comforts that Christmastide of 1076. He moved only with difficulty, and she was glad to see there was a brazier in his little cell. Glad for herself, too, since it had been a cold ride in midwinter, her escort grumbling about ice and the horses' legs, all the way. She stretched out grateful hands, in sodden woollen mitts, to the warm glow.

"Just as well the boy should do so," Father Petroc wheezed. "It will be many years before England speaks with one tongue again, and the young had best cleave to the winning side, if they can. You have done well for him, lady, to give him such a chance. I am glad."

She was silent, knowing he was right. Jean spoke of building a new manor at Ketil's Thorp, for their son. Why not? It was a good position, safer from the river floods than the manor at Neutone. If he – or, more like, John, when he was old enough to take a wife – ever got round to building on the ruins, she knew what she would do. She would choose her moment to secrete her cross in the stonework, in physical memory of Erik.

She had just lit a taper for him in the Minster. Where had he found to shelter, these bitter nights? Could he make an outlaw's life worth living? What would he want, for his son?

Father Petroc looked at her thoughtfully. Then he suddenly sat up, bright with recollection. "Daughter, listen. I sleep little now, in my old age, and use the darkness for reflection. And a few weeks ago, I remembered that I wanted to tell you the story about the sparrow."

"No," he went on, hasty to explain, "not Our Lord's promise, that the least of us is in his hands – the parable I told you of the falling sparrow, all those years ago, to comfort you when your trouble came. Not that story. It was something else that I recalled, and that I think, perhaps, might give you solace now."

Albertha waited. You could not hurry Father Petroc, these days. But he spoke fluently enough, if he could take his time.

"It was in a history written by a great servant of Our Lord Jesus Christ. These days, they call him the Venerable Bede. He lived a long time ago – three centuries or more. God rest his soul."

The afternoon was almost gone; she should be getting home, before the snow started once more. But she waited.

"And by God's goodness," Father Petroc continued, his eyes, milky as they were, still shining with pleasure, "I recalled we still have a copy of his great work here, though all else has gone to Lincoln. A treasure! There are few of us left to read it, but Father Bernard is a kindly young fellow. He found the time to humour an old man. And once he had read, it came back to me, almost word for word. I learnt it when young, and the words taken to heart in a man's youth stay with him, in old age, though later things fade. I have it by heart, more or less, and can give you the best, at least. Listen well, daughter."

He paused, drew breath, and began to recite, haltingly at first. But, warmed by the image he was creating, his creaky voice soon grew more fluent.

"The present life of man upon earth, O King, seems to me, in comparison with that time which is unknown to us, like to the swift flight of a sparrow through the house wherein you sit at supper in winter, with your ealdormen and thegns, while the fire blazes in the midst, and the hall is warmed, but the wintry storms of rain or snow are raging abroad."

He paused again, while Albertha thought of the fading light outside, and the prospect of just such a storm tonight. Then he went on, carrying her imagination with him.

"The sparrow, flying in at one door and immediately out at another, whilst he is within, is safe from the wintry tempest; but after a short space of fair weather, he immediately vanishes out of your sight, passing from winter into winter again. So this life of man appears for a little while, but of what is to follow or what went before we know nothing at all."

She listened, entranced. And then she said:

"Poor lonely sparrow. What if she had a mate, out there in the winter storm? Might they meet again, when she leaves the hall?"

Father Petroc smiled. "Perhaps."

But what the story tells me, she thought, is: not in this life.

1066–1217

There is no mention of the settlement of Ketil's Thorp in the Domesday Book, but Torchesey features, as does Neutone, and Ketil's Thorp may simply have been too small or too hidden to merit separate attention. Or maybe, as I have imagined, the great battles had taken their toll. The casualty rate was high.

The "pacification" of the country by Duke William also spread destruction. Torchesey, less than a mile away, lost half its population in one brutal episode that may have wiped out the nearby hamlets. Lincolnshire was, as so often in our history, rebel country. And it was treated as such.

In 1072, after dealing with embarrassing accusations of simony, Bishop Remigius de Fecamp began building. The new castle and cathedral in Lincoln soon made Norman dominance clear to the countryside for miles around.

There was barely a breathing space between the final subjugation of England to Norman rule and the struggle between two rival grandchildren of Duke William that dragged the country into over a decade of civil war. At Lincoln, in 1141, the army of the Empress Maud roundly defeated King Stephen. But their fortunes were soon reversed; and the war between cousins dragged on.

Eventually – in the 1150s – the nobility on both sides agreed that Stephen should be succeeded not by his own son but by Maud's. So *began Plantagenet rule, with two of the largest characters of early medieval history, Henry II and his wife Eleanor of Aquitaine. Their quarrelsome sons, however, lost much of their inheritance, and in the early thirteenth century England faced invasion again.*

Kettlethorpe* emerges from the mists at this time, in the light provided by church records. In the early thirteenth century we find the manor in the hands of a Norman family semi-anglicised from de Caen to de Ken. John de Ken tries to present his brother to the Rectory, but is told he lacks the necessary Latin. On such glimpses of the inhabitants of the manor have I have built my story.

It is the time of Magna Carta, rebellion and invasion. A confrontation is pending between the rebel barons and their French allies on the one side, and the dwindling band of supporters of the Plantagnet dynasty on the other. It would prove to be the last great battle against a foreign invader ever to take place on English soil.

On Lincolnshire soil – just ten miles east of Kettlethorpe.

---

*   From now on I have used the modern spelling – as I have for Torskey (Torchesey), Laughterton (Leugttricdun), Newton (Neutone), York (Jorvik) and Marton (Martone).

THE KNIGHT'S DEMOISELLE

KETTLETHORPE MANOR: *1217*

John de Ken shifted restlessly on his stool. Weighed flat with his left elbow, on the bench in front of him, was his rent roll; to his right, tipped out of his purse, a pile of coins. Try as he might, he couldn't marry the two up.

He sighed, and stretched, glancing around the chamber that had been his mother's solar, and now bore the uncared-for look of a young man's chamber. It was littered with broken pieces of harness, clothes discarded where they fell rather than folded in a press, hounds quarrelling over a bone at his feet.

He was an active young man, with a big frame that did not fold easily into a clerkly position at the bench. He hadn't had much time for letters or reckoning – or, to be honest, much appetite. His father had tried sending him to Lincoln, for some schooling at the Cathedral; but since he had persisted in playing truant with the urchins of the lower city, skating on Brayford pool or fishing in the Witham, he had soon been allowed to stay home instead and make himself more useful.

The reeve had dealt with the rents in his father's day, well enough; since both their deaths, however, John had not been able to find a replacement he trusted. There was that rogue Roger Wale who had offered to collect the lot in return for being relieved of rent for his own bovate, but John doubted his honesty, and disliked the way he kept threatening to sell his rent-collecting services to the Archdeacon in Stow instead.

There was no lettered priest to help John now, either. When his brother Richard was a year or two older, John, who held the Advowson at Kettlethorpe, was thinking of presenting him, since the Rector's position was well worth keeping in the family. But he wouldn't put it past the Archdeacon to challenge this, demanding someone who had some church Latin, could read the bible and keep the parish records. And the Bishop, Hugh de Wells, was known to have high standards.

John shifted uneasily. Maybe he should send young Henry to Stow, to get some learning from the priests there. It was closer to home than Lincoln. With the boy at Stow, he could keep an eye on what he was up to: once some Latin had been beaten into him, he could stand in for Richard if need be.

John had inherited his manor and his responsibilities for his brothers sooner than he would have wished. His mother had died giving birth to the youngest of four sons, whom "she had taken with her into eternal life", according to the Archdeacon, a man much given to reproving his flock for grieving at God's will. John's father had ignored all such reproofs; he had his own way of dealing with grief. He lasted only a few weeks longer than his wife, refusing to eat and turning his face to the wall.

They had been doting fond, John's parents, though the sparks flew between them, and more than sparks when his mother was in a rage. When they married she had been a young widow, whose son, only two years older than John, became his closest friend. The pair of them, so different in disposition and looks, had become like twins in their understanding of each other.

John had his father's bluff good humour, blue eyes and head of light brown thatch; Odo de Sainte Croix was dark and finely made, like their mother, her fire tempered in him into something more tranquil. When he was a child, their mother told them, Odo had been as blond as his half-brothers, but now his hair was black, and curly, and it seemed hard to believe.

While it was John who looked a farmer's boy, Odo a troubadour, their characters were the reverse. Odo had no desire for the wider world, finding happiness in the lands he knew and loved. He was no weakling, using skill in their boyhood battles to floor a sibling who soon topped him by a shaggy head; but he had no appetite for combat. John, meanwhile, yearned for glory.

Odo had lands only a few miles north, at Upton: John's father had managed them when Odo was a child, disdaining to exploit the benefit as most guardians did. He had, as he always said, a fine enough property of his own at Kettlethorpe, built on the ruins of a Danish settlement, and more lands closer to Lincoln.

He farmed them well. Harvests were good and bad, but his flocks of sheep were built up over the years, and only unusually bitter weather at lambing interrupted their steady improvement in quality. The reopening of the Fossdyke, after dredging ordered by old King Henry, carried his flax, beasts and wool to Lincoln and beyond.

Wool, he told his eldest son with conviction, was the best thing: it was what had made England wealthy. It had made this shire rich.

"Mark my words, John, wool will make this family rich too. Lindsey's ports carry good Lincoln staples to Flanders, or down to London. My Longwools are much prized for breeding, too."

He had been to Lincoln to borrow enough to buy good breeding stock, as soon as he took the lands over from his father. "I went to the house of Aaron the Jew," he told John later. "And they dealt fairly with me, whatever others may say. I'm repaying it as I promised, there'll be no debt left to burden you. Of course, I was small fry there, Master Aaron lent to the greatest in the land. But they treated me courteously, all the same. Don't listen to all they say about the Jews, boy, I'd never be where I am now without them. Look at whose ewes."

But John had barely listened: he didn't care for the land, for farming or his father's prized flocks. He longed only to be a knight, and win fortune from success in the tourney. Perhaps the Jews would lend his father what was needed to equip him for that, too.

His hero – his idol – was William Marshal, "the greatest knight in Christendom". Marshal, the younger son of a minor court official, had by his sheer prowess at arms become the champion of the tournament circuit in Europe, the companion and counsellor of Kings, the Earl of Pembroke. His was still the name on the lips of every young man aspiring to the heights of chivalry.

But John knew the world had changed since Marshal's youth. The greatest days of the tourney, the mock battles ranging across leagues of French countryside, were over. Chivalry was certainly not dead, but it had begun to be codified and civilised. A violent war game with few rules was developing into a semi-religious military calling, infused by Arthurian legend, requiring a show of skill before an audience, competing for a lady's favour.

Nothing in that to dampen a young man's ardour, maybe, but it looked harder now to hew your way to the top through sheer force of arms. Long dead now was chivalry's arch-patron, the eldest of the bellicose brood of Henry II and Eleanor of Aquitaine, who had been Marshal's lord and rival. Dead too, by the time John de Ken was growing up, were not only old Henry himself, but also his second son, Richard, who had succeeded him.

"Lionheart", they called him: his reign had been spent almost entirely outside England, much of it on crusade. But Jerusalem had fallen to Saladin some thirty years ago, and King Richard's efforts to recapture it had ended in failure. And then his younger brother John, who succeeded in his turn, managed to lose much of the Angevin empire to his Capetian rivals.

All of which, as John de Ken was growing up, left little enough on the European stage to satisfy a young man's hunger for glory.

Nor did King John inspire him with a desire for royal service: a hated tyrant, brutal, greedy and quixotic, he had driven his barons into open revolt. All young John de Ken could hope for – all he had hoped for – was through hard training to become qualified to join some great lord's mesnie, where knights were needed for a show of power. And he had driven his father to distraction, begging for the chance to try.

Appleby, barely more than a day's ride north of Kettlethorpe, had been the first honour granted to William Longsword, Henry II's bastard son. John's father knew the steward there. Through this acquaintance, John had been taken on as the lowliest of squires, in the household of the great man, who through marriage was now Earl of Salisbury.

John had been found some harness, and the best courser his father could afford – yes, he had been to the Jews again, but not for too much. The boy would have to earn enough to buy the hugely costly trained destrier that a knight needed.

John's hopes had risen when he had been allowed to travel south with Salisbury's mesnie, but those hopes had soon been snuffed out. He had only been there long enough to learn of the disputes that were convulsing the country, when his mother and father had died.

Salisbury had remained loyal to King John all the way to the field near Runnymede, where the King was cornered into putting his seal to a charter of rights. "Great" this Charter came to be called, "Magna Carta," but to begin with, it was anything but great. The King repudiated it within weeks and drove its drafting genius, Archbishop Langton, overseas, when he refused to excommunicate the barons. The King had the Pope's backing, but still, in England, his support continued to drain away.

In his time down south, John de Ken had seen his hero William Marshal once, striding out of Salisbury's chamber with a face like thunder, having learnt that even the King's half-brother had finally deserted the crown. Mere squires were wise to shrink out of range of Marshal's anger. Stiff with age and old wounds, he was still upright and formidable.

When King John died at Newark last year, few mourned him. Foul as hell was, they said, it was made still fouler by the King's arrival. Nothing could be expected of his spawn: in any case, the boy, another Henry, was still a child. And so when Prince Louis of France laid claim to the English throne, making much of his marriage to old King Henry's granddaughter, it was generally assumed – considered certain, even, in London and the east of England – that his coronation was only a matter of time. Marshal's own son and heir had been quick to give his allegiance to Louis, in return for promises of court position, and it was said that King John's death would finally free the Earl to do likewise.

But that all came to John de Ken only via traders' gossip: he was far away from great events, now. He had left Salisbury's service, and done his best to shoulder his responsibilities. He had to care for his brothers and his other dependants, such as the impoverished Cistercian sisters at the Fosse Priory, a scant mile from Kettlethorpe. Locally, they now called him Sir John, out of courtesy to the new Lord of the Manor; but it was not how he had wanted to win his knighthood.

He had gritted his teeth when his tenants, and the older and bolder of his villeins, bemoaned the loss of his father. He had blocked out of his mind events in the wider world, even when word came that Prince Louis had stormed up the Vale of Belvoir, marched along the ridge and taken Lincoln, all but the castle, which would surely fall soon. What could John do, to help or hinder? In that spring of 1217 he sowed his crops, and guarded his lambs, and learned to hope, almost, that the world would pass him by.

As he struggled to manage his manor he had discovered which of his tenants' excuses to accept and which to reject. He had learnt which of the wool traders in Torksey could be trusted, and who to listen to, in deciding when to cut the hay. If he could just make his accounts tally, he would be happy, or at least not unhappy, with the good fortune of his inheritance. He must cease to dream of glory. He set to again with his tedious calculations.

*

A full half-hour later, and he had just reached that miraculous point where the pile of coins on the right and the scruffy parchment on the left were beginning to produce the same answers, when he was distracted by the drum of hoof beats on turf. He got up to peer through the window slit, and caught sight of his brother Richard flinging himself off his blowing palfrey. Before John could go out to meet him, the boy was bounding up the steps to the hall.

"They're at Newark! In force!" He was breathless, with excitement as much as haste. John gripped his arms, and sought to calm him. "Sit, and tell me slowly – who is at Newark?"

Richard broke his grasp, but only to clutch at his brother himself. "John, it's the new King's army, come to break the siege at Lincoln and defeat Prince Louis. I heard it from two merchants, who'd come downriver from Newark to Torksey this very morning. And believe it or not, they say the Lord Salisbury is with them – and that the Earl Marshal is leading the force himself! You must go, at once!"

John shook his brother off. "That's naught to me, now, Richard, you know that. Father was right. Why should we care whether Capetian or Angevin rules? Neither of them is worth a harvest."

Richard glared at him. He was the mirror image of his elder brother, though still not fully grown, and with only a boy's down on his cheeks. They were flushed now, and stained with the dust thrown up by his fast ride.

"We do not want to be ruled from Paris! We are Normans, and England is ours!" There was pleading in his voice, as well as passion in his eyes.

"You told me yourself, the Charter has been reissued, the barons have no excuse for dragging in the Capetians! We must fight, John, we must! And if the Earl Marshal leads us, we will win! Surely we must win!"

John shook his head, shaking off such thoughts. "You talk like a fool. How can a child rule? A puny child, the new so-called King! He's younger than your own little brother – and by all accounts, feeble. With Louis, at least we may hope for some order in the land. We can trade our wool, unhindered. And his army's not French – most of its knights are Norman like ourselves."

He tried not to look at Richard's stricken face. Angry at his own longing for action, he spoke roughly. "Stop this folly, now, and tell me you did something of use at Torksey, other than pick up alehouse gossip."

Richard stiffened. He stepped back, pulling together some shreds of dignity. "I have bartered fleeces for barges for the end of the month; Jankyn told me we could finish the shearing by then. But I will go now and talk with him again, to make sure; he is wont to tell us what we want to hear."

John nodded, and softened his tone. "Do you find Edgytha first, and bid her heat you some pottage; you'll be famished, I'll wager." It did not mollify the boy. Richard bowed, with stiff formality, and left, his rigid back view registering his hurt and disappointment.

Doggedly, John turned back to his rent roll. After another half-hour, he gave up, sweeping the coins into a leather purse, tossing it into a trunk and the rolled-up parchment with it. He'd go and see Jankyn himself.

Richard must still be with him, and Henry too. John would help them to understand why he was acting as he did: it was for them, he'd explain, much as he would fain take up arms. It was to protect their interests, keeping clear of the battles of great men that could only impoverish lesser folk. And then he'd charge them with bringing the sheep in, and the cattle too, out of harm's way; that would give them something to think about.

He strolled down to the Sallie Bank, and found, as he expected, Jankyn his shepherd, with two of his boys, and Henry. But no

Richard. Jankyn shook his head. "I've not seen hide nor hair of him today, Master," he said slowly. "He were away to Torksey, weren't he?"

John cursed. "God's teeth, the fool boy, where's he gone? Jankyn, I must look for him, I fear mischief. Look you to make all safe, and hurry. Take some of the men, and round up the cattle, and young Henry, you can drive the flock into the sheepfold close to the hall. Bring all within, shut the gate to the palisade, and stay there."

He paused, and spoke more deliberately. It didn't do to hustle Jankyn, he'd only get confused. "Don't come out, even if you are provoked. I doubt the army will come this way – if it does you can do naught. I would not have you put yourselves in danger. But you can hold off a few stragglers, I'll be bound. I must away to find Richard."

He searched the demesne, with care, lest the boy was hiding away, brooding on his wrongs. To no avail: his instinct had been correct. No sign of Richard, anywhere. He shouted for the stable boys to harness his courser, and chiding himself for foolish thoughts, turned back to the hall to collect his harness.

For all his suspicions of Richard's intentions, it was a shock to find some of his gear missing. Boiling with rage, he shouted for his horse. A scared boy led the fidgeting horse out, hanging on with difficulty until John grasped the reins; but just as he put his foot in the stirrup, he both heard and saw a small group of mounted men approach the gate. Flinging the reins back at the boy, and shouting for aid, he ran to close it, checking only when he saw who was there. God be thanked, it was Odo.

He was riding a fine new bay stallion, and had a useful-looking retainer at his elbow. But that was not all. With them, white-faced, muddied and fearful, was John's brother Richard.

"Look you on what I found, on my way home with my new mount," Odo said. He looked quickly from brother to brother. "A boy's escapade, no harm has come of it."

But John's eyes went to his helm, mail, and lance, bundled and strapped on to the sumpter led from Richard's palfrey, and they hardened with anger.

"I left your sword," Richard cried out defensively. "I only took father's."

Odo broke in, before John could do more than raise his hand to the boy. "Peace, John, it was for you he went. The lad told me you wanted to join My Lord Salisbury, but had held back out of care for your brothers. So he was going in your place – in your honour."

He handed his reins to his man, and dismounted lightly to fling his arm round John's shoulders, easing the anger from them. "He didn't get far, poor lad. I found him at Newton, after a bruising fall. I think it was the lance strapped to the sumpter that unhorsed him! He said it poked his palfrey in the rear."

Many times, these past dismal eighteen months, a sense of the ridiculous had saved John from despair or folly. He relaxed, letting out a great shout of laughter.

"I would it had poked Richard's! Get down, boy, and tend to your horses. I'll deal with you later. Odo, I am in your debt. Come, take ale with me, and tell me what you have learnt. Is there truly an army at Newark?"

"It is, I warrant, as Richard recounted to you," Odo said, once they were alone, stretched out companionably beside a brazier in the solar. "The word is that the Earl Marshal – 'swounds, I'll never learn to call him Pembroke – went to meet the child-King Henry, who flung himself on the old man's mercy."

Watching the tension ease itself out of John's angry body, Odo kept talking.

"Marshal himself was once a child at the mercy of great men, did you know that? King Stephen paraded him to the gallows, threatening to hang him, when he was only five – after his father had broken faith. Mayhap it was such a memory that bound him to young Henry's cause. For there is no doubt, the Earl Marshal has pledged his allegiance yet again to the Plantagenets."

"And has that brought the others back to his side? Is Salisbury truly with him?"

"So I am told. Louis has waited overlong for his reinforcements, and given Marshal time to win over others. And the Pope has declared it a holy war against the Capetians, a new crusade."

Odo set his beaker down, and drew breath. "John, as I know you and love you, you must go and join Salisbury or rue the lost chance for ever. Take young Richard with you, to mind your horse and armour. Have no fear for Kettlethorpe – I'll stay here and see all well."

John flushed, but shook his head. "Odo, you cannot stay – you have your own lands to protect. You should be on your way, you have done me kindness enough in rescuing Richard from his folly."

"You owe me naught – nor will you. My steward is a good man, I can leave him with confidence. I do not have your prize flocks – I sold most of my sheep after lambing, thinking to buy better from you. And the army is not like to come as far north as Upton. It will surely head for Lincoln up the Fosse Way. From Newark, it's the shortest route."

John sat up. "They'd be fools if they take it – it would bring them into Lincoln from the south, with the hill in front of them, and a steep climb to the castle. Louis's men would have all the advantage."

Now it was his friend's turn to laugh. "Then go tell them that at Newark, John! I say again, I will answer for all here. I owe it to your father, who took such care for me. Forgive young Richard, take him, and go."

*

It was not a great force: that was all too plain. A few hundred knights, perhaps, John guessed; fewer crossbowmen, all camped just to the east of the town of Newark. John left Richard and their mounts near the horselines, and sought news of the Earl of Salisbury.

He found Salisbury's tent close to the Earl Marshal's. One of his household was emerging just as John appeared, a cheerful, red-haired young man, who checked in pleased recognition. "John de Ken, by all that's holy! Have you come back to your service? I thought you'd gone to look after your lands!"

"Aye, I did – I have. But word has it you cannot make do without me, Roger. Can you hit the quintain yet?"

Roger de Coursey bunched his fist, and thumped John gently. "Sir Roger now, I'll have you know. I'll tell my lord you're here to save us, when I have the chance. Now, by your leave…" He sketched a courtly bow.

John checked him. "Roger, in all truth, I do have a warning to give our great men. They must not try to take Lincoln from the south, it would be fatal. Do any of them know the city? I mean, know it well?"

Roger shook his head. "Archbishop Langton was a Lincoln man, but he is still overseas. My Lord Salisbury may have visited, but I doubt he was there long. I will beg an audience: methinks he may have need of you, after all."

And so it came that John found himself where he had so often longed to be: at the councils of the great, a step behind his one-time lord. In the torchlight he saw, for only the second time in his life, his hero the Earl Marshal. With him was the Papal legate, Guala, and a churchman, big, bustling and self-important. That was Peter de Roches, the Bishop of Winchester, according to Roger, who had somehow slipped in close along with John, and was muttering in his year.

"Those two are from Marshal's household – his son, and John d'Earley, you'll have heard of him. And see, on the Earl Marshal's right, even greater folk? The Earl of Chester, and Falkes de Breauté, who commands the crossbowmen. A brute, but a valiant fighter. Still, it's the Earl Marshal who leads, ancient as he is."

John nudged him to silence. Salisbury was speaking. "My Lord, I have a squire here familiar with the city, who urges us to avoid the direct route. Will you hear him?"

The Earl Marshal's gaze swept round to Salisbury. "Where is he? Let him come forward, and speak plainly."

"Loudly," hissed Roger in John's ear. "He means – speak loudly. His hearing is not so good, these days."

John stepped forward, dropping to his knees. "Stand up, young man," Marshal said irritably. "I am not your Sovereign. Tell us now, how should we approach this? You know, I suppose, that the invaders have the city, but the castle is held for the King."

"The Castellan is a brave lady," the Bishop added, eagerly, "the Lady Nicholaa de la Haye. We must find a way to reach her, before the fighting begins. To relieve her of command."

Marshal looked a little irritated. "To free the castle we must take the city, My Lord Bishop. And do you say, boy, that this cannot be done from the south? My Lord of Chester – did you not tell me the Empress Maud's army came from the south, when it defeated King Stephen at Lincoln? Has so much changed since then?"

John did not wait to be asked again. Before Chester could respond, he plunged in. "Sir – My Lord – King Stephen lost because he came down from the castle to fight on the plain below. He threw away his advantage! They say he wanted to make it a fair fight." Chester expostulated, but subsided at a look from Marshal. John ploughed on.

"Lincoln is built on a rise, and the walls run up the slope to the castle, which is in the upper part of the city. If you enter through the south gate, you will have to fight your way a long way up inside – and it's steep going."

Marshal rubbed his chin. "So they tell me. But what choice do we have?"

John hesitated. "Go on," Roger hissed, "you must, now."

"My Lord, I'd take the track north from here along the river, on the eastern shore of the Trent. I know the way well, it goes through my lands. Go to Torksey! You can cross the Fossdyke there and then turn east from the river to Stow. From the Minster there, you can march straight up to the ridge above Lincoln. It's an old road, a good one! Then you can press down into the city from the north, close to the castle, with the slope in your favour."

Falkes de Breaute could not contain himself. "This is folly. Doubtless this lad is a rebel – they are thick as fleas in these parts. For sure, he wants to lead us away from Lincoln, to give the Capetians more time to reduce the castle. Give the rascal to me, and I'll get the truth out of him."

Roger's little intake of breath frightened John as much as Falkes's words. "Once in his hands, and you're a dead man," his friend muttered.

But at the same moment, Salisbury moved. Just a slight shifting of his weight, and a hand dropping to the hilt of his sword.

"This young man was in my service for a year and more. I know him to be loyal, an honest fellow. I have questioned him, and that should suffice."

Marshal raised his hand for silence. "Enough now, all of you. Do you leave me, and get some rest. I shall ponder on what has been said tonight, and seek guidance in this Godly endeavour. Have your men ready, to march at dawn."

Roger whistled with relief as they slid away. "A narrow escape, that. You should stay close to us, tonight – Falkes's men are too numerous for comfort, and they'd like a little sport with you, if they thought it had their lord's blessing."

"I must first find my brother, and the horses," John said anxiously.

Roger slapped him on the back. "You did well tonight – you convinced me, anyway. I'll come with you to find them, you're too precious to lose."

*

A few miles north of Lincoln, the knights and mounted squires checked, to allow the crossbowmen to deploy in front of them. John had stirred Salisbury's memories of the city, and he had pressed the same argument with Marshal, to good effect. So they had marched north along the eastern side of the Trent, as John had suggested, cutting inland only to avoid marshland.

They had set out from Newark early on the morning of May 19th. A few more knights had joined them at Newark; there might be 400 of them now, and more crossbowmen than John had realised – perhaps 200. A puny force to take on the Capetians and rebels, all the same.

The Earl Marshal and the Papal Legate between them had done their best to raise the men's spirits in the early hours. The one had spoken of honour, country, wives and children; the other had given Communion, and promises of paradise. Guala reminded the warriors of the crusaders' crosses on their surcoats, and the excommunication of the enemy. But perhaps the army was most cheered by Marshal's assurance that Prince Louis was not in Lincoln, having unwisely split his army; even so, they knew the French forces were far greater than their own.

As they passed through Kettlethorpe lands, John had looked anxiously from side to side, but had seen no sign of his precious sheep. He was his father's son enough not to want to sacrifice them to hungry crossbowmen. Let the army raid the Archdeacon's stores at Stow, he'd plenty to spare.

They had crossed the Fossdyke a scant mile farther north at Torksey, and camped a night close to Stow. In the dawn, after Mass in the chilly darkness, they had made the final distance through the dawn promise of a fine May morning. As they marched up on to the ridge, the eastern sun caught their armour, outlining a glinting snake of men and revealing their pitifully small number to any who came out from the city to see.

Now they were north of Lincoln, and could see the formidable task ahead of them. Lincoln was a fort within a fort: the old Roman walls were still standing around the city, but within them was the Norman castle, the Cathedral close by. The city was full of the rebel army and its French leaders, and its gates would be well defended; only in the castle was there a small party loyal to the crown. How, John wondered, would Marshal deploy his relieving force?

They could hear the Capetians' siege engines at work on the castle. The Earl Marshal's force had no such heavy weapons. And now Roger, riding beside John, exclaimed, pointing at a group of knights emerging from the city.

"They've come to take a look at us – see their standards in front of the North Gate? Perchance they'll attack, and save us trouble."

John shook his head. "They could have done so a while back, when we were climbing the ridge. They were watching us then, too. But why should they leave their strong position?"

He heard his name called: Salisbury was beckoning him towards the group of commanders. "If my memory serves me, young squire, there is a gate from the countryside through the castle's western wall – am I right?"

John nodded. "Aye, My Lord."

"The Bishop of Winchester is anxious to make contact with the Lady Castellan, if he can. The Earl Marshal has given him leave to try, while the crossbowmen get ready. Will you show him the way to the castle gate?"

Pausing only to tell Richard to stay back with the sumpters, John dug in his heels and cantered to where the Bishop and his mesnie stood, Roger close on his heels. Young Marshal followed, at his father's command.

"This way, Your Grace!" John called out. He led them well clear of the north-west corner of the city wall, curving in again to approach the steep rise to the castle entrance directly.

The Bishop's herald trotted beside him, and someone on the battlements must have recognised his device, for the gate opened and a knight and squire rode out down the earth ramp to meet him. The two were immediately in danger, John saw, for a small party of men had spotted them and rode up from the south, bent no doubt on capturing such easy prey.

The Bishop led his party forward with a shout, and the French sheered off. The two emissaries from the castle fled west, their pursuers at their horses' heels. John saw the Bishop hesitate. Then he rode forward to the castle gate, and dismounted to enter the wicket, since the gate had been shut at the sight of the French party.

John grasped his friend's rein. "Roger, I beg you, take care of my horse, I must go with him." Young Marshal and one of the Bishop's knights had also dismounted, and were following him cautiously into the castle, with unsheathed swords.

Inside the gatehouse, they found, to their astonishment, a girl waiting for them, an anxious sergeant at her heels. She made an obeisance to the Bishop.

"Your Grace, My Lady bids you very welcome. As you can hear, we are hard-pressed." Her words were calm, though a tremor in her voice betrayed her. She knew the danger, had lived with it, John realised, overlong. Missiles hurled by the siege engines were thundering into the castle ward from the east.

"Can you take me to the Lady Nicholaa, my child?" She bobbed again, and led them close along the inside of the castle wall to the steep motte at the south-west corner. "My Lady is up within the tower."

As they crowded into the chamber at the top of the tower, they found Nicholaa de la Haye sitting by the small arched window. It was a vantage-point high above the castle walls from which she could look out over the city, stretched out below her down to the river plain. The Bishop joined her, and John, peering past him, could see the haunts of his schooldays.

To the east of the castle, a street of houses ran downhill, southwards, to the wall that ran east–west, dividing the upper city from the lower. Below the gate in that wall, the street ran on down again to the Stonebow, in the lowest, southern wall of the city.

Cathedral and castle, the Bishop's palace, the timbered houses of the burgesses, the fine stone house once lived in by Aaron the Jew – they, he remembered, were all in the upper city. The urchins from whom he had learnt how to fish and fight, when he should have been at his lessons, had all lived in the ruins and shacks that made up much of the lower part.

The Lady Nicholaa was safe enough up here in the tower, John thought: there were no siege engines that could reach so high from the south, where the ground fell steeply. He studied her, as she turned back to the room. The clear morning light was not kind to her ageing features, but illuminated the strength of character etched upon them.

She was dignified, though clearly exhausted, and no wonder: she had carried the defence of the castle on her shoulders for so long, since King John had made her Sheriff and Castellan. But there was still an iron will in control of her own and the castle's fortunes.

The girl went to stand behind her, placing her hand in an almost heraldic gesture on the back of Lady Nicholaa's chair. Turning to face them, too, she revealed the resemblance between the two women, the one fair and hopeful, the other grey and experienced, but with the same wide-spaced eyes and strong brows.

Nicholaa smiled, softening the lines of authority in her countenance, and reached up to pat the girl's hand. "You see behind me, Your Grace, my faithful squire. My youngest daughter, Amabila."

The Bishop bowed, briskly, to them both. "Madam, you have carried a heavy burden, and we are here to relieve you. We will do battle this day, and with God's help rid this city of His enemies. I am come to bring you comfort: to assure you that your safety – and your daughter's – is my chief concern."

Nicholaa smiled again, a sceptical smile this time. She was too civil, or too tired, to tell him how little she believed him; or how little she relished the thought of relinquishing authority. That would be a battle to come, John thought.

"There is no safety for any of us, I fear, unless you can take the city. And we can give you little assistance – we have suffered many losses. Since they brought up the catapults, it has been grievous. There are few enough of us to maintain our defences, now. But we are still holding, for all our stores are running low."

"We will bring crossbowmen, and place them on your battlements. And we had thought to mount an attack through the castle, as well as through the North Gate into the town."

Nicholaa shook her head, doubtfully. "Both ways are heavily guarded. The French forces are strong. Simon de Perche is a doughty captain, who deploys his men well. He has brought many engines into the open space between the castle and the Cathedral, where they can fire in either direction."

"Is there no other point of entry?"

"There is the East Gate to the city, but that will be well defended, too."

Amabila made as if to speak, but her mother pressed her hand for silence.

"My daughter will tell you that in Roman times the West Gate into the city was farther north, above the castle itself. That would lead directly into the city, sure enough. But it was blocked up long ago – when Duke William ordered the castle to be built, with its own entry from the west."

Peter de Roches looked at Amabila. "Demoiselle, do you know where the old gate was? Could you tell us how to find it?"

John watched her flush with eagerness, and his heart went out to her. "Your Grace, I can do better, I can show you. If my lady mother permits me, I will gladly take you there."

Nicholaa sighed, and spread her knotted hands in resignation. "You will be disappointed, I fear. But if you go under protection, I will not forbid you, daughter. Cover yourself with your cloak, and go with His Grace the Bishop, but do not stay outside the castle for long."

She rose, leaning just a little on her stick, but straight-backed and a force to be reckoned with, by friend as well as foe. "I pray you, sirs, take good care of her." Was it John's imagination, or was she looking straight at him?

Amabila snatched up her cloak, and led them again, down out of the tower and, close in under the protection of the walls, back to the gate where they had entered. John went out the wicket first, and handed her through, the Bishop hot behind her. The men guarding their horses had drawn back north up the hill, closer to the Earl

Marshal and his army for safety: they started forward when they saw the little party emerge, but the Bishop flung up his hand to halt them where they were.

The sun was up now, but the walls still cast a shadow westwards, and Amabila kept within it, moving lightly along the very top of the slope on which the castle had been raised. More heavily accoutred, they stumbled after her, slipping on the slick, dewy grass. She reached the corner of the castle, where it joined the city wall. A holly bush obscured the join, but she pushed behind it, freeing her cloak impatiently. And beyond it, sure enough, was an old round archway, filled with stone and rubble.

The Bishop shouted now, to the rest of his men. "Leave the horses, and come help us here. Bring axes. One of you – William, he'll trust your word – go beg the Earl Marshal, of his love, to send crossbowmen to the castle gate. And you, demoiselle, you have our thanks: get you back now to your lady mother." He looked round, and his eye fell on John. "Escort the lady, and see her safe into the tower."

John held out his hand, but she ignored it, moving light as a doe back along the top of slope to the gate. "You need come no further, sir, I am safe enough." But he followed her through into the castle ward again, and just as they entered, a thunderclap presaged an avalanche of stones from the top of the gatehouse. A lucky long shot from the engines beyond the eastern wall.

Without thought, he flung himself upon her, taking them both to the ground. A buttress afforded just enough protection: the stones rocketed harmlessly past. In the silence that followed, he thought he could hear her heart beat. He looked into her wide eyes and shocked countenance. And was lost.

He helped her to her feet, brushed down her cloak, and they exchanged words of concern and reassurance almost mechanically, mere cover for more important things they could not say, not then. He escorted her to the tower, left her with her mother, bowing awkwardly, and saying he would return, as if that were not in question. When he got back to the Bishop and his men, Roger gave him a puzzled look, and he realised he had not even heard what his friend had said.

"Were you caught in that blast?" Roger asked him again, and John nodded, glad to have an excuse for his confusion. "Well, we're nearly done here – we've made a way through, we only need to make it wide enough for horses."

The Bishop stepped back. "Owen and Giles, you stay to finish the work. The rest of you, mount up and get back to the Earl Marshal. We must tell him the good news. Get the rest of your harness, you that are still unarmed. Now we can begin, in God's name."

They did not have far to go. In response to the earlier message, Falkes de Breauté had brought his crossbowmen round, and a group of knights, led by the Earl Marshal himself, had followed. He raised his arm to the Bishop. "Chester is attacking the North Gate. We will meet him within."

John searched for Richard, found him and hastily pulled on his hauberk, mailed gloves and helm. He belted his sword back on, wishing he had chausses to protect his legs, watching with envy while others where laced into these; he'd been only half-equipped when he left Salisbury's service.

Richard was struggling to hold John's horse, which was excited by the swirling mass of warriors now armed and mounted. John hauled himself on, and grabbed the reins. "Get back, now, Richard, to the baggage train, and stay there till I send for you." He saw Richard wanted to argue, and shouted: "Go now, before I give you the flat of my sword."

The Earl Marshal had had himself armed beforehand, and was waiting impatiently for the Bishop's men. He swung round to address them all. "Let me see no cowards here. We fight for a victory that will drive the false claimant from England, and send Frenchmen to hell." He dug in his spurs, and his horse leapt forward, towards the open arch.

A horrified shout forced itself unbidden from John's lungs. In his excitement, the Earl had forgotten his helm: his squire stood dumbfounded with it in his hands, rooted to the spot where Marshal had spoken to his men. John had only an old-fashioned, small helm with a bar running down the bridge of his nose, leaving him free to shout an unmuffled, clearer warning now.

He thrust his horse to the front of the string of knights, bellowing as he went. "My Lord! My Lord! Your helm!"

To his relief, the group of knights checked, and Marshal himself swung round angrily, looking for the cause of the interruption. With realisation of its cause, his anger faded. His squire came running, and Marshal looked closely at John. "You are our young pathfinder, are you not? It seems I am doubly in your debt."

*

John sat slumped on his exhausted horse, his mouth full of bile. It had been nothing like the battles of his imagination. And its aftermath had been shameful. He could still hear the screams of women and children as the crossbowmen rampaged through the city. The Bishop had declared the inhabitants' lives and goods forfeit, even the clergy, as excommunicated rebels. De Breaute's men had needed no further encouragement.

Few knights had been killed, apart from Prince Louis's captain, Simon de Perche, an event that had shocked both sides. Knights were too valuable for ransom to kill: many had been captured and taken to the castle for safe keeping, away from the mayhem. But the people of the city had been pillaged, and raped, and carelessly slaughtered at any sign of resistance.

At first John had found the battle glorious. The Earl Marshal had defied age to lead them from the unblocked gate to the Cathedral. John and Roger, stirrup to stirrup, had followed Salisbury in this mad scramble. When they burst out of the narrow street, the men manning the siege guns before the castle had thought they must be allies, arriving so unexpectedly, and had learnt otherwise the hard way.

The crossbowmen had rained arrows down from the castle walls on to the Capetian army. Chester had, with difficulty, forced his way into the city through the North Gate. They had joined forces on the open ground before the Cathedral.

Even so, victory had hung in the balance; the Earl Marshal's forces were well outnumbered, and they were pushed back more than once. But after de Perche's death, the tide of battle turned, and the Capetian army began to flee down the hill.

They were followed, soon enough, by the inhabitants of the city. As the victors began pillaging houses and churches, even the Cathedral itself, fear took hold and all tried to flee south, some scrambling on to boats to escape along the Witham. Many did not get that far.

Some died as they were caught, or were trampled by the crowd struggling through the gate in the inner wall; more were trapped further downhill at the Stonebow Gate. Later, John learnt that many, overfilling the boats in their panic, had drowned.

Roger had come across John trying to intervene, and pulled him away by his bridle. "Leave them, or they'll turn on you, too. 'Tis always this way, after a battle – and the Bishop has sanctioned it. There's naught you can do. Find something for yourself, John, you'll need a new horse, by the look of that one, at the very least. There's no time to lose. Come."

But John could not. In the trampled crowd he had, he was sure, seen faces he knew: faces he would see in his dreams. At the Cathedral, too: faces he remembered from his boyhood, trying to teach him his lessons – now struggling to defend the church's treasures.

One elderly cleric had clutched at a jewelled cross, wailing about its precious relic, and was spitted like a pig. Others had sought safety by clambering up the scaffolding – the Cathedral was only half-rebuilt since the earthquake – and had been brought down like crows by the crossbowmen.

Hardly knowing what he did, he turned his weary horse towards the castle. He must find Richard, and take him home; he could get through this way to clean fields outside the city. The battle was won, but everything else was lost. He would go through the castle, look up at the tower and wonder if Amabila was there. He had dreamt of coming to her in triumph, but now he was sick with the destruction of all his dreams. He dismounted and led his horse through the gate.

As he passed through the castle ward, John d'Earley was climbing down from the tower. He checked, in surprise. "You come very timely, young man. The Earl Marshal was asking for you."

The older man watched John shake his head, and looked at him shrewdly. "Was that your first taste of battle? Aye, I can see it was. And it was not what you imagined. Well, that is a lesson learnt, and one you must not waste."

He shouted for a boy to take John's exhausted horse, and firmly pushed him up the steps to the tower. The Earl Marshal had taken over the high chamber; there was no sign of Lady Nicholaa and her daughter. Only the Earl, and his son, two servants, and the Earl of Salisbury, who sat relaxed in the Lady Nicholaa's chair, with the air of a man in possession.

John bowed, and Marshal looked at him, a moment, in silence. Then he nodded briskly, as if coming to a decision of minor importance.

"I saw you fighting well, young squire, but I do not know how you fared. Did you take any knights captive?"

"No, My Lord."

"Horses? Armour? Chattels?" John shook his head.

Marshal gave a short laugh. "When I was nineteen, and in the service of the Lord of Tancarville, I fought in a skirmish at Neufchatel. I acquitted myself well, and was proud of it. But I was the poorer for it: my warhorse was killed, and I took no booty nor captive. That night the older knights in my lord's mesnie taunted me with my failure, and my poverty."

He picked up a cup of wine, and with deliberation, drained it and set it down. "I learnt then that glory does not fill your belly: the chances of war must never be wasted. If you cannot stomach that, become a monk."

He paused, smiling with his lips but not his eyes. "A priest. Like His Grace of Winchester, perhaps?" He rubbed his chin, with a fleeting expression of distaste. "A fine warrior, with God on his side."

Now he glared at John. "Learn it now, young man: life is a battle, better fought for right, and in God's name, but hallowed or not, in battle no one will pick you up if you fall."

He called over his shoulder. "D'Earley, have we many to ransom?"

"Aye, My Lord, as many from the rebels as the French."

"Then I would give this young squire his share. I am in his debt. I would not have him wait, and perhaps go unrecompensed. Can you find me a purse that will serve the case?"

D'Earley passed him a leather pouch, its contents chinking. John realised he must have several of these ready, to settle his lord's debts. He opened his mouth to refuse, but the Earl Marshal stared him down. "Take good fortune where you find it; you will do so rarely." The Earl pulled himself to his feet, with a grimace of pain, and reached out impatiently to d'Earley again. His sword was put in his hand.

Somehow John found himself kneeling, and the Regent of England slapped the flat of his sword on the young man's shoulder.

"I dub thee knight, Sir John. Never traffic with traitors, give evil counsel to a lady, or break the commandants of Holy Church. There, that's done."

John stumbled to his feet, muttering incoherent thanks, but Marshal brushed them aside. "I have little time for such courtesy; in my youth you told a man he was a knight, and dealt him a blow, and it was done. But nowadays we are supposed to sing like troubadours and pray like saints. You should have fasted through a vigil. Ah well, you heard Mass this morning, that will do. Chivalry! They don't know the meaning of the word. Blood and sweat, that's what chivalry means, not fine oaths and fancy verses. Now go home, and tell the story as you will."

John bowed again, incapable of speech. He was pleased, no denying it, though it was not as he would once have felt such an honour. His innocent dreams of glory had been trampled in the gutters of Lincoln. All the same, the Earl Marshal had helped him to face the reality that he had found there.

He had made it plain that war and cruelty were inseparable, and that in pursuing the one he practised the other, without pleasure but without regret either. So John had discovered that his idol of chivalry had feet of clay – no, not clay, iron rather, stamped on the neck of the defeated. To be sure, Marshal had found time, money and honour for John – but not out of generosity, rather because he did not care to be beholden. And somehow, in the sickened aftermath of battle, John found that easier to accept. He found his voice.

"Aye, My Lord, I will. But pray you, will you do me one more favour?"

His benefactor grunted, but not unkindly. "It seems you have learnt your lesson already, and too well. What is it that you wish for, young man?"

"Can you tell me, My Lord, where I can now find the Lady Nicholaa and her daughter?"

1217–1399

*F*or all I know, the real-life John sat out the battle at home or had joined the rebels. But it was an irresistible temptation to give him the part of the squire who did indeed – according to the Life of William Marshal – warn the seventy-year-old warrior-Regent that he'd forgotten his helmet. And, of course, to introduce him to Amabila.

For everything else about this battle, I have kept as close to truth as I can. Or, at least, to truth as portrayed in the Life, written for Marshal's son within fifty years of the old man's death.

This, naturally, skates over the darker side of what became known, with bitter irony, as the Battle of Lincoln Fair: the brutality of the retribution meted out, egged on by a "crusading" Bishop. That said, it was a remarkable victory against a superior force.

The Life also skates over Marshal's demotion of Lady Nicholaa; it seems he had promised the position of Castellan to Longsword. Undaunted, she petitioned the new King's council for its return and, surprisingly, succeeded.

It was highly unusual to kill the enemy's commander in a battle, and of course a waste of a good ransom opportunity. The supporters of young Henry did not attempt to follow up with the capture of Prince Louis, who would have been a rich prize indeed. But even after Lincoln Fair, Marshal did not have a strong enough army to *be sure of victory. In the end it took a sea battle, off the coast of Kent, to destroy the last vestiges of the Capetian prince's English ambitions. By 1218, Louis was gone.*

The child, Henry III, reigned for an astonishing fifty-six years, though with no great distinction. He fathered a far more formidable royal champion in the huge person of Edward Longshanks, the "Hammer of the Scots".

Longshanks came to the throne himself in 1272, the first of the three Edwards who ruled England over the next century. In this period, Kettlethorpe passed from the de Ken to the de la Croix families, the final echoes of the Conquest. But then, in 1356, it was conveyed to the Swynfords – the family that was to give the house its brief lustre of royalty.

Edward III outlived the eldest of his sons, and was succeeded by his grandson, Richard II, still a child. Richard's early popularity faded as the years passed and his favourites became hate-figures in a country exhausted by plague and war. His uncles and their families were frequently at odds, with each other and the King.

Even so, it was not until the death in 1399 of the third and most powerful of Edward III's sons, the Duke of Lancaster, that support for Richard finally collapsed. Lancaster was loyal to the end. But his exiled son, Henry of Bolingbroke, decided that his time had come.

No group of men had a keener interest in the outcome of Henry's challenge than his half-brothers, the Beauforts. They were the children of Lancaster's mistress and third wife – Katherine Swynford, Lady of Kettlethorpe.

Lancasters, Beauforts and Swynfords – the families of John of Gaunt and Katherine of Kettlethorpe

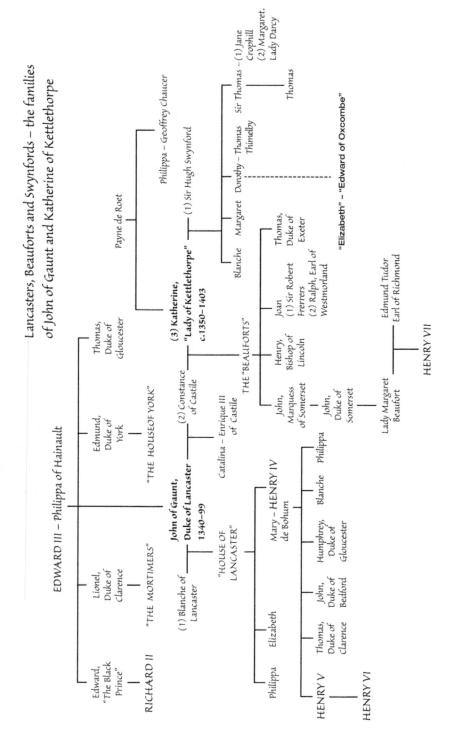

PORTRAIT OF A LADY

KETTLETHORPE MANOR: *1399–1403*

Elizabeth checked, her hand on the churchyard gate. On the parched grass between her and the moat stood her Uncle Thomas. He had his back to her, but she did not need to see his face: every inch of his solid frame expressed satisfaction with the scene in front of him. From new gatehouse, the standard of his mother the Duchess hung limply in the warm and windless air. It made a statement of the importance of this small manor. Sir Thomas Swynford seemed to find this very pleasing.

Elizabeth drew back, letting the latch on the gate drop noiselessly into place. Surely he would not stop long. He was stout for a man still young, with a colouring that did not take the sun well, and like Elizabeth he was formally dressed, in expectation of guests. She hoped her uncle would head for the shade of the buildings soon, without seeing her.

It was not that she feared his disapproval, since her errand was irreproachable. Dame Margaret Dymoke, having caught her dallying with Edward of Oxcombe in the Great Hall, had briskly handed her a laundered altar cloth, and bidden her return it to the vestry. It had been most annoying of Dame Margaret, since

Edward had clearly been taken with Elizabeth's new, close-fitting gown.

It was a deep red, which Elizabeth considered a very grown-up colour. Her friend Alice told her she should wear blue, like the Duchess used to, or perhaps Lincoln green, with her colouring, but Alice knew nothing. The gown was cut in a deep square across her breasts, with an embroidered girdle hanging enticingly low around her hips.

Edward had played with its tassel, and she had smiled back at him, well aware of his meaning. She wondered if she dared give her girdle to Edward, as the Lady did in *Sir Gawain and the Green Knight*. But Dame Margaret would be shocked beyond belief if she found out, and Hawise Maudelyn, who had been with the Duchess from way back, was sharp-eyed, and bound to ask where it had gone.

Sir Gawaine was Elizabeth's favourite poem, though in this household the works of Master Gower and Master Chaucer tended to be preferred, being close to the great family of which Elizabeth was so proud to be part. Master Chaucer, indeed, was the Duchess's brother-in-law, Elizabeth's great-uncle; he had always been kind to her, on his visits, which had grown more frequent since his wife died. She wished he was here now, to help her find her way to her heart's desire.

Furious at being sent on an errand, Elizabeth had turned with what she hoped was an elegant swaying of her hips. But the twitch of Dame Margaret's lips was disheartening: it made Elizabeth fear that that it had looked more like a childish flounce.

No point in hurrying back, since Dame Margaret would no doubt have sent Edward about his business too. But that was not why Elizabeth had stopped. Nor because she was afraid of Uncle Thomas. It was simply because he was there, where she endlessly, privately, and silently, accused him of being, without the right to be so. He was standing between her and Kettlethorpe.

Elizabeth was an orphan, the eldest and only surviving child of Thomas's sister, Dorothy Thimelby. The Thimelbys had died within days of each other, nine years ago, when a pardoner carried a recurrence of the plague in Lincoln out to their manor in the Wolds. In this outbreak, the grim reaper had seemed to have his eye bent on children, and Elizabeth had been the only survivor of four. Since that day, when she was only six years old, Elizabeth had lived as part of her grandmother's household.

She was proud of her descent from this grandmother, a lady who had risen far out of the sphere of the Thimelbys. But when Elizabeth had first come to live with her, Katherine Swynford had been no more than a royal mistress, once repudiated, often defamed, with a brood of bastards to provide for.

Hawise had told Elizabeth that a gang of Dame Katherine's detractors had once stormed the courtyard of her house in Lincoln, calling her foul names and stealing her goods. It had made Elizabeth dream of heroics, standing between her grandmother and the mob. "So young," they would say at her funeral, "and so brave." And the mobsters would kneel weeping by her bier, begging forgiveness and pressing a strand of her long, loose hair (Elizabeth particularly enjoyed this part of the dream) to their lips.

But Dame Katherine had shown little need of championship, setting an example of brisk resilience, complaining boldly to the Mayor and demanding restitution for the damage. The name-calling she had become well used to. There was much less of it now. She was the esteemed Duchess of Lancaster, widow of the greatest – and richest – of the sons of King Edward III.

Grandmother was old now, of course, nigh on fifty, but even the critical eye of youth could see the traces of an astonishing beauty. Whether it was this, her intelligence, or her strength of character, that had sustained Lancaster's affection for Dame Katherine through the storms of public anger, the very public parting to appease the mob, the fading of passions in old age, was beyond young Elizabeth's understanding. But whichever, when his second wife Constance of Castile died, the Duke had astonished – no, outraged – the Court by marrying his mistress.

They had been wed quietly in Lincoln Cathedral three years ago. Elizabeth, self-conscious in her new finery, had not then understood how much of a change this joining of two elders would make to all their lives.

Most significantly, she had soon come to see, this marriage had been accompanied by the legitimation of My Lord Duke and Dame Katherine Swynford's four children, long since given the name of Beaufort. ("Why Beaufort?" Elizabeth had asked Hawise, who had pursed her lips. "One of his castles in France. Long way away. And a handsome name for a handsome pack of rascals!")

The Beauforts too had now risen way above young Elizabeth, with great titles and lands – one, Henry, to the Bishopric of Lincoln, at the indecently youthful age of twenty-one: another cause for outrage among the nobility and clergy. But soon, the Court taking its lead from Lancaster's nephew King Richard, the muttering had stopped. The ladies who had threatened to ostracise the new Duchess came to treat her with the respect her husband's position and her own courtesy merited. The new order settled over the old.

Elizabeth had not grudged the four Beauforts their advancement in the slightest. They had always been kindly to her, and – most importantly – their raised ambitions took them way above contention for the only thing that mattered to her.

Kettlethorpe.

Proud as Elizabeth was of her ancestry, she was enough the Duchess's grand-daughter to know that pride took you only so far. Property, land, wealth: those were what gave you assurance against the turbulence of life, as the former Dame Katherine Swynford had taught her. Elizabeth's hunger for these these was directed simply and solely towards her grandmother's lands at Kettlethorpe. An impoverished holding inherited from Sir Hugh, it had been slowly and carefully built up by his widow into a substantial estate.

Lately, Elizabeth's land-hunger had been sharpened by love. She had first met Edward of Oxcombe as a page, and then a squire, in Lancaster's retinue. He was gently born, but a landless younger son, with his way to make in the world, lucky to get a place in so great a household.

That need for advancement he had until recently shared with his close friend Thomas Beaufort, the Duchess's youngest son, until Thomas's legitimation had raised him to semi-royal status. Indeed, to wealth as well as status: after the Earl of Arundel's execution, King Richard had granted Thomas the traitor's lands at Castle Acre, in Norfolk, in one of those strange bursts of generosity with which he sought to placate his Uncle Lancaster.

Edward, by contrast, still needed to marry well, a lady with lands and title, and at present Elizabeth had neither. She was fifteen, marriage-ripe, and to achieve what she wanted she had only had her hunger, and her hopes.

Now the Duke was dead and his heir, the Beauforts' elder half-brother Henry of Bolingbroke, had been banished by the King. And all was uncertainty again. Edward, Elizabeth knew, longed to join Henry of Bolingbroke in his exile, but could not do that without the Duchess's support.

The Duchess's household was not often at Kettlethorpe. While the Duke of Lancaster was still alive, she had spent much time at Leicester Castle, or with the Court, where she had been chief of the ladies deputed to care for King Richard's new little wife from France. In autumn, they came to Kettlethorpe to hunt, either here in the 300-acre deer park Richard II had given Katherine permission to enclose, or in the Bishop of Lincoln's deer park just across the Fossdyke. But now, as a widow, she liked to spend most of her time in Lincoln, where she rented a fine canon's house in Minster Yard, and had made it still finer to suit herself and her household.

But she still visited Kettlethorpe in high summer. They had arrived only last week, on the church's feast day of St Peter and St Paul. Falling at the end of June, this took them to Kettlethorpe each year when the scents of roses and lavender could drive the city out of their nostrils, and the younger members of the household put off courtly dignity to help with the haymaking.

Dame Margaret and Roger Stow, the Duchess's chamberlain, much disapproved of this, but the Duchess only laughed and said it was good to be reminded they had not always ridden so high. She liked to point to the wheel on her coat-of-arms. It was there for her name saint, of course, for whom it had been an instrument of torture. But it should also, she said, remind them all of the spinning wheel of fortune.

She had retained a great affection for her old manor, as well as a careful interest in its affairs. Her chamberlain had told Elizabeth, in an unusual burst of confidence, that despite all her new royal titles, the Duchess still insisted on signing herself "Lady of Kettlethorpe".

The hall had been substantially rebuilt, of cut stone, and its internal plaster painted with hunting scenes. The tower had been rebuilt, too, and the solar hung with tapestries. Extra chambers had been added – small ones, little to Dame Margaret's taste, but well appointed.

The group of buildings that made up the manor was now fronted by this new impressive gatehouse, so approved of by her eldest son. But the Duchess had not, as yet, handed either the manor or the Advowson of the rectory over to Thomas Swynford. Only this summer, she had herself chosen young William Wylingham as the new priest.

In the nature of things, when the Duchess died, this Swynford property, together with her manor at Coleby, must pass to Thomas. Many would argue it should have done so on her husband Sir Hugh's death, or at least when Thomas Swynford came of age.

But his mother seemed in no hurry, preferring Thomas and his wife to live at Coleby Manor, or now at nearby Somerton Castle, which had been granted to Thomas by the King. No one cared to argue with the Duchess of Lancaster, who was – after the little Queen – the first lady in the Kingdom. And on this evidence of reluctance, Elizabeth rested all her hopes that she might be recognised as the Lady of Kettlethorpe's heir.

She thought about it much. Surely she was the only true claimant? Of the Duchess's four surviving babies bearing the Swynford name, Blanche – the eldest of three girls – had had no children and was, like Elizabeth's mother Dorothy, long dead. Margaret, the middle sister, had entered a convent favoured by the royal family, at Barking. The fourth child was, of course, Thomas. But gossip cast a shadow over his paternity. Was he the last of Sir Hugh's children, or – as Elizabeth firmly believed – the first of My Lord Duke's?

There was much confusion over Thomas's birth. Only a few years ago, in proof of his inheritance rights, various good citizens of Lincoln had been asked to swear they had been present at his baptism, and had done so with much detail and enthusiasm, recalling such personal events on the same day as a broken bottle of wine or a birth in their own family. But that, Elizabeth had whispered excitedly to her closest friend amongst the Duchess's ladies, would make his bastardy certain. For the date they recalled, she had been told, was in 1373.

Alice Deyncourt, a year older than her friend Elizabeth, had entered the Duchess's household only a few years ago. She was much in awe of the Duchess, and had not been inclined to doubt her word. But Elizabeth had persisted. "Sir Hugh Swynford had died too long before!" she had pointed out. "How could he have fathered such an infant?"

Alice had shrugged. Every country counted years differently, and Sir Hugh had died abroad. Or perhaps, she had suggested, those witnesses confused the occasion with the baptism of Her Grace's next child – was that not Sir John Beaufort, Marquess of Somerset, who now stood so high in King Richard's favour?

Elizabeth had been furious. How could Alice be so stupid? "For sure my grandmother knew the difference! Why then did she pretend it was Uncle Thomas Swynford? There could be but one reason!"

Alice had been sitting on their bed, admiring the glinting waves in her unbound hair. She had brushed it away over her shoulder, dismissing Elizabeth's arguments with the same strokes. Everyone in the Duchess's household, she pointed out, knew that in My Lord Duke's petition to His Holiness the Pope, the Duke had admitted to his own adultery, but not to any such offence by his bride. Elizabeth should be ashamed to suggest otherwise.

They had all been puzzled by talk of this petition, hastily dispatched to the Pope after the marriage of the Duke and Duchess, and had been eager to know what was in it. Elizabeth had not dared to ask her grandmother, but had gone, as usual, to Hawise. Was it because of the Beauforts?

Hawise had sniffed. "Nay, they're no secret to the world. It's your Aunt Blanche, God rest her soul – His Holiness had to be told she was the Duke's godchild."

That made Elizabeth even more confused. "Why did that matter?" she had asked, but Hawise either didn't know or wouldn't say.

"His Holiness makes the rules, not me. Now, stop your pestering and get to your duties, or Dame Margaret will be after you."

Elizabeth had explained all this to Alice, who had brushed it aside as quite unimportant. What really mattered was what they had been told about the petition: that the Duke and Duchess had sworn to the Pope that the couple had not lain together until after Sir Hugh Swynford was dead.

Her Grace, Alice had said to Elizabeth with reproach, was a most religious lady, and would never have committed so grievous a sin as to lie to His Holiness. And why, Alice had asked, with an abrupt lowering of her pious tone, should the Duke deny fatherhood of a Swynford or two, while owning to all those other Beaufort bastards?

Elizabeth's exasperation had boiled over. How dared Alice suggest she was casting a slur on her grandmother? She loved her deeply, but the Duchess was, she had told Alice sharply, no plaster saint: she had lain with another woman's husband, after all. "And only imagine, Alice, how much harder it would have been to admit to her own adultery! How could she do so publicly, when she'd already been called witch and whore?"

Alice had clapped her hands over her ears in horror. These were not subjects for maidens to discuss: Dame Margaret would have them severely chastised if she heard whisper of it.

It was impossible, Elizabeth realised belatedly, to make her friend see things her way. Of course, she had tried to explain, when her grandmother was only My Lord Duke's mistress – a mistress who had been discarded once, and might be again – she had insisted on Thomas's claim to Swynford property. For security. But now, Elizabeth hoped, that the Duchess was secure beyond all question, perhaps she would admit the truth.

Even to her own ears, though, that had sounded over-hopeful, and Alice had been unkind enough to laugh. "It's folly. Forget it, before it leads you to disgrace. How could you dare even mention it to the Duchess? Especially now that she has asked all those good burgesses to swear to the date of Sir Thomas's christening!"

She had looked at Elizabeth with pitying exasperation. "Her Grace has always dealt with you kindly, tell her of your love for Edward, and I am sure she will see you well dowered. But ask her for something it is easier for her to give away than her own good name."

Alice had tossed her hairbrush aside, bored with the topic, and it missed the coffer, falling to the rushes on the floor. If Hawise found it there in the morning, there would be trouble.

Hawise had brought up young Elizabeth, and still had no hesitation giving the girls a sharp talking-to, for lesser offences than chatter about the Duchess's chastity. In Elizabeth's view, they were far too old to be so demeaned, but she knew Hawise had the Duchess's ear. And the hairbrush was silver-backed, a present from the Duchess herself, and so in Hawise's eyes nigh on sacred. Alice was in for a scolding.

Seething with resentment, Elizabeth had contemplated that prospect with some pleasure. It was bad enough that her friend had golden hair, the very colour Elizabeth would have loved to inherit from the Duchess, instead of the mouse-brown that Hawise had told her dismissively she had from the Thimelbys. It was worse that, after all the vows of eternal friendship they had sworn, Alice still refused to share in her friend's hopes.

You can, Elizabeth had thought crossly, be too honest with your friends, sometimes. She had turned away from Alice, tugging their coverlet with her and pretending sleep. She would not give up. And now they were at Kettlethorpe for the summer, surely something would happen to turn things her way.

*

Sir Thomas Swynford's admiration of the new gatehouse seemed to have ended abruptly: he was striding forward, shouting for the porter as he went. Elizabeth followed, curious to know what had alerted him, and found the manor courtyard busy with grooms, leading spent and sweaty horses to the stables. A party must have entered from the south, through the old farm gate: a party that knew its way here. Their guests? Fine coursers, if so, but no – the grooms wore the Beauforts' livery.

Which of them could it be? The eldest Beaufort, John, Marquess of Somerset (a title that Hawise said was outlandish – nay, downright foolish), was with the Duke of York, and the King's forces in the west. Bishop Henry Beaufort was with the King himself in Ireland, taking care of Henry of Bolingbroke's eldest son, Harry. King Richard had taken the boy with him on his rebel-hunting expedition. Why? When the girls asked Hawise, she sucked in her cheeks: doubtless, the King wanted to keep his prize hostage under his eye. He was a fool to leave the kingdom, but that was enough, she'd say no more.

It couldn't be the Duchess's daughter, Joan Beaufort: she was now married to the Earl of Westmorland; her servants would wear his livery. So it must be Thomas Beaufort, her youngest uncle, Elizabeth thought, quickening her step with pleasure.

This handsome young man was only five years older than Elizabeth, and he was one of Edward's heroes; so she tripped eagerly up the steps to the door of the manor, slipping into the Great Hall behind the other, older Thomas. But he strode on briskly towards his mother's solar, entered – and pulled the door to behind him.

Frustrated, Elizabeth looked round for an excuse to follow. A boy was staggering from the buttery, with a tray of drinking mazars, and jugs of ale and Rhenish, to wet the travellers' throats. Elizabeth took it from him, ignoring his protests, and motioning him to open the solar door.

Eyes turned towards Elizabeth as she entered, not all of them approving, as she thankfully lowered the heavy tray on to the coffer. How dreadful it would have been to drop it! She saw Dame Margaret preparing to dismiss her. But the Duchess looked amused, and beckoned her granddaughter to stand beside her, turning at the same time to ask Dame Margaret to take the other ladies away.

"You have all heard what the messenger had to say, and now I must speak alone with my sons. Hawise, do you take these young fellows to the kitchen, and see them well fed. Take your ale with you, masters, and then take your rest. You have surely earned it."

She checked her chamberlain. "Roger, you must stay and hear, in case there are dispositions we need to make. And Elizabeth, you shall stay to look after your grandmother." The chamberlain bowed, stiffly; looking at him out of the corner of her eye, Elizabeth could see he was gratified, but shocked to his staid soul by what the messengers had told.

Hawise went willingly enough: she would learn all from her mistress, soon enough. Dame Margaret was not so pleased to be dismissed, and the Duchess hastened to appease her. "Our guests will be arriving soon; of your kindness, would you welcome them for me?"

Dame Margaret was careful of her dignity, as the elderly widow of a knight of the Duke's retinue, Sir Hugh Dymoke. She had come to give tone to the Duchess's household, or so she clearly believed, after Lancaster's scandalous marriage. She had remained with them after the Duke's death, "as a favour to Her Grace," or so she told the girls, since the Duchess had no one else who knew how a royal widow's household should be run.

The girls thought, and Hawise said, that the Duchess was more than capable of running her household herself, and had done so for many years; indeed, the Duchess's skill in managing her affairs was a by-word, a further proof of witchery in the eyes of her detractors. But age, and security, had only reinforced her kindliness, and Dame Margaret was, the Duchess told the girls when they had recently shown a tendency to rebel, a lady to be admired. "She is much to my taste: independent and courageous, and I will have her treated with respect in her old age."

So she had smiled sweetly at Margaret Dymoke and blessed her goodness in saying she would stay. Life was not as comfortable or well found at the Dymokes' remote manor as it was in the Duchess's luxurious residence in Lincoln. The girls just had to accept that, now into her seventies, Dame Margaret was always bad-tempered at Kettlethorpe, which she compared unfavourably with Scrivelsby.

She now swept the ladies out with as much dignity as she could muster, Alice rolling her eyes at Elizabeth as she went – which earned her a sharp push from Hawise. The messengers got to their feet, bowed, wiped the sweat out of their eyes once more, and reached thankfully for the mazars as they departed. The Duchess was left confronting her two sons, the two Thomases, youngest of each of her two litters of children. Her chamberlain was still at her elbow, his back rigid with disapproval.

These two sons did not, Elizabeth reflected, look very like. Sir Thomas Swynford resembled his mother, though only as base metal can resemble gold. His brass-yellow, close-cropped hair and beard were dull and rough, his complexion ruddy, the sweetness and roundness of the Duchess's face in him flattened and squared. And even now, when her cornflower irises had faded with age and sickness, they were a truer blue than his.

Her widow's robes, dark – and rich, today, in honour of the expected guests – paradoxically made her look younger. They absorbed the light, leaving her pale face in its white wimple and barbe strangely disembodied, the floating vision of a girl's countenance trapped in the skin of age and grief. In widowhood she was no longer quite of this world, though she still had a shrewd and hard-earned understanding of its follies. Could she shelter her sons from them? Never, but for all that she would still try.

Thomas Beaufort looked not just a decade, but a generation, younger than his half-brother: for all he had ridden hard, there was still, Elizabeth thought admiringly, a look of court fashion about him. He wore a rakish chaperon, a brooch glinting in its folds; an embroidered linen shirt, still damp with sweat, cinched at the waist with a jewelled leather sword belt. A short paltock was thrown over his shoulder. His shirt, too, was short enough to leave his thighs and much else outlined to view in his hose.

His fine leather boots and gold-worked spurs completed the image of the young noble, comparing, in Elizabeth's eyes, very favourably with Swynford's knee-length tunic of sober quality. Dowdy, Elizabeth thought contemptuously, but then so was her Uncle Swynford's new wife. They were a dull couple, Thomas and Jane. But very settled, which was fine, if only if they would settle somewhere else.

Beaufort was far from settled. He was unfinished work. His features still had some of the softness and changeability of youth, but with angular Plantagenet contours showing through: the aquiline nose of his father, high cheekbones, and a pointed chin, on which he was struggling to grow the neat short beard favoured by Henry of Bolingbroke.

There was little of his mother in him, except, Hawise always said fondly, the vitality and gift for life that the Duchess had had in her youth. Right now, he looked a warmer spirit than his sharp features suggested in repose: his face was flushed with excitement, his eyes sparkling with the adventure on which he was so eager to embark.

Not so his mother, for whom it was clearly not welcome news. She spoke with caution, and concern.

"So. You tell me Henry of Bolingbroke has defied his cousin the King, and landed on English soil. At Cromer, did you say? Was that well done?"

Her voice was low, and a little strained with age and care. It still carried traces of her Hainaulter childhood, though she spoke English with the confidence of long use. Even the largely Norman court had followed the lead set by Edward III and switched more or less to the English tongue, Frenchifying it as they went.

Her youngest son nodded, eagerly. "There had been rumours he would land in the south. But when the news came to Castle Acre that he had come to land so close, he was already headed on to the Humber. He'd only stopped for supplies. He can count on much support in the North. Northumberland, for a start – Harry Hotspur was ever his friend. And Westmorland, naturally, now he's wed to sister Joan."

The Duchess's thin hands grasped the arms of her siege. "There is nothing natural about treason, my son. Richard is our King anointed, and My Lord Duke stayed loyal to him to the end, despite much provocation. Your father would never have broken his oath of fealty."

Young Beaufort shifted restlessly. "Richard forfeited his right to Bolingbroke's fealty, when he extended his exile. Extended it to life, mother! How could he do such a monstrous thing? And the King broke his oath to my father, too, seizing the Lancaster estates, and arresting Bowet."

Henry Bowet, Archdeacon of Lincoln, had been appointed, with the agreement of the King, to take control of the Duke's vast estates on his death, in the name of his exiled heir.

"Now Bowet lies in the Tower, threatened with execution!"

Elizabeth was horrified. Archdeacon Bowet, that learned but kindly man, in the Tower? He had been her tutor before his rise to eminence, since her grandmother had insisted on Elizabeth having the education she herself had lacked. Even Elizabeth's great-uncle Geoffrey Chaucer, much inclined to poke fun at the clergy, had admired Archdeacon Bowet; though that may have been because he had rescued Chaucer from at least one of his frequent financial embarrassments.

The Duchess sighed. "It is not so grievous as you fear, my son. I heard he had been released, and gone to join My Lord of Bolingbroke in his exile. Pray God he gives wise counsel."

Her voice had become stronger with concern, and she raised a hand in admonition.

"I blame the Archbishop for this rash venture. He has encouraged it, for his own ends! My Lord Duke never trusted the Arundels, prelate or noble: they are no friends to the House of Lancaster. They would have murdered My Lord Duke, and his heir, had they been given the chance. No, hear me out, my son! Richard was full wise to get rid of the Arundels, or so My Lord Duke thought. But I'll warrant the Archbishop and his worthless nephew are both at Bolingbroke's side now, urging treason. And you should beware, Thomas – the Arundels will have Castle Acre from you, should they return."

Thomas Beaufort looked uncomfortable. She was right, of course. But his mother smiled at him, softening her shrewdness, which she usually took pains to conceal. "Richard is ill-advised, but he will come to his senses. Has he not assured us that he will hold the Lancaster inheritance only until his cousin Bolingbroke has earned his forgiveness? And Richard has already granted me all my widow's rights and monies."

She straightened her back, and looked at both her sons in turn. "Whatever else he may have done, he is still King. My son Somerset will stay loyal, I warrant."

A smile flickered between the two Thomases. Everyone knew that John Beaufort – Sir John, as the world still called him, rather than Marquess of Somerset – was the Duchess's favourite son.

But Swynford could not suppress a snort. "I'll warrant John is writing news to Bolingbroke, even as he serves in Richard's army. He's no fool, mother. But Richard is, or he would never have left for Ireland after robbing Bolingbroke of his birthright. Madness!"

His mother made a small, dismissive gesture, but he ploughed on.

"It was asking for trouble, and now this treacherous King will have to answer for his folly. You know Bolingbroke came back privately, after his father's death. I spoke with him then, and I knew he would not wait long to claim his own."

He shifted his weight slightly, squaring up to his decision, and spoke with the determination necessary to challenge his mother.

"Yes: I grant you, His Grace of Lancaster was ever loyal to Richard. But with his heir exiled for ever, all bonds of loyalty are broken. With your leave, mother, we'll be on our way tomorrow, to join him."

The Duchess, always graceful in defeat, made peace with her sons.

"You were ever his loyal henchmen, from childhood, and I would expect no less of you than you would support him now. I would you were at his elbow, not Arundel. But what about young Harry of Monmouth, poor child? King Richard holds him close, and his father is putting him greatly at risk with this foolhardy landing!"

Swynford shrugged. "If the worst befall, Bolingbroke has a quiverful of sons."

Elizabeth had stood still as marble, terrified of drawing too much attention to her presence. But at this a little gasp escaped her. The Duke's grandchildren were a merry crew, often seen by her at Leicester during the time of his marriage to her grandmother. Surely thirteen-year-old Harry was too precious to be used as a pawn by his warring elders! Thomas Beaufort caught her eye, glanced quickly at his mother's bleak countenance, and hurried into reassurance.

"The Bishop's with Harry, remember." The Bishop! That was how the family all referred to Henry Beaufort: his mother with pride, his siblings, like Thomas, with amusement.

"He'll not let the boy be harmed. And Richard has a fondness for young Harry, despite all. What's more, Richard won't fight – he's a coward! His troops know that, too. They will desert to the

Lancastrian side, and Richard will never provoke vengeance by harming Bolingbroke's son."

The Duchess sighed. "And what does My Lord Bolingbroke intend by coming? You tell me, to claim his rights, but will he stop there? I misdoubt it. How far will you go with him?"

Another flicker of intelligence passed between the brothers. For a long moment, neither said anything. Then Swynford, heavily, spoke for both. "Richard has governed ill, and taxed without mercy: he has forfeited support. Henry has the country behind him. There is the prophecy, too, remember. That may sweep him to the throne, whether he wills it or no."

Elizabeth shivered. Edward and Alice had both tried to explain Merlin's Prophecy of the Six Kings to her, and swore it meant the triumph of the Lancastrians. Of course she believed in prophecies! But she had found this one horribly confusing, a muddle of boars, and dragons, lambs and eagles. If she had understood it aright, Henry of Bolingbroke was represented by a mole – hardly a Kingly beast! But Alice said she was being stupid, prophecies were always like that.

Young Thomas had meanwhile chimed in. "The crown for Lancaster! That's what the mob cries in the streets of London."

There was a sudden movement behind the Duchess, from her chamberlain. She put up her hand to him, in acknowledgement. "Aye, Roger, you and I both know the temper of the mob. We saw the Savoy burnt – a palace. Ruined. Burnt to the ground, by a rabble of Londoners that demanded the head of My Lord Duke! Your brother was there with him, young Thomas: he can tell you what a mob is like."

Again she softened her tone, trying to gentle them into listening to her.

"Be wary, my sons. They may shout Lancaster today, but who knows where their fancy, or their bloodlust, will take them tomorrow? There are other heirs to choose from, when they grow tired of Henry. God love him, he will never sit secure on the throne."

"He was named as Richard's heir by old King Edward," Thomas Swynford repeated, doggedly. "In secret, maybe, but before witnesses."

"And Richard unnamed him. There are others who will press their claims!"

"A child," Thomas Beaufort said. "Young Mortimer. That's all there is, between Richard and Henry. England cannot be ruled by a child again."

Elizabeth was lost. How could a child be a threat to Henry of Bolingbroke? Who was this Mortimer? She scratched desperately at her memory of the royal family. Old King Edward had had five sons: everyone knew that. There was the Black Prince – Richard's father, the first of those sons. And the Dukes of Lancaster, York and Gloucester. All now dead save York. There must have been one more. Clarence! Yes: the Duke of Clarence, dead so long he was easily forgotten.

Perhaps Mortimer was Clarence's son – no: his grandson. That must be it. And wait a minute, hadn't Clarence come second, after the Black Prince? He was senior to Lancaster! This child then had a claim to the throne, as her grandmother was warning.

"My son, you have so much still to learn. Richard a coward? Be not so sure: he showed great courage as a child. I remember when he rode amongst the mob, and charmed them. Maybe little Mortimer will be the same. And he'll not be a child for ever. Meanwhile one of Richard's uncles is still alive to defend him, and commands his army."

"The Duke of York will not stand for Richard against Henry," Beaufort said stoutly.

His brother nodded, and came to his support. "He'll not put his army to the test."

"And how long do you think Bolingbroke will rest easy, if he snatches the crown by force? If you set cousin against cousin, where will it end?"

She was shaking, Elizabeth saw, and reached for the silver cup on the tray that held her cordial. It smelt of elderflowers, but Elizabeth had seen Hawise add drops of poppy juice, scolding the girl for prying.

Her grandmother waved it aside. "I've done, my sons, you must make your own ways through this tangle. Roger, my old friend, our time is past, and we must leave these great matters to others. Pray only that they leave us in peace."

Her chamberlain bowed. "As His Majesty has done, My Lady – I mean, Your Grace." The Duchess smiled. "Aye, I am still Lady of Kettlethorpe, however high My Lord Duke raised me! And Richard has indeed dealt fairly with me. I have a fondness for him, for all that he hastened My Lord Duke to his death."

"Richard is a tyrant," Swynford said. "He pays no heed to the Great Charter. Demands to be called Majesty – faugh! There was none of that nonsense in great King Edward's days."

"My dear son, you were but a child in those days! Believe me, the old King ruled with a firm hand, humble though he might appear. And what matter that Richard likes us to use these new titles? Folly, perhaps, but no harm in it."

She had silenced them at last, but not brought them to agree, she knew. It was time to do more than acquiesce: to take their part.

"Henry of Bolingbroke is very dear to me, as God knows he was to his father, and I wish him well. He has been as a son to me, and good to all my children. I loved his motherless daughters as my own. I fear for him, that is all."

She looked at her ardent youngest son, and smiled, wryly. "I remember, before My Lord Duke and I were wed, how Bolingbroke paid for your first suit of armour, so you could joust at New Year. I reproached him at the time, for you were too young. Then he reminded me that he had first jousted at fourteen, and said practice was the source of his prowess. It was generous: I have not forgot. Now I will go to say prayers for all of you, in these perilous times."

She rose to leave, but Thomas Beaufort stayed her a moment. "Mother, there is a squire in your household I would beg you to release: my friend Edward of Oxcombe. Give me leave to ask him if he will come with me."

Before she could answer, the elder brother took charge. "And for yourself, mother, I am not happy that in these turbulent times you stay here on the Trent. We will escort you to Lincoln, if you would command your chamberlain to make ready. And I will send Jane to you, from Coleby, to bear you company in my absence."

The Lady of Kettlethorpe sighed again. The company of her daughter-in-law was a doubtful pleasure. "It would be kindly of Jane to come. In truth I am loth to move now that I am settled at Kettlethorpe, but – yes, I will be guided. But you need not stay for me. Roger can sort all. I know you are hot to join Henry, and yes, if Edward wishes, he may of course go with you."

The brothers looked relieved. "If we leave tomorrow," Beaufort said, "it will be soon enough for me. Some gentlemen of Lincolnshire are strong in the Lancastrian cause; Bolingbroke was born here, after all, and they will fight for his rights at need. But they'll take time to gather. We can wait to escort you to the city, when you are ready."

"As you wish, my dear sons. We can be ready, Roger, can we not?"

"We can, Your Grace, if I leave some of our trappings to follow." Roger was still stiff with disapproval, but she knew he would not let her down.

Edward was waiting in the Great Hall as they left the solar, a boy on the brink of manhood, with limbs that had grown too fast for him to manage gracefully. He dropped clumsily to his knees before the Duchess, and she shook her head gently, giving him her blessing. "I cannot reproach you, Edward, for wishing to go with my son. God go with you, and keep you both safe."

She saw Elizabeth's face, and her smile embraced them both.

"My granddaughter, I see, is wishful to bid you her own farewell. Ah, here is My Lady Dymoke come to find me. She will escort me to church, and you may join us, Elizabeth – soon. You may tarry the time it takes me to tell one mystery on my beads. A sorrowful mystery, I fear, though."

Hawise joined them, shaking her head over her mistress's determination to cross to the church. "You should rest, Your Grace, if you are to travel tomorrow, and say your prayers before your altar in your chamber. And you, maiden, bid your farewells speedily, there's work to be done if we're to be ready tomorrow."

She bustled on to the now-empty solar, calling for the maidservants, leaving Elizabeth and Edward briefly on their own. He flushed painfully – with embarrassment? Or excitement? – took her hand, and kissed it awkwardly. "Give me your blessing, too, my heart, for this may be the making of my fortunes, if we are early to Henry's cause. And pray God it is successful, for if not we are all lost."

Her heart lifted as he hesitated, willing him to say more. "Elizabeth, I have no right to ask you, but…" She lifted her face to him hopefully. "… I cannot take my talbot or gyrfalcon with me, will you see them both cared for?"

Ah well. She had longed for him to say he would be back to claim her, but this was a start. She could see his mind was already on his great gamble.

"I will, never fear. And I will be waiting for you, praying for your victory." It was all she could find to say in turn.

But what she was praying for, except Edward's safety, she did not know. What did victory mean? What answers would it bring? To England, or to her?

*

The Duchess sat by the window in her solar, in the soft light of the late sun, filtered through the greenish glass of the little panes. Hawise was placing her treasures in chests to be taken to Lincoln, muttering disapproval as she went about it – though whether of the manservants, the move, or the conjunction of the stars that had brought Henry of Bolingbroke back in arms, it was hard to tell.

All was now quiet at Kettlethorpe. Their guests from the south – a Lancastrian knight and his lady homeward bound – had arrived, dusty, dry and tired, to a disordered household, and to Roger's mortified apologies. At the news Sir Ralph had quickly expressed a tactful desire to hurry on north, and they had retired to their chamber for a night's rest.

They had brought the Duchess's brother-in-law with them, Geoffrey Chaucer. Hearing the rumours on the road, he had thought to turn back to London, if his kind sister would be good enough to lend him the wherewithal – he had somehow unaccountably mislaid the warrant for his pension.

Such a thing had never happened to him before, he assured her. He would apply to King Richard for a new one, or maybe – he looked at his sister speculatively – to Henry of Bolingbroke, who had always treated him kindly. But if her sons were leaving her, perhaps his sister would prefer him to stay?

The Duchess assented, warmly. Geoffrey would be a welcome dilution of Jane's dull company.

They sat together now, Dame Margaret having gone to her rest. Chaucer watched Hawise with amusement. The Duchess too smiled at her.

"Peace, now: you must be weary. Leave those chessmen, Master Chaucer and I may have a game."

She touched Hawise's arm, in gentle admonition. "There, leave the rest. The men can pack up all that is left tomorrow. Come and sit with us, and tell me: am I too fearful? They see their fortune, my boys, in this landing by Bolingbroke, and who am I to hold them back?"

Before Hawise could answer, she turned to Chaucer. "What do you think, brother? My Lord Duke was from a different mould, cast in a different age. And he gave his oath to King Edward, his own father. The young are not so bound. Do they do right? And will the country be with them?"

Geoffrey Chaucer stroked his forked beard, now white with his near-sixty years, then linked his fingers over his paunch, as if abdicating all involvement. "The country must choose between tyranny and loyalty on the one hand, freedom and treason on the other. If it chooses the latter, and I'll wager it will, its choice will not long be called treason."

He met the Duchess's anxious gaze, and sighed a little. "But you are right, sister; whether it will truly be freedom is another matter. The crown rests uneasy on a usurper's head. If he triumphs, sooner or later Henry will be pushed to harsh measures to keep it there."

Hawise sniffed. "Praise be, that My Lord Duke didn't live to see this."

The Duchess nodded. "He truly cared for Richard. Even in his last will, he left the King treasure that meant much to him. The chalice I gave him, our last Christmas together. My Lord Duke left that to Richard!"

Geoffrey nodded, noncommittally. It had truly been a strange bequest, given all that had passed. The Duchess went on, as if to herself.

"And yet it was Richard's sentence of exile on Henry that killed My Lord Duke, sure enough. His poor sick body could not stand the grief."

Now it was Hawise's turn to bite her tongue. That sickness of the Duke's had been an unwelcome part of the Duchess's inheritance from Lancaster, a disease which his physician told Lancaster came from his travels, when he had slaked his appetites unwisely. Much as Hawise had admired the Duke, there were nights of the Duchess's suffering when she silently cursed him, though the Duchess herself never complained.

She was dreaming now, Hawise saw, back through the twilight to her youth at the court of Queen Philippa, a Hainaulter herself, who had a kindness for the orphaned children of a compatriot in her service. A beautiful child, Katherine had been, an even more lovely girl. And the Duke had been the finest prince in Christendom.

"When I first saw My Lord Duke," the Duchess mused, "he was only young Thomas's age, and as full of life and pride – and I dare say as rash, too. The Lady Blanche, God rest her, taught him patience and duty, and he worshipped her. As did we all. Even you, Master Chaucer."

She smiled at the memory. "Especially, perhaps, you, or maybe it was just that you alone had the genius to express your worship."

Blanche of Lancaster, the greatest heiress in the Kingdom, had been the duke's first wife. The plague had snatched her, tragically young, while her husband was fighting in France. All who knew her had mourned her, deeply, and for many months Lancaster would not be comforted.

Chaucer shook his head, acknowledging the worship but not the genius. "I did my poor best. Poets can give nothing except, perhaps, a whisper of immortality. It was the first thing I wrote of which I have any reason to feel proud, and it was the subject, not the scribbler, that made it praiseworthy."

A little silence passed, in which even Hawise was still. Then Chaucer spoke again.

"If I bring her back to us as I saw her, gentle, teasing, dancing, singing, it is to her credit, not mine. She was, truly, fresh and fair and free. An early rose, plucked untimely."

And her husband, and Katherine? The question hung between them. Chaucer had written no poems in praise of Katherine – though her granddaughter thought there were less worshipful glimpses of the Duchess in his *Canterbury Tales.*

Geoffrey thought about Katherine now, seeing her arrival in Lancaster's life from the distance of age. They had all been so very young! When John of Gaunt and Blanche of Lancaster had wed, he had been nineteen, she fourteen; she had been only twenty-three when she died.

And I, Geoffrey thought, not yet thirty, and newly married to Philippa de Roet, a herald's daughter dowered by the Queen, God rest her soul. Katherine, Philippa's sister, had been a child-bride to a knight in the Duke's retinue, Sir Hugh Swynford, and had become governess to the Duke's two daughters.

The greatest man in the Kingdom, young, handsome, lusty; a beautiful, charming girl, in his own household – how could they not have been drawn to each other? But whatever accusations were later levelled at Katherine Swynford, he recalled, and there had been plenty, no one truly believed there had been anything between her and the Duke in Blanche's time. Whatever came after, what disrespect was there in that to his first wife?

Chaucer was a kindly man, for all his sharp wit, with a generosity towards human weakness, and an unusual sensitivity to women's feelings. In silence, he disentangled his painful loyalties, and finally made peace between them. He took the Duchess's hand, and gently kissed it.

But Katherine scarcely noticed, still lost in her own train of thought. "She taught us all so much, and it is right that he lies with her in death."

Hawise looked at her mistress, sharply, wondering at what she had heard, and Chaucer lifted his heavy head towards her, slowly.

Katherine, he reflected, had always had a talent for blocking out what she did not like but could not change; it was the source of her great strength in adversity, delaying sadness until she was strong enough to bear it. She had accompanied the Duke's hearse to London, and seen him buried with Blanche in their great sepulchre at St Paul's, with all the royalty and nobility of England there to see it done.

But this, he sensed, was the first moment that she had acknowledged her own tomb would be solitary. The Bishop – like the rest of the family, Chaucer was amused by Henry Beaufort's elevation to the See of Lincoln – will no doubt ensure her burial matches her status, or rather his: but there will be no connubial, hand-fast effigies for her.

The Duchess's voice was fading, with the light. "She was a great lady, and she brought him so much. Beauty. Wealth. An heir. She taught him to be a great lord. He adored her, and they lie together in glory."

A whisper, only, now. "But I think I taught him how to love."

*

Even Elizabeth, with her love of Kettlethorpe, usually enjoyed being in Lincoln. The city was not what it was, the older folk moaned, since it had lost the staple to Boston thirty years before. The Duchess said – though she took care there were no churchmen present to hear her – that in truth, the decline went back much further, to the expulsion of the Jews who had brought such wealth to the city. Had they never heard of Aaron of Lincoln, the greatest financier in the Kingdom, in the early years of the Angevins? Kings had borrowed huge sums from him, and his wealth had built many of the great abbeys!

Her family all shook their heads, doubtfully. Surely the Jews were hostile to Christ and Christians both? But then they knew the Duchess understood money; it was the most unwomanly thing about her. Why, on occasion, Hawise had once indiscreetly told the girls, she had had to lend some to the great Duke himself, when for all his great wealth he had found himself short of ready coin.

For all that talk of decline, however, Lincoln was still a lively place, full of craftsmen making a good living serving the guildsmen, burgesses and clerics with which the city abounded. The Cathedral added the excitements of its own annual pattern of feasts and rituals, music and mysteries to the busy trading centre, drawing pilgrims to the shrine of St Hugh and clerics from all over the Bishop's huge diocese. And there were always minstrels to enliven the evenings spent there since the Duchess was well known to love music, and any travelling troupe would likely try for her patronage.

There were markets and fairs, as well as the workshops and traders Alice and Elizabeth loved to visit, some producing the finest wares, and enjoying the Duchess's patronage. There was a cordwainer who made boots from the softest Spanish leather, where the girls could not only satisfy their own modest desires but giggle at the monstrous long-toed men's shoes made fashionable by Richard's courtiers. Not much call for them in Lincoln, where the proud owner would be flat on his face as soon as he essayed

Steep Hill, but a pair had long been kept on display to show the cordwainer had the grandest of clients.

There was a mercer who specialised not only in delicious scents, but also in aids to the complexion, though Hawise did not permit the girls to use those. Down Steep Hill there was a goldsmith patronised by the Duchess: she had taken Elizabeth there on her fifteenth birthday. There was a cloth merchant where ells of velvet and silk could be bought, and even cloth-of-gold, as well as good Lincoln wool.

The sumptuary laws might seem to restrict the market for finery, but in truth they were rarely enforced, if the wearer was reasonably discreet. And the Duchess, of course, was expected to dress richly; though nowadays she had little appetite for finery, she still took pleasure in the girls' apparel.

But this time they were more confined, and their unexpected arrival meant there were no minstrels waiting. High summer had brought sickness to the lower part of the city, so the girls were restricted to what the Bail and Close had to offer to the burgesses living there – though they managed to wheedle permission to visit the fair still going on at Newport. But it was not a good time to beg the Duchess for a purse to squander on adornment or sweetmeats, Hawise told them firmly.

For the present, however, it seemed that the Duchess's fears had been ill-founded. When the Duchess's party had arrived in Lincoln, the city had already been buzzing with news that Bolingbroke had landed at Ravenspur, on the northern tip of the great Humber estuary. His force might be tiny – barely 300 men in all, and a mere handful of knights – but it was said to be rapidly growing.

Anxiety had been, Elizabeth opined to Alice (in what she hoped to be a very adult manner), only natural in a lady of her grandmother's age. But Alice was not impressed.

"Are you not fearful for Edward?"

"Certainly not," Elizabeth said staunchly, though this bravado obliged her to pretend sleep at night rather than reveal her anxiety to her friend.

The very next day, Alice and Elizabeth had gone to the Bail, to watch the lords and knights of the shire assemble under the shadow of the castle – of which My Lord Duke had so long been Constable, by inherited right. Loyal to Lancaster's heir, this party was planning to ride north to join him.

With the Duchess's sons ("… and Edward, of course," Alice said to Elizabeth, politely), the girls recognised some of the great men of the county – Willoughby, Roos, Darcy and Dymoke. Roger, who had escorted them, unbent to identify others. No sign of Bussy, the chamberlain reflected; it was not to be expected, since he was one of Richard's closest henchmen.

Only a few days later, the Duchess's household learnt that Northumberland and Westmorland had come to Bolingbroke's support. It was said that he carried all before him. Elizabeth's spirits rose. But the Duchess still looked grey with worry, and Master Chaucer advised against counting chickens before they were hatched.

What had Bolingbroke come for? Only to claim his rightful inheritance, his supporters said. Word came he had taken an oath to that effect, at Doncaster. The same story came back from other points on his progress, as he built up an army and gave assurances he was not planning to use it.

Yet slowly, ineluctably, that inheritance came to mean more than the Lancastrian lands. Soon he was reported to have taken oaths that he would not raise taxes, except in time of war. What value could such a promise have, if he would not be King?

And now the Duchess began to be proved right about the ambitions of the forces behind him. If Bolingbroke's resolve needed stiffening, Archbishop Arundel, his eye on a return to the See of Canterbury, was said to be very willing to bolster it, as well as to provide the supporting texts.

The story began to run that Bolingbroke, not Richard, was the rightful heir to the Plantagenet throne. How so? Because, so the tale went, Henry's great-great-grand-sire, Edmund of Lancaster, had been in truth the eldest of Henry III's sons. He had been put aside in favour of his brother Edward, only because he was crippled. They had substituted Longshanks for Crouchback. Which meant that Edward I was no true King. *Ergo*, Richard, his great-great-grandson, was no true King, either.

Well, everyone likes a good story, and the lawyers did their best with it, but few gave it much credence. In reality, it was all much simpler: a popular leader was overturning an unpopular one. Tyranny, not illegality, was the main charge against Richard. Provoked by injustice, Henry of Bolingbroke seemed to be carrying the day. And doing so to acclamation.

The Yorkshire strongholds went over to him; some – like Knaresborough, which belonged to the Duchess herself – after a nicely judged show of hesitation. Bolingbroke then moved south. Would Richard's last remaining uncle, the Duke of York, defend his Kingship? Bolingbroke's force was by now superior, and they soon learnt York had made peace. In that prediction, at least, the Duchess's sons had been right.

In Lincoln, they waited to learn when Richard would return from Ireland to fight for his Kingdom. But when he did, the odds were already stacked heavily against him. He was rumoured to be fleeing from fortress to fortress, seeking the protection of his Cheshire archers, but to no avail. Eventually Northumberland enticed him out of Conwy Castle, with false promises cooked up by Archbishop Arundel. To his eternal credit, Richard left his hostage, Bolingbroke's son, young Harry of Monmouth, unharmed.

The Bishop, with Harry safely returned to his father, had come back to Lincoln. He told his mother and his uncle Chaucer all. Elizabeth was sitting with them again, trying to make herself invisible, but the Bishop missed nothing.

"Well, niece, you are here, are you, and busy with your stitchery? I dare say. You may stay, and learn, provided you guard your tongue." She nodded, dumbly, furious with herself for flushing, as if she had something on her conscience.

Henry sat at his ease in the solar of his mother's house, still in his riding gear, looking more soldier than priest. He was more like her than any of his siblings, with her colouring, and finer-built than Thomas Swynford.

A clever boy, Chaucer reflected, watching him with appreciation, he had become a formidable young man. Ireland would have held no terrors for Bishop Henry Beaufort. He looked fit and well, and energised by events.

"It was an ill-judged expedition from the start," the Bishop opined. "Richard was so heedless of advice that I feared he had lost his reason, and we would all suffer for it. Be sure I kept close to young Harry, but give Richard his due, he never meant the boy harm. And Harry had – has – a great affection for him."

Before the Duchess could question that little slip, Hawise came bustling in, with refreshments; she was no respecter of her nurseling's eminence, and told him briskly to tell his mother what he knew, and let her rest: she had been sick with worry. The Bishop laughed, a mite relieved at the distraction. He would not welcome questions as to Richard's fate. "Peace, Hawise, I will do so – and Lord bless you for your care of her."

"Your brother Somerset?" The Duchess pressed, anxiously.

"Oh, John stayed loyal to Richard, until his surrender; and some of the scum Bolingbroke brought back with him called for John's execution, along with Bussy. But fear not, mother, our stepbrother has brushed John's accusers aside."

As Thomas Swynford had rightly guessed, Somerset had been sending information to Bolingbroke even as he served King Richard. All he had suffered, the Bishop explained, was a minor demotion, from Marquess to Earl.

The Bishop himself, it seemed, had managed a skilful change of allegiance, dismissed with an airy wave of his hand. He had kept his Lincoln See, he told his mother: his servants were even now readying the Palace for him. Thomas Swynford and Thomas Beaufort were enjoying royal favour.

For now it was, as this confident young man explained to the Duchess, no longer King Richard, but King Henry, the fourth of that name, who handed out the prizes. The deed, the young Bishop explained, had been done at Michaelmas, at a Parliament called in Richard's name, then brilliantly invested with its own authority. Chaucer, well versed in such matters, smiled dryly.

Those assembled were asked if they knew any more worthy than Henry of Bolingbroke, and were wise enough – the Bishop gave a most unholy grin – to give the right answer. It was a process, he said admiringly, carefully orchestrated by Archbishop Arundel, ready with his sermon on the evils of child rulers, and his scrolls displaying the genealogical efforts of his clerks. And it culminated exactly as the Archbishop wished.

The head of the House of Lancaster became King. It had, the Bishop concluded, been an almost bloodless handover. Chaucer smiled again at that mellifluous description, but forbore to speak. Richard had been well alive to witness his own humiliation.

So they must, the Bishop told them, all now go south for the coronation, in mid-October. He was staying himself only a few days, on diocesan business. He would beg his mother's leave, now – there was much to do. He rose briskly, embraced the Duchess, nodded to his uncle, and with a dry smile, held out his ring for Elizabeth to kiss.

"Remember my words, niece. You can do much, and learn much, in the coming days if you show you have discretion."

Curiously, amongst all the Duchess's household, it was Dame Margaret who greeted the news of the coronation with most excitement. They did not realise why until the great day itself.

To be sure, Dame Margaret had told Alice and Elizabeth often enough that Scrivelsby, the manor she had brought to her marriage, carried with it the hereditary role of King's Champion. But they had given little thought to what that meant.

The whole Court was soon to discover. At Dame Margaret's urging, her son, Sir Thomas Dymoke, arrived unannounced at King

Henry's coronation feast, in full armour, demanding to know if any would take up his challenge.

It was a magnificent performance, earning roars of approval from those furthest into their feasting. But it took the new King himself to bring Dymoke's splendid but disruptive display of loyalty to a peaceful conclusion, which he did with great tact. He knew Dymoke from old, of course. After all, he was Henry of Bolingbroke, born only a few miles from Scrivelsby.

*

And Richard? By the end of September, after he had been brought to London and bullied into abdication, he was lodged in the Tower. Though not for long.

Sir Thomas Swynford sent word to his mother he had been ordered to take Richard north, to Pontefract, where Sir Thomas was to remain as Constable. It was a Lancastrian stronghold, one of her favourite residences in the past.

She would not go there again. "How long will the K... will Richard stay at Pontefract?" she asked the messenger. He shook his head; she asked no more.

All that was soon known for certain was that Richard was dead by mid-February, 1400, after the Epiphany rising, a rebellion that had given Henry IV the first of many scares during his reign. Were the two events connected? Was Richard deemed thereafter to be too much of a danger to the new King, alive? Or had his death always been inevitable?

Thomas paid for a good horse, to get the news fast to King Henry. For rumour spread on wings: the Duchess and her household, in Lincoln, learned of it within a fortnight. Richard died of starvation, it was said. By his own choice, the world asked, or Swynford's? Who could say?

It was some time before Sir Thomas came to see his mother again. Least said, soonest mended, seemed to be their tacit agreement.

Here was a very dark doubt, about her eldest son, one for her to block out from her mind, for ever.

By the time he came, her forebodings of a turbulent reign were proving all too correct: Henry was struggling to defend his scarcely won Kingdom, and it was no time for recriminations. Richard's body had been shown to the people; there was no mark on it. What did that prove?

And what did young Harry of Monmouth think of the death of his once-beloved uncle? Years later, they got some clue. When Harry came to the throne, Richard received the burial place his "Majesty" warranted, and his remains were moved from a mere Priory at King's Langley to the Abbey at Westminster.

Meanwhile King Henry IV ruled with, as the Duchess had foretold, much difficulty. But for all that, also with success. The country remained at precarious peace, and his Lancastrian relations were found plenty to do, helping to maintain it.

The new King continued to treat his stepmother with the greatest of respect, and her Beaufort children became his trusted lieutenants – trusted, that is, so long as they posed no threat to his heirs. Suspicion became a habit of mind with Henry IV, and that may have been the only reason a statute was passed banning the Beauforts from laying claim to the throne. That done, the King raised them to the highest estate.

But maybe it was the Pontefract stain that held Thomas Swynford back, for while he became a Knight of the Chamber, and carried out a number of missions for his stepbrother, he never achieved the highest office. Yet Henry did not forget him, nor discard him altogether, as men so often do with the instruments of their crimes.

For when some lands due to Thomas in Hainault proved difficult to claim, the King came to his stepbrother's aid. Counterclaimants had raised doubts about Thomas's legitimacy, given his mother's long relationship with Lancaster, and the confusion over the year of his birth. At Thomas's request, King Henry wrote robustly in defence of his claim. So far as the King of England was concerned,

Thomas was the true and rightful son of Sir Hugh and Dame Katherine Swynford.

Which was, in turn, the final extinction of young Elizabeth's hopes of inheriting Kettlethorpe. But for her, too, life had moved on. Edward had been knighted on the occasion of King Henry's coronation, among a crowd of excited young men, made members of the new Order of the Bath, hopeful of great things for themselves and the new reign. Elizabeth stayed with the Duchess, cared for Edward's unruly hound and malevolent gyrfalcon, waited and hoped.

And she was rewarded for her patience. Enough came to Edward, in honours and lands, and came soon enough for him to hurry home to Lincolnshire in triumph, and marry Elizabeth. Her grandmother did not forget her: she gave Elizabeth a handsome dowry, as Alice had predicted.

Less predictably, shortly before the Duchess's death, in 1403, she let Elizabeth know how much she had understood.

The young woman had come to visit her grandmother, at Hawise's urgent request. It was spring, but there was still a chill in the air, and a north-west wind whipped along Minster Yard. The Duchess no longer had the strength to rise, but her chamber was blessedly warm, with a fireplace served by the new chimney to the side of her solar wing.

She lay in the nuptial bed left her by the Duke, with its magnificent black velvet coverings decorated with compasses, garters and a turtle dove – a frail figure now, almost insubstantial against the luxurious residues of her ducal marriage. But she spoke to Elizabeth first not of the Duke: instead, of her first husband, Elizabeth's grandfather, Hugh Swynford.

"I committed a great sin towards him. No: I do not speak of the one I know you hoped I would reveal. My chief sin was that I did not love him. I married, as most women do, without love, and I tried to do my duty. But many succeed, with God's help, in turning duty into love, and I never did."

Elizabeth put out her hand. Her grandmother pressed it, and put it gently aside.

"I did not even ask for God's help. My heart was elsewhere, and I never tried to reclaim it for my husband."

She stopped, and Elizabeth thought she was too sick and weary to go on. With obvious effort, she did.

"But I did give him an heir, and the continuance of his name – of Swynfords, at Kettlethorpe."

Another pause, and a longer one, as she gathered strength.

"I want you to try to understand. I know you love Kettlethorpe, as I do, and dear child, I would be glad to see you there. It is no great estate, even now; there are others of far greater worth, with finer buildings, that I could give Thomas, leaving Kettlethorpe to you. And maybe he would prefer that! But that would be a betrayal of my duty, however poorly I performed it, and a slur on my husband's name. So I say to you: ask no more. Question no more."

Hawise moistened the Duchess's lips with a little cordial.

"You have something now much more precious even than a place you love. You have Edward, to whom you can give your whole heart. Give it without wishing for more, and you will be at peace with yourself, and with God."

A long sigh. "As I am, now, at the last."

All her life, Elizabeth would be sustained by the memory of those moments with her grandmother, before pain and delirium took the Lady of Kettlethorpe on her tortured last journey to death.

To be sure, her words were not foremost in Elizabeth's mind in the early days of her marriage, for she had so much else to think of, then. Only two months after her grandmother died, her husband would be at Shrewsbury, playing his part in the defining domestic battle of Henry IV's reign; and that was but the beginning.

In Thomas Beaufort's retinue Edward of Oxcombe served Henry, and then Henry's son, young Harry, too. He followed Henry V through his French wars to the battlefield triumph of Agincourt, and saw Beaufort made Duke of Exeter.

There was little time for tranquil reflection in those years of danger and drama, fame and family, advancement and achievement, that came to Elizabeth and Edward. But her grandmother's words would come back to her, to nourish her, in the days of loss and pain that were ahead.

As in our transitory, fragile lives, such days must always come.

1403–1536

*S*ome historians have been less than romantic about Katherine, arguing that Lancaster's marriage to her was about dynasty, not love. He had only one legitimate heir. And here were three more ready-made (Beaufort) sons…

That's a bit churlish, I think. After all, by the time John and Katherine wed, the eldest of the Duke's four legitimate grandsons was rising eleven. Indeed it could be argued that legitimising the Beauforts might create a dynastic problem, rather than solve it: that was what Henry of Bolingbroke (otherwise very fond of his half-siblings) seems to have thought.

But a true love story still may have its darker side, easier for the historical novelist to explore now than it was sixty years ago. Anya Seton does not, for example, tell the reader that Lancaster probably gave Katherine venereal disease. And then there's the puzzle about Thomas Swynford.

Critical to Anya Seton's portrayal of a "moral" Katherine is the assumption that she did not begin her relationship with Lancaster before her husband Hugh Swynford's death. But a woman's marital status does not seem always seem to have inhibited Lancaster. And there is a question mark over the date of Thomas Swynford's birth.

Katherine's biographer, Alison Weir, points out that the petition the Duke sent to the Pope (to have his marriage confirmed) admits *that he committed adultery, but says no such thing of Katherine. To have lied to His Holiness, even by omission, would – Alison Weir argues – have been a fearful thing, to the fourteenth-century mind: it would have risked Katherine's immortal soul.*

But it would also have been a very big thing for Katherine to confess publicly to her own adultery. It was a sin so much worse for a woman, in the eyes of the fourteenth century, than the adultery of a man. And particularly in this case. Pope and world alike would allow a good deal of licence to a royal duke; none at all to a woman of Katherine's reputation. Who could blame her if she had kept some things for her own confessor?

Others argue, in defence of Thomas's legitimacy, that Henry IV would never have supported Swynford's claim to the Hainault lands if he knew it to be unmerited. But in pursuing his own claims, Henry's conscience seems to have been pretty elastic. So in telling this part of Katherine's story I have left the question just a little bit open.

But now for my own confessions, starting with the fact that there is the barest, questionable mention in the records of a daughter Dorothy for Katherine, and of a Thimelby marriage for a Swynford of (probably) the right age and parentage. Elizabeth is an imagined granddaughter, who enables Katherine to share her last thoughts. Edward of Oxcombe is pure invention; his name honours a particularly magical valley in the Wolds. But Katherine's son Thomas Swynford, for all his disputed birthday, was real enough, as was his wife Jane, Geoffrey Chaucer, and all the other members of Katherine's family in my story.

Her Beaufort descendants played their part, more or less successfully, in the governance of England and the Wars of the Roses. Henry VI, the last, mentally fragile, Lancastrian King, was murdered by the rival Yorkists; who then fell out amongst themselves. Mayhem followed. And the son of Margaret Beaufort (Katherine's great-granddaughter), Henry Tudor, managed to pluck the crown from the shambles.

Margaret gave Henry his only claim to royal blood. Not a drop of royalty ran through the veins of his opportunist father, Edmund Tudor, who married Margaret Beaufort as a child and got her pregnant when she was barely thirteen.

Henry Tudor spent much of his first twenty-eight years in hiding or exile, until in 1485 came his showdown with Richard III. The battle of Bosworth Field was won when Margaret Beaufort's third husband, Lord Stanley, finally swung his support Henry Tudor's way. He took the throne as Henry VII, then married a Yorkist princess and coloured his Tudor rose both Lancastrian red and Yorkist white.

For all his family's associations with the county, his son Henry VIII had no love for Lincolnshire. It was, he told its inhabitants, "one of the most brute and beestlie shires of my realm". That condemnation came after the Lincolnshire Rising, which heralded the Pilgrimage of Grace – the most serious rebellion of his reign.

The rising brought Lincolnshire a brief taste of revolution, a longer taste of the Duke of Suffolk, and much grief.

A BRUTE AND
BEESTLIE SHIRE

KETTLETHORPE MANOR: 1536

It was the face of nightmares, powerful and malevolent. Brutal, commonplace features. Ruddy face, puffed cheeks, deep grooves of temper running down from the nostrils.

Chin broader than forehead: more jaw than brain. Clipped, square, grizzled beard. The small, black, chancy eyes of an angry animal.

To pin your hopes on the mercy of this man must be folly – unless, of course, you had nowhere else to pin them. And it had all been hope and folly, from the very beginning.

*

It seemed to have been raining for ever. For the first four days of October it had been relentless – heavy, vertical rain, slashing on to ground that was already waterlogged. Agnes unlatched the casement, and peered out on a sodden world.

Her mother's herber was a dismal sight. The neat brick paths were underwater; the straggly, overgrown herbs, overdue for their autumn trim, were beaten to the ground. And the cloud was heavy as ever. "Black over Will's muther's," as her nurse would mutter, when heavy cloud hung over the flat Lincolnshire countryside.

Her spirits as damp as the weather, Agnes pulled her head back in, shaking moisture off her coif. Her thick, dark hair curled in the misty air. She smoothed it down, and turned to meet her mother's mildly exasperated gaze. "If wishes were horses, daughter…"

There was a convulsion at her feet. "Beggars would ride!" Francis shouted, clambering up on to his mother's knee and waving his little wooden horse at her, at grave risk to her embroidery frame.

She put it carefully aside, and settled him into her lap. He beat her with the horse for a bit, then lent back, sucking his thumb.

Dull as this weather might be for them all, it was dullest for a five-year-old. Agnes stretched out her arms. "Shall I take him to the hall, and play with him there a little?" Dame Catherine smiled. "Bless you, daughter: that would be a kindness to us both. But go softly, I thought I heard your father's voice: he may have guests."

"I want to go too!" Elizabeth whined. Dame Catherine leant over to examine her youngest daughter's grubby sampler. "Not till you have finished that row of cross stitch." Elizabeth pouted, but knew there was so use in arguing with her mother. She bent her head again, sniffing reproachfully, and Agnes perched Francis on her hip, escaping before Dame Catherine could relent.

Since Francis had usurped Elizabeth's prized position as baby of the family, she was forever complaining. With her red-gold curls, and bright blue eyes, she had been her father's pet until another boy appeared. But it was ever thus. Agnes lacked her mother's patience with Elizabeth's grievances.

Dame Catherine had the gift of tranquillity. She had been married at the age of sixteen, and had borne John Meryng eight children so far, of which five had survived infancy. She ran her household lightly, her husband skilfully. She came from out of Nottinghamshire, from a comfortable home for a large and prosperous family, just the far side of Newark – a busy market town, very different from the shabby old port at Torksey or the faded grandeur of Lincoln.

John had done his best to reconcile her to life on the Lincolnshire side of the Trent. He had persuaded his father, Sir William Meryng, to modernise the medieval manor of Kettlethorpe. It had been well appointed for its time, in the days when it had been the summer retreat of the Duchess of Lancaster, and Sir William was immensely proud of its acquisition from the Swynford family. But as Dame Catherine had quietly pointed out, a century and a half had passed since then, and buildings had changed much.

William, or rather John, since his father had promptly moved to his townhouse in Lincoln, had built on to the hall in brick, making a new entrance, with internal stairs rising to the hall and chambers, and added two new chimneys. The animals had been driven out of the undercroft, now used for storerooms and dairy, with new windows to bring light. Best of all, here, at the bottom of the tower, he had fashioned a fine parlour for his wife, with a low door leading out to her herber, a fireplace feeding into one of the chimneys, newfangled casement windows and oak-panelled walls.

Beside the parlour a passageway led from the new front door to the oak staircase. Agnes set Francis down. He was too heavy to carry for long, and certainly not up the stairs. And it seemed her mother had been right: she could hear voices in the hall. Loud, angry voices. Whoever had come with her father, they did not sound like welcome guests.

She pressed her finger to her lips and Francis fell silent, round-eyed at her urgency. She took his hand and crept quietly up the stairs. Her father's voice was raised above the rest. "Your duty is to your King, not to some scurvy ruffians from the Wolds!"

That seemed only to inflame his visitors: there was a roar of dissent, loud enough for her to risk unlatching the hall door. She peeped in. A group of men faced her father, who was seated at the high table with his bailiff at his left shoulder, and her brother, young Thomas, on his right, almost close enough to the door for her to touch.

"You must take the oath now! And lead us to Lincoln!" Agnes thought she recognised the voice of the blacksmith from Drinsey Nook. "Or have you sold your soul to that devil Cromwell?" There was an ugly murmur of support, and Thomas shifted slightly. She saw his hand move towards the dagger at his hip.

But her father must have seen it too, for he flung out a restraining hand. His anger was under tight control again. "Goodmen, I spoke in haste. I know you for loyal subjects of His Majesty. Did we not march together for King Harry, Jack? We both bear the scars still, I warrant."

As boys, he and the blacksmith had run away together, to follow Sir William Meryng to Northumberland, where the Earl of Surrey had trounced the Scots. They had been left with the other youngsters to guard the baggage. But they had returned home with their heads held high, having been bloodied in a skirmish. Agnes's father limped still, from the wound he took in his thigh.

Now he was giving a shrewd reminder to them all of where their loyalties lay. Surrey, the champion of Flodden Field, was a hero in the eyes of the North. And it was his son, the present Duke of Norfolk, who was rumoured to be bringing an army to put an end to the present disorder.

What's more, His Grace of Norfolk was no reformer, and no friend to Cromwell. Or to Cromwell's Commissioners, who had been working their way around the churches of the county, assessing their income, fingering their treasures, and raising tempers as they went.

Jack Smith nodded, and Agnes saw him grin reluctantly at the memory of their escapade. Her father pushed his advantage. "I know you are fearful of what the Commissioners may do. But I will not put my head in a noose, nor yours, without learning more about this cause."

He lent forward, shouting them down.

"Treason carries a fearsome penalty. D'you want to see the butchers pull out your guts afore they chop you in pieces? Go home to your wives now, and be at peace, and let me find out what I may."

They did not like it. The hotter heads were still muttering. But Jack began turning away, and with him the curate, Robert Carbott – dragged here, surely, against his will, for he was a quiet little fellow. Agnes slipped back down the stairs again, catching up Francis at the foot of them, and carrying him protesting back to the parlour. No time to dally; the men would be coming out of the hall, and her father would not be pleased to see an eavesdropper.

Her mother looked up anxiously, alarm deepening at Agnes's white face. But before she could explain, her father and brother had joined them, bringing the sharp stir of danger into ordered quiet.

John's temper was not improved by having had to restrain it. "Jesu," he spat, "what possesses these madmen? Have we not troubles enough without flouting the King's will? Can our simpletons not see that these wild men are after plunder, not salvation? They are terrorising the countryside when we are already late with the ploughing, thanks to this vile weather! They will bring poverty and hardship, if not death, to the fools who follow them!"

He checked, thought overtaking anger. "They will be back, or others will come. We must be ready. Agnes, do you go bar the shutters – there's a loose one in the kitchen, it must be attended to. They'll be after horses: we must send men to guard the barn. Walter can bring his family into the house, for safety."

He turned to his son, brisk in his instructions. "And Thomas, you must ride to William at Meryng. Ask him to send to My Lord Hussey at Sleaford, to warn him of this trouble – they'll be looking to him for leadership, and he'd be wise to get away."

But Thomas did not move. And Agnes knew, or feared, what was coming.

He had poured his allegiance out to her, as they rode back from their grandfather's in Lincoln, on the last golden day of summer. Sir William had talked to them of old days and old ways, as old men do. Days when King Harry was the handsomest prince in Christendom, the Pope's favourite and England's too, and his Spanish wife beloved throughout the land.

A time of victories, Grandfather said, and feasting, of saints' days and Our Lady's blessings. A time when the new young monarch had brought enchantment to a country that had been wearied by the long wars between cousins, and then by the sour, penny-pinched rule of the victor, the young King's unlamented father, Henry Tudor.

Sir William had had an unusually willing audience in his grandson. All this talk of the good old days, of the old religion, had been music to Thomas's ear.

"And now King Harry's proving worse than any of them," Thomas had said, as they jogged back along the line of the Fossdyke. "Turning off the Queen for the Boleyn whore, and yet now she's gone to the scaffold and Cromwell's found him another doxy. The poor Princess Mary declared a bastard, as well as the Boleyn spawn. And he's letting Cromwell squeeze every penny he can out of us, as well as shutting our churches and monasteries. What will a village do without its church, answer me that?"

Agnes stayed silent, hoping Thomas's wrath would blow itself out, but he had warmed to his theme.

"Don't think we'll be spared, either. The Priory at Torksey will be closed, and so surely will the convents at Heynings and the Fosse. And what will the Sisters do then, thrown out to starve?"

"Are they not promised pensions?" Agnes had asked, diffidently.

Thomas's horse sprang forward, as he clamped its sides angrily, startling the nag ridden by the old groom sent to accompany the two youngsters.

"And what pensioner would put trust in Thomas Cromwell and Richard Rich? Agnes, they are striking Holy Days out of the calendar next, saying they make men idle. That will set a match to the unrest. And we must be ready, as Edward says."

Agnes had sighed, and pricked her little jennet to catch up. Her father was glad to see some of the Holy Days go, the ones that interrupted harvest and ploughing. As for Edward Dymoke, she did not think he was as thirsty for action as all that. His grandfather had learnt the cost of rebellion: he had been beheaded by Edward IV.

To be sure, Edward's father, King's Champion to three successive monarchs, had been close to the Spanish Queen, and there was always lots of angry talk about Cromwell at Scrivelsby. But when she and Thomas had gone there in June, Edward's fine eyes had kept wandering across to where Agnes had sat giggling with his sisters, while the other men inflamed each other's anger. Still, he would be swept up into action with the rest of them, no doubt.

Ah well: no use thinking of Edward. He was married, with two hopeful children already, however his thoughts strayed. And Thomas had moved on to another hero.

"Lord Darcy says that Yorkshire is ready to rise. He told Dame Margaret so, when he came to see to his property at Knaith – and she told Dame Agnes here at the Fosse."

Thomas had spoken with awe, and Agnes had sighed again. Lord Darcy was nearly as old as her grandfather, yet he was still held in the greatest respect in these parts. And Dame Margaret, Prioress at Heynings, the convent at Knaith, would take as gospel every word the old Lord said.

As for Dame Agnes at the Fosse, young Agnes's own godmother, her nunnery might be small and poor, but its Prioress was chief intelligencer to the villages along the river, and no tale would lose in the telling with her. Agnes would wager that whoever did or did not secure a pension, Dame Agnes would be sure to do so.

She had tried again to lighten Thomas's mood. "They say the Sisters will be allowed to marry when their houses are dissolved, those that were handed over to the religious life when they were but children. Sister Cecily might make a bride for you, Thomas, she is very comely, and they say Dame Agnes was delighted with her dowry."

"Sacrilege!" Thomas had exclaimed, though he had had the grace to grin. Sister Cecily was indeed fair: blue-eyed, sweet-faced, and in a careless – careful? – moment had let a golden curl slip out from under her veil when the two Meryngs came to visit Dame Agnes. But in truth, Thomas had little interest in girls; all his passions were for young men, and the causes they espoused. Tall and well grown as he was, he was still only fourteen, so his father dismissed it as immaturity. His mother quietly cherished her better knowledge of her best-loved child.

But now, two months later, there was – sweet Jesu – no way to lighten Thomas's mood. The confrontation she had feared had all too clearly come. Pale as parchment, the boy faced his father. He spoke unhappily, but doggedly. "Father, I must tell you, I share the rebels' cause. I have already taken their oath. I will go – I must go – to Lincoln to support them."

Dame Catherine made a little sound of distress. John Meryng let all his pent-up rage explode. "God's wounds, boy, what treasonous oath?"

Thomas laughed, though without mirth. "God's wounds it is, Father. I have sworn by the Five Wounds of Christ to be true to the Commons of Lincolnshire. We are loyal to the King, I have sworn that too, and we are not for the Pope. But we will rid ourselves of those false creatures, Longland and Cromwell. We will demand that the King has done with them."

John gripped his son by the shoulders, as if to try to shake sense into him. "Thomas, you fool boy, I'm no lover of our Bishop in Lincoln, still less of Cromwell, God rot him, but no one can stand against them. What do you think the King will do? Say, as you will, good people, here's their heads on a pike?"

"Father, we must – we shall – stand against them. We cannot stop now! The whole countryside has risen. And it's not just the common people – Edward Dymoke has joined them, and other gentlemen, and they've added the Statute of Uses to their grievances. You know how wrong you thought that was, to take away your rights to dispose of your property as you wish."

His father tried to check him, shaking him again, but Thomas pulled away. "It's too late, Father, the die is cast. They've taken the Commissioners by force and made them write to the King. John Heneage, for all he's Bishop Longland's man, has been sent to His

Majesty, by the leaders of the Commons, with the letter of their demands. We will hear his answer any day now. And we must join with the Commons, or lose everything."

John thumped his fist into the panelling, barely able to contain his anger. Elizabeth uttered a wail of terror and flung herself on her mother, but no one had time for her. Francis silently buried his head in Agnes's shoulder. Thomas blenched, expecting a blow, but stood his ground.

Their father checked himself, again. "Thomas, speak no more of this, unless you want a thrashing! You know nothing of these matters. And child though you are, I have need of you. Would you leave your mother and sisters in danger? Do you help secure the house and bring in the horses. I'll send Walter to William instead, with a letter for Lord Hussey. He must go soon, while there's still light, and before the rabble returns."

He checked at the door, looking back to his wife. "Madam, look to your children, and give your son no encouragement – nor you, Agnes. You are both too fond of this boy, as I have been. God send I still have one loyal son."

*

In another dark, wet dawn Agnes was woken by a scratching at her chamber door. She slipped out of the bed she shared with Elizabeth, hugging her shawl around her shoulders, and went softly to lift the latch. Thomas stood outside, in hose and jerkin, with his riding boots in his hand.

Agnes glanced nervously at the truckle bed, but their nurse Betsy was still snoring away, and Francis still slept beside her "No…" she whispered fearfully, "Thomas, I beg of you, you must not go, you heard what Father said…"

Thomas touched her lips to silence her. "Agnes, you heard me also, I am sworn. Will you ask our mother to forgive me? She said not a word of reproach, and I am fearful for you all, but I must go."

"How are you going? When will you come back to us? Thomas, I am sore afraid for you, you cannot just run away alone!"

"Hush now, enough; I'm taking no one from here, not even Rob, though he pressed me hard. I'm taking the grey cob, so rest assured he's not been stolen, and I'll stable him with Grandfather in Lincoln, so he'll be safe. But I'd as lief you told them naught, or they'll blame you for helping me."

He was breathing hard, Agnes saw, white with excitement or fear. As dark as she was, a tall, thin boy, but well made, he looked older than his years, and brave enough for anything. "I'll not be back till the King has agreed to our demands. I may have to go north, the gentry are bolder there, they'll pick up the torch if we drop it in Lincoln. Agnes, you must agree, surely – you hate what they have done, don't you, how they treated the Queen and the Princess Mary?"

"You must not call her that – it's treason, Thomas, you know it is!" Betsy, disturbed by Agnes's raised voice, snorted and turned over.

Thomas looked quickly, and kissed Agnes's cheek. "Christ be with you, Sister, I must go."

"Christ be with you, Thomas, and keep you safe," she whispered. His eyes were shining, with passion, or perhaps tears.

"He is with us. By his Five Wounds, I know that he is."

She dropped the latch and turned away, shivering and half-blinded by her tears. Through them she saw that Elizabeth was sitting bolt upright, mouth open, ready to cry out.

Agnes ran swiftly to her, and clapped her hand across her sister's face. "One sound, and I'll throw Lucy in the kitchen fire." Elizabeth breathed in sharply, clutching her doll to her. "Not one word of what you heard, or I swear it, she'll burn like a witch."

Agnes took care not to come down until Thomas would be well away. She protested that she was still asleep when Betsy scolded her to hurry, the house was in turmoil, young Master Thomas was gone, and the Good Lord knew who else.

"A horse is gone too, and the Master in a rare state. He's blaming Rob, as if the poor lad could tell the family what to do. Minding the horses, that's his task, not minding the fools who ride them."

Elizabeth was struggling to dress without letting go of Lucy, looking anxiously at her sister. Feeling guilty, Agnes helped her, and took her hand to lead her down, squeezing it partly in admonition, partly in reassurance. At the foot of the stairs they met their father.

"Agnes, I care not now what you knew of this, but I tell you, it is a grave matter. Thomas has endangered us all, curse the boy. I must to Newark, or Nottingham, to the King's men, to show my loyalty, or this whole family will be under suspicion. When Walter returns, tell him Thomas was sent after him, to ask William to come take charge here. I'll stop to see William on my way, to tell him what's amiss, but better no other knows of this."

He looked, bleakly, at Agnes, speaking to her as if she were a woman grown. "He was always a wayward boy, at times I found him unnatural. But I loved him, as I love all of you. I do not doubt his courage – he has more than his share of that. But for all he's still a child, I must disavow him now, if I cannot catch him quickly. Agnes, you must help your mother to understand."

His eyes dropped to Elizabeth. "And you, miss, mind your manners – and your elders. If strangers come, hold your tongue."

He embraced Agnes. "Take care of your mother, and Francis. Give the rebels nothing, unless to save your lives. I'll be back as soon as I may. God willing, it will not be long."

Agnes stood silent at the door, holding Elizabeth's hand. Dame Catherine joined her, watching her husband mount his courser, while Walter's deputy, Will Fenton, scrambled on to Agnes's beloved jennet to accompany him. Seeing her expression, John looked at her, again. "I don't know whether the horses are more at risk with me, or here – all armies are thieves. But I'll take care of your mare, girl, if I can."

No one came that day – a long day, when they struggled to get used to the fear and disorder that had engulfed their secure little family world. Agnes and her mother kept busy, between kitchen, storeroom and still room, until the evening, when they retreated to the parlour and tried not to jump at every sound.

Neither of them slept that night: Agnes lay awake beside her sleeping sister, listening to Betsy's tossing and turning on the other side of the chamber – even she, it seemed, could not lie easy. Finally, Agnes crept down to mull some ale, and found her mother there, about the same task.

Dame Catherine plunged the glowing poker into the pewter tankards of ale, and handed one to her daughter. Agnes curled up in a chair by the kitchen fire, wrapping her shawl tightly around her, and felt the warm intimacy with her mother drive fear away for a while.

"Agnes, I have not asked you what Thomas said before he left, for it's best I know nothing I cannot tell your father. But..." Dame Catherine's voice lost its habitual calm, "... I would that he knew, that he is always in my heart."

"He begged your forgiveness," Agnes said quickly, knowing how dear this second, troublesome son was to her mother. Dame Catherine sighed. "Of a surety he will have that, but not, I fear, his father's. This must end ill for one of them. Blessed Virgin, save us, that it is not both."

She straightened her back, and glanced over to the pallet in the corner, where the kitchen wench slept. "Come, we must try to get our sleep now, and leave others to theirs. God will give us the strength we need today, but we must do what we can to help Him."

She gave Agnes a conspirator's smile. "I shall tell my beads, while there is no one here but Our Blessed Lady to see me do so. They oft bring slumber, I am ashamed to say, before I finish." The rosary was frowned on by the reformers, as was all veneration of the Virgin Mary; but women like Dame Catherine did not readily give up the small, comforting rituals of their lives.

*

Just when Agnes had begun to hope the unrest might pass them by, the rebels came to Kettlethorpe. It was Saturday evening, and the end of that first week in October. Dame Catherine was with her children in the parlour, Elizabeth leaning against her, trying – not very hard – to read from her prayer book.

Francis, sensing the general unease, had been furiously refusing to go to bed, and his mother had been putting off the battle, hoping he might fall asleep by the fire. Betsy waited, glad of the excuse to sit and warm herself by the parlour fire.

Dame Catherine laid aside her stitching, and straightened her back, preparing to order her younger children up to their beds. Looking at her mother, Agnes thought, with a shock: how this has aged her. All the content that made her round face comely had drained away, leaving it dragged with anxiety. She had barely eaten, Agnes recalled, that day, and had looked grey with tiredness this morning.

For the first time in her life, Agnes thought: my mother is growing old. If anything goes amiss with my father, or my brother, it will go hard with her. And Agnes's own anxiety vented itself in a spurt of anger against Thomas. How could he bring her such trouble, and leave her defenceless?

Dame Catherine caught her eye, and smiled, her spirit still unbroken. "Don't fear for me, daughter, I am well enough. It is only, I think, that I am breeding again, and I am not as young as I was."

Before Agnes could say anything, they heard the sounds at the gatehouse: a thundering at the barred door, as of a beating with staves, and shouts demanding entrance. Dame Catherine rose, put Elizabeth gently from her, and went out to find Walter, who was trembling with fear. "I doubt me the door will hold, Mistress, against so many."

"Tell the porter to open it," Dame Catherine said firmly, "and I will speak with them."

"Mistress…"

"Do as I bid you. But first light a torch, so they can see me clearly."

She stood stock-still on the highest step before the hall door, twenty yards from the gatehouse, a small, unimposing woman, plain with weariness, but with the dignity that courage can bring. Agnes stepped forward, to stand beside her mother; Walter held the torch, shakily, on her other side.

When the gatehouse was opened, the first of the little army surged through, staves in hand. One was clutching an arquebus as well. But they checked at the sight of the two women, and a middle-aged man pushed his way to the front. The torchlight picked out his breastplate, but he did not look the soldier: he wore his harness as if it were unfamiliar and unwelcome.

He spoke, however, with an air of authority, civilly enough. "Madam, we seek your husband. Be so good enough to bid him come to us."

"Sir John is not here," Dame Catherine replied calmly. "He has gone to my son's at Meryng. What is your business with him, Sir?"

"Gone to join the King's men, more like!" A voice shouted from the back of the crowd. "Burn his house, for a traitor to the Commons!"

Walter gasped, the torch shook, and Agnes swiftly took it from him. Dame Catherine did not flinch. "I ask you again, Sir, what is your business with him? I can send him a message, if you wish. Who are you, and what is it that you want?"

Their leader looked at her, uncomfortably. "Madam, I am Abbot of Barlings, commanded by the Commons to pursue their just cause. The gentry are needed, to lead them in pressing their case with his Majesty. Many are already in Lincoln. And I am charged to collect provisions, for the great assembly of men who have joined them."

"Then there is no need for harsh words. My husband is not here to greet you, but we can do so in his place. Do you need food? Ale for your men? Agnes, do you take two of these fellows to the storeroom, and let them take what they will."

She paused, to let the offer sink in, and went on smoothly. "We do not keep our packhorses here, but there are two mules you can take, to carry part of the load. And if you, My Lord Abbot, will step into the hall, we can find you a pen to write a message to my husband."

She half-turned, with a gesture of welcome. "My bailiff will take care of the rest of your men, while the business is done. Walter, stay here, help Agnes, and let the men load up as they will."

Somehow, Agnes thought, she has hypnotised them into doing as she says. The Abbot beckoned two of his fellows forward, and pointed them towards Agnes. One doffed his cap, a little uncomfortably; the other sheepishly followed suit. Agnes led them to the first of the storerooms, Walter following with the torch, breathing heavily. She unlatched the door.

"Take what you will," she said, struggling to match her mother's calm. The first of the men looked at her with a mixture of guilt and truculence; she found anger replacing fear, and fought to suppress both. The men were very close to violence, and it would be easy to provoke it.

She and her mother had planned all this, of course, the first long, dreary day of anxious waiting. Making their plans had helped them hold the household together, giving them all some sense of usefulness and order.

The storerooms must be full, Dame Catherine had said, or the marauders would lay waste to the manor and torch the barns. And they must hide what they could, at the same time, food, as well as valuables: under the floorboards, suspended in the well, under the flower beds in the garden.

Everyone had been kept busy, to their unspoken relief. Do this, do that, choose this, hide that: and all will be well. The cook had wept, to see how much was being sacrificed; but Dame Catherine had been firm. What was sacrificed must be credible, or marauders would lay everything to waste. So while sheep, kine and hogs had been herded down to marshland on the Trent, where only their herders knew safe ground, and the scrubby woodland afforded hiding places, the goose-girl was told to take only part of her flock, hens were left scratching in the farmyard, and there was a house cow in the barn.

And as a plan, it seemed to be working. Once the rebels were busy emptying the stores, Agnes left Walter to it, and returned to support her mother. The Abbot had followed Dame Catherine into the hall. Once out of hearing of the others, he spoke rapidly.

"Mistress, you do wisely. Their temper is easily roused, and one poor soul they suspected was hung before my very eyes. They have forced many reluctant souls to take their oath and join them. I myself," – he made a despairing gesture towards his harness – "I and my brothers were left no choice but to take up arms with them, though it is against our calling."

"I am sorry for you," Dame Catherine said, a little perfunctorily. A weak man, Agnes could see her mother thinking. "Would you stay the night with us," she asked politely, "and recruit your strength?"

The Abbot shook his head. "We are too close to Nottingham here, in this corner of the shire. They will want to withdraw closer to Lincoln, and the safety of their fellows, and praise be, we have a clear night at last. Of your goodness, give me pen and parchment, and then we will be gone."

Not all that quickly, of course; disputes broke out over the stores, and a few of the men, following the Abbot into the hall, pushed through into the kitchen, pulled jars off the shelves and the roasting fowl off the spit. Dame Catherine saw the infuriated cook reach down for a red-hot poker, and spoke sharply, just in time. The dairymaid wept as the house cow was slaughtered, and the cockerel and his chickens soon suffered the same fate.

The men split a few barrels for the fun of seeing the waste, relieved themselves where they pleased, and scared the kitchen wenches witless. But as Dame Catherine counted up the damage with Agnes afterwards, it could, she said briskly, have been far worse.

She decided to leave their valuables where they had been hidden, for fear of a return, and most of the rest of their stores, but they recovered what they needed for daily life. Agnes wept over the poor mules, and prayed her jennet was still safe. Best leave the stock in the marshland where they were for now.

On Sunday, Robert Carbott appeared sheepishly to carry out his curate's duties. With his eyes shifting nervously around his congregation, he prayed for men of goodwill to join together, losing himself in contradictions as to the direction in which such union of thought should take them. Dame Catherine listened patiently, and went home to wait for news.

They had none for four days, and their spirits were sinking low again – and then all too much. On Wednesday, William came from Meryng, bringing news of his father.

"He has been ordered to join the forces of His Grace of Suffolk, who is leading an army to Lincoln to bring the rebels to book," William said with relish. "His Majesty's answer was to be read to the rebels there yesterday, and it will not have made good listening for them."

Seeing Dame Catherine blench, Agnes cried out at him. "Brother, for shame. Cannot you not see that we are in fear for Thomas? Mother, take heart, it must all end soon. And His Grace must surely be merciful to those who have done no wrong."

William laughed, unkindly. "No wrong? When Lord Burgh's servant was beaten to death, and they say another man bound in hides and fed to the dogs? No wrong?"

"But Thomas has done none of those things, William, you can be sure of that."

"Sister, you're a fool, do you think Suffolk will make distinction?"

"Thomas will flee to Yorkshire, at need," Agnes said, to comfort her mother, regretting she had spoken as she saw the sharp look in William's eye.

"If you are party to Thomas's folly, sister, beware. Women are burnt for treason. Am I to regret I did Father's bidding, and brought you back your jennet?"

This roused Dame Catherine. "Agnes is grateful to you, William, and you need have no fear. There is no treason in this house, son, nor will there be. We are loyal servants of King Henry, and for all anyone here knows, Thomas is with you at Meryng."

William was small and stocky, with bristling red hair and round features, a plainer copy of his mother. The twins were far from identical: the contrast with Thomas, who like his father was long-legged and sharp-featured, always annoyed William. But he was secure in his position as first-born, that all-important half-hour older than Thomas. At thirteen William had been sent to Meryng to learn to manage the estate that would be his, under the watchful eye of an experienced bailiff, and had justified his father's trust.

"I'll not lie for Thomas, Mother, that way lies ruin for us all. And have you no refreshment to offer me, or have you given it all to Thomas's friends?"

Their second gobbet of news came a couple of days later, just after William had saddled up and set off back to Meryng, urgent to hurry on the ploughing now the ground was drying out. Rob came to the house, twisting his cap in his hands, and asked for Agnes. "The mare's come back lame, Mistress, will you come and see?"

Agnes hastened to put on cloak and pattens; the yard was still churned and rutted. "Has she strained herself, Rob, or is it an abscess? Is her leg swollen? Shall I make a poultice?"

He shook his head, silent till they were out of anyone else's hearing. "Rest easy, there's naught amiss with the mare, Mistress, but I had summat for you I'd as lief none had sight of." He handed her a crumpled piece of paper. "Come in the stable, where you cannot be seen."

Agnes struggled to decipher the message: Thomas had obviously written in haste, he had a poor hand, and the paper was of the poorest quality. They had gathered in Lincoln, and taken over the Cathedral. But after the King's message had been read out at Lincoln, the gentry had taken fright, "even Edward". Agnes smiled, wryly.

The rebels had disbanded, Thomas told her, and he himself had ridden with a group of them to the north. He had found a moment to write while he was waiting to cross the Humber, aiming to find his way to Templehirst, to offer his services to Lord Darcy. I must burn this at once, Agnes thought, it's a death sentence: how can he take so little care? She struggled to read the last few words, gave up and opened the catch on the stable lantern. "Bring tinder, Rob, quickly."

He looked at her, took lantern and scrap out into the yard, and round behind the midden, where they were out of sight. It was soon ashes, and she breathed again.

*

It was November before John Meryng came home, on a cold grey day carrying warning of winter. He dropped wearily off his horse, his face drawn, but embraced his wife and children fondly. At a nod from her mistress, Betsy took Elizabeth and Francis away, despite their protests, so their father could talk freely.

Stretched out in a chair before the fire in the parlour, he let Agnes haul off his boots. "Bless you, girl, that's easier. Now tell me what's been afoot here, and how you've fared."

Dame Catherine told him about the Abbot's raid on their stores, and he snorted. "That weak fool. He's already in hold, in Lincoln Castle. But I fear we'll not see the mules again – no, wife, you gave only what you had to. And 'twas well you did, hiding so much beforehand. We'll not starve, for sure."

Nervously, Agnes asked: "Who else do they have in captivity?"

Her father looked at her narrowly. "Many rash fools, misled by rascals. The babbling priest from Louth, who started the fire. Thomas Moigne, poor fellow, though he nearly lost his life to the rebels himself; 'tis not a good time to be prominent in the city. Now he is reviled by both sides, and locked up as so many others have been."

He paused. "But not, so far, your brother."

"What about Edward Dymoke?" Dame Catherine asked. Her husband laughed. "A busy fellow, Edward. He's got on to the right side, and is scouring the shire for rebels to hand over to His Grace of Suffolk."

"And how did you fare, father?" Agnes asked, greatly daring.

"God be thanked, I joined My Lord Shrewsbury's muster soon enough to be judged loyal, and it was in my favour that our men here did not join the rebellion. Lord Hussey was not so fortunate. He still goes free, but it is said he was exchanging messages with the rebels, even if he swears it was to trap them. I fear it will go ill with him. The King will have the lives of many such, for all he talks of mercy."

"William came to tell us you had been sent to join His Grace of Suffolk," Agnes prompted.

"Ay, I rode with his men to Lincoln, where he is housed in the castle. The Bishop's Palace has been all but destroyed, but otherwise there is little damage. Your grandfather is safe enough, and talking less of the old religion – he was badly scared by the rioting, living where he does."

"Will My Lord Suffolk now leave us and go north?" Dame Catherine asked hopefully. "They say the rebellion is stronger there, and has spread wide from York."

John shook his head. "He is to stay in Lincoln, and show us the King's vengeance, a task much to his taste, I fear. They say the King has demanded a hundred deaths. He has no fondness for our shire, that is certain – he has condemned it roundly, for the impudence of its ignorant peasants. We will suffer much for this."

He looked at her sombrely, not saying what they both feared, how close that suffering might come. "But you are right, wife, there is much disturbance now across the North. One Robert Aske is the leader, and other gentlemen and lords have joined him. They call it a Pilgrimage, the sacrilegious rogues, a Pilgrimage of Grace. Faugh! His Grace of Norfolk has gone to deal with them. His force is small, and ill-paid, but he's a wily fox. Those 'pilgrims' will learn that, soon enough."

*

It would not be long before they learnt just how wily Norfolk was. In December, word began to drift south that His Grace had made terms with the northern rebels, and indeed that Aske had been invited south, with fine promises, to explain the Northerners' grievances to the King himself.

Before Christmastide, Rob pressed another missive into Agnes's hand. It was brief, and ill-written, but all was well. Thomas was coming home.

False promises, of course. Come the New Year, and the Yorkshire leaders were soon arrested, as the men of Lincolnshire had been. And Thomas never arrived. He was scooped up off the Humber ferry by Suffolk's men. No missive came from him this time, just a message from his grandfather, whose servant came to tell the family Thomas was in Lincoln jail, and like to suffer a traitor's death.

Her mother had collapsed at the news, and had been put to bed with a draught by Betsy. But she was awake now, and John had gone up to her. Darkness fell, and he did not return.

The door to her parents' bedchamber was latched shut after him. There was a unquiet sound of voices within. Agnes crept close in the darkness, to try to hear better. Then there was a creak on the landing, and she whipped round. She could just make out Elizabeth's small figure in her skimpy white shift. Stretching out her arm, she cuddled the shivering child to her, wrapping her shawl around them both, and miraculously, Elizabeth did not make a sound.

Their mother's low voice came to them only as a murmur, but in his rage and grief their father shouted loud enough for them to hear every word.

"A child! Aye, I know he is, but the King's men will not deem him so. I can do nothing for him, without putting us all at risk, and nor can you. We are still suspect, as all are in Suffolk's eyes. Catherine, I forbid you to go to Lincoln."

Agnes could hear her mother's voice rising in agony, but her words were still indistinct. They had not long to wait for her husband's reply.

"No, I cannot send William; have I not taken care to keep him clear of all this? We must just wait, and pray, that the wretched boy is too small a prey to be deemed worth the full rigour of the law. They have set the trial for early March; time for tempers to cool. My father will make sure he gets fed, at least."

Again her mother's voice, keening like an animal in pain.

"Wife, put the thoughts from you, and pray it does not come to that. If it does, God save us, my father can send a bribe to the hangman, to see he is dead before they cut him down for the butchers. More than that we dare not do."

Elizabeth was shivering again, and Agnes had heard all she could bear. She lifted the child in her arms and bore her back to their bed. At least, now, she knew what she had to do.

In the morning, she found Rob, and with him made her plans. She slipped back into the house for what she needed, then walked through the village as far as the rectory, where the curate was allowed by their Rector, comfortably ensconced in the Cathedral, to reside in his place. Carbott greeted her cautiously. "How may I serve you, Mistress?"

She walked past him into his bare little parlour, and sat down. "I wish you to write a letter for me. I have brought good paper for you."

He looked surprised, and slightly resentful. "I understood Dame Catherine to have taught all her children a fair hand."

"I have sprained my thumb," Agnes said calmly, "and my mother is busy."

He submitted, with an ill grace, and sitting at his desk dipped a poor, ill-sharpened quill into the battered inkwell.

"Sweet cousin," Agnes began, "now that the days lengthen and the roads are quiet again, I dare to ask if your lady mother would spare you to us again at Scrivelsby."

He stopped. "Mistress, you mean 'at Kettlethorpe'."

"No."

He looked at her, baffled.

"When you have finished writing this letter to me, in a hand my lady mother will not straightways recognise as my own, you will have a secret to keep for me. Just," Agnes continued, before he could protest, "as I have already a secret to keep for you."

"No such thing! I have shared no secrets with you, Mistress!"

"I know," Agnes went on steadily, "that you were last year in correspondence with Thomas Kendall, of Louth." She let this now-notorious name drop into the sudden stillness.

"My brother showed me the letter he sent you. I can recall it perfectly, because he left it with me. But of course it is a secret, just as the writing of this letter will be. Pray, shall we continue?"

It was the following day when Rob came to the door of the hall, with a message for Agnes. "A lad brought this letter for you, Mistress. He would not stay: he had another to deliver, but he said he'd be back for a answer on the morrow."

Agnes opened it, taking care to break the seal so it was unrecognisable. She handed it to her mother, sighing. "It is kind of the Dymokes, and I fain would visit Scrivelsby again, but I cannot leave you now."

Dame Catherine was reading the letter, but at Agnes's words she looked up. "What foolishness is this? We must not bury you here, however great our sorrow, when you should be learning how to go on in the world, with people of rank, if they are good enough to invite you. A most flattering invitation."

She read on. "It is prettily worded, indeed, though I should be ashamed if a child of mine wrote such a poor hand. But the Dymokes are an old family, perhaps they do not care to educate their daughters." She frowned, considering.

"It is a pity William cannot escort you, it would do both of you good." Neither of them mentioned Thomas, who had gone to Scrivelsby so blithely with Agnes last year: it was too painful.

"But Rob is a steady lad, and you can take him, and young Avice as a maidservant: she can ride pillion with him."

"I could stop the night in Lincoln, and take Grandfather more of your potion for his ague," Agnes suggested. Her mother looked at her, quickly. She nodded, slowly. "That is indeed a kind thought, daughter."

For a moment, Dame Catherine sat silent, thinking. Then she stiffened her back, and rose. "Come with me."

Agnes followed, a little puzzled, to her parents' bedchamber. With a key attached to her waist, Dame Catherine opened a small carved box that lay in the press under the window. Her modest trinkets lay within, and she removed them, to slide open the false bottom to the box. Below that were her pearls, and a small piece of silk, wrapped around a little cross.

It was gold, with delicate, trefoil endings to its four arms, and a blood-red gemstone set in the centre, fine work to Agnes's untutored eye. Her mother held it up to the light. "It was found when your father made his alterations to the house. It was buried in the old stonework. But why it was secreted there, no one knows. It would suit you well, I believe."

She did not meet Agnes's eye. "I dare not give you my pearls, your father would think me reckless, but this I never wear."

Now she looked at her daughter, almost blindly. "I think you should take this with you to the Dymokes, to... to give you countenance. You are old enough now."

She looked down again at the cross. "And one never knows when such things may be needed." She pressed it into Agnes's hands. "Use it if you can... find occasion for it. No need to trouble your father about it, though."

"No, mother – no need at all."

They understood each other passing well.

*

Lincoln was a sad city. It had had troubles enough, before the rising. Ever since it lost the staple to Boston, nearly two centuries ago, it had been in decline. But the wealth brought by the Lincolnshire Longwools had left its mark: the great Cathedral – the tallest building in the world, so it was said – the fine stone houses around it, and a profusion of priories.

Agnes was used to the decay in the half-deserted lower city, but not to the bitterness on people's faces. The gentry had failed them, had run away and left the Commons to suffer, and there were dark looks at Agnes's little party. Rob hurried them through the Stonebow, up Mikelgate and Poultry, and Agnes slipped off her jennet's back to lead her up the steep hill that led to castle and Cathedral.

Sir William Meryng's house was at the top, one of a fine group of half-timbered modern houses in Bailgate. The castle was in plain view, and Agnes shivered at the thought of the brooding presence of the Duke of Suffolk. She handed her mare to Rob, and rapped on her grandfather's door.

It was opened quickly enough, and Edwin, her grandfather's manservant, beamed down at her. "Well, by Our Lady, it's the young mistress come to lighten our sorrow. Come in, and this young wench you've brought, she's Betsy's kin, from the look of her. Who's with the horses? Rob? Ay, well, he knows his business."

Agnes found her grandfather in the little panelled front chamber of his comfortable townhouse, wrapped in a blanket, before a bright fire. It was a shock to see how he had aged since the summer, but his mind was still sharp.

"If it's that young brother of yours you've come about, girl, well, he's come to no harm yet. Edwin has a friend amongst the jailers, and he's getting as well-fed as I am. If you've a mind to see him, Edwin can no doubt get you in. But mind, I know nothing about it. Your father don't, I'll be bound. Christ alone knows what story you have told him."

Agnes plumped down on her knees, stretching out her hands to the fire. "My lady mother knows I'm come to see you, and has sent you her hyssop syrup that gives you ease. And honey. And her damson wine, this year's already, and the finest cheese the rebels did not help themselves to."

"She's a good woman, and I bless the day I found her for your father," the old man said complacently. "Give them to Edwin, and make your plans with him. Not too proud to borrow a serving-wench's garb, are you? Safer that way: and it'll cost you less. Tell Edwin I said so."

The kitchen was small and dark. Most of her grandfather's meals came from cook shops in the city. A skivvy came in to scrub, but she was fearful of Edwin, and left his mess untouched.

"I take young Thomas a meal at sundown; you can go instead, if you're not afeared. I've sent young Suky here a few times, so they'll not be surprised at a serving-maid. That young niece of Betsy's come with you, she's up in your bedchamber now. Go change into her kirtle, and I'll go fetch the vittels."

Avice was enjoying the biggest adventure of her young life, but she was aghast at the thought of Agnes wearing her clothes. "I didn't have time to wash anything but me apron, mistress," she protested. "Betsy'll kill me if you pick up me little strangers."

"I'll tell her I caught them from the dogs," Agnes promised, but she kept on her own shift.

Rob escorted her to the castle gate, then slipped out of sight. It was a comfort to know he was waiting for her: she felt vulnerable and afraid as she entered the gatehouse. But the guards waved her through with no more than a lewd jest, though one stuck out his foot for the sport of seeing if he could send her tray flying. She steadied herself, and scuttled across the castle ward, thankful they did not follow.

At the prison, the sergeant looked at her shrewdly. "Edwin taking his ease again tonight, is he? Well, whoever you are, you don't look much of a threat. In you go, Halkin will take you."

An elderly man heaved himself to his feet and took a ring of keys from the wall, pocketing the pence Edwin had placed on the wooden supper-tray. He pushed her ahead of him down a low corridor, with a stairway down at the end. Agnes's pattens slipped on the rough steps, and encumbered by her load, she would have fallen had he not grabbed her arm. "Careful, m'duck, it's mucky down below."

He put his lantern on a ledge to select a key, covering it with his hand. and smiled when he saw Agnes watching hopefully. "Nay, duck, I'm too old a hand to show you the key. Now, in you go, to see your master, or lover, or what you will; there's another gentleman with him, but you'll have to put up with that."

The cell was not as bad as Agnes had feared: it was a fair size, with a hearth on which a fire smouldered, taking the edge off the prison chill. There were two truckle beds, with well-stuffed straw pallaises, against the wall. In the middle, a table bore two platters and a branch candlestick. Three candle stubs were as yet unlit, for there was some natural light, from a high barred window, at ground level outside.

The middle-aged, grey-bearded man seated facing the door she vaguely recalled as a visitor to Kettlethorpe: he had stayed there last year on his way to London, newly elected as Lincoln's Member of the Parliament. Thomas Moigne, who by all accounts had tried to cool the rebels' temper, but had earned no royal thanks for that.

He had a book in his hands, having evidently eaten already, and looked up with only mild interest as the door opened. "Come in, wench," he said kindly.

Young Thomas, seated with his back to her, immediately swung round. Fed and clothed he might have been, but prison, or failure, or fear, had taken its toll: he was pale and unkempt, with heavy shadows under his eyes, and none of the older man's composure. His eyes lit up at the sight of his sister, and he leapt to his feet.

"Agnes…" He brushed her embarrassment aside. "We need have no secrets from Master Moigne. Sir, this is my sister, come with news from my father."

Agnes put her tray down, gently. "Eat, while it's still warm. Sir, there's enough for two if you would like some."

Moigne shook his head. "Thank you, Mistress, I have had more than enough: my good wife sees I do not lack."

Agnes turned back to Thomas, and spoke quietly. "Thomas, Father does not know I am here. He thinks I am paying a visit to the Dymokes."

Thomas swore. "That cursed turncoat, fool I was to trust him. He's eager for our deaths, to save his own skin."

"As I wish to save yours, and I would do as much if I could!" Agnes exclaimed. "Edward is wiser than most."

She looked, shyly, at Moigne. "Sir, I trust we do not disturb you! But you are wise in the ways of the world, can you tell me, what is to come? Is there anything I can do to help Thomas?"

Moigne looked at her sadly. "I am not so wise, I fear, Mistress; for a surety they will make an example of me. The Duke of Suffolk has had enough of Lincoln, and left for his new home at Grimsthorpe. Sir William Parr is sent to do the business for him. He is not a merciful man, he is hungry for lands, and I am in his way."

He paused, and Agnes thought he would say no more, but he roused himself, smiling bleakly. "I am a dead man, so I will do what I can to defend all the other poor souls caught in his net. But your brother, for all his rashness, is not known to His Majesty or his counsellors; nor, I think, would his death bring rich pickings. If you can get Thomas's name struck off the list of those to be tried, I do not think his absence would be noted."

"But Sir, who could do that? Only tell me who can alter the list! Is it His Grace himself, or Sir William, perhaps, or even some clerk I might be able to persuade? He is only fourteen…"

Thomas snorted. "Fifteen, now, and so I told them."

Moigne caught Agnes's eye, and almost smiled. Despairingly, she continued. "I would plead, I have something of value to give such a man, if only I can reach him…"

Thomas interrupted. "What thing of value? Agnes…" She shook her head, blushing. "No, I don't fool myself that my maidenhood is worth anyone's life! I have this to offer." She tugged out the cross to show him.

"In God's name, how came you by it? I've never seen you wear such a thing! If you stole for my sake, I'll not have it…"

"Rest easy, Thomas, my lady mother gave it to me, and for this purpose, and Father knows nothing of it."

She turned back to his companion, pleadingly. "But Sir, who can I give it to? Who can help me?"

Moigne looked up at the barred window, as if even the fast-fading light might bring answers. He was, Agnes thought, a quietly heroic figure: marked for death, awaiting agony in his own garden of Gethsemane, yet still with the mental strength and generosity of spirit to help others if he could.

Of an impulse she asked him: "Sir, how came you here? My father told us you tried to calm the rebels. Did you not read them His Majesty's reply, and urge them to go home?"

She stopped in confusion, appalled at her own presumption, but he took no offence.

"Yes, Mistress, I did indeed read it out to them, harsh as it was. We were gathered in the Chapter House, the gentry forced to join with the rebels, and the mood of the Commons was dangerous indeed. I tried to leave out the parts of His Majesty's reply I thought would most inflame them. But some fool of a clerk, reading over my shoulder, cried foul! The crowd grew angry, and made me tell it all – how His Majesty decried our shire as one of the most 'brute and beestlie' of his realm. A foul calumny, full of contempt."

He checked, slapping his hand on the table in recollection. "But now I remember it, there was one there on that day, the message-bearer indeed, who could aid your brother, had he a mind to do so. He is certainly known to your father – the Bishop's man, John Heneage. That family has the ear of the King himself."

*

In the upper guest chamber of her grandfather's house, Agnes lay awake. Avice's rhythmic snoring punctuated the unfamiliar town sounds, loud as bedlam to a country girl. Even in the night hours, after curfew, sounds carried along the cobbled alley outside the house. Agnes's thoughts clattered along with them around her brain, evolving into more and more fantastical schemes for waylaying one of the Heneage family.

In the way of wakeful nights, she finally fell into an exhausted sleep just as dawn was breaking. Avice woke her early, as promised, but she came downstairs to find Sir William had already breakfasted, and was waiting impatiently for news of her visit to the prison.

He grimaced at the Heneage name, screwing his elderly face into a monkey's pout. "I'm no help to you there, girl, they've no cause to do me a favour. I beat Thomas Heneage to a parcel of land – years back, but they're not ones to forget."

He shook his head, doubtfully. "Coming men, the Heneages, with Thomas now so close to the King, John so close to Cromwell through our Bishop Longland. George is the best of them, our Dean here at the Cathedral. He kept away while the rising was on, wise fellow, for the Chapter were up in arms, and His Majesty's had his eye on them for many a year. The family'll be looking to pick up attainted lands, I'll be bound. Pray God they don't have eyes on Kettlethorpe."

"Master Moigne said Thomas Heneage was to have Lord Darcy's lands at Knaith," Agnes ventured.

"Then Darcy's a dead man. But hey ho, he was anyway, poor old fool." His Lordship was younger than her grandfather, Agnes reflected, but it wouldn't help to say so.

Frustration and helplessness were making Sir William fretful. "Be off with you, girl, there's nothing you or I can do, and your father would put his head in a noose if he tried. Where's Edwin? This fire's no good – tell him to bring some dry logs, the idle fellow."

Agnes went to find him, glad to escape. The fire had indeed been smoking, badly. Edwin muttered that they were out of dry wood, but there was a much better fire on the kitchen hearth, and when he saw her look at it Edwin went grumbling to the woodshed. He had been stalwart, but Agnes could see he was growing tired of it all, the worry and its effect on her grandfather.

Desperate for fresh air herself, Agnes pulled her cloak off its hook in the hallway and reached for her pattens. Calling for Avice to follow her, she pushed the heavy door open and stepped out into the Bailgate.

Winter had whipped back, with a cutting wind, after the mild days that had given a deceitful promise of spring. Even here in town, frost had rimed the cobbles, though the constant traffic had rubbed most of it into slush. Almost without thinking, Agnes turned left, towards the deep sound of bells.

The nave of the great Cathedral of St Mary's was quiet, with little groups huddled together, talking softly, looking round nervously, anxious not to be overheard. This was still a place of fear: fear of the future as well as the past. She slipped off her pattens, whose smack on the stone floor earned disapproving glances, and sent Avice home.

Agnes walked quickly up the south side of the nave. She was heading for her favourite refuge, along the side of the Angel Quire: the tombs of Katherine Swynford and her daughter. This daughter, Joan, Countess of Westmorland, had fulfilled her parents' wish and endowed a chantry for them. Agnes knelt at the little chantry chapel, and tried to lose her fears in fervent prayer.

At first it was just an outflow of grief, but gradually she formed it into words of supplication: to Our Lady, Christ's mother, to whom the Cathedral was dedicated, and to the two women, daughter and mother, who lay at rest there. Katherine, Duchess of Lancaster, had still styled herself the Lady of Kettlethorpe, even when far grander honours came her way. Would she not have some care for her successors in that place?

Pouring out her heart, Agnes lost all sense of her surroundings, until brought back to them by a small shock. There was a man close by, watching her, and he had clearly been standing there for some time.

He was not, she realised with relief, at all threatening. He was small, with the slightly stunted look of so many who had had too little to eat in childhood. He was shabby but neat, with brown close-cropped hair, and shrewd, disillusioned eyes.

He lifted his hands, in benediction or perhaps just reassurance. "Forgive me, daughter, for my besetting sin of curiosity. It is my duty to pray for the soul of Her Grace of Lancaster, her Lord and their daughter, but I did not know others still did, and in such distress. Means she so much to you, this great lady, dead as she's been for more than a century?"

Agnes scrambled to her feet, her own curiosity breaking through the blankness of her misery. "Are you their chantry chaplain, Father?"

He was smaller than her, she found, and had to look up, smiling wryly. "I am, and have been for two years, though the Blessed Lord knows how much longer I will have a living as such…"

He checked. "How my tongue runs on. Another failing, though not perhaps one I will burden my confessor with, in these dangerous times. So tell me, daughter, why do you pray for the Lady Katherine, and weep for her too?"

Agnes blushed. "Father, I confess I was praying for the Lady's intercession, not for her soul. If I did wrong, forgive me, but I come from Kettlethorpe, and I hoped she might still have a care for those who dwelt there."

"What care do they need?" He checked again, a faint twinkle in his eyes. "There, you see, my curiosity is incurable. It is you who should forgive me."

She shook her head quickly. "It is no secret, I fear. My brother is taken up on suspicion of playing a part in the rising." Not even to this kindly priest would she admit more than suspicion. "He is but a child! He may have spoken foolishly, but nothing more than that, I swear."

She had the priest's full attention, now. "Is he held in the castle?" She nodded. "Has he been tried?"

"He will be, on March seventh, they say, with the rest of them – unless I can find someone to hear my prayers." Her voice wobbled. "Only five days from now."

He bowed his head. "Then I will pray too, and if Her Grace the Duchess cannot hear me, Our Lady of Sorrows will. Come, now, and walk with me in the cloisters, it's bright enough to dry your tears – and you can tell me how this all came about."

They crossed to the north side of the Cathedral, and out into the cloisters, where the wind did not bite as keenly as in the Bailgate. He was a good listener, this shabby little priest, and Agnes lost her suspicions and found herself telling him the story, straightening it out as she went.

"Where did he go from here, your young brother? You say he was taken up coming back into the county, across the Humber: where had he been, after the meeting here in the Chapter House?" She hesitated, knowing this was the weakness in her tale. She knew little enough about Thomas's time in Yorkshire. What could such a boy have done, at worst?

"I do not know," she confessed miserably. The chaplain rubbed his nose, thoughtfully. "But in Lincolnshire, daughter, he has nothing to answer for?"

She shook her head, firmly. Jesu grant Thomas had written no more letters than the brief missives to her! He had received some, she knew, but surely he had not been foolish enough to keep them? She had searched his chamber, after he had left, and found nothing – certainly not the evidence with which she had threatened the curate. And even a hot-headed boy like Thomas would not have taken such dangerous material with him.

But what about letters he might have written? Pray God there were none: he had been lazy with his copybook; he got Agnes to write for him, as a rule, and she had penned no letters for him on these dangerous matters. As to actions, in Lincolnshire at least he had been too late even to witness them: the riots and murders happened before he left home, and he had got to Lincoln only in time to see the rebels disband.

All this the spry little priest teased out of the tangled wool of her story. But then, looking quickly at the sundial on the cloister wall, he withdrew his attention.

"Daughter, I am sorry, but in listening to you I have overspent my time here! No, no cause for apologies, it was needful. But I have other duties: I earn half my living at the Deanery, helping with the books. I was due there nigh on an hour ago. We could meet on the morrow, if I can serve you further?"

But Agnes was staring at him, eyes shining with hope. "The Deanery! Have you then a way to talk to Dean Heneage? Master Moigne said that family is my only hope, they are close to His Majesty. His Grace of Suffolk will listen to them! If I could but speak to the Dean, if he would receive my petition…"

Her voice died away. She knew she was asking too much. Listening to herself, she could hear how hopeless it was. The Dean would not see a foolish girl, at the request of a lowly priest, barely more than a clerk. She bobbed a curtsy to him, ducking her head to hide her new tears of self-realised disappointment, but he checked her.

"Wait…"

Looking up, she saw his pupils dilate with calculation. "Yes," he said, but not to her, rather as if concluding an argument with himself. He gazed at her, still thinking. "Where are you staying, daughter? Have you any finer raiment?" He looked away, embarrassed. "I mean no offence, but…"

Taken aback, Agnes almost giggled, despite everything. "No need to spare my blushes, Father! My shame that I cut such a sorry figure, I have given little thought to it since these troubles started. But my grandfather lives close, and it would take only moments, if…"

He smiled back at her. "That's better." Did he mean her laughter, or her attention to dress? He chafed his hands against each other, as if dusting for action. "Go put on your best, and come a fine lady to the Deanery. You know where it is? No? I'll show you, as we go."

He had set off briskly, talking as he went. "Have you a maidservant with you, or can you borrow one from your grandfather? Anyone to give you countenance?"

Before she could answer, he was off on another tack and walking even faster. "When you get to the Deanery, ask for me. Oh yes, my name: I am Robert Parsevall, remember that. Be persistent, they will say I am busy. Ask several times. Make a nuisance of yourself. When I come out of the Great Chamber, insist on speaking to me. That's all for now, but I promise you, you will get your turn."

He stopped, to focus her attention. "One more thing. Do not be dismayed if I seem sceptical, or reluctant to believe you. I know the Dean. I know how his mind works. He is cautious, that is how he himself has survived. But he is not unkind. And he has good judgement."

A pause. He is wondering, Agnes thought, how much to say to a foolish girl. Then, as if in a deliberate act of trust, he continued.

"The Dean knows that if this city is made a slaughterhouse, there will be another rising. Executing so young a boy might just kindle the flame. And I have heard Sir William Parr concede to the Dean he will seek to satisfy His Majesty with fewer than the hundred deaths he asked for."

Father Robert paused for breath, before the door leading out of the cloister. "There, you can see the Deanery, in Eastgate. Now run back to your grandfather's. And remember what I say. The Dean likes others to do the testing for him. So tell me the story again as you told it just now, and expect me to ask the same questions, but with more suspicion. Keep going. Do not give up, or stop, until you see me do thus."

He crossed the third finger of his right hand over the second. "Then he will have heard enough. Make your reverence then, and say you leave it in his safe hands." He grinned. "And, of course, God's."

"Father…"

He turned back to her, a little impatiently. "What now?"

"Why are you doing this?"

A sad, private, fleeting smile. "Too long a story for now. But once, I had a younger brother, who put his life at risk by taking on a fight he could not win. To my grief, and shame, I did not save him. It means nothing, except that you can trust me. By Christ's wounds, I will do all I can."

It was only afterwards she remembered that those wounds of Christ were the symbol of the rising.

The porter at the Deanery looked at Agnes and Avice doubtfully. Avice had laced her into her best petticoat and kirtle, with fine slashed sleeves, and bound her hair into her new green French hood. She had worried about that, wondering if the fashions favoured by Anne Boleyn were now dangerous to wear; but a linen coif would have done little to give her maturity or status, and she did not possess one of the old box hoods – even her mother had thankfully discarded those.

She had made the right choice, it seemed. On consideration, the porter judged her to be a gentlewoman, and reluctantly doffed his cap, though the look he cast over Avice was contemptuous. Agnes had had no time to do more than tie her maidservant into a slightly less grubby apron, and stuff most of her hair into a kerchief round her head. Avice returned scowl for scowl, and the porter, reluctantly, stepped back.

Father Robert, he told them reprovingly, was with the Dean, Mistress, and she was not, he added with finality, on the list of expected guests he had been given this morning. Agnes looked at his scrap of paper, and pointed confidently at an indecipherable scribble in the corner. "There it is – I see it now. They have written 'Lady Annis' mistakenly, for 'Lady Agnes'."

In truth, the scribble looked like neither, but the porter was sufficiently confused for her to get past the door. "I will wait here," she said, seating herself on the long settle, and beckoning Avice to stand beside her. The porter opened his mouth to protest, then sighed and shrugged. Let Robert Parsevall deal with it, he thought, as he did with most things round here.

Ten minutes passed, and Agnes rose. "You must tell Father Robert I am here, or he will be angry." The porter shook his head. "I dursen't disturb them, Mistress."

She began to walk restlessly around, simulating extreme annoyance. Avice gazed at her, bemused. Mistress Agnes was usually so quiet, and gentle. At the fourth turn, a door opened and Robert Parsevall appeared. Before he could speak, the porter pointed at Agnes.

"This young gentlewoman, Father, she says you are expecting her. She's been most insistent..."

The chaplain looked up, as if annoyed at being distracted from his papers. "Of course. Yes. I had forgot. Forgive me, Mistress, would you come back tomorrow?"

Agnes drew herself up. "Father, I have come today, at your request, and some trouble. I demand you see me, as you promised."

Robert Parsevall sighed. "Very well, come with me, but we may be interrupted by the Dean. I have much business with him today. He looked at Avice. "Come with your mistress, girl, but stay you quietly by the door."

In the chamber, he drew up a chair for Agnes, and to her relief gave her an encouraging wink. The far door, opened, and a well-dressed, surprisingly young man came in, more papers in his hand. The chaplain looked up, and began apologising. "Reverend Sir, I am greatly at fault in forgetting Mistress Agnes Meryng was to visit me, with some papers for me to study. In truth, her questions are more than a lowly cleric like myself can answer..."

Dean Heneage looked at him, a little sceptically, but with good humour. "I know you, Robert, and I misdoubt this is a mistake. Would you have me hear Mistress Agnes's complaint?"

"I would be thankful for your judgement, Dean, I am uncertain of mine."

"Humph." He perched on the desk, brushing aside the chaplain's efforts to give him his chair. "Well, Mistress?"

Agnes told the story again, gaining confidence from Father Robert's challenges along the way, however hostile he made them appear. Yes, her brother had foolishly gone to Lincoln to join the rising, but no, he had taken part in no violence, neither to person nor property. No, he had not come home after they dispersed, but he had caused no other trouble in the shire.

"And further north?" This was the dangerous question.

"Sirs, I know nothing of his time there, but he has sworn to me he took part in none of the fighting. He is very young…"

To her shame, her voice broke. She glanced at Robert Parsevall: he face was blank, but his eyes gave her courage. "He was only fourteen, and foolish, maybe, but never wished to make war on his Sovereign, to whom his loyalty is undoubted."

Agnes swallowed, and took the gamble the chaplain had advised. "I dare to pray your aid because, I am told, His Grace of Suffolk was commanded to mete out punishment here for deeds done in this county?"

"It is not your place, Mistress, to question the Duke of Suffolk's mission." But the Dean spoke without heat, almost absent-mindedly.

Then Agnes took her own gamble. "Sir, if gold is needed to help make inquiries, I can pay." She pulled the cross out of its hiding place between her breasts, untied the ribbon, and laid it on the table.

There was silence. A long silence. Heneage frowned, and she wondered if she had fatally offended him. It looked a little thing to offer for a life, a small gold thing, with one gem. She dared not look at Robert Parsevall; she had not shared this secret with him.

Then the Dean stretched out a long, well-kept hand, and took the cross.

Afterwards she never remembered how she got out of the Deanery, blinded as she was by a gut-churning mixture of terror and hope. It was only when she was back in the Cathedral cloisters, sitting on a cold stone ledge in the dying afternoon, that she could begin to take stock.

She had had said no more after the Dean had picked up the cross, seeing the chaplain make his pre-arranged sign. As they left, he said that it was he who would be tasked to make inquiries, in what little time there was before the trial. How would she would know the result? He shook his head. Not, he feared, until the names for trial were pasted outside the castle, the day of the trial.

In four days' time. Four days!

*

March the seventh dawned winter-bright, with that fickle clear sky that is so quickly overcast. Agnes was up early, filled with febrile, fragile energy; she had not slept, but lain listening to the night sounds of the city.

She was so tired that she found herself making simple, stupid mistakes – forgetting to lace her shoes and tripping on the stairs, burning her hand as she tried to revive the kitchen fire.

Edwin came in from his frowsty little chamber, grumbling to himself. He was looking old, she realised, like his master: no wonder if he just wanted the worry over, for good or ill. He would be glad to see the back of her, and life returned to its even tenor: to sorrow, maybe, but also to undemanding normality.

They heard Sir William thump his stick on the floor of his chamber, and Edwin sighed deeply as he went to see what her grandfather wanted. Sir William was now shouting for Agnes, and she followed Edwin in to see him.

He had propped himself up in his bed, and dismissing Edwin irritably, muttered to her to open the hidden drawer in its base. "Press down the little panel at the bottom of the bedpost, that will release the catch. Best someone knows, and I'd not trust Edwin to keep his fingers off it when I die. That's it, girl, now give me the iron box. Do the same on the other side of the bed, and you'll find the key."

She did as told, and he fitted the key in the lock, turning it with a little grunt of effort. He counted out five gold sovereigns, and a handful of silver coins, pushing them into an old leather pouch. "Take that, girl, hide it well and keep it safe. If he's condemned, seek Edwin's help to find the executioner, and bribe him well for a quick death, but don't give him the money till after."

His eyes blurred a little, and his wrinkled face drooped. "No: it's no task for a maid. I'll tell Edwin. He'll know what to ask for, should all go badly. Not for you to think about. Give Edwin the money, if need be. Now go."

Avice was downstairs now, holding their cloaks ready, looking scared but resolute. Agnes thanked her, but sent her to the stable for Rob to come with her instead. His broad frame at her back, she thought, would be a greater comfort. But even with him behind her, it took all her courage to step out into Bailgate, and force herself to make the short walk to the castle's east gate. Our Blessed Lady, she prayed with desperate fear, hear my supplication and help me. Let this dark day end well.

Outside the castle, a small, shivering crowd was already waiting. The clouds were yielding a thin, spiteful drizzle. There was no notice pinned to the wall. "They're still making the list," said a man near the front. "The sergeant told me. We'll not know who's charged until the trial."

Anxious faces turned towards him – women's faces, mostly, mothers, wives, sisters, daughters. His tiny bit of information made him, in their eyes, the source of all knowledge, and they besieged him with questions. But before he could disappoint them, the castle gate opened, and the crowd abandoned him to surge forward, stumbling over each other in their anxiety to get to the great chamber to be used for the trial.

They were packed into a small pen in the building that ran along the castle's north wall, heavily guarded. Agnes could see little, but Rob towered above most. She had told him about Robert Parsevall, and he hoisted her up on to the barrier to see if she could see the little chaplain.

"He's there," she muttered, and caught Father Robert's eye. Her heart lifted, but he spread his hands. Holy Mary, he did not know either; that did not bode well. Her gorge rose, and her heart beat faster. Rob tightened his arm around her. She thought, with a fleeting wisp of gallows humour, how before this turmoil, such presumption would have earned him a thrashing from her father. But the pit of terror made nonsense of such distinctions; she leant against him gratefully.

The guards straightened up, slamming their pikes on the floor, setting Agnes's heart jumping again. The door groaned open, and two men of authority strode in. The first had the unmistakable look of the lifetime courtier, assured, brisk, well dressed, cold-eyed: Sir William Parr, he must surely be. But with the second came power. The room stilled, and chilled, as he dropped his hefty frame into the seat of judgement.

About fifty, too, but of a very different cut to Sir William. A face to haunt your nightmares. Brutal, commonplace features. Puffy cheeks, deep grooves of temper running down from the nostrils.

Chin broader than forehead: more jaw than brain. Clipped, grizzled beard. The small, black, chancy eyes of an angry animal.

To pin your hopes on the mercy of this man must be folly, unless, of course, you had nowhere else to pin them. A whisper went round the courtroom. The Duke of Suffolk had come back to see the King's will done.

A man with a lifetime of command behind him, the King's friend and brother-in-law, son of Henry Tudor's standard-bearer at Bosworth Field. Agnes remembered, with a shudder of empathy, that a girl of only fourteen had recently been married to the Duke, after Mary Tudor's death – Lady Willoughby de Eresby, heiress to the estates at Grimsthorpe, in the south of Lincolnshire. A brutal bunch, her mother always called them, the Tudors and their friends.

Sir William called the court to order, and waved an impatient hand at the clerk who had entered behind him. He bowed, and handed a parchment roll to the court usher. "Call these men to stand trial."

The usher unrolled it, and read.

Fear made it so hard to concentrate. She caught a few familiar names on the list, above all Master Moigne – and then the usher was done, the parchment handed to the sergeant, and he was gone to call those ill-fated men to trial.

Could she have missed Thomas's name? Had she missed it? Her eyes sought Father Robert's, again, but his face told her nothing. It was a mask: what did that mean? He dared not show joy, of course, but surely, if Thomas's name had been called out, he would have shown grief?

She could feel Rob relax, and turned a face of appeal to him. He shook his head. "No mention of the young master." But she was not reassured until, an interminable time later, the forty-five men were squeezed into the court, and asked how they pleaded, one by one. Praise God, no Thomas. Not this time.

She and Rob could not get out. They had to stay there right through the trial, hear Thomas Moigne plead bravely for those around him, hear them all condemned to execution by Sir William. An elderly woman fainted; Agnes clasped the poor creature before she fell, and cradled her head, sinking down with her.

Others screamed or shouted for mercy, until Sir William terrorised them into silence. There was a boy amongst the forty-five, even younger than Thomas: he collapsed too, and was dragged away by the guard. The courtroom stink intensified: fear and sweat were overtaken by vomit and excrement.

The Duke of Suffolk had sat unmoved while Sir William concluded the business, occasionally casting his malevolent gaze over prisoners and relatives alike. Then, with a grunt, he pushed himself to his feet, and led the way out, the soldiers driving the crowd back again to make way for him. Sir William followed, with the air of a man relieved to have discharged dull but necessary business, and now with his mind on greater things.

Rob was tugging at Agnes's sleeve. "Come away, Mistress, quickly." She was loth to leave the old woman, but a man struggled through the crowd to carry her away. Father Robert had somehow made his way across too, and was urging Rob and Agnes to hurry.

"Your brother's not been condemned, but he's not been released, either. You must get him away now, before someone bribes the guard to exchange him for one of those unfortunates. Follow me, quickly. Have you money ready?"

There were into the castle garth now, and Agnes pulled the pouch from inside the waist of her skirt. The chaplain looked at the coins inside. "Give me two sovereigns, and some silver. He'll need the rest to get out of the country."

Outside the prison, it was a chaos of grieving, pleading families. Father Robert slipped through, and it seemed eternity until he emerged with Thomas, in shirt and hose, with a piece of coarse sacking over his head and shoulders. "Pull it up, boy, and keep close to me. Mistress, do you and your groom go in front of us, and don't look back."

They crossed to the west gate of the castle. The sergeant on guard looked suspiciously at Rob, but waved him through with Agnes. They heard an altercation behind them, but obeyed Father Robert and walked steadily on, slipping on the muddy path down from the gate. Turning right along the line of the hill to the solitary church of St Bartholomew's, Agnes dared a quick glance back, and saw with a flood of relief that her brother and the priest were safely through.

In a shed behind the church, Edwin was holding two horses. Avice stood with him, clutching a bundle. Agnes gaped at Rob, recognising the cob he had ridden from Kettlethorpe.

"I dursen't tell you, Mistress: when the message came from Father Robert to bring him here ready, Edwin told me not to breathe a word, for fear of raising your hopes."

Edwin nodded, lips pursed. "Least said, soonest mended. Not a word have I said to your grandfather, either, he's had enough to bear."

The chaplain drew a long breath, and turned to the maidservant. "Well done girl, did you bring what I asked?"

Avice nodded, her eyes wide in her frightened face, but could not speak. "She did," Edwin assured him gruffly. "I saw to that."

Father Robert took Avice's bundle, struggling to strap it on to the back of the cob's saddle. Edwin took it from him, but gently, listening with unusual respect to what the chaplain had to say.

"Touch and go, and it took a bit more of your master's money at the gate, but we're clear. There'll be many bribes asked and given today, and few will escape, all the same."

The chaplain turned back to Thomas. "There's a cloak and thick doublet, food, and ale, enough to get you on your way to a port. Ride hard, young man, and get you a ship, soon as you can."

He glanced at the western sun. "Not much light left now, I fear; still, get as far as you can from Lincoln tonight. Don't go home, or anywhere you're known, whatever you do."

Agnes thrust the pouch into his hand. Thomas pushed it away. "I'll take naught but a horse, I've caused you trouble enough.

She persisted. "Grandfather sent it for you, and I have more to give you..." But at that he got angry. "No, I'll take nothing from you. Nothing. Pay this good father for my food and clothes, and my father for the horse, for I fear you'll not see him again."

The chaplain shook his head, in silent exasperation. But Edwin spoke up bluntly. "Pride's a fine thing, boy, but only if you can afford it. You'll take the purse, or risk all our good work. I'll not face your grandfather and confess we let you go empty-handed. A boy like you will need all the help he can buy. Now take it and get you gone, quickly, as the good Father says."

Reluctantly, Thomas stuffed it inside his jerkin.

Father Robert tightened the girth on the cob, quickly and neatly. "Rob will come with you till you're at the coast. And mark me now," he added seriously, "send no message home until you are safe abroad, it would bring danger both to you and your family."

He smacked his forehead. "By Our Blessed Lady of Lincoln, I almost forgot. You must take a new name – choose it now, to comfort your sister. She would know who to pray for, and whose letters to trust."

Thomas looked at him, hesitantly. "I'd thought of that. If it would not endanger you, Father – I'd fain choose yours."

Father Robert smiled. "Robert. Not Parsevall, I thank you, but Vagus, there's a good name for a wanderer. Take it, Robert Vagus, with my blessing, and go, with God's!" He hugged Thomas roughly, and turned him to his sister.

"Where will you go?" Agnes asked, anxiously.

Cold, weary, and still in fear of his life, Thomas yet had not lost all his spirit. "I'll go to Italy. Was that not where Lord Cromwell served his apprenticeship? You may see me at the White Hall, yet!"

*

Agnes sat in her bedchamber, at Kettlethorpe, grateful for the midday solitude there. She thought again of Dean Heneage.

That day in Lincoln, he had taken the cross from her, looked at it closely, and with a surprisingly gentleness had put it back in her palm and closed her fingers over it.

"It is a fine thing, Mistress, and ancient, but it is both too little and too much to give for a life. Keep it; I see no reason for Sir William Parr to add it to his treasure chest. I will see that inquiries are made. And if what you say is true, and there is no cause in this shire to pursue your brother..."

He had paused, and looked at Father Robert with the ghost of a smile. "What I can do, I will do, or I will have no peace from this troublesome fellow." Only a look passed between them, but afterwards, Agnes thought: he was repaying a debt. It was hard to imagine what a despised chantry priest could have done for the Dean of Lincoln, but there was something there, all the same, some small service in the dangerous politics of the time.

He had turned back to her then, though she had sensed he was still talking to Father Robert. "I am not, myself, entirely free from the suspicion that attaches to my Chapter, but I have a voice, and a family that has the ear of the great. And that family will do well enough in these times, without depriving a maiden of her little treasure."

So she had kept the cross to give to her brother, as her mother would have wished. But he would not take it. Nor would her grandfather, who became crotchety when she tried to thank him for what he had done. "Think shame to offer me your mother's trinket! You give it back to her. Don't you go offering it to Edwin, mind you, either, however he may have helped you!"

She had told her mother all, and tried to make her take the cross back, before her father realised it was missing – but nor would Dame Catherine accept it. "Daughter, I owe you more than I can say. How can you imagine I would take this back from you?"

But Agnes could not look at it without pain, and the memory of fear. That would linger, even if, or when, they heard that Robert Vagus was safe in Italy.

She had told her father only as much as was needful, to rest his fears. When Rob returned, he faced no questions, only a nod of thanks, for a job well done. But Agnes knew it would be long, perhaps lifelong, before she saw her brother again.

She did not want to give her treasure to the church, since King Harry and Master Cromwell were busy scooping up even such little treasures. So she scraped a hole in the plaster, in the corner of the hall, where it might be a mouse hole. And she pushed her little treasure back to lie, more or less, where her father had found it.

Maybe, someday, it would be offered for a life again.

1537–1642

The Lincolnshire Rising and the Pilgrimage of Grace were crushed ruthlessly. The King used the excuse of the second flare-up of unrest in Yorkshire to renege on Norfolk's promises, and the body of Robert Aske was soon hanging in chains from Clifford's Tower in York.

He was by no means the only "Pilgrim" to go to the scaffold. Both Lord Hussey and Lord Darcy were executed, as was the luckless Abbot of Barlings, Matthew Mackerell, and at least 200 others. Thomas Moigne was condemned at the trial in March 1537 to suffer the full penalty for treason, and was hung, drawn and quartered in Lincoln the following day. However, the Duke of Suffolk was indeed anxious not to provoke a further uprising in Lincolnshire. He stopped well short of the King's target of a hundred executions in the county.

It was the east of Lincolnshire that took the greatest part in the rising, and even there, the gentry were lukewarm at most about it. So I thought it unlikely that John Meryng, whose family lived at Kettlethorpe at this time, was actively involved. However, amongst his large brood, of which we know at least the names, it was possible there was one hothead, and I have chosen his teenage second son for this role. But that is all imagination, as is the courage of his sister.

The Pilgrimage did not much disrupt the economic process of Reformation, though a few concessions were made to placate the *gentry. But the Pilgrimage dented Cromwell's reputation as a safe pair of hands, and in three years he too was dead.*

There were enduring pockets of the old religion in the North. They were suspect. Henry's daughter Elizabeth I may have declared that she would not make "windows into men's souls", but her spymasters did not believe they could afford to be so nice. Many souls' windows were wrenched open in the Tower to expose conspiracies, real as well as imagined, during her reign and that of her successor, James I.

And then his son, Charles I, brought a Catholic Queen to England from France, and encouraged his Archbishop to impose practices on the Church of England that caused ferment and suspicion of Popery. He also wanted money, badly. He lacked Elizabeth's gift for managing an uppity House of Commons, and the tension between King and Parliament grew.

It would be felt even in Kettlethorpe, now owned by the Hall family. In 1564, John Meryng's eldest son William had parted with the manor, which then passed through a number of hands in quick succession until, by Abigail Bellamy's marriage in the 1620s, it passed into the hands of Charles Hall.

The records paint a picture of a man of some means, with his finger in many pies, keen to get on but not particularly successful, busy in the county, not always too scrupulous about how he deals with money or acquires land, but a kindly widower who loves his home and is good to the poor.

And, one thing more, so significant in the mid-seventeenth century – the time of the turbulent birth of constitutional monarchy and representative democracy. While most (though not all) of the Lincolnshire gentry were Royalist or indifferent, Charles Hall was neither.

He was a Parliament man.

THE MIDDLING SORT

KETTLETHORPE HALL: 1642–45

Watched by their womenfolk and children, the men filed up the nave of St Peter and Paul. On the chancel step, Isabel saw that her cousin Gervase Hall sat at a small table, quill held ready, inkwell and scroll in front of him. Some men signed for themselves. Others he wrote for, handing over the quill for them to add "x" beside their names, with confident flourish or doubtful scrawl.

Why, Isabel wondered, had this commitment been demanded of them all? All the good folk of Kettlethorpe knew was that Parliament – a newly assertive, righteous but frightened Parliament – had determined to take control of the country's destiny.

Gervase had read them the oath beforehand, in the same voice in which he pronounced the Lord's Prayer. It was the Rector's duty. And it was supposed, Isabel surmised, to flush out the Papists, the secret service of the Bishop of Rome, the foreign Queen and King Charles's other evil advisers. But the Papists would not be caught that way: everybody present seemed to be trooping up to sign, even those who she knew full well clung to the old ways. And she didn't think anyone was missing.

Perhaps they were afraid not to come. Or perhaps they were just confused, as she had been, when her father had read the oath to her yesterday. It was very long, and complicated, and seemed to her to contradict itself, stressing allegiance to both King and Parliament, when even Isabel knew they were at loggerheads. Had not her father himself read her a pamphlet railing at His Majesty for flouting Parliament's privileges, marching in on the Commons and demanding that five of its Members be handed over to royal arrest?

Isabel's father, Charles Hall, loved to explain great matters, and since his wife had died, Isabel had been his loyal fireside audience, struggling with first her sampler and then her stump work while he read or held forth to her. But he had not appreciated her questioning the oath, replying irritably that Parliament was no enemy of King Charles, only of his false counsellors. So it was, Isabel concluded, just another example of the lengths to which adults would go to insist that all colours were the same, up until the moment they insisted that one was white and the other black.

Isabel had had much opportunity to observe the ways of adults, having been constantly in their company. She had no brothers or sisters. When her mother Abigail had died, Charles had imported an unmarried sister to run the house. But when Isabel reached her twelfth birthday, he had sent this fussy spinster back to Derbyshire in high dudgeon and secret relief. Since then – nearly two years ago – Isabel and her widowed nurse, Goodwife Barton, had run the household between them, to their mutual enjoyment and Charles's entire satisfaction.

The file of jurors was thinning out. She had watched a stream of her father's tenants troop up to sign: John Raynor, William Smithsone, John Harrison, Richard Smith, all farmers in Kettlethorpe, Laughterton and Fenton.

Now, just in front of where she sat – in the Squire's pew, at the back on the south side – the eldest of the Stow brothers rose to follow their father up the aisle. She watched him with admiration:

they were all big men, the Stows, but Daniel topped his father by a hand's width. He caught Isabel's eye, and winked broadly: the oath clearly caused him no crisis of conscience.

After the Halls at Kettlethorpe, and the Coles at Fenton, the Stows were the wealthiest family in the parish, and Daniel, for all he was five years older than Isabel, had often sought her out. She knew she was an heiress: even if her father were to remarry, Kettlethorpe had come to him through her mother, and Isabel would inherit house and land.

But she also knew, even if her father had not so often reminded her, that she was not ready for marriage: she was small, and undeveloped, having suffered from ill health all through her childhood. He would, he said, not look for a husband for her for some years yet. Just the same, it was pleasant to talk with Daniel, and imagine a future with him – if her father would permit it, and not hanker after a greater match.

As they walked back to the house through the churchyard, in the chancy spring sunshine, she found her father's natural good humour fully restored. This view of his beloved home always cheered him. He had inherited bigger properties, but none had touched his heart as Kettlethorpe had done, and he was hefted here, for life. And for the hereafter: he had already bought the stone that was to bear his name when, in the chancel, it covered his mortal remains.

He had rebuilt the house in fine red brick, and made a good job of it. He had reconstructed Katherine Swynford's gatehouse in front of the house, with more enthusiasm than historical accuracy, perhaps: the gargoyle sticking out of the top always made Isabel want to giggle. But he had attached a fine new brick wall to the arch, circling the front of house and its demesne on one side, connecting with the new barn on the other, and the whole was very pleasing, at least to its owner.

This wall was punctuated by three fine gates, with Charles's own initials and part of the Hall arms carved below one of the ball finials that topped the gateposts. "A*rgent, a chevron engrailed between* *three talbots' heads, erased, sable"* – Charles liked to recite his arms to her, the mark of a gentleman: the talbot was crudely carved, but it made his point.

Inside, panelling and arches over the central doorways added a style to the old house that gave Charles further satisfaction. The final touch had been to top the arches with small carved heads that, to her mortification, he told everyone had been modelled on Isabel as a baby.

When they had knocked down the old stonework, they had found all manner of things from the house's past. Some Tudor coins, and one much earlier, from the time of King John. And a small package containing an elaborate little gold cross, with a gemstone in the middle, which Charles had given to Isabel on her tenth birthday. She did not wear it, now: it looked Papist.

Warmed by pleasure and the sun, her father sought to make amends for snapping at Isabel last night. Would she, he asked, like to pay a visit to the Willoughbys at Knaith? He had a pamphlet new come from London that he was sure would interest His Lordship. He would read it to Isabel this very evening. He knew she would agree with him.

Isabel tried not to smile. Her father much wished to improve his acquaintance with Lord Willoughby of Parham, although that did not stop him fighting furiously with His Lordship over enclosures at Kettlethorpe – with Charles, his property always came first, even before politics or social advancement. He was a good master, and generous to the poor of the parish, but he had made more than one enemy through sharp dealings over land, or small abuses of positions he held in the county.

Nonetheless, Isabel knew Lord Willoughby valued him, and they were of like minds as to the dispute between Parliament and King, which is to say that they were on Parliament's side. In this Willoughby was a rarity: almost all the leading families of the county – the Monsons at Burton, Towneleys at Nocton, Pelhams at Brocklesby, the Fanes new come to Fulbeck, the Husseys at Doddington – were shocked at Parliament's temerity in challenging their sovereign. And, closest of all to Kettlethorpe, the Jermyns at Torksey were closer still to His Majesty. Henry Jermyn, in particular, was close to the Queen – Charles's pamphlets said, scandalously close.

Many others of the gentry, Isabel suspected, were simply uninterested: they were more exercised by the disorder caused by the rioters in the Fens, protesting against their landlords' drainage schemes, than by disputes in London. But Lord Willoughby had made his support for Parliament plain, and, together with the lawyer William Ellys, had had a great influence on Charles.

And meanwhile Isabel herself would love to go to Knaith. It was so short a ride that it would not tax even her slight strength, and the Willoughbys' eldest daughter, Diana, was always kind to her.

Diana was of the same age as Isabel, but much taller and more robust. Isabel – small, and pale, with hay-brown hair and green eyes – looked a shadow of a girl beside Diana, with her blue eyes and bright complexion, her mane of black hair, and her breasts already straining her girl's bodice, to Isabel's deepest envy.

But Diana was not ready for marriage, either, even if her body was. She had shocked her mother by declaring she would not be wedded, bedded and buried until she had had a life. Isabel always came away from seeing Diana feeling a little bit bigger, stronger and braver than when she arrived, if also exhausted by the strain of keeping up.

*

In the event it was not until late April, in the week after Easter, that the visit to Knaith finally took place, as the Willoughbys had been down south. The original purpose of the Halls' visit had obviously been overtaken, since old pamphlets had little value to a man of influence new come from London. But that, of course, made Charles all the keener to attend on him.

What Lord Willoughby had had to tell Charles, however, was grievous news. All knew that His Majesty had left London for the

North: he had passed through Stamford, Newark and Doncaster before pressing on to York. His purpose had been a matter of much debate, with optimists reassuring themselves the King was merely seeking to discover the feelings of his people.

Lord Willoughby had quickly disabused his visitor. The King was raising an army. He had sent his wife overseas to drum up the money. And Parliament, now relying on the London Trained Bands, would be forced to do the same.

"His Lordship tells me he expects Parliament to appoint him Lord Lieutenant of the county, and he will review the Trained Bands in Lincoln as soon as he may," Charles told his daughter, as they rode home in the late, mild afternoon.

"He has ignored the King's summons to raise troops for the Royalist side. Willoughby will need support, for the Mayor will give him none, foul Papist that he is. I may have to be away from home much this summer."

Reluctantly, Isabel dragged her mind away from the delightful day she had spent with Diana and her sisters, wandering along the Trent at Knaith, gossiping and making their own very different plans for the summer.

"Surely it won't come to war, Father? Nobody wants that! For sure, you told me yourself Parliament wishes the King no ill…"

Charles shifted impatiently in his saddle, and his horse broke into a nervous trot. He was pulled up sharply. "If the King takes up arms we must defend ourselves, or lose our liberties! His wife is the worst of his counsellors, and she has led him into tyranny!"

So, thought Isabel, all colours are become black and white. What would war mean? What would men be fighting for? She would ask her father again, when he was readier to explain.

The next day, Goody Barton told Isabel there were men at work in the cellar. Puzzled, she went to find her father. Surely the cellars were in good repair? Only a few years ago, he had had the brick repointed, and channels cut in the floor to carry flood waters away.

"They're digging a tunnel," Charles told her, a little brusquely. "To the church. From there, at need, you can run to Gervase at the Rectory. It'll ease my mind, to know you have that recourse, should ruffians come to Kettlethorpe and I not here. There are dark days ahead, and I would have you safe."

When Diana visited, she shrieked with excitement at the tunnel, and vowed she would have her father dig one at Knaith. When Charles came looking for them, he found them giggling halfway down, frightening each other with talk of rats.

After Diana had gone he was sterner with Isabel than she could remember: foolish maid, he said, the tunnel must be kept secret, for her safety. That did not, she noted, prevent him showing it with pride to Daniel Stow and his father, when they next came to call. She was emboldened to point this out.

A quite different matter, he retorted stiffly. He had asked the Stows to have a care for her in his absence – as good neighbours, he stressed, not meeting her eye, nothing more. She had no quarrel with that, but it was a pity that the day Daniel chose to call again, in high summer, was when Diana was with her again.

With a sinking heart, she saw his eyes light up, as whose would not, she thought ruefully – Diana was so beautiful, so vital, and unlike Isabel, a woman grown. Isabel wished she had not seen Daniel's eyes drop from Diana's vivid face to her creamy, round breasts, and the deep cleavage between them, or heard his voice grow husky as he spoke to her.

But to her surprise, Diana came the grand lady with Daniel, depressing his pretensions, and treating him with a contempt that caused him to behave like the boor she knew he was not. When he had departed, his cheeks burning, Diana noticed Isabel's stricken face.

"Dear heart, did you think I would stoop to steal your lover from you? Though in truth, I think you would be well shot of him – cannot your father find someone more gentlemanly than that yokel? I must speak with Mr Hall!"

Seeing Isabel stiffen, Diana laughed, but held her peace. After her carriage had swept her back to Knaith, Isabel trailed disconsolately round the house. She finally found Goody Barton supervising the maids in the dairy. The goodwife looked at her shrewdly. "Yon fine lady left you discontented? Well, you can make yourself useful, taking this butter to the Rectory. They've but the one house cow, and all those children to feed."

Goody Barton treated the Rector's wife with an exasperated mixture of admiration and contempt. Anne Hall had borne six children, all of whom survived infancy, but she had, the goodwife said, no idea how to run a household.

Isabel took the basket willingly enough: she liked Mistress Hall. But any hope of confiding in her faded rapidly: the rectory was bedlam, the screaming children quite out of the control of their mother or the slut hired to manage them, the Rector hiding in his little study. Isabel would usually have offered to help, but in her present disheartened mood she accepted Mistress Hall's distracted thanks for the butter and escaped as quickly as possible.

Daniel did not visit again for some time after his humiliation, and it was a long, dreary summer with little visiting or pleasure. An anxious time. In June they heard that Parliament had sent the King nineteen "propositions", and very soon after that, they learnt he had rejected them outright, saying he would be King only in name if he did otherwise. Then, in July, to the delight of his local supporters, he came to Lincoln.

Drawn by the excitement, Charles rode in to watch the royal arrival. Isabel begged him to be careful: he had made no secret of his views, and he had told her that the Mayor and his friends had already arrested a few known Parliamentarians. But he came back full of scorn.

"His Majesty was well received, sure enough. They were all there, the Royalist crew — Monson, Fane, Pelham and the rest. And there was fine talk of raising 400 cavalry, but even the Mayor — Sir Charles Dallison, as he now is — only pledged four! And they daren't touch Lord Willoughby, for all he's ignored the King's commands and is recruiting for Parliament under their noses. Most of them, I'll warrant, just want a quiet life, and if they do raise troops they'll keep them to protect the county."

The summer dragged on, without action or resolution. Isabel and Goody Barton harvested and dried their herbs, made preserves and cordials of the abundant fruit, took baskets of provender out to the men struggling to rescue some of the battered harvest from the foul weather. And prayed for better times.

But even prayer was difficult and confused. Gervase's sermons spoke less and less of the goodness of God, and more and more of the wickedness of men. He was no zealot, but a cheerful, good-living country parson wishing only to occupy the comfortable, loyal ground that the Church of England had marked out for itself between Puritans and Papists.

But now the safe ground seemed to be narrowing, and the great divisions in the body politic were forcing him towards choices he did not want to make. So he preached hellfire, removed the angel carvings and the communion rail from the church, and waited for the days when the high church rituals he loved might be acceptable again.

And then, after a wet and windy day in August, they learnt that King Charles had raised his standard at Nottingham. Isabel's father came back with the news from Newark, where the town was in ferment.

"They say it was raining so hard in Nottingham that the King's Herald could barely read his proclamation," Charles told his daughter contemptuously, "particularly as His Majesty had amended it so much by his own hand, and the ink had run!" As if, Isabel thought, it mattered what the words said. It was action that would plunge us into war.

Now it was as her father had warned: he was away a great deal, on business around the county in support of the Parliamentary cause. He came home only to eat and sleep. There was no more reading aloud of pamphlets, no more disquisitions on the nature of privilege, Royal or Parliamentary. Somehow, the more serious affairs had become, the less he wanted to talk about them. The barest facts he shared with Isabel, and not all of those. It was some time before she learnt of the first serious battle of the war, a defeat for Parliament, at a place called Edgehill.

Late in the year, war came much closer, as the Royalists seized Newark. This cut the Great North Road, and was a vantage point for raids into Lincolnshire. With Royalist strongholds all around them, they felt vulnerable indeed. This land along the Trent had become hotly contested, with its critical points of passage between north and south. The closest of these pinch points was little more than a mile away, at Torksey, where a bridge crossed the Fossdyke.

The Halls made as merry as they could that Christmas, with Gervase bringing his numerous family over from the Rectory, joining a little nervously in a celebration of which he knew the Puritans disapproved. But the New Year brought worse news. The Royalists had garrisoned Gainsborough. No visits now from or to Diana, for Lord Willoughby had deemed Knaith unsafe for his family, and sent them south to London.

However, Daniel had started visiting again. and Isabel, at last, was growing up. She would be fifteen in the spring: her woman's courses had started, and her breasts, if they lacked Diana's voluptuousness, were at least budding. She and Goody Barton sewed busily at new clothes to fit her altered state.

Isabel looked sadly at her mother's finery, folded away with lavender in a press. She extracted some lace, a roll of linen, and a black shawl of fine wool, then closed the lid on the bright colours again. Praise be, her nurse said, you could still get good cloth in Lincoln, if only in the sober hues suited to the times. The precious dyes needed for brighter stuffs were in short supply, and needed, they said, for the soldiers' coats.

When Daniel came, she walked with him in the garden in the conscious dignity of her new grey gown, and the black shawl, her face framed by her coif and the white linen lace-edged collar she had sewn so carefully that even Goody Barton had approved. Daniel and Isabel wandered along the path below the brick garden wall, where the survivors amongst her mother's roses had been pruned ready for spring. They could see their breath in the chill air, and when they were out of sight of the house, his kiss softly brushed her lips.

He came a week later to see her father: and she hoped it was to ask for her hand. Her father would refuse, of course, saying she was still too young, but it would be a start.

It was not what Daniel had come for. Yes, he told her, he had wanted to ask: but he could not. He had something he must do first. He was going to join the army.

She should have known. His boundless energy had overflowed into restlessness. "Will you join Lord Willoughby?"

He shook his head, decidedly. "There's a colonel from Huntingdon, in the Eastern Association army, who I want to join. He commands cavalry: Godly men, I'm told."

This did surprise her. Daniel had never been a zealot, indeed had skipped Sunday attendance when he could. But he had not finished.

"And," he went on a little truculently, not looking at her, "they also say he chooses his officers on their merits, not their pedigrees. He likes men of the middling sort, he says, yeomen and gentry, not noblemen. I want to fight with him."

Greatly daring, Isabel had whispered: "I am of the middling sort, too. Will you write to me?"

Daniel turned to her, startled, and his face broke into a smile. "You know I'm no great hand, but yes, Mistress Isabel, if you wish it, I will write."

He took both her hands. "And my family will watch out for you when your father's away."

To her joy, he kept his word. His first letter took time to come, but come it did, and it lit up her life. It had little to tell of the war, but it seemed that Colonel Cromwell was all that Daniel had been told, and more, though his men were still not as disciplined as he would like. They had run amok in Peterborough Cathedral, and stabled their horses within.

She read quickly, then took the precious letter down the track to Laughterton, finding Daniel's mother at work in her big farmhouse kitchen. Mistress Stow bore Isabel no ill will that she had been written to first. "My hands are all dough, bless you. And my eyes aren't what they were. You read it to me, like a good girl."

Her husband Robert snorted, but fondly. "It's well he did write to you, Mistress Isabel; Martha can read a receipt, maybe, but not much else. Daniel's hand is well enough, as it should be, after his time at the King's School."

His wife looked indignant, as well she might, at such plain speaking, so Isabel hastily started to read again. Daniel told of his training, of how his horse had gone lame, and he was coming to terms with another, a brave but obstinate beast that was learning to accept his commands. There was a bit at the end she did not read out, but repeated to herself every night before sleep.

Then, late in May, came another letter. The first words told her Daniel had been in a battle. This time she ran down the lane to the Stow family, even before reading more, anxious to share the news with them as soon as possible.

It had been in the south of Lincolnshire, at a village called Belton. Daniel's father grunted. "Aye, I know it." The boys listened, wide-eyed.

Colonel Cromwell's force, Isabel read, had joined forces with Captain Hotham's contingent from Nottingham, near Sleaford, over to the east of the county. She looked questioningly at Robert Stow, and again he nodded.

"South-east, towards the fenlands, on the way to the Wash. The last of the good ground. I've heard the Eastern Association was camped there."

They had been joined, Daniel's letter said, by the scattered men of Lord Willoughby's regiment, which, he added scornfully, had been routed by a Royalist force. Then they were all ordered west again to attack Newark, and had camped on the way, at Belton. There they were taken by surprise, by a murderous Royalist attack.

But, wrote Daniel with a triumph that made him almost illegible, Colonel Cromwell's cavalry had saved the day. "God be praised, we charged uphill and drove Cavendish's forces from the high ground." His brothers banged the table, cheering, and setting their mother's pots rocking, to her immediate protest.

"And did they march on to Newark?" Robert Stow asked. "I've heard naught of another battle there."

Isabel shook her head. "He does not say."

"But is he safe? Does he say if he was wounded?" Daniel's mother cared little for Newark, much for her son.

Isabel shook her head, in turn. "He says he is well, praise be. And acting as a scout, so he cannot have taken hurt, can he?"

In early July another message came to Isabel: but this time, from the Stows. Isabel was in the garden, cut lavender piling up in her lap, when the second Stow boy, Samuel, came looking for her, breathless with excitement. "Mistress, Daniel's home! He asks to see you — will you come?"

Would she come! She tugged off the sacking tied round her waist, and followed him back to Laughterton, doing her best to keep up.

Benjamin Stow, the youngest of the brothers, was hanging on to the bridle of a big, heavy-footed stallion, restless away from his troop, outside the farmhouse door. In the kitchen, she found Daniel surrounded by the rest of his family, his "lobster" helmet on the table, buff coat unbuttoned and one leg stretched out so his mother could salve an angry scar above his knee.

When he saw Isabel, he pushed his mother gently aside and unrolled his breeches over the wound. "Enough now, it's mending, I promise. It was naught, and healing fast." He got to his feet, and with a strange new courtesy, bowed.

"Mistress Isabel, it is good to see you, and I thank you for your letters, they have been a comfort indeed." He stopped, and grinned, more like his old self. "You've grown again."

She smiled back at him. "So have you." Not in height, perhaps, but in maturity. His soft boy's face had hardened; his thick shock of dark hair had been clipped short.

"Can you stay?" Daniel's mother asked hopefully, but he shook his head.

"We are camped just short of here, and likely moving north. With Newark in the King's hands, the Great North Road's blocked. Gainsborough is ever more important. I asked leave only for a few hours, to see how you fare. He looked down at his mother, with a boy's grin. "And to beg one of your pies – it's hungry work, soldiering!" He flung his arm round her, in a gesture which made him look both old and young.

Given a welcome task, his mother revived, and started bustling around the kitchen, chivying her family out of the way, calling for her maidservant. "Daniel, you take Mistress Isabel outside, and the rest of you, get out from under my feet, if I'm to get baking in time. Get on with you all, now."

They were moments Isabel was to remember for the rest of her life, dream-like moments, listening to the sudden flood of words Daniel had been storing up for weeks. He had been wrong, Daniel told her, to believe their love could wait on his time as a soldier. The forces of Parliament and King were too well-matched for him to believe any longer that the war would be over soon. He must go now, for they must secure Gainsborough, but when that was done, he would be back to ask her father for her.

He had shed his coat, and held her close against his chest. She could feel his heart beating strongly, and his embrace this time was fiercer, no longer a boy's kiss but a passionate man's. And she responded as a woman should, not a girl, though as his arms tightened she gasped a little, and he released her at once. "Sweetheart, I can wait for you, but not for longer than I must."

*

Her father was indeed away, now, most of the time. He was one of Parliament's Commissioners for the county, raising troops and supplies. No easy task, at the best of times: he was in furious dispute with a Presbyterian of some repute, Captain Edward King, who had accused Charles of abusing his position to save himself land taxes. But King was notoriously quarrelsome; he had fallen out with Lord Willoughby, too.

The news from further afield was confused, and turbulent. In the spring, some of the Marton folk, trading the other side of the river, had actually seen the Queen, returned from the continent with money for the Royalist cause. She had been riding with Henry Jermyn towards Newark, at the head of new troops she had raised in the North. "Generalissima," she was said to call herself, which delighted the Royalists, but added fuel to the flame of Puritan hatred – and the Commons voted to impeach her.

They voted many other things too, most of them to raise money, like the hated new excise duty on beer. And they were desperate enough for help to appeal to the Scots, making concession to their vision of organised religion, which divided opinion at home.

At home at Kettlethorpe, Charles was still a kind father, and good master, but Isabel could see the struggle was taking its toll. And through the summer, the news did not get any better. At the end of June, they learnt that the Earl of Newcastle had inflicted another defeat on Parliamentary forces in Yorkshire, at Adwalton Moor. Rumour came on wings to Lincolnshire, that he was bringing his army south to take control of the county.

Lord Willoughby and Colonel Cromwell had moved north, as Daniel had foretold, and – Praise the Lord – they did succeed in taking Gainsborough. No sooner had this news brought relief to Kettlethorpe, however, than they learnt the town had been lost again, and learnt it from Daniel himself.

This time he could pause only to eat, and collect supplies, and tell them what he knew. They had been surprised by Royalists just south of Gainsborough, which Daniel put down to Willoughby's poor scouting. But again, he said, the discipline of Cromwell's troopers had saved the day. The Royalist cavalry was driven off, and Parliamentary forces entered Gainsborough on July 20th.

Still, it availed them little: they could not hold the town. On a sortie north of there, just three days later, they had clashed with what they thought was just a small Royalist force. Then, to their dismay, they had found the whole of Newcastle's great force in front of them.

"Had it not been for my Colonel, it would have been a rout," Daniel said. "But he is the Lord's anointed. We held firm for him. And we held Newcastle's army! Troop by troop, we retreated in turn, on the Colonel's command. So the infantry could draw back to Gainsborough, in safety."

He paused, to drink deeply of the ale his brother held out to him.

Impatiently, his father asked: "What then?"

Daniel lowered his tankard, empty, and wiped his mouth with his sleeve. "Against such numbers, we could not win. We cannot hold Lincoln, either." He looked at his father, and spoke harshly, with the taste of defeat still in his mouth. "You must guard yourselves here as you can, for we are headed south. Pray God we can return, but it will not be soon!"

They did pray, fervently, as news came soon enough that Newcastle's troops were in Lincoln, and meting out their idea of justice. Willoughby and Cromwell were rumoured to be clinging on south of Boston. But one more push, and Newcastle would drive them out of Lincolnshire altogether.

So Charles told Isabel, sharing his thoughts once more. Then, he said – as much to himself, she saw, as to her – the Royalists' way would be open down to London. And to victory for the King.

It was the bleakest time yet. Charles struggled to raise money from a county that had lost faith in a Parliamentary victory, and was already suffering much hardship. She had given him her own trinket box for the cause, with her mother's pearls and the gold cross he had given her himself – he had thanked her, but hesitated, and she guessed he was not going to hand either of them over. He had made contributions of coin and plate, she knew, and the church vessels had been handed over for melting down, to the Rector's carefully suppressed regret.

At Kettlethorpe they struggled to get in the harvest, late, with men and boys gone to join the army – any army, if it could promise them pay, or at least a full belly, a coat and pair of boots. Harvest in, the village struggled to hide it from the constant raids to fill those soldiers' bellies. They stored the grain, ill-dried, behind hay stacked high in the barns.

But hay too, they knew, might be taken any day, to feed army mounts. No point in keeping it to feed the cattle, the Quartermasters told protesting villagers: the beasts would be needed to feed the army, too. There would be hunger across England, this winter of 1643–44.

And then one day Charles came home with the news that – inexplicably – Newcastle had turned north, not south. "God be praised, he's abandoned Lincoln!"

Isabel was dumbfounded. "But why, Father?"

Charles shrugged. "The Lord alone knows. He's taken his army into Yorkshire. They say he's gone to besiege the Parliamentary garrison in Hull."

A breathing space, but only a short one, since Samuel, Isabel's faithful messenger from the Stow family, brought warning that a Royalist force had been seen heading east from Newark. It was rumoured to be heading to take John of Gaunt's old keep at Bolingbroke, and so complete the King's command of the rest of the county.

They waited for news of another battle, though the work of building winter stores could not wait. Isabel was in the orchard with the kitchen maid and the stable boys, stripping the apple trees before the autumn storms brought the fruit down, when her father brought the next momentous piece of information.

Restless with worry, he had ridden south and east to learn what he could, taking – at Isabel's persuasion – old Jacob the groom with him. Going cautiously through the woods near Doddington, they had seen two cavalrymen cross the track ahead of them. They were on the wide, straight avenue through the woods, along which Lincoln Cathedral could be seen from Doddington Hall. And it was to the Hall, it seemed, that they were headed. Royalist soldiers, then, most likely: it was not a Parliamentary house.

Cautiously, Charles and Jacob trailed them, pistols primed, though without much fear, for both troopers and horses were so clearly spent. When the two fugitives reached the gatehouse at Doddington, and were admitted, Charles and Jacob turned back, and found themselves in the path of a small troop.

These men – in pursuit of the two Royalists they had seen before – were from Sir Thomas Fairfax's cavalry. They were ready enough to share their news, once Charles had convinced them of his Parliamentary credentials.

They had been in Hull, they told him, preparing to defend it against the Royalist army. But it seemed that Newcastle, in moving north, had left the Lincolnshire shore of the Humber unguarded. So Cromwell had crossed the estuary, and slipped into Hull, to confer with Fairfax. Then the pair of them had broken out of Hull again, taking with them cavalrymen and horses that were only a burden to the besieged. They'd crossed the Humber southwards again.

"We joined Manchester's army outside Bolingbroke," the sergeant said. "There's a nest of Royalist vipers there that the Newark Royalists had hoped to relieve. We gave them battle close by. A small village – Winceby, I think they call it."

"The Earl of Manchester?" Charles asked. "Commanding the Eastern Association army? Where was Lord Willoughby?"

The Sergeant shrugged. "I know nothing of him. Lord Manchester is our commander, though it's Black Tom and Cromwell that do the fighting."

"It was a slaughter," he added with satisfaction, accepting Charles's offer of a drink from his leather bottle. "A great slaughter. Few escaped, and we've hunted down most of them. Pity to lose these two." He handed the bottle back regretfully and, Charles noted, empty.

"Doddington's a Royalist household, and will be well guarded," he warned. "You'd be wise to wait for reinforcements."

He'd said enough to dent the sergeant's valour. "We'd best be getting back. There'll be easier pickings on our way."

"No," Charles said later, answering his daughter's unspoken question. "They knew nothing of Daniel. But they were not Cromwell's men. And trust in the Lord, daughter, they said our casualties were light. He'll come home, safe enough."

She trusted God little, and men less, but her father was right. A long month later, Daniel came home.

Again he had changed. The war was consuming him. But Cromwell was still his hero: he had been immensely proud to have been chosen to form part of the Colonel's small bodyguard, on his journey to Hull and back, and to have been close behind him at Winceby. It had clearly been a chancy business.

"After the dragoons had engaged, the Colonel charged, with all three cavalry divisions. Had we been repulsed, it would have gone very ill with us. And we nearly lost the Colonel when his horse was shot, but I found another mount for him, and he drove Henderson's force back."

Sir Thomas Fairfax, however, seemed to have earned as much of Daniel's admiration. It had been Black Tom's troops, Daniel said, held in reserve, who had completed the rout of the Royalist cavalry, with a flank attack.

"It panicked them. Into headlong flight. Too many of them tried to escape down this deep, narrow lane. There was a farm gate across the bottom. There was such a press, they could not open it," he told his family, and Isabel, all gathered again in the Stows' house in Laughterton. "Hundreds of God's enemies, and their beasts, died there. Slash Hollow, they're calling it now."

Isabel thought of all the obstinate, heavy farm gates she knew, with broken hinges that made them so hard to open, and shuddered. Daniel's mother moaned a little, but her husband's hand on her shoulder pressed her into silence. Daniel pulled himself up from the table, stretching limbs stiff with weariness. "I'll sleep here tonight, mother, but on the morrow I must be gone again."

Then, at last, he looked at Isabel, and with a chill she saw his eyes were blank. Involuntarily, she stretched out her hand. He grasped it, like a drowning man, and emotion came flushing back into his face. With his other hand, he tugged a sweat-stained paper out of his coat. "For your father," he said.

She took it home, and gave it to Charles that night. He would not read it in front of her, and she regretted the niceness of her conscience, that had prevented her from reading it first. But he came back to her soon enough, and handed it over. "He says he is to be made an officer – and can then support a wife." Charles sighed. "If ever he gets paid."

Isabel, wise in her father's ways, said nothing.

"It's not what I hoped for you, but these are not times I hoped for either. And I grant you, he's a good lad."

Isabel spoke only with her eyes.

"Mark you, I'll not let you be betrothed until you are sixteen, and so I shall tell him."

And now she did speak.

"But will you also tell him, father, that you will not promise me to anyone else?"

He looked at her, with tenderness, and gently touched her cheek. "I will reflect on it."

And she knew she had won.

*

Winter set in, and brought as much hardship as they had feared. Parliament's levies bore heavily on men of means, while those

173

without means struggled to keep their families from starvation. Isabel heard Goody Barton mutter, though not in Charles's hearing, that there was nowt to choose between Roundheads and Cavaliers, they both took what they wanted, though one gave thievery a lawyer's name and the other didn't bother.

Isabel fell ill, with a fever that wasted the last of her childish roundness, and Charles wanted to call the doctor to her. But Goody Barton resisted, saying he'd only bleed away the last of her strength: the bouts of fever had left her weak enough. Through the short, dark days she lay abed, drifting in out of sleep, conscious only of the small fire her nurse somehow kept going, and the goodwife's comforting presence, puffing at her clay pipe.

When Isabel was finally let out of bed, and dressed shakily, she burst into tears: her new gown hung on her like a sack. It was lucky it did, Goody Barton said briskly, or it would have shown her ankles – in her illness she'd somehow grown, an inch or more. Now she must leave worrying to the goodwife, and eat, and rest, and wrap up to walk in the garden, and get the roses back in her cheeks before Daniel came home.

But he did not come, and instead Samuel went to join his troop. Robert Stow confided to Isabel that he'd had the devil's own job, beg pardon, Mistress Isabel, to keep young Benjamin from following, "and him but twelve years old. It'd break my good wife's heart to have all three gone to this cursed war."

Still, Isabel had two letters from Cornet Stow, full of pride in his new role, holding the troop's guidon, but also, she noticed, now full of a religious zeal he had never shown before. It disquieted her: as the war got more savage, so, it seemed, did the need to proclaim the slaughter to be God's work.

She asked her father about it, for he, she noticed, had become less zealous, not more. He pulled a long face. "Young Daniel is right, Cromwell is a coming man, but he is also a zealot, and promotes those of his kind. Independents, they call themselves, who reject not only the Archbishop and his Popish tricks, but a Presbyterian church as well. Oh, they'll work with the Scots Covenanters, for they need them: I'm told the Scots are already marching south. I dare say even Cromwell will sign the Covenant himself if need be, but they'll fall out once those malignant Royalists are defeated."

"And what about you, father? Who will you side with?" But he would not be drawn.

"Time enough to worry about that when we've won. Now, finish that muck Goody Barton brought you to drink, or she'll be here bothering us till you have."

These days, she knew, he was talking much with his old friend William Ellys, a Member of the Commons of steady, Presbyterian bent. He was keeping his political powder dry.

He had said "when" the King was beaten, Isabel noted, not "if". 1643 had seemed like a year in which the King was sure to win, for all the fervour of his opponents. But he had not. Now, with the help of the Scots, they dared to hope for a Parliamentary victory. To be sure, the King had brought in forces from Ireland, to counter the Scots; but that was a wicked thing to do, which must harden the hearts of God and man against him.

So 1644 started with renewed hopes of success for their military leaders. But at Kettlethorpe, the weather tested them sorely: it was bitter cold, with every pond frozen iron-hard and snow piling in drifts across the tracks and against the house. At the end of January, the snow fell continuously for over a week, a heavy, persistent fall on top of hard-crusted December snow that had never thawed in the fitful sunlight.

There was little food stored, that winter, with which to fight the cold; even at the Hall, it was short commons, while in the village many families starved and children perished, for all the help Charles tried to give them. And the churchyard ground was too deeply frozen to bury them.

Death came close to home when Gervase's youngest, a pale and silent child, slipped away; and his wife, depriving herself to nourish the others, feel ill and quickly followed. Then the Rector himself came down with a fever, and died before Charles could even send help. The remaining orphans were collected by his wife's family, though they too were hard-pressed; and soon there was a new Rector at Kettlethorpe, a widower with a small son, and a sister to housekeep for them.

Isabel could not warm to John Smythson, a small, angry zealot whose sermons on the King's iniquities covered the front pew with spittle. Her father defended his choice, saying Mr Smythson was strong for Parliament, but Isabel could tell Charles was regretting it. Smythson was a descendant of the famous architect who had been responsible for so many of the great houses around, but there was no greatness in him, Charles conceded.

To add to their sorrows, when the snows melted, faith in the Parliamentary leadership was sorely tested, very close to home. In March the arch-Cavalier Prince Rupert humiliated Lord Willoughby and Sir John Meldrum outside Newark, leaving the castle and town even more securely in Royalist hands. Willoughby, her father told Isabel sadly, had been blamed for his men's refusal to take Meldrum's orders.

The Royalists, emboldened by their success, garrisoned Lincoln, putting young Sir Francis Fane of Fulbeck in command. At Kettlethorpe they felt more threatened than ever.

The days lengthened, though spring played with them, with sunny days followed by sharp little flurries of snow. April was cruel: so many of the old, who had struggled through the coldest months, died quietly even as better weather came, for stores were almost completely exhausted now, and nothing yet was growing.

But Isabel regained her strength. She lived in hope of another visit from Daniel, as the army of the Eastern Association, increasingly known as Cromwell's army for all that Manchester remained in command, returned to Lincolnshire. They had marched up Ermine Street and massed, Isabel learnt later, on Canwick Hill, overlooking Lincoln from the south.

History could have told them it would be a hard fight that way in to Lincoln, and indeed it was. They took the lower city with ease. The upper city was more of a struggle, with Steep Hill slippery in heavy rain. Undeterred, they stormed Lincoln Castle, and took it, in a short, sharp tussle with Fane, its brave but untried commander, early in May.

They did not stay there long to enjoy their victory. Manchester sent Cromwell and his cavalry on smartly to Gainsborough, to build a bridge of boats across the Trent. Lord Goring was said to be commanding a Royalist force on the other side: they were to drive him south, and get themselves to the Great North Road to await the infantry, who would not be long behind them. Then they were to move on quickly, to besiege York. Or so Charles surmised, from all the news he gathered; the one letter Isabel had had from Daniel told her of the battle, but not the future.

They left behind them, in Lincoln, only a small garrison. But also, to Charles's disapproval, a trail of destruction.

Isabel went to Lincoln with her father, when the county committee met there again. Much as she rejoiced in the victory, she was saddened at the sight of the Cathedral, windows smashed, brasses ripped away, tombs violated – including Katherine Swynford's. To Puritans, Isabel reflected sadly, Katherine was probably no better than any other royal whore.

The Halls were heartened to learn that the Mayor, stout Puritan though he was, had protested against the despoliation, saying bluntly and truthfully that Lincoln was nothing without its Cathedral. Blasphemously dedicated to the Virgin it might be, but would the garrison please stable their beasts elsewhere?

That summer, Isabel spent all the time she could with Daniel's mother, who was sore in need of comfort. After Daniel and Samuel were gone, her maidservant had suddenly disappeared: they had traced her south of Collingham, where rumour had it she had been swept up by a Royalist trooper, whether by her choice or no. Martha had taken in a starveling from a poor family in the village, but the child was little help yet.

And then, in late May, Benjamin had gone, taking his father's last sound riding horse and a purse from his chest. When Robert had recovered from his rage, and stopped swearing that he washed his hands of the boy, he came to Isabel's father for advice. Charles could only guess that Benjamin might have tried to join his brothers, and told Robert that Manchester's forces were said to be outside York. It was an anxious few weeks for the Stows before they learnt that guess was right.

In June there came a brief letter from Daniel, telling them Benjamin had arrived half-starved, both purse and horse gone, and tried to enrol as a drummer boy. Daniel would send him home as soon as he could, but for the moment the boy was safer with him.

Safe? Nowhere was safe, they knew, with both sides boiling up for the biggest battle of the war so far. The King's chief commander, Lord Newcastle, was bottled up in York; Prince Rupert and Lord Goring, the ogres of God-fearing children's nightmares, were both rumoured to be hastening to his relief. Under Manchester's command, Cromwell and Fairfax must stand against them – but where, or how, nobody could guess.

At the end of the month, alarming news came. Near Newark, the church bells had been heard, pealing – in celebration of what? It could only be a Royalist victory.

There followed a strange silence, until fugitives were seen coming from the north along the Trent, fleeing from both armies. No sense could be got from those it was safe to challenge – they spoke only of panic, disorder and death.

No sense came until, miracle of miracles, Daniel himself appeared. He had been sent south with reports for London, had handed his packages to a fresh troop at Gainsborough, and got leave to bring Benjamin home.

His father's anger died in him the moment he saw Benjamin: a little scarecrow with dark shadows under his eyes. His mother hid her relief under a rumpus of hot broth, and warm nightshirt, first sending her little servant off to the attic with a warming pan, then bustling to do the job herself. Benjamin was asleep almost before he finished the broth, and she came down white-faced to hear Daniel's news.

"He's taken no hurt, mother, and Samuel is well too. But Ben's seen what no child should have to see, and been in fear longer than he could stand. I tried to keep him out of harm's way, and praise God, he survived, but it was a brutal fight, to the bitter end, and no mercy shown."

He turned as a peremptory knock sounded at the door, and Isabel saw how quick his instinct now was to reach for his sword. But it was only her father, come to learn the news at first hand, and Daniel relaxed.

"Where did you do battle?" Robert Stow asked. "And tell us the worst, was it truly a Royalist victory?"

Daniel shook his head, wearily. "Praise God, no, though for a time it seemed it would be. We had a hard time of it, against that devil's spawn, though we took his cavalry by surprise."

"Prince Rupert?"

"Aye. He came to relieve Lord Newcastle in York. And he would have caught us unready, had Newcastle come to join him sooner, but instead the fool let his troops spend the day ransacking our camp, God rot him. I feared for Benjamin then, but he escaped."

He was so tired it was, Isabel could see, a huge effort to go on. But he wanted to tell it now, and be done.

"It was evening before the King's army assembled. They supposed we would do nothing more that day, especially as it was raining torrents – their commanders left the field. But our Colonel and Black Tom made nothing of the weather or the lateness of the hour. And our men raised their voices, and sang psalms. It was like the trumpets outside Jericho!"

Daniel shook his head, like a dog getting water out of its ears. "It was hard – far harder than I'd known it. Both our cavalry wings attacked, but only ours got through. Colonel Cromwell was wounded, and had to retire for a time, but our captains held steady. Just the same, I do not think we would have made it through without the Scots."

"The Covenanters?" Charles asked, sharply. Daniel nodded. "Doughty fighters, and we needed them. We broke through on the left, but Fairfax's horse on the right were driven back by Prince Rupert, and many of them ran." He smiled, mirthlessly. "I fear it was our own cowards who brought the tale of Royalist victory south."

"So how did you recover?"

"Black Tom got word to us, and rather than chase Royalist cavalry on our wing, our leaders wheeled us round to charge back again on the other side. The Colonel was back with us by then, and it's where our training held: only Cromwell's cavalry – Ironsides, the enemy calls us – can be pulled back from pursuit, and kept under such tight control. The Cavalier scum fight savagely enough, I'll grant you that, but the devil himself could not hold them, once they've charged."

Silently, Daniel's father handed him another tankard, and he drank gratefully.

"In the end there was only Newcastle's infantry standing firm – his Whitecoats. Godamercy, they were brave men. They were cut down where they stood. Black Tom ran in at the end, trying to strike up our swords, crying it was Englishmen we were killing, but they had refused quarter, and so we gave them none."

No one moved. There was a chill in the room, that no summer sun, leaching through the casement, no sullen kitchen fire, no warmth of humankind, could lift from this reality of civil war.

They were fortunate, they knew, to have lost no one, and to be undivided. Many wives had a husband on one side, a father on the other; some mothers had son fighting son. But still: Englishmen were killing Englishmen. And were asking, and showing, no quarter.

Isabel sat as still and cold as stone. But warm tears were streaming down Martha Stow's cheeks. In rough comfort, Robert shook her by the shoulder. "Brace up, wife, all your sons are unharmed. Tell me, Daniel, how did you keep that young fool Benjamin safe? Your mother will ever bless you for that!"

Such provocation steadied her, and she wiped her eyes on her apron. "As if you were not as glad to see the young scoundrel as I!"

Daniel smiled again, but now with greater warmth. "In truth, Samuel and I were at a loss when the camp was raided; we had to leave Ben with the reserve. But all reserves were drawn on during the battle, and when we came to an end we could find him nowhere. I thought he must be lost – there were boys as young as him among the slain."

"How did you find him?" Isabel asked quickly, before Martha could cry out.

"He was in the Lord's hands – and I was in the Colonel's! When I was searching the battlefield for the boy, I came across a woman on the same task, in search of her husband's body. Malignant she may have been, but she was a brave lady. Colonel Cromwell saw her, and me, and bade me escort her to safety, for fear our men might insult her."

Charles nodded, approvingly. "A gentlemanly thing to do."

Isabel saw a flicker of annoyance pass across Daniel's face. "She said she had friends near Marston who would give her shelter. She would not give me their names, for fear they would be marked for sequestration, but I escorted her safe to Marston village."

"But – Benjamin?"

"By God's grace, I found him on the road to Marston. He was walking blindly, I don't think he knew where he was or where he was going. He did not know me, when I called to him; I had to dismount and lift him on to the horse with Lady Towneley, who treated him very motherly."

"God bless her, poor lady," Martha whispered.

"When I reported back to the Colonel, it was he who said we were truly in the Lord's hands. He asked me where we lived, and after thought, he said I could take his dispatches as far as Gainsborough, and deliver the boy home thereafter. I was commanded to take a trooper with me, so I took Samuel. He is at Gainsborough now."

"Colonel Cromwell is a kindlier man than I supposed," Charles said thoughtfully.

Daniel shook his head. "He is a Godly man, with much love of family. But you should warn your friends in Parliament, Sir: there is a hardness in him, for this war. He will show no kindness to their treacherous King."

Another chill, as clouds moved across the sun. The room darkened. None of Daniel's audience, Isabel reflected, had given thought to the time after the war, daring only to hope of winning. Except, of course, her father, and he was ever the optimist, happy to imagine a world in which Charles Stuart would have learned his lesson.

Surely, her father had said to her – or was he talking to himself? – the King would then deal amiably with Commons as well as Lords, making common cause with Presbyterians but allowing freedom of worship to Independents. But what, she wondered, if the King, even in defeat, would not bend?

Daniel and Samuel were given leave to stay home a fortnight, to help with the harvest. Samuel stayed close to home, but Daniel gave Kettlethorpe a share of his time, and Charles was grateful. Short of men, he had been obliged to hire unknowns: vagabonds, deserters from the Lord knew which army. They were grateful enough for the work, asking little more than to be decently fed, but the presence of an Ironside officer was a useful caution against thievery or violence.

They were long, exhausting days, but when the light faded Isabel and Daniel could snatch time together, sitting against the south wall of the Hall in its now-neglected garden, watching the summer insects dance in the light of Goody Barton's candle. Charles insisted on her keeping the lovers under her eye, though he had finally consented to their betrothal. But the goodwife sat apart, remarking frequently on how hard of hearing she was these days.

Isabel was harvesting her own private store of memories, food for the bleak winter of Daniel's absence. Precious amongst them, the feel of Daniel's arm round her, warm and sunburnt, the dark hairs bleached to gold. His hand strayed to fondle her breast in the darkness, and Goody Barton moved her candle further away from them, muttering about the light needed for her sewing.

Isabel lifted her lips to Daniel's, and in a little while he plucked at her skirt, tugging it up to slide his hand up between her thighs. She gave a little gasp, and Goody Barton was not so deaf, after all. She folded her mending and rose, commenting on the lateness of the hour, and sweeping a flushed Isabel ahead of her to bed.

They had made their betrothal vows in the church, the Rector with a sharp eye out for any "Popish" festivity or adornment, but they did not care. All their thoughts were forward, to hopes for next year.

Daniel had shared his ambitions for a captaincy with Isabel. She, in turn, had told him of his father's offer to her of the cottage next to the Sallie Bank.

"For though I know Kettlethorpe will be your home, m'duck, your father has it for life, and he may marry again when you're wed. It's good to start on your own, and it's a fine new building, I always had Daniel in mind for it."

Goody Barton had said much the same to Isabel about her father, and approved. She was training a girl from Fenton to be Isabel's maidservant. Prudence was smaller even than Isabel, but strong and hardworking, grateful beyond saying to be rescued from her hand-to-mouth existence with her old father and his doxy. She was, Isabel's nurse said grudgingly, a quick learner, "though you can rest easy, I'll be with you at need, you've only to send for me." Isabel knew Goody Barton's hopes and anxieties, and felt a flutter of longing for children.

Next year, Daniel hoped, the war could be brought to an end. "If they will but give our Colonel his head. He knows what must be done with the army, if we are to finish this business properly. Too many of our commanders are playing at war. Manchester. Essex. Cursed noblemen who'd make peace with the King and go back to their comforts if they could." He spat.

"But do we not want peace?" Isabel asked. "If His Majesty will but agree to Parliament's requests?"

Daniel shook his head. "He will never agree. He'll pretend, and speak fair, and play our fractious leaders against each other. But he is a serpent, and a tyrant, and there is only one way to deal with such." She hoped Daniel would not speak as freely to her father, or all her persuasion to let them marry might go for nothing.

Charles had refused their pleas for an early wedding, but finally agreed they could be wed next summer. Isabel would be seventeen, and not even her father could pretend that was young to marry.

*

When autumn came, Charles was as restless as his daughter. He did his work for the Association, but he yearned for more. Eventually he decided he would take William Ellys's advice, and travel to London, to the heart of things, taking Isabel with him; it should be safe enough, now, if they headed east and kept well clear of Newark.

To Isabel's relief, he decided their old-fashioned coach was not up to the long journey, and failed to hire another for the first stage, deciding they would ride by easy stages: she had dreaded the thought of a long, jolting coach journey on the overgrown track that once was Ermine Street, until they could risk joining the Great North Road near Stamford.

He begged an escort from the militia, who accompanied them as far south as the county boundary. Jacob and Goody Barton he left behind, to watch over Kettlethorpe; instead he took his manservant Thomas, a young man whose crippled leg made him of no use to any army.

Charles had taken Thomas into his house when the abandoned boy was barely ten years old. He had repaid his master with the utmost devotion, made light of his deformity, and sat his horse throughout their long day's travel with determination, doggedly ignoring the pain it caused him. Prudence rode behind him, and Isabel saw how she watched him at the end of the day, discreetly and delicately, but with an eye on Isabel as well. Goody Barton, she suspected, had lectured the girl fiercely on her mistress's frailty.

The season was kind, stretching soft weather into November, and they rested their first two nights with friends. At the second of these, Sir Thomas Trollope, with a fine house south-east of Grantham, they heard of another victory for Manchester's Parliamentary forces down at Newbury.

Sir Thomas passed this news on with easily restrained enthusiasm; Charles had warned Isabel their host's loyalties were suspect, and he clearly lived in fear of sequestration now the tide had turned against the King. But that was true of so many; nearby the Thimelbys of Irnham, avowed Papists, were no longer a suitable stopping point. And Sir Thomas's daughter, a quiet, fair woman ten or more years older that Isabel, made them very comfortable.

Isabel saw how her eyes rested on Charles, and how he took pleasure in the young woman's company. She remembered Goody Barton's warning, and, testing her feelings cautiously – for she had never had to share her father since a child – was relieved to find herself hoping he would find a love to match her own.

The third night they reached Stamford, without encountering any of the Royalist raiding parties that were still common in the area. They found the town buzzing with rumours that the Royalist army down south had slipped out of Manchester's hands. Even worse, it was said the King's forces had been allowed to snatch their arms and stores from under the noses of the victors, losing little from their defeat.

The landlord of the George, a big, busy coaching inn, was full of gossip. "They say the business was so mismanaged that there's been a great falling-out between His Lordship and his General of Horse," he informed Charles, not without some satisfaction – Stamford's sympathies, if now suppressed, had been with the King. "That's a man we know well here, of course," he added importantly, "seeing as he comes from Huntingdon."

"You mean Colonel Cromwell?" Charles asked, but the landlord shook his head. "You're behind the times, friend, he's a Lieutenant-

General now, and as high in Parliament's esteem as Manchester himself, if not higher."

"Did General Cromwell lose many men at Newbury?" Isabel asked fearfully. The landlord looked at her kindly. "You've a sweetheart in the Ironsides, have you? No, I heard the casualties were light on Parliament's side." Unfortunately Isabel saw him give her father a furtive wink. It would be weeks, even months, before she knew the truth, since Daniel, if he wrote at all, would send his letter to Kettlethorpe.

She sat by the welcome fire in the little parlour, loth to drag herself upstairs to the small bedchamber she must share with another traveller, a stout, angry lady who seemed to take the war as a personal insult. Isabel had begged a pallet from the landlord for Prudence, causing her bedmate further affront. There was plenty of room in the hayloft for servants, she told Isabel crossly, when they finally retired.

Once decked in bed gown and nightcap, and with the weight off her feet, Isabel's bedmate became a little more mellow, deigning to explain she was a widow, travelling south to stay with her daughter. Her son had inherited the estate, but she had been left very well provided for, and hoped to make another match of her choice. This son, who had escorted her this far from Yorkshire, felt she would be safer in the south. He always had such care for her, unlike his wife, who was not what she had hoped for.

Isabel fell asleep before she had finished, which was a blessing, since every word made her think how her father would dislike their companion on the journey ahead. Her last thought was to resolve that that she would tell him how much she had liked Anne Trollope.

She need not have worried: Charles took one look at Mistress Wormald, arrayed for the journey, and announced he would ride beside the coach the landlord had found for his travelling guests. And his resolve was strengthened by a sudden flurry at the inn, causing the landlord, full of insincere apologies, to announce that the great coach had been commandeered by another guest, of the highest standing, whose own conveyance had a broken axle.

They need have no concern, the landlord hastened to assure them. He had, he told them proudly, persuaded Sir Harry to allow them places, should they contribute to the cost, though their servants would of course have to ride outside. "Sir Harry", Isabel's father soon discovered, was young Sir Henry Vane, the Member for Hull, a leader in the Commons and a great supporter of General Cromwell; he and his secretary had also opted to ride rather than sit with Sir Harry's wife and children, and Charles was thrilled by the opportunity to make his acquaintance on the journey.

Isabel was ready to think well of a supporter of Daniel's hero, though she thought Sir Harry had an unpleasant air of self-importance. His wife was an exhausted-looking young woman, with a whining small girl, an exuberant toddler and a baby, who was strangely lacking in servants.

Mistress Wormald, who with ill grace had also paid up for a seat, looked at them all with profound dislike. This became acute, and vocal, when the toddler placed two sticky paws on her knee. He took no notice of her reproof: he clearly had all his father's self-confidence, and continued to demand attention.

The lurching movement of the coach seemed to quiet him, and eventually he fell asleep. But by evening even Isabel's fondness for children had been slaked. The baby was very fretful, and Lady Vane, a gentle woman without hauteur, told her in quiet desperation that her wet nurse had died of a fever, early on their journey, and had given it to the rocker, too, while her tirewoman had slipped on the inn stairs at Stamford and broken her leg.

Lady Vane was coming to London with her husband because she was fearful to stay on her own in Yorkshire. Raby Castle was not fortified, and her husband had fallen out with his father. The baby had caught the same fever as the wet nurse, and though he had seemed to be getting better, God be praised, she still feared for him, and her own milk was gone.

For that first day, Mistress Wormald had retained a furious silence, watching Isabel's feeble attempts to help with scorn. But on the second, to Isabel's surprise, she unbent, demanding the baby be handed to her. Treating his mother to a brisk recital of her errors, only thinly veiled by respect for rank, Mistress Wormald wrapped the infant tightly in a cloth and gave him another to suck, steeped in milk and smeared with honey.

Isabel was sharply commanded to wipe the toddler's face and hands, give him some bread to chew and threaten him with a whipping if he did not sit and eat. Pulling out a small book of prayers, Mistress Wormald then told Isabel to read them to the company, and Lady Vane was advised in minatory terms to close her eyes and get some rest. Happy to exchange chaos for tyranny, she did meekly as she was bid.

At Hatfield Mistress Wormald showed her mettle by bullying the landlord into finding another wet nurse, and commanded Sir Harry to pay the exorbitant sum required to get the woman to travel to London with them. The baby improved rapidly, and by the time they reached Holborn, they were all on excellent terms.

Lady Vane had told them of her husband's travels on a mission to Austria, and then to the King of Sweden, before his reforming zeal took him to America, where in his early twenties he had been made governor of the Puritan colony of Massachusetts. "But that, of course, was long before we were wed." Was that regretful? Isabel could not be sure.

Since then, Sir Harry had been much engaged on Parliamentary business, his wife said, travelling to Edinburgh to secure agreement on the Covenant. But these were grave matters, of which she must not speak – indeed, she did not fully understand them.

A dejected silence fell on them, until Mistress Wormald picked up the distaff with stories of her journeys to the Low Countries, when her husband was building up his trading house. "That, of course, was in his early days, before we took our place in the county." She drew her fine wool shawl closer around her shoulders, and contemplated the rings on her left hand, obvious signs of her spouse's progress towards prosperity and position. "Though what will become of us all, if this war is not brought speedily to a conclusion, the Lord alone knows."

Even Isabel was cajoled into telling of her betrothal to a Cornet in General Cromwell's cavalry, and his hopes of a captaincy. Lady Vane promised to speak to her husband, and introduce Isabel to others who might be helpful, for it seemed that all appointments at that level must now be approved by Parliament. Isabel shrank from the thought of interfering in Daniel's life, but was told briskly by Mistress Wormald that it was her duty. "My husband would never have got anywhere in trade without me."

She disembarked at Holborn, with parting admonitions both to Isabel and, in rather politer tones, to Lady Vane, as she still insisted on calling her: by Hatfield, Frances had given up begging Mistress Wormald to use her Christian name. The rest of them travelled on the short distance to Charing.

The Vanes had a fine modern mansion to the north of London, near the village of Hampstead, and Frances had said how much she was looking forward to getting there; but at Hatfield her husband had decided to send his secretary on to command lodgings in the City itself, saying she and the children would be safer there.

It had indeed been a little alarming to see the defences flung up by Parliament around London, manned by the Trained Bands, but built – so the coachman claimed derisively – mainly by London's women. Within these rather sketchy fortifications there was, however, little sign of a state of war. Indeed, when the coach pulled into the famous Golden Cross Inn, it seemed as busy as if normal life were completely undisturbed.

There they parted. William Ellys had written to Charles promising lodgings close by, in one of the alleys behind the Palace of Whitehall, close to Parliament itself. There were plenty of lodgings vacant, he had asserted, since almost all of the King's hangers-on had fled. But London had swollen so rapidly since Charles's youth that to the Halls' eyes, it still seemed to be teeming with life.

"Nigh on 400,000 people, now, so they say," the coachman told them, loquacious now the journey was over and he was looking to have his palm greased. Isabel was amazed. "How many are there in Lincoln, father?"

He shrugged. "A few thousand – six or seven, perchance."

There were hackney carriages waiting outside the Golden Cross – a new thing, Charles said, since his youth – but it was such a short distance to their lodgings, and a fine day, with the thoroughfare dry underfoot, that he decreed they should walk. While their baggage was loaded into a handcart, Isabel begged her father to let her go to see the Charing Cross itself. She had heard about it since her childhood, the last of the twelve Eleanor Crosses marking the way from Lincoln to London.

"Why Eleanor?" she had asked her father, knowing he would love to instruct her.

"After Queen Eleanor, the wife of Edward I, who died just up the road from Kettlethorpe. At Harby. The King, they say, was heartbroken. So he had crosses carved and erected at each point where her coffin rested, as it was carried to Westminster Abbey. Charing Cross is the last of these – a wonder to see…"

"… if you care for that sort of thing," Charles had added hastily, remembering that they were now considered Popish.

It was a great disappointment to Isabel to find it boarded up. Through the rough wooden planking she could just see that it was a magnificent memorial, of marble and stone. But the carved images of Eleanor and the saints were now deemed idolatrous, and Parliament, Charles told her, had decreed it should be knocked down.

So too, she learnt, the Queen's chapel at Denmark House, halfway between here and the City, had been stripped of idolatry. A fiery gentleman called Sir John Clotworthy, Charles told her, had himself slashed into Rubens' painting of the Crucifixion. Isabel had the impression that her father did not entirely approve of Sir John.

Disappointed, she accompanied him through Scotland Yard to the rambling Palace of Whitehall, looking for further marvels. She was confronted by one, soon enough: a magnificent modern building, in a style like nothing she had ever seen.

"Built only twenty-odd years ago," the carter said, obviously used to inquiries about this amazing construction, with its seven bays of windows between carved pilasters, its roof defined by its balustrade. "Meant to be the King's new Banqueting House; his father's old one burnt down. Don't fancy it, meself."

He stopped, to let them get a better look. "Foreign, isn't it? Classical, they call it – Popish, I say. Lots of shocking paintings inside. On the ceiling, too! They can't do much about them, not without scaffolds."

He sniffed, disapprovingly. "The King wanted to build a whole lot more like that. Got some designs done, by the same fancy fellow, only five years ago. Jones – that's his name. Inigo Jones. That's what the King spent our taxes on – palaces and pictures! Not much chance of him doing that, now."

He gave the cart an extra push over the cracked paving stones. "Now then, where're we taking this lot? Haven't got all day."

Charles told him, and he headed on through a small arch in an impressive brick building, built across the thoroughfare, at right angles to the modern Banqueting House. This was older, built in a style with which Isabel was more familiar. It was clearly the gatehouse to the old palace. "The Holbein Arch," Charles said, knowledgeably, and followed the carter right into a little warren of alleyways on the west side of the palace, beyond the disused tennis court and tiltyard.

They were sore glad to reach their lodgings, and Charles professed himself delighted with the rooms. But Isabel found them dark, and the alley dirty and noisy: she was bitterly homesick.

✳

In a few days, however, her good spirits reasserted themselves, and she thought better of her surroundings. Prudence had cleaned the rooms to her good country standards, Thomas had quickly fetched fuel, and unloaded their stores: between them they had made the lodging comfortable enough. At the end of their street, beyond Axe Yard, there were steps down to parkland, where Isabel could walk – if she obeyed her father's wish that she was always escorted.

The air was better here than in the City, which was thick with the smoke that hung heavy on windless days: she found that out soon enough, when she and Charles accepted the Vanes' invitation to join others concerned with the Parliamentary cause. She was excited to visit the City, and had made Charles promise to take her to the Exchange: but she was disappointed at what else she found.

The City was so old, built of soot-blackened wood and plaster, much of it falling down. The houses seeming to lean on each other, so far did the upper stories overhang the streets. They had taken a hackney carriage this time, whose driver grumbled much about the narrowness of the thoroughfares and the traffic jammed into them. But they persevered: Charles had confided to Isabel his hopes that William Ellys might one day support him for a seat, and was anxious to use this visit to the Vanes to increase his chances.

There was a crowd in the house the Vanes had taken, and Charles quickly spotted, to his excitement, that it included Cromwell himself. The men clustered round him and Sir Harry, and as the next room emptied of all but the women, Frances Vane introduced Isabel to a lively girl only a little younger than herself.

Her new acquaintance, Bettie Cromwell, was only too ready to make it clear that she was the great man's daughter. But she was friendly, and chattered away happily, until they were interrupted by another girl, whose presence caused Isabel real pleasure. It was Diana Willoughby.

Her father was about to leave, Diana said in a whisper, but Isabel must visit her, the very next day. A fond embrace, but only a cool nod to Bettie, and she left.

Isabel looked quickly to see what effect this rudeness had had, and observed a faint flush on Bettie's face, and a pursing of her lips. But she was easily distracted by Isabel's questions about London, sharing gossip and advice freely, and promising, with a slanting smile that betokened mischief, to introduce Isabel to Godly people of true value to the cause. Her charm was irresistible, and Isabel found herself promising to visit Bettie soon.

Next morning, Diana treated Isabel to a very different view of the Cromwell family: churlish upstarts, she was told, who would rid the country of all the nobility if they could, though only too ready to take their place. "His wife is a real plain Joan. And the children – his son Richard is a fool, Bettie a spoilt brat, and the others dull as ditch water."

Diana's father, it seemed, had been treated monstrously by Cromwell and his cronies; they had turned the Earl of Manchester against Lord Willoughby, too, but Lord Manchester, Diana said bitterly, would find out soon enough that there was no place for him in the New Model Army, either. "Harry Vane is plotting against him. All members of the Commons and the Lords will be forced to agree that they should resign from their army posts. But I'll warrant Master Cromwell finds a way of keeping his."

It was clear that Diana had no time for the new leaders of the Parliamentary cause. "They'll not stop until the King is dead, and then where will we be? Subjects of King Noll! I tell you, Isabel, the Lords will have to stand up to Cromwell, and soon."

Isabel looked around, nervously. "Diana, please do not tell me any more, it's dangerous talk. You may get your father arrested!"

Diana shook her head. "He's safe enough, for now. But the sooner he acts, the happier I'll be."

That evening, Isabel asked her father cautiously about the changes in the army. "Indeed, the Commons will pass a Self-Denying Ordinance," Charles said confidently. "And in the end the Lords must agree. No member of either House may then command, and we will have better order in the pursuit of our cause. No more Manchester, or Essex, who have become only half-hearted for war."

"But who will command, then, when they have gone?" Isabel asked.

"They say it will be Black Tom Fairfax," Charles said. "Everyone trusts him, including Cromwell."

As the days passed, it became clear that was indeed the way things were headed. Charles and Isabel stayed in London past the New Year, and she saw plenty of Diana, but with less and less pleasure.

The Willoughbys were lodging in one of the modern brick houses built shortly before the war, north of the Strand, beyond the fine piazza developed at Covent Garden. The area had, like the palace, a semi-deserted feel; the houses had mostly been built by noble families, granted the right by the Stuart kings, and now fled from London. But it was still a nicer place to visit than the noisome, smoke-heavy City.

The problem was with Diana herself. She had always been larger than life; now there was a violence in her emotions, and a rancour, that made Isabel uncomfortable, even fearful.

Much as she disliked the City, she found the gentle company of Lady Vane more agreeable, and was flattered that such a great lady seemed to welcome her visits. She played with little Frances and Henry, the baby Edward now securely in the care of the wet nurse. She still could not like Sir Harry, the less so when Charles told her how the falling-out with his father had occurred.

Sir Harry had taken some confidential papers of old Sir Henry's, which showed that the Earl of Strafford had been planning to bring in an Irish army. It had served a great purpose, Charles said, to help secure Strafford's execution, but she could hear the doubt in his voice.

Christmas passed almost without them noticing; celebrations were much disapproved of, now, and the shops obliged to stay open. In the New Year another man hated by the Parliamentarians was also, finally, executed: Archbishop Laud. Charles went to watch, taking Thomas with him for a treat, but came back saying he must be getting old, for he was losing his taste for such excitements.

"It was a shambles," he said. "The little man was so hemmed in with abusers that he had to push his way through to the scaffold. Clotworthy was there, shouting and spitting at Laud to the end." Charles's face was wrinkled in disgust.

Missing the country, Isabel took to walking every day behind their lodgings, in St James's Park. Charles did not worry, provided she took Prudence and Thomas with her, and promised not to stray towards Westminster, and the den of thieves surrounding the old Abbey. If Diana accompanied her, the two Hall servants would walk companionably behind, ignored by Diana's most superior tirewoman.

Once, when they went close to St James's Palace, soldiers brusquely waved them away. Isabel was puzzled, until Diana hissed in her ear that two of the King's children, Henry and Elizabeth, were being kept there. "They were left behind, when he and the Queen fled from Whitehall. They say she feared for her life, she is so hated. She is a foreigner, and men…" – Diana looked contemptuously at the soldiers – "men always find it easier to hate a woman."

"How old are they?" Isabel asked.

Diana shrugged. "Elizabeth is nine, I think – and Henry, four, perhaps?"

"Poor little things."

"They suffer less than others," Diana said. "They are protected from the soldiery. Other women and children are not so lucky." She saw Isabel's expression. "Oh, I know you want to think well of them, with your swain one of Cromwell's men, but in truth, they are mostly brutes."

"But Daniel says General Cromwell demands Godly men."

Diana laughed. "They are zealots. Levellers. Men who use religion to justify their worst abuses, claiming to fight a Holy War. They destroy all that is beautiful, befoul the churches, and hate women. Especially Catholic women. And there are men in the Commons, and the county committees, who are just the same. Have you not heard of the witch trials in Essex? Harmless old women, burned and hanged to satisfy men's cruelty."

"But surely," Isabel ventured, "the Royalist troops are worse? Prince Rupert's men, I've heard, have no pity for young or old!"

Diana pulled her friend's arm through hers, patting Isabel's hand. "Keep your faith, sweetheart, I do but jest. For sure, the King has scoundrels on his side. Men who deserved to die. Women like My Lady Carlisle, who slept with both sides and betrayed the Queen."

Isabel gasped; she had had Lady Carlisle pointed out to her by Charles as one of the greatest ladies in the land, and a friend to Parliament, and had admired her from afar. Diana smiled, faintly.

"Did you not know? She was mistress to Strafford, he who the King gave up for execution, and also to John Pym, one of the five in Parliament whom the King tried to arrest. Her husband was a scheming fellow, who peddled her services while he lived."

"Poor lady," Isabel ventured.

"Oh, you need feel no pity, she is quick enough to sell her favours to the winning side! She was close to Queen Henrietta Maria, and betrayed her. She learnt from her of the King's plan to arrest five Members of the Commons. Such folly! It hardened hearts against him. Still, it was traitorous of Lucy Carlisle."

She spoke confidently of a world beyond Isabel's comprehension. If there were rules, she did not begin to understand them. But Diana had been taken to London as a child, and as they passed a deserted courtyard told Isabel how she had stood with her mother watching the King's gentlemen and yes, some ladies too, play a game with wooden ball and mallet there.

"Pell-mell, it was called, and the ladies all pretended they could not hit the ball, so that the gentlemen would hold the mallet for them – intimately!" Diana smiled, disdainfully. "Such coquetry."

"Ah well," she continued. "Pym's dead now, too, but My Lady Carlisle still enjoys favour here. My father says she shares his disillusion. I only hope she does not share his bed. She betrays all her friends, and her lovers."

She looked at Isabel, with, for once, no emotion more complicated that genuine affection. "You have had enough of London, dearest.

Keep your innocence, and your love for your trooper. But mark what I say: war falls hard on women. And it will be worse, before all this is over. My father has had the scales lifted from his eyes. We will be leaving soon too, and I am glad."

Isabel did not tell Diana that she was also becoming friends with Bettie Cromwell. Despite the girl's airs and graces, Isabel had taken to her: there was an innocence about her pretensions, an enjoyment at being in the limelight, that was endearing. And she soon had Isabel's betrothal out of her, revealing in turn that she was in love with a young gentleman, John Claypole, from Northampton, whom she hoped to marry next year if Father could be persuaded.

From the confidence with which Bettie spoke, it seemed to Isabel that however iron-hard the General might be in public affairs, he was clay in the hands of this daughter. And the second time Isabel visited the Cromwells, she had proof of that.

Isabel had been sitting with Bettie and her mother, trying to forget Diana's scathing indictment of this kindly but dull woman. To Isabel's surprise, Elizabeth Cromwell showed the same fascination with the royal family as any goodwife; she disapproved of Henrietta Maria, of course, but would discuss the children with as much excitement as if her husband was not at war with their father.

In this bizarre if harmless discourse she was, however, interrupted by Oliver's return, with Vane in tow. It struck Isabel then how light a man Sir Harry, for all his rank and experience, his wit and influence, appeared beside the big, ugly, shabby and graceless General. The slightness of the one, the greatness of the other? Or was it Daniel's hero worship that made her think like that?

Isabel rose, thinking she should leave, but Bettie protested that her father must hear her story. "Her betrothed is in your regiment, Father, and I vow he should have his captaincy, from what I have heard of his deeds." Isabel blushed deeply, and waited for a reproof that would no doubt encompass her as well as Bettie, but Cromwell only smiled at his daughter and asked how many more times she would beg favours for her friends.

Bettie tossed her curls and said it was no favour, to treat a good soldier as he deserved, and shaking his head at her presumption, the General turned to the shrinking Isabel. "Mistress, it is no longer my regiment, I serve only at Sir Thomas Fairfax's request, but tell me, what is the name of this young fellow?"

"Sir, it is Daniel Stow," she whispered, praying she would not have harmed him through Bettie's rash intervention. To her relief, Cromwell nodded, abruptly but benignly, "Stow? Indeed, I know him for a fine, Godly officer. He has been with me for nigh on three years. The cavalry has been in winter quarters, near Reading; they were in a sorry state after the mismanaged affair at Newbury. But now it is being divided, into new regiments, and some troops are being joined with local forces, to help bind them into our new army. Young Stow has every chance of a captaincy, in these times."

Isabel dared ask no more, but Bettie was persistent. "Will you find out where he has gone, father? Or where he is going? It would be a kindness! And will you urge his promotion? You know a word from you would make all the difference!"

Her father sighed. "I'll not mislead this maid with rash promises, but I will mention Stow to his commanders, when I write. Now leave me in peace, daughter, Sir Harry and I have more weighty matters to discuss."

Isabel embraced Bettie warmly, before taking her leave. "I dared not think you could achieve so much, and I trust your father will not be angry with you for troubling him so."

Bettie giggled. "I have known him angry, but seldom with me, thank the Lord. Go, now, tell your father, and come again soon. I am sure I will have word of where your Daniel is."

Isabel did as she was bid, and Bettie was not mistaken. She was big with news when Isabel came again. Her father had been as good as his word, and had had inquiries made. He had told Bettie that he thought Cornet Stow might be with the troops that had been sent to Lincolnshire, where they were needed to guard the crossings on the Trent. "Isn't that where he comes from, like you?"

Daniel on the Trent! Had he come looking at Kettlethorpe, and found her gone? Had they told him that she was in London? Charles had had messages from home, only a week ago, but there had been no mention of Daniel.

Isabel visited the Cromwells once more, but only to say farewell. She had worked hard on Charles, fuelling his restlessness, so that even in bitter March weather, with the days lengthening, he was ready to travel north.

Bettie wailed that she would not have tried so hard with her father, had she known it would end with her friend hastening away. But then she kissed Isabel fondly, saying she understood – she would do the same to see John.

Saying farewell to Diana was more painful, for Isabel feared she might never see her again.

"Father has promised it to me," Diana whispered. "Unless he is better treated, this coming year, soon he will leave the country altogether."

*

It was a harder journey north, with less agreeable company, than on the way south. Bad weather had deepened the wheel-ruts, so that the unwieldy coach skidded and the wheels jammed. Slanting rain, turning now and then to sleet or wet snow, made everything worse.

The Boston merchant's family with whom they travelled grew ever more ill-tempered, and Prudence and Thomas grew numb with cold on the back of the vehicle. With depressing frequency, as they reached marshy ground, they all had to get out and stand shivering in the wind while the post-boys jammed branches under the coach's wheels and the horses strained to pull it out of the sucking mud.

All the same, they stayed with their co-travellers as far as they could, the coach leaving the Great North Road at Norman Cross and heading east. The Royalists were still raiding from Belvoir, and it was a relief to find a large Parliamentary garrison at Bourne, where they stopped for the night.

They would carry on up the old Roman road past Ancaster, before parting company at Byard's Leap: the Boston family heading east in the coach, Charles and his family north-west on the horses that would hopefully be waiting. He had finally persuaded the commander at Bourne to provide a couple of troopers to escort their small party on the last stage of their journey.

They made their final day's ride on an unexpectedly fine day, when the wind whipped a little dryness across the surface of the sodden countryside. The sight of the Cathedral, constantly ahead of them as they rode north, spoke to them of home. They turned west before the Witham floodplain, skirted Doddington and made the final few miles in the fading light of a chill, still evening in which all whisper of spring had gone silent.

The haze of tiredness that enveloped Isabel left her with only a vague memory of their arrival, of candles lit and ashes blown up into roaring fires, hot possets and warming pans, the sweet sound of recognised voices, the scent of lavender and the comfort of her own bed. She slept for two days, waking uncertain as to where she was, until she pulled back the bed curtains and saw, through the casement, the dear remembered view of archway and church.

She was stiff, and sore, but dressed as quickly as she could, anxious to visit the Stow household. She had been too tired when they arrived to do more than scan the two letters from Daniel that Goody Barton had handed her, discovering the last had been written over a month ago and made no mention of a return to Lincolnshire. Indeed, he spoke of trying to come to London and find her there, leaving her with the dreadful thought that he might have done so just after they left.

Surely his parents would know, if she did not. But now Goody Barton arrived, with an anxious Prudence in tow. Isabel had to summon all her determination, against a barrage of objections from her old nurse. Isabel should stay and rest – Mistress Stow would surely come and visit. Or Prudence could take a message.

Well, then, if she must go, Jacob would take her, pillion or cart – she must not walk, in this weather. But at last the goodwife gave way to Isabel's pleas that she was too sore and jolted to relish either of those options, insisting only that if she would have her way and walk, Prudence must go with her. In vain did Isabel protest that Prudence must be as weary as she was: Goody Barton's expression said plainly that it was not Prudence's place to be tired.

The two girls set off under the goodwife's disapproving gaze, wrapped in cloaks and shawls, the wind whipping their hair across their faces; and in truth, short journey though it was, Isabel was breathless by the time they reached the Stows' farmhouse. But the news she was given made it more than worthwhile.

She had heard from Samuel, Mistress Stow told Isabel: "You can read it yourself, my dear, if you can – he writes as bad a hand as Daniel." Worse, Isabel thought privately, peering at the scruffy note, but she could still make out the crucial information.

Daniel's troop was being sent to Gainsborough. They should be there by April. As soon as they could, they would come home.

They were as good as their word, and before the end of the month, Benjamin came running to find Isabel with news of their arrival. She found Daniel in good heart, buoyed up by expectations of his captaincy – aspirations that were, however, in conflict with his growing hope that 1645 might just possibly bring peace.

Prince Rupert was still a force to be reckoned with, Daniel said, the King's army was battle-hardened and the Royalists maintained a firm grip on Newark. But God be thanked, time and tide were running against them. The New Model Army was serving its purpose, binding the raggle-taggle of Parliamentary forces into one.

True to Diana's predictions, General Cromwell had stayed in effective command of the cavalry, under Sir Thomas Fairfax's leadership, without giving up his seat in the Commons. His forces were being deployed across the country, wherever there was need.

Colonel Rossiter was replacing Lord Willoughby in command of Lincolnshire. "And I am to take command at Torksey," Daniel told Isabel, "watching over the Fossdyke crossing. Captain Peart is in charge, until my captaincy is approved, but he will be at Gainsborough."

So began the happiest period of Isabel's young life. No May Queen could be crowned in 1645, but to Isabel it felt as if the private coronation of her love was affirmed daily by the unfurling of spring. Every bud, every young green leaf, sang to her of her own blossoming, the promise of fulfilment.

Charles had agreed they could be wed after harvest, at the beginning of September. Work was started on the house by the Sallie Bank, putting in a new stone floor, replastering the inner walls, fitting new casements – as much, Robert Stow said to Charles, as anyone could afford in these straitened times.

For Isabel, it was more than enough. When she could not be with Daniel she spent her time stitching for her bride chest, assisted by Prudence, though Goody Barton was inclined to say that the girl would never learn to sew a straight seam. Her criticisms slid off Prudence like water, so excited she was at the prospect of her own domestic kingdom in Isabel's new abode.

For Prudence this prospect had been made perfect by Charles's generous decision to hand Thomas's services on to the young couple. Isabel had protested, knowing how fond of Thomas her father had become, but he had brushed her aside, saying there would be good servants aplenty to hire when the war ended, and the Malignants' properties were sequestered.

*

In June came a setback to Isabel's hopes. Daniel sent word, scribbled hastily before his departure, that troops from all along the Trent had been summoned to Leicester, where the army was massing for battle.

Even in this short note, Isabel could see, he had done his best to reassure her. Parliament's army now was truly a force to be reckoned with, trained, united, and blessed by God. And General Cromwell would command the horse.

Thankfully, she did not have long to worry. Only days after she had she received this news, Daniel was back, in person, with more. And this time, great news.

They were gathered at the Stows once again, where Isabel felt she had spent all too many anxious days. Daniel had dropped exhausted into his father's chair; he looked grey and, for the first time, not just matured but aged by the war. Parliament, he told them, had won its greatest victory. The Royalist army had suffered a terrible defeat. Daniel did not believe it could recover.

"The King may still duck and weave, God rot him, but sooner or later, he must sue for peace. God send he knows that, soon."

For all the sweetness of victory, Daniel seemed deeply reluctant to talk about this latest battle. He was war-weary, of course, and all men's courage, Isabel knew, had its limits: perhaps it had been one battle too many for him. It had been going on so long, the war, and the bitter winter in camp had drained Daniel's health and strength. But she sensed something more.

Maybe, though he was still full of courage for the fight, he was sickened by it. Englishmen were still killing Englishmen. And there were no tales, this time, of kindness to weeping women.

Unbidden, Diana's words crept back into her mind. This cold, starved country was being turned into a slaughterhouse, a butchery in which hatred was hacking away all human decencies. She caught Martha Stow's eye: sensitive to her son's mood, she did not seem to want to hear more, either.

But Robert Stow persisted.

"Where did you fight? And did this New Model Army prove its worth?"

"At Naseby, Father. Not far from Leicester. And aye, our new army more than proved its mettle."

"And how went the battle? Was the enemy there in force? Prince Rupert? And the King?"

"Both of them. It was a foggy morning, June or no. But my troop were on a slight rise, and when the mist cleared, I could see we outnumbered the Royalists. Still, we'd done so before, and knew we could still be defeated."

"Did Prince Rupert charge?" Benjamin asked, and Daniel looked at him, quickly. Isabel knew the boy still saw the Royalist cavalry in his nightmares.

As if aware of this, Daniel replied with a studied calm, "A fierce charge, sure enough, and we were scattered, but when his men carried on in search of plunder, again he could not turn them. All the same, we took time to recover, so it was the infantry's chance to earn glory, and they did."

"Against even the King's own troops?" Robert Stow asked.

"Aye. Veterans. Hardened men. They died bravely enough. But as a fighting force, they're finished. We took his guns, too."

He looked at Charles, standing quietly beside his daughter. "And, Sir, your friends in Parliament will rejoice. We took the King's cabinet. We have his papers."

Those papers: how they were to haunt the King. Parliament used them, time and again, to fight the propaganda war against him. The letters were filleted, to whip up still more hatred against Henrietta Maria. Other papers were used to prove the King was bringing in Irish Catholics. And this was deemed by his enemies to justify the slaughter of women in the Royalist camp at Naseby.

When the story of that butchery came out, the women were swiftly denounced as Irish whores. But rumour had found its way down the Trent that they had, in fact, been Welsh. It was that sorry business, Isabel surmised, which had left Daniel so grey and taciturn.

Well, it must soon be over, surely: pray God, before worse atrocities. In this summer of 1645, it was nearly three years since the King had raised his standard, and he was running out of everything: ordnance, cavalry, heartlands, time. Surely he must give in. She found herself hating him – she, who seldom hated – for prolonging the torture of his country.

There was a bitterness throughout the land, as well as poverty and hunger. Word came from Norfolk that the fashion for witch trials was spreading; Isabel hoped the witch-hunters would not come north. An old woman in a hutch on Laughterton marsh, whom the children feared, was sometimes called a witch; but Goody Barton said she was harmless, just confused with age.

"She knows her herbs," – a great compliment, that, from the goodwife – "though she is just a little too ready to help foolish girls in trouble." She glared at Prudence, blamelessly sewing the hem of Isabel's nightgown.

Prudence was betrothed now, to Thomas, but Goody Barton had ruled the they should not marry for another two years, at least. "Mistress Isabel will need you to have all your wits about you, when she marries."

Isabel's wedding was still planned for September, war or no. She had heard from Diana, that she too was wed; a letter, much delayed, found its way to Kettlethorpe, written with Diana's typical self-mockery; Isabel hoped it concealed some happiness, wanting nothing to mar her own.

Daniel had been sent back to Torksey, to guard the Fossdyke crossing, since the Royalists still firmly held Newark. Daniel's troop occupied the Jermyns' house, which was only a mile down the Trent, so he was with Isabel often. And slowly, he seemed to come back to life.

Charles was again much in Lincoln, and Goody Barton seemed content to leave the lovers to themselves. Fierce as she might be with Prudence, she no longer kept strict watch over her nurseling.

If they went further in their loving than a Puritan would approve, well, the wedding was so soon that there was no risk Isabel would come to church with a swollen belly. In the soft summer evenings, she and Daniel came to know each other free from fear, or guilt, or constraint, their enchantment subject only to the relentless intrusion of an angry world.

For the war had not done with Kettlethorpe.

*

The Newarkers had been growing steadily more desperate in their raids for men and supplies along the Trent. Every day brought a ripple of fear, with a new story of murder and pillage. And one day in late July a gang of them, as many as thirty, came to the village, setting about it in their usual fashion: seizing the livestock, ransacking the cottages, striking down those stalwarts who resisted them, trying to take some others captive.

Charles was away, but Isabel did as she had long promised him and Daniel. She sent Thomas to Torksey for help, told Jacob to bolt the doors and led Goody Barton and the maidservants down through the tunnel to the church. There she found other village women huddled together for protection, but peeping out she could see the Newarkers were not having it all their own way.

Thomas had done well. A small Parliamentary troop had arrived from Torksey. With the support of the villagers, armed with billhooks and scythes, they had engaged with the raiders on the green between church and hall. Three or four of the Newarkers lay unmoving on the ground. A few had already panicked and fled.

Now the rest were being driven out of the village. Soon the clash of fighting men was over, and then all that could be heard of them was hoof beats, as the raiders scrambled back on their mounts to head south. They were pursued by the triumphant little troop from Torksey.

Was Daniel, or Samuel, amongst those who had come to their aid? Isabel could not be sure: it had all been so quick. She called to Goody Barton and Prudence, and they went to the aid of those on the green still groaning with painful life.

Two were from Kettlethorpe, one with a bad gash to his head. Prudence ran for linen and they soon had his wound bound, and had sat him against a tree while he gathered his wits. The second was clutching his arm, from which the blood flowed freely, and Goody Barton bound it as tightly as she could.

The third, a stranger, was clearly dying from terrible wounds to his groin, and for all the harm he had brought to Kettlethorpe, Isabel could only pity his youth and pain and hold his hand through his agony, as he cried out to Christ and his mother. The Rector came, and said a prayer with him, though Isabel suspected the young man was a Papist, since he begged for the Sacrament. He died before Smythson could refuse him, to all their relief.

It was some hours later before they could count the cost, which would have been so much worse, they all agreed, but for their brave troops from Torksey. Four of the Newarkers lay dead: the sexton was already digging a grave. But none of the villagers had lost their lives.

They did not, however, then know the whole of it.

In the evening, the little Parliamentary troop came back from their pursuit. Samuel Stow came to give Isabel the news. One look at his face froze her heart.

They had chased the marauders beyond Collingham. To go so far, that had been their mistake. Just three miles short of the garrison at Newark, they had been surprised by a Royalist patrol.

All six of the Parliamentary troop had come back, but two of them as dead men, strapped across their saddles. One of these was their commander. Samuel's brother. Isabel's betrothed.

Daniel, a soldier of the Lord.

1645–1796

*A*bout the real Isabel Hall all I know is that she died young. I can only hope that her little, unrecorded life lasted long enough for her to enjoy the sweetness of first love, as I have imagined, as well no doubt as its sorrows.

A small Parliamentary troop did come to drive the "Royalist rabble" out of Kettlethorpe in July 1645, according to a contemporary account in a Parliamentary journal. There was a skirmish, with casualties, and then the troop did indeed chase the raiders and lose two of its number just beyond Collingham.

I cannot pretend there is any evidence that they included one of the real-life Stows, but the family were there in Kettlethorpe Church to take the oath administered in 1642 – the moment with which this story started – and it was not a long stretch of the imagination to have the eldest of the sons join up, and serve along the Trent.

I have a soft spot for Charles Hall, despite his obvious (minor) venality, because he clearly preferred Kettlethorpe to all his other properties, and was good to the poor of the parish. But his was not a successful public career. Although he was elected to Parliament in 1654 and again in 1656, he and six other Lincolnshire MPs were excluded by the Council of State as enemies of Cromwell's Protectorate.

These suspicions of Charles can only have been sharpened by his second marriage – to Anne, the daughter of Sir Thomas

Trollope, who was suspected of Malignancy and arrested in 1651. It would be nice to think this resulted in recognition for Charles at the Restoration, but it seems not: by 1662 he had been removed from all Commissions of the Peace.

Lord Willoughby of Parham, who lived at Knaith, played the part in the war I have ascribed to him. He was one of the very few of the local aristocracy who sided definitively with Parliament, but later, when dismissed from command, he became disillusioned. Other great names who featured in this story do not need me to affirm their existence.

At the Restoration, the English establishment may have welcomed back their Stuart dynasty, but they did not welcome its religion. In 1689 they began an extraordinary series of invitations to Dutch and German princes to come and rule the country, rather than continue with a native line of kings tainted with papacy.

These uninspiring, but – in most cases – reassuringly unpretentious immigrant rulers, with their poor command of English, were tailor-made for the evolution of a unique system of government. Power passed from Sovereign to Parliament, and military heroics from Kings to generals who (more or less) won their right to lead armies through their own achievements. Butcher Cumberland was the last member of the royal family to win a major battle, at Culloden; the Prince Regent's leadership of armies in the war against Napoleon existed only in his own imagination.

Protestantism, in the mild form espoused by the Church of England, became entrenched in the political system, reinforced by a series of penal laws that drove adherents of the old religion out to the fringes of society. Roman Catholics could not purchase land, hold a commission in the army or a public office, take a seat in either House of Parliament, inherit property or practise their religion openly without civil penalties. As Samuel Pepys found, to be accused of papacy in the seventeenth century was to risk livelihood and liberty.

A few grandees escaped the penalties imposed on lesser folk, while many of the Catholic gentry in the north of England diluted *their recusancy – refusal to attend the local church – with the compromises necessary to preserve their estates. They sent their sons to be educated abroad, and to pursue military careers there, too. They disguised their chapels as libraries or follies. They followed Lord Baltimore to Maryland in hopes of religious freedom. But throughout the north of England, there remained pockets of the old religion.*

Despite the Trollope leanings, the Hall family remained firmly within the Church of England, and prospered at Kettlethorpe until Charles's grandson – also Charles, and also a Member of Parliament – ended the family connection. He left his property to the son and daughters of his half-brother, Vincent Amcotts, rather than to his cousin and Rector, Gilbert Hall.

When her brother Charles died childless, Anna Maria Amcotts and her husband Wharton Emerson inherited the Kettlethorpe estate. In her brother's time it had been further increased by a succession of Inclosure Acts, private Bills put through Parliament to transfer ancient parcels of common land to a series of "interested parties". It was a substantial estate, better than the other Amcotts property at Harrington, which went to Anna's sister. It was the late eighteenth century, the heyday of the English country house, and the grandest phase in the life of "Kettlethorpe Park" was about to begin.

GRAND DESIGNS

KETTLETHORPE PARK: 1796

Sir Wharton. The title was still new enough to give him deep pleasure. A baronet. And, he thought happily, if I say it myself, I look the part. That tailor knew his business: the coat was an excellent fit. He turned a little sideways, to catch his half-profile in the pier glass. The new fashion for wearing boots on such occasions, that suited him too. A hint of the military man. He made a slight leg. Not bad; not bad at all.

He caught his wife's eye in the mirror, and smiled a little sheepishly. "Just considerin' my new coat, m'dear. Ridiculous sum to pay, I don't know how I let that feller talk me into ordering it."

"It looks very well," she said loyally. They had married when he was a handsome twenty-two-year-old ensign, pockets to let, and she an ageing spinster of thirty-seven, heiress on the death of her brother Charles to his fine estate at Kettlethorpe. It was hardly a love match. But mutual gratitude for meeting each other's greatest need – he for land, she for a husband – had strengthened into genuine affection.

Their union had been blessed with only one offspring, and a girl at that. But both of them had derived such profound delight from Elizabeth that disappointment at the lack of a son had been fleeting at most. In Wharton's eyes, Elizabeth had been, and still was, perfect. Her mother had retained, in company at least, some pretence at a more detached judgement of Elizabeth's qualities, but in private was inclined to share her husband's views.

Elizabeth had survived this lack of parental astringency remarkably well, growing up neither spoilt nor capricious. A governess of exceptional ability, respected even by Sir Wharton, had undoubtedly helped. Miss Anstey had established her domain rapidly. Entering the schoolroom in her first week, Sir Wharton had found a furious Elizabeth in tears over some scholastic misdemeanour. Opening his mouth to protest, he had encountered his new hireling's frosty gaze, and retreated without a word.

Miss Anstey had not, to her public regret and Sir Wharton's private relief, succeeded in making a scholar out of Elizabeth, who continued to prefer the stable to the schoolroom. But her governess had had the great good sense to ask Lady Amcotts to invite two of their close friends' daughters to share Elizabeth's lessons. This had brought out the competitive streak Elizabeth might otherwise have reserved for her hunting with the Burton, and she emerged into society with all the necessary accomplishments, and with her character unspoiled.

Even more surprisingly, she had become firm friends with her governess, and had borne her off to Yorkshire to educate her own children. For Elizabeth had continued to fulfil her parents' hopes by receiving, in her very first London season, a suitable proposal of marriage. She was, of course, quite an heiress, but her father was still young, and John Ingilby, owner of a fine estate in Yorkshire, seemed a highly eligible suitor.

Lady Amcotts might wish Elizabeth could have found happiness closer to home – with one of the Heneages, Monsons, Fanes or Neviles, perhaps – and she worried that there was something shady about John, if she could put her finger on it. But Wharton hugely enjoyed his visits to Ripley Castle, and declared the day of Elizabeth's wedding in Kettlethorpe church to be the happiest of his life so far.

Anna was right, of course – she was always so acute – but Wharton saw no need to enlighten her. That was all in John's past, was not his fault, and was best forgotten: he was, after all – long before Wharton himself secured such a prize – about to receive a baronetcy.

True to her admirable form, Elizabeth had presented Sir John with two sons in the first three years of her marriage. And now, with his own baronetcy, Wharton had secured a special remainder, which would enable it to pass through his daughter to the second of her sons. This boy William would, like Wharton himself, adopt the Amcotts name. Wharton also intended to pass on his Parliamentary interest, in the constituency of East Retford to which he had just been returned unopposed, to this fortunate grandson.

The only cloud in the sky was the boy William himself. He was undoubtedly difficult. At the age of thirteen, he displayed a fascinated enthusiasm for the revolutionary ideas that were convulsing the new French Republic. He was not of course alone in that, though by the time William started chanting the slogans (in his very poor French) older heads were becoming alarmed by the bloodletting.

Sir Wharton had had his radical moments: he was a Whig, and indeed at one point was even rumoured to be a supporter of Charles James Fox. This was going too far, and it would be truer to say he was a supporter of the Duke of Portland: but truer still to say that his politics were a matter of interests rather than ideas. His opposition to William Pitt was driven less by opposition to the war than by the prime minister's pesky plans to increase taxation to pay for it, which were much resented by Wharton's East Retford supporters.

Wharton had tried to ascertain Miss Anstey's view of William, but without success. She clearly preferred talking about the girls; but then she had, in an unguarded moment, professed an admiration for Mary Wollstonecraft, and consequently could be expected to take much greater interest in female education. Or so Wharton had comforted himself. Perhaps he could have another word with her when she arrived with Elizabeth.

With a start, he realised he had been gazing into the pier-glass for several minutes. He made a hasty recovery. "My dear, I think we really should be going down to receive our guests."

Her eyes twinkled. He had the grace to look slightly abashed, and held out his arm. She rose, still straight-backed at seventy-one, and placed her hand upon it.

The new staircase was wide enough for them to progress down together. Wharton looked at it with satisfaction. All the improvements he had made to Kettlethorpe – and they were definitely his, though his wife had encouraged him – gave him pleasure. He had entirely remade the house, doubling it in size; the exterior, he had to admit, was not particularly distinguished, but at least no one could now suppose it had been built over a hundred years before.

The little breakfast parlour he had left unchanged, though its panelling was no longer fashionable: there was a fine marble fireplace there, not more than fifty years old, that gave it some distinction. He was particularly pleased with the newly built morning room, with its stucco ceiling: the design was bang up to the minute, with Chinese influences, despite having been crafted by a workman from Doncaster. The ballroom beyond it had as yet no such embellishment; if that fellow Pitt wasn't too grasping, he'd see to that in a year or two. The church needed updating too, when he could find the funds.

A small irritation intruded on his inward recital of improvements. Brampton was waiting, as he should be: but he was not one of Wharton's successes. A local man, he knew all the tradesmen from here to Grimsby, and could always be relied upon to find a new kitchen maid from amongst his extensive family. But nothing his employer could do had succeeded in turning him into a butler worthy of a baronet.

Deeply ingrained in Brampton were the down-to-earth, slightly cross-grained, incurably humorous attitudes of the yellow-belly, and he continued to display a cheerful lack of deference and mild pugnacity. Brampton took everyone as they came, insulting squire and servant alike.

His employer had taken him to London, to see if he could acquire a little town polish, but it had not been a success. Brampton, who had never previously been further south than Stamford, complained that walking on the newfangled pavements made his feet hurt and he couldn't sleep for the noise. He quarrelled royally with the French cook they had hired for the season, and had to be sent north after startling a Peeress by addressing her as "m'duck".

A harsher man would have sent Brampton back to the stables, or turned him off. But Wharton combined an innate kindness with an incurable optimism, and continued to believe Brampton could change. Lady Amcotts, both more realistic and less demanding, merely put up with Brampton's unchanging ways in gratitude for his dogged loyalty.

As Wharton reached the bottom of the stairs, he could see that Brampton was eyeing his master's boots with disapproval. Any second now, and he would ask if his master was thinking of going hunting. Wharton hoped he wouldn't; it would necessitate a put-down of his butler, and that was never very successful. But Lady Amcotts had, with suspicious alacrity, intervened.

"How nice everything looks, Brampton. Thank you for all your hard work."

Brampton ducked his head – it could hardly be called a bow. "Thank you, m'lady." And that was a step forward, Wharton noted with relief: without having anything as advanced as Republican views, Brampton didn't much hold with titles, and had had several times to be told not to address Lady Amcotts as "missus". But then Brampton had no wish to insult his mistress, whom he regarded, not of course without reason, as the true owner of Kettlethorpe, and adored her only slightly less than her daughter.

Elizabeth should be here by now, Wharton thought. She had promised to come to stay for the event, bringing some of the children with her. She did not seem to think the affair quite as inappropriate as her mother did, Wharton reassured himself. Anna had ventured to demur quite strongly when Wharton first proposed that his baronetcy should be marked at Kettlethorpe by a Publick Day.

"My dearest husband, such a notion may be very fitting for the great houses – indeed, I have been to more than one at Belton, and you remember when we were obliged to miss the one at Welbeck last summer, we consoled ourselves that there would certainly be another soon. But this house, splendid as you have made it, surely does not carry the same responsibilities. I fear we may be overreaching ourselves a little."

Seeing Wharton looked a little affronted, she tried another tack. "And in these troubling times, too, my dear – and in your important position…"

It was no use. The war was of course a matter of grave concern, particularly now those damned Spaniards had sidled over to the French side. But in a newspaper report of his recent re-election to Parliament Wharton had read that "at no place was the old English hospitality kept up with greater spirit than at Kettlethorpe Park", and he was determined to live up to his billing.

"I am confident that enough of the Quality will come to give it distinction," he had said. "I will write to our particular friends to say how glad we would be to see them. The Neviles will certainly come from Thorney, and the Huttons from Gate Burton. And I shall write especially to Lord Delaval: it would be splendid if he were to honour us, although of course he does not spend all his time at Doddington. And perhaps I should also write to Joseph at Revesby, bidding him spend the night with us should he care to make the journey."

He stopped, a little uncertainly, while his wife tried not to smile. Wharton venerated Sir Joseph Banks, who tended to feature on all her husband's lists of "the Quality". Joseph had become a national celebrity over twenty years ago, after he and Captain Cook had come back from their travels to outlandish parts. Of course, Wharton found all of what he called "Jo's plant life" a bit tedious

– he had thankfully forgotten all his Latin after leaving school. But he recognised that Joseph had greater interests and aspirations than most country gentlemen, and admired him for it.

When Joseph had presented him with a specimen from his Antipodean adventures, Wharton had handed it hastily over to his head gardener, with threats of instant dismissal should it expire. Kyme took the threats with as much seriousness as they deserved, but somehow failed to kill this strange foreign weed, which flourished on the south side of the house, tumbling clusters of yellow flowers down the wall.

Despite his elevation – Joseph had become a Knight of the Bath at much the same time as Wharton had received his less distinguished baronetcy – Banks still played a full part in Lincolnshire life. Only a few years before, he had commissioned the artist Claude Nattes to produce exquisite line drawings of every notable building in the county. Though this exposed the extraordinary disrepair into which so many churches had fallen, while the clergy had taken themselves off to baths and pleasures in spa towns, the houses looked very fine – and Wharton was greatly relieved that his extensions to Kettlethorpe had been completed in time.

He had also greatly enjoyed acting as Joseph's aide-de-camp in the development of the Stuff Ball, an idea he had picked up from a well-meaning parson without the cachet to bring it off. It was to be an annual ball, which ladies could attend free provided they were wearing gowns woven from the fleece of Lincolnshire Longwools, in order to support the ailing manufactory of these once-prized fabrics. Gentlemen faced a similar request, despite having to pay for tickets, although of course their dress required less "stuff" – and an exception was made for the wearing of silk stockings. The Stuff Ball proved so successful that it packed the Lincoln Assembly Rooms each year, and attracted approving comment in the London press.

To ensure no lady used the same ballgown or petticoat twice, each year's patroness of the ball was required to decree a different colour, but this had proved a less happy idea: even Anna had been heard to protest that she would rather give a purse to every weaver in Lincoln than make a figure of herself in orange to please Dorothea Banks. And Elizabeth had been still less happy with Lady Monson's choice, writing to say that she would sooner stay in Yorkshire than go to a ball in brown.

Attending the Stuff Ball, however, was one thing; expecting Joseph to make the trip from Revesby to Kettlethorpe for a Publick Day was quite another, and Wharton knew it. He had moved hastily on. "And you could always," he had continued, with somewhat less enthusiasm, "invite your sister to come over from Harrington."

But Frances, Anna's younger sister, who had inherited the second of the Amcotts estates, had sent a polite refusal, into which Wharton tried not to read a similar view to his wife's as to the seemliness of this event. He was not sorry his sister-in-law had stayed away, anyway: a clergyman's widow, she combined holiness with avarice, and always appeared to be inwardly calculating the difference between the sisters' properties, to her own disappointment.

As Wharton and Anna entered the Kettlethorpe ballroom, he was forced to admit that not many of their more distinguished friends had turned up. But then, it was still early. While his tenants could be counted on to be more than punctual, the Quality could equally be relied on to be fashionably late.

So he looked round with unalloyed pleasure. Most of his tenant farmers were excellent fellows, and it was good to see them in his house, or patrolling the gardens in their Sunday best and showing off their families. The farms had recovered from last year's disasters, when the Trent had broken its bank at Stapleford, and land had been flooded all the way east to Lincoln and north to Torksey. Even the house here had nearly been swamped: floodwater in the cellars had topped five feet.

There had been much distress in the countryside, and riots in the towns, as people went hungry in the bitter cold last winter. He had done his best for his tenants, to be sure, but there had been many deaths from starvation and sickness.

However, the weather had been kinder this year, and the harvest looked promising: a few more blazing hot days like this, and it would be time to start. He saw Jim Turgoose from Fenton surreptitiously loosening his stock when his tartar of a wife wasn't looking, and grinned in commiseration. It was hot be to wearing broadcloth and a starched collar.

He was pleased to see them all – well, nearly all. Here was poor Joseph Tomlin, who had lost wife and son in barely more than a year; there was the Baker family, and the Seneschalls, the Watsons and Ardens. And there was the Rector, Hugh Palmer, but talking to him was something Wharton avoided doing whenever he could. It was never a brief conversation with Hugh, and always resulted in Wharton feeling intellectually as well as spiritually inferior, a feeling that greatly annoyed him. He'd presented the man with his living, dammit, he needn't be so condescending.

Never mind: he'd catch up with the Rector later. He was even less enchanted to see Jem Clifton, the landlord at the posting inn just down the road at Drinsey Nook. Every piece of thievery in the district was plotted in his taproom. But Wharton had needed his stables for the occasion, and so had to view his presence with complaisance.

At least, it now transpired, Elizabeth had arrived without mishap. In the hall behind him he heard her being greeted by Brampton in his inimitable fashion.

"And what time do you think this is to arrive, Miss Elizabeth? There's your father worriting himself silly about you, and me telling cook not to put the vittels out for all the riff-raff to guzzle, you'd not be here while dusk if I knew anything. Give me that cloak, now, and you young'uns too, and get yourselves through to where the Master can see you. You leave nurse to me, yes and Miss What's it, and the baggage, you've brought half the house, I'll be bound. Get along with you all now."

Really, Wharton thought, Brampton had missed his calling. He should have been on the stage, in some comedy of manners, playing the eccentric retainer. Not for the first time, he wondered if Brampton kept himself amused by seeing how far he could push the role without disaster. He felt his wife's silent laughter and squeezed her arm.

Before the Amcotts could make their way back to greet the Ripleys in more seemly fashion, Elizabeth had burst into the ballroom, her family behind her, and had flung her arms round her mother's neck. Well into her thirties now, she seemed untouched by age or child-bearing, or by the worry her husband's financial difficulties must have caused her.

Having spent too much on the restoration of Ripley, Sir John had resigned the Parliamentary seat Wharton had vacated for him, and taken himself abroad to avoid his debtors. Elizabeth's letters suggested things were now repaired, and his elder son had gone to visit Sir John with the intention of accompanying him home; but she was always an optimist, her father reflected – an inherited trait, or so his wife foolishly alleged.

Just now Anna was gently reproving her daughter, shaking her head at travel-crumpled muslins, and encouraging the travellers to repair to their rooms to refresh themselves. But Elizabeth put out both hands to her father, saying that she could not rest until she had thanked him for what he had done for William.

"And father, he has been bursting to thank you himself, have you not, William? I vow, he has talked of nothing else all the way here!"

Wharton did not think his grandson had talked of that or anything else, to judge by the mulish look the boy had given his mother. He certainly did not look enthralled at the prospect of his inheritance, and Wharton wondered if this reflected his proclaimed Republicanism. Perhaps the remainder had been a mistake.

But in this he misjudged William, who had in fact been deeply gratified, and was anxious to express his gratitude – just not with his mother's arm around him, pushing him forward like a child. He had been rehearsing in his head a few dignified sentences, which he felt would show him properly seized of the honour of his inheritance, and could be delivered man to man, if only he could get his grandfather away from all these women.

But his mother was hanging on to her father's arm, and now there was Gussie simpering at her grandfather from the other side, when she should have been sent upstairs with Miss Anstey. He would have to wait, and meanwhile was not going to indulge his mother by saying anything.

William's awkwardness sprang from an acute realisation that he was, in all things, and to all members of his family, incurably second best. He had all of his mother's passion, but none of her easy charm, and a tendency to the kind of hero-worship that inevitably ends in disillusion.

He had first idolised his father, and some of his professed political ideas had been a cack-handed attempt to demonstrate an independence of thought he hoped would win his parent's respect. A landowner with money troubles rarely appreciates Republicanism, however, and Sir John had merely been irritated. His obvious preference for the company of William's elder brother had completed the younger boy's humiliation.

This brother, with his easy confidence, good looks, excellent horsemanship and sporting prowess, was William's next idol. But then William had joined him at school, and found that, far from protecting him, Ripley Major sided with the older boys who bullied and humiliated his younger sibling. William dimly understood that he was abandoned out of an instinct of self-preservation, not out of viciousness – that he, William, was somehow a natural victim and siding with him would have been suicidal. But his adulation of his brother could hardly survive this betrayal.

At this moment, the worst in William's life so far, his grandfather's promise of position and title came like a godsend, and William had a new deity to worship. In vain his father warned him not to count too much on this one either. In letters scribbled poste restante from Antwerp and Brussels, Sir John pointed out that if (God forfend, he hastily added) William's grandmother were to die, Sir Wharton would likely marry again, and was quite young enough to sire a son and bring all these expectations to an end.

It was a waste of pen and paper. In William's eyes he was already the owner of Kettlethorpe Park and its acres, a Member of Parliament and a baronet. With a guilty concession to his now-fading Republicanism, he decided he would be a generous landlord and open a school.

He looked a little anxiously at his grandmother, all the same. She was, he had to admit, really quite old. But she seemed sprightly enough. Having gently detached Elizabeth and Gussie from Sir Wharton, she had led them away to do their duty amongst the guests. William heard her remind his mother that of course, she remembered Mrs Cole – Mrs Wells-Cole, she should say, for Elizabeth would remember brother and sister had married sister and brother, such a happy arrangement.

Well, to judge by all that, William thought, his grandmother still had her wits about her, and she looked in good pin. He turned back to his grandfather, hoping he could now say his piece, only to find Sir Wharton's attention was elsewhere. More than that: his grandfather looked, William thought, as if he were in shock.

*

It could not be her. Of course it could not. These past five years, Wharton had caught glimpses of her, time after time – only to find, when the figure that had set his heart racing turned around, that it was not her. It was not even like her.

Once he had been so certain that he had approached the tantalising back view uttering – even without realising it – her name. "Rose," he had muttered, and the young woman gazing into a shop window in the Bailgate had looked round, alarmed, clutched her companion's arm and edged swiftly away. He must not make the same mistake again, here at his own house.

But through the window overlooking the lawns he could see, with this girl, a couple that were — how could he not recognise them? — Rose's parents. Why had he never imagined that they might come? They were, after all, his tenants, for at least some of their acres. Why should they not come? But why — how? — after all this time, had she suddenly decided to come with them?

He had called on them after Rose had disappeared, a courtesy visit in which he could learn frustratingly little without destroying his pretence of polite indifference, keeping her secret as he had sworn to do. How kind of Sir Wharton to inquire after her, Rose's mother had said: she had gone to live with a friend who was a schoolmistress — Rose too was teaching children their letters, she had always had a way with young ones. No mention, in this conversation, of a "little one" of her own.

He forced himself to move slowly towards the garden, greeting his guests as he went, suppressing the fear that they might leave before he got there. The Rector was again trying to catch his eye, but Wharton ducked behind a stout pair of farmers, and slipped down the short flight of steps to the garden door.

He reached the family as slowly as he could contain himself, and greeted them without obvious incoherence, trusting he found them well. Rose's father, he could see, had taken this as an invitation to give his views on the harvest, but while he was drawing breath, his wife got in first.

"In very good heart, Sir Wharton, thank you, now our dear Rose has come to visit us, as you can see. She is living in York now, so we do not see as much of her as we would like."

York! Why had he not thought of York? He had made inquiries of schoolmistresses in Lincoln, and Newark, Sleaford and Gainsborough, but had not looked outside the county. Yet of course — he now recalled her talking fondly of a friend who had gone to join the Ladies at the Bar. Her mother still had a fondness for the old religion, which she had shared with Rose, who had told him with shining eyes of this brave group of Catholic women. Until recently they could not openly call themselves nuns, but for a century had been living in a house in York, to follow their double vocation of prayer and the education of women.

Sir Wharton had no leanings to Rome, and little time for prayer or women's education, but all the time in the world for Rose. That enchanted summer he would have listened to her talk of anything, even Catholic emancipation, just for the magic of hearing her voice, seeing the flush rise in her cheeks, restraining himself to let her share her thoughts before catching her in his arms. It was first love for her, while he, having been accelerated into maturity by his advantageous marriage, was making up for lost youth.

The idyll had ended, as such idylls do, when she had told him in the autumn that she was with child. She would not let him find her somewhere to live close by; she did not want to shame her parents, or wound his elderly wife; she wanted to disappear. She took his money, for she had none of her own; and then she had gone.

At first he could not believe it. His hopes rose and fell every time the post arrived. He made his discreet inquiries. He took to visiting schools, professing an interest in education that surprised his household. He learned nothing.

Five years. Of course he had not spent them thinking only about her; his boundless energy had been channelled into so much else. He was still very fond of Anna, he loved his family, he enjoyed his place in the world. And of course she was right: her disappearance had saved him from embarrassment, from his wife's distress, and part of him could not help feeling some relief. But on sleepless nights his imagination had tortured him with what might have happened to her, as well as bringing back to him the sheer, searing pain of loss.

Now her father was talking – about the harvest, of course – but Wharton did not take in one word in ten. With enormous self-control, he turned courteously to Rose, and asked how she was liking York. His voice sounded strange, even to him, but she answered steadily enough, and he dared to look at her. No longer a girl, her dark curls were smoothed back under her bonnet, her expression grave; but as he searched her countenance for clues to her well-being, he did not think it was marked by grief. Her grey eyes held his, steadily. And then he knew what to do.

*

Wharton was wrong, again, in thinking that no one had marked his passage. William, waiting anxiously for his private moment, had cheered up when he saw his grandfather go into the garden. Much easier to talk to him there. But of course everyone out there wanted to talk to him, too, and he seemed to have got stuck with that fellow – one of his tenants? – chatting with his wife and daughter.

No: his grandfather was breaking away now with a polite bow, but curse it – just as William started forward, Gussie appeared, bursting with self-importance. "William, Mama wants you. Grandpapa has disappeared, and here is Lord Delaval arriving, and only us females to greet him! She says you must find him – at once!"

Exasperated, William pointed at his grandfather, who was now heading purposefully for the house. He grabbed his sister's arm. "Leave him be, Gussie, Mama will see him soon enough, and he won't thank you for running after him like a hoyden."

Gussie pouted, but did as he said, trailing disconsolately after her brother towards the house. William could clearly see, through the windows, that Brampton was already ushering Lord Delaval and his party into the ballroom, with all the style of a farmer bringing cattle to market. The boy arrived at the ballroom door in time to see his grandfather greeting the newcomers, but in a slightly distracted fashion that brought a puzzled crease to his grandmother's brow.

As soon as His Lordship had professed pleasure at meeting other of their guests, and started on a gracious peregrination around the room, Wharton slipped away again. William tracked him to the library. Wharton had been in too much of a hurry to close the door, and William saw him pull out his watch chain, to use a little key attached to it on a drawer of the desk.

It looked like a fistful of Treasury bills that he was now stuffing into the pocket in his coat-tail, and William wondered who needed paying so much in such a hurry. But the boy barely had time to hide behind an urn before Wharton emerged again. He hesitated, looking round, then stepped firmly out of the open front door, as if to welcome some favoured new arrival.

He was through the gatehouse, and had turned right up the avenue of elms before William dared follow him. A few yards that way, and his grandfather cut right past the succession houses and orchard towards Ice-House Wood.

Now deeply puzzled, William trotted after him. Surely a footman would have been sent, if more ice were needed? He saw his grandfather crest the slight rise in the land to the wood, so familiar from chilly, sparkling hunting days: Ice-House Wood was always the first they drew. And William had found the wood a useful hiding place in summer, when he wanted to escape from adult demands – you had good visibility from the rise, and could always see whoever was sent in pursuit well before they got in range.

He crouched at the edge of the wood, behind a thicket of elders and brambles, while he got his breath. Now, at least, he could talk to his grandfather in private. Ever afterwards, as the awful discoveries of the afternoon ran through his mind again, he was thankful for one small mercy. He had stopped, once more, to rehearse his speech, and so was saved the ultimate humiliation of bursting in on the pair of them unawares.

For in that short moment he realised his grandfather was not alone. William heard him speak, though it was impossible to make out what he was saying – a thick, tumultuous flow of words, checked finally by another voice. "Hush, my dearest, I am here, as you see – and I am well. And the child is very well – a fine boy, four years old now. I have called him Joseph, after your hero, and he thrives."

Wharton spoke more calmly, now. "Thank God you understood. I was afraid you might have forgotten this place, or could not slip away from your parents. But where have you been? How have you managed? You had nothing from me!"

"I had the money you gave me. And the cross. I have it still. It was enough."

Enough! How could it have been enough, even if she had sold it? It had been Anna's, but she had asked her husband to sell it: a "Popish" little thing she'd inherited, and had no liking for. He gave it to Rose, salving his conscience by taking it to Retford, to get a price, and spending the same out of his own money to buy Anna a brooch.

"I searched everywhere I could think of for you when you left, but fool that I was, I never thought of York."

"It was far enough to protect me from gossip. I pass for a widow, of a militia officer. The Sisters have looked after me – which was good of them, for their enemies are always looking for scandal in a convent. A woman in the town cares for Joseph, and I teach in the Sisters' school."

She smiled. "I can wear a cross, when I am within walls there."

Wharton was not diverted. "Can you not move closer to home, now? I would find you a house, could support you and the boy…"

William had crept nearer to the two of them, and could see her firmly shake her head.

"And risk the scandal I have taken such pains to avoid? No, my dearest, that would be folly indeed. I have come back only in the hope of telling you to your face what I will tell my parents tomorrow, that I am going still farther away. My sister has come to live nearby, so I need not fear for them any more. Joseph and I are booked on a passage to America next month."

"No, dear God – no… not now I have found you again, you cannot go. You would be much at risk. The French – and those damned Yankees are not to be trusted! Stay in York, if you must, I can visit you privately, no one need know…"

He took her hands, clinging to them, and she did not protest. She lifted her face to him, and her voice was shaking, but she did not give way.

"Wharton…"

And, to his eternal shame, William saw an embrace that seemed to last a lifetime, between his revered grandfather – an old man, in his fifties – and this young, beautiful stranger who had borne his son.

His son. The boy who should – who could – be the master of Kettlethorpe. Illegitimacy was not, after all, an absolute bar. That was something that William had learnt, only this year, in a way he could not forget.

In one of those quarrels that spring up from nowhere, in the middle of a game, when tempers are high, a boy at school with him had suddenly shouted: "You son of a bastard!" Common enough abuse, but there had been an edge to his voice, enough to make William see red. He had charged his tormentor, pummelling furiously if ineffectively. On hand to save him for once, William's brother had plunged in, and torn the two younger boys apart.

Mopping William's bloody nose with his kerchief, he told his brother that though Royston shouldn't have said it, it was true. Their father was, in truth, a bastard. It was widely known. Sir John had told his eldest son, before he left for school, but no one had bothered to tell William.

Their father had been legitimised, the elder boy explained to William with impatient embarrassment, so he could inherit Ripley. Yes, it could be done.

※

William was still at school when, three years later, his grandmother died. When his grandfather came to Ripley for Christmas, William was disgusted by his grief, seeing this genuine emotion as sheer hypocrisy. He waited, expecting every day to hear news of his grandfather's remarriage, but when such news did finally come it disgusted William still more.

Not Rose, but a Miss Amelia Campbell, a lady Wharton had met in London, was to be his bride. When his mother dragged

William along to meet the new Lady Amcotts, he bristled with so much hostility that this inoffensive creature, only glad, at last, to have a husband, shrank back and begged her dear Sir Wharton not to invite "that awkward boy" again.

"Of course he may fear for his inheritance, I realise that, but he should learn manners, surely, my dear, if he is to profess to be a gentleman?"

Wharton could not disagree: and he was hurt by William's behaviour. He had not confessed it to Amelia but he had, in fact, told the boy that he would still leave Kettlethorpe to him, whatever new family he had. This, he said, was only right, since it had come to the family through his grandmother. And it should have settled all William's fears.

But it seemed to make no difference. The young man came as little as possible. His excuse was that he was now also the heir to his father's estates in Yorkshire, for his elder brother had been purchased a commission, left proudly in his regimentals, and died of his wounds after his first engagement.

When his grandfather died, in 1807, William succeeded to Wharton's baronetcy, and his interests in East Retford. And on her next journey to Kettlethorpe, his mother insisted that William accompany her.

It was a sad visit. Wharton's widow had gone south again, back to her family, taking only as many of her husband's possessions as Brampton would permit. He was skilful at hiding things, or pronouncing them damaged beyond repair. Lady Ingilby giggled a little at the trophies he produced for her, but then wandered sadly around the empty rooms, alone with her memories of a cherished childhood.

She spoke to the Rector, the agreeable Charles Massingberd, presented to the living by Wharton shortly before his death, and offered to dig into her own pocket to rebuild the church. She urged William to take an interest: it would be his estate, after all. But he evaded her, wandering indifferently around the park, wondering how easy the house would be to let. He looked at the great avenue of elms with something close to hatred: perhaps they could be sold for timber. Ice-House Wood, too.

Walking back along the drive, he encountered Brampton, who pulled up short and waited for him to approach. "Your mother says you'll be here while Sunday. Anything you want to see?"

William shook his head, not looking at Brampton.

"Gone off Kettlethorpe, have we? Or do we prefer Yorkshiremen to us yellow-bellies, nowadays?"

William hunched his shoulders and made to walk past, but Brampton blocked his path. "You'd best tell me what you have in mind for the place, since you won't tell your mother, poor duck."

"This place," William said. "It isn't mine." He breathed in, and with the expulsion of that breath let go what he'd never voiced in over a decade. "He had a son."

Brampton nodded, quite unconcerned. "That he has, and the boy's growing up in America, with a different name and that. Your grandad saw him right. He'll not be coming back to bother you."

William was astonished. Was there anything Brampton didn't know? "How did you find out?"

"Didn't the Master send me over to find him, after your grandmother died? He had some daft idea of marrying the boy's mother, making all right and tight, he said. But she'd married herself by then, smart girl as she was, to a farmer like her own kind, and the boy took his name. I'll remember it in a minute."

He scratched his head. "Carroll. That was it."

It was too much for William to take in. Brampton looked at him, more closely. "I'm telling you the plain truth, now, lad – young Sir." He snorted, anything but respectfully. "The lad has no claim on you and yours."

"Her mother told me where to look for young Rose, as I still think of her. I told the Master, leave it to Brampton. I went to see her kin afore I left, told them Sir Wharton had business in Maryland, and was sending me to attend to it. So I'd had the idea that while I was there, if she lived convenient-like, maybe I could pay a call on their daughter. Didn't say I would, mind, only I might be able to. So they gave me her address, I remember that well enough: Good Fellowship Farm. Near a town called Butler."

He blew out his cheeks. "Fancy sort of names they go in for. Good Fellowship! Can't see one of our farmers nailing that on his gate. And it was quite a journey, I can tell you. Sailed to Baltimore, dodging the Frenchies and the privateers, and me sick as a dog all the way. Bit of a hunt through Maryland, to find where this fancy-named farm was. But they were civil enough to me when I got there, she and her husband, though he was glad to see the back of me. Told me fair enough, he didn't want to see or hear from us again."

"What about the boy?" William asked.

"Joseph, he's called. Jo Carroll, now. Dead spit of your grandad, only he's dark as his mother. I gave her the money, to spend on setting him up. Wants him to go to college." Brampton sniffed. "They'd do better to buy more farmland with the money, it looked good pasture for beasts. Fine hunting country, Miss Elizabeth would've loved it, I reckon. Anyway, nowt more to do. You can forget about young Joseph."

He poked William in the ribs. "And stop blaming Sir Wharton, he wasn't the first, he won't be the last, and she was willing enough, young Rose. She did the right thing, too. They didn't want to hurt your grandma, either of them, and that's to their credit, to my reckoning. She was a fine lady, and your grandad loved her too, in his way."

William could think of nothing to say. Brampton hesitated, then went on, surprisingly gently. "Don't you go carrying this house on your shoulders, lad, nor blaming it for what you feel. If your heart's not in it, you'll not be happy here. This was a good place, in your grandad's time, and he was a good master. Liked to make a bit of a show, and puff off his rank, but no harm in that, and I could always take him down a peg or two, at need."

Another snort, but a kindly one this time. "But nothing lasts for ever. I know that. You look after your mother, and I'll look after

Kettlethorpe, so far as I can. You see her right, and you'll not find me complaining as to what happens after. Like as not I'll be gone first, anyway."

Brampton looked at the sky, always a useful diversion for a man who's said too much. "Black over Will's muther's. Best be getting on before the rain comes."

He swung round for his parting shot, more like the old Brampton again. "But you leave them elms alone. No money there: they won't make the cost of felling 'em. I'm telling you, lad. Leave 'em be."

1808–1914

*I*t was Gussie, not William, who secured the future of the Amcotts family. The unsatisfactory boy became a thoroughly unsatisfactory adult – at least in the view of the Reverend R.E.G. Cole, Prebendary of Lincoln, writing his history of Kettlethorpe a century later. William had, he wrote disapprovingly, "advanced Liberal principles and a decidedly eccentric character". His ownership of Kettlethorpe was "disastrous". And though he married twice, he fathered no children, so his two baronetcies died out. The Reverend Cole seems almost relieved.

Whatever the truth of his character, William clearly never had much time for Kettlethorpe, and allowed it to fall into disrepair: he did indeed try to dispose of the elms in the long avenue, stopping only when he learnt the timber would fetch less than the cost of cutting it down.

I have burdened William with a childhood trauma to help explain all this, but of course that is pure imagination, and I warmly apologise to the Amcotts family for presenting Sir Wharton with the love child. I needed Rose and Joseph not only to excuse William, but to start a vital new thread my story.

They are figments of my imagination, although Rose's refuge is not. The oldest surviving Catholic convent in England started educating girls in York in 1686. It was a secretive business. The convent chapel, built thirty years later, is hidden at the top of a disarmingly plain Georgian building, with eleven separate exits through which those hearing Mass could escape.

During the eighteenth century, despite occasional anti-papist violence, persecution had gradually faded into discrimination backed by law and taxation. Even so, it was not until 1791 that George III's fanatical opposition was overcome, and the Catholic Relief Act removed most of the restrictions. Not, however, until the late twentieth century was the last barrier removed to a Catholic holding public office – the Lord Chancellorship – a mere twenty years before that office itself was effectively destroyed.

By the middle of the nineteenth century, thanks to William's neglect, Kettlethorpe was a wreck, and in the 1860s it was cut down to the size of a modest Victorian vicarage. The grandiose "Park" disappears from the address, and it now becomes plain "Kettlethorpe Hall". It was then let to a variety of farming tenants. Gussie, heiress to the estate, lived with her husband, Robert Cracroft, and her large brood, fifteen miles away at his house, Hackthorn.

The family did not entirely abandon Kettlethorpe: they still, after all, owned a considerable estate there. The great stone escutcheon, bearing the Amcotts arms, was saved and cemented into the facade of the new one. The gatehouse, much-restored relic of Katherine Swynford's time, was preserved. And in 1874, one of Gussie's grandsons came to live in the large Victorian house on the other side of the church.

His arrival was the product of one of those family networks of gentry and clergy so familiar to the readers of Trollope or Austen. Two of Gussie's daughters married two clergymen sons of the Jarvis family, owners of Doddington. And so it came about that one of their sons, Francis Amcotts Jarvis, was appointed, or "presented", by their uncle Weston Cracroft-Amcotts as Rector of Kettlethorpe.

But the Hall itself was not brought back into the family until 1883, when Weston's son Edward made over house and estate to his *younger brother Frederick ("Fritz"). Fritz's wife Emily was to live there for over forty years.*

She would see more changes in her time than in any previous century. Cars. Electricity. Phones. Mains water, ending dependence on wells and the deep Victorian water tanks dug to the side of the Hall. A bathroom – the first in the parish. Tractors, to replace the shire horses that ploughed her lands. Aircraft, passing overhead, not least from the national training college on the heath, RAF Cranwell.

And, in the world at large, great social changes too: the heady scent of revolution, trade unions, strikes, the birth of the Labour party, the Old Age Pension, the subjugation of the House of Lords to the will of the Commons. The shrivelling of two vast workforces, which between them had absorbed the vast majority of Kettlethorpe's inhabitants: domestic service and agriculture. The incursions of women into the professions. Female emancipation, if not yet equality; universal suffrage. Short skirts and shorter hair. Riding astride. The bicycle, the typewriter, radio and the movies.

All these, and more, would come to Kettlethorpe in their time. But in 1914, much of it was still ahead – along with slaughter on a scale that would earn the military expedition that was supposed to be over by Christmas the well-deserved title of the First World War.

LITTLE WILLIE

KETTLETHORPE HALL: 1914–1936

Lincolnshire folk always turned out for a funeral. St Peter and Paul was packed. The county was there in force for old Mrs Amcotts, as well as her family, overfilling the little Kettlethorpe church on a dull autumn day in 1936.

Elsie hadn't been sure whether to come, all the same. She'd had a bit of an argument with herself. Of course there'd be a pew reserved for the servants, but she wasn't one of them, not now. But then thanks for that, at least in part, went to Mrs Amcotts. So on that late autumn day in 1936, Elsie had told Arthur she needed the motor car today, put on her best black coat and hat, asked Dot to give the children tea, and made her way to Kettlethorpe. Now, though she was squeezed in behind the font and couldn't see much, she was glad she had come.

She was seated just under the war memorial plaque, and the names of the fallen, familiar from so long ago, took her straight back the wartime years. Despite all that had come after – marriage, a comfortable home, a growing family – they were still so vivid to her. A time of suffering and loss, but also, for Elsie and many girls like her, a time of change and opportunity. In her corner perch she found herself crowded by memories as well as people – memories of Kettlethorpe, yes, but still more of the year she had left.

She could feel again the optimism of a naive sixteen-year-old, determined to make her way in the world. Today, she thought, she could never summon up the mixture of courage and bluff she had brought to her adventure. She could taste the excitement and terror of her first day in her new job. But above all, what came back to her was the elation of that night in September 1915, when the "proud parents" had announced the successful delivery of their mechanical baby. The night when she and Patrick had in their turn delivered the news to the Admiralty. A time when she, Elsie, a smallholder's daughter, a skivvy, had been a little part of history.

*

Daylight soaked through the thin, faded curtains, into the little back servants' bedroom. Mary stirred, muttering, but to Elsie's relief she did not wake. She knew Mary thought her room-mate strange enough, without seeing Elsie creep out of bed to perch on the window ledge, and scribble in her notebook. Elsie did not much mind what the other girl thought; after all, Mary was leaving today. But she was nosey and talkative, and a stream of questions as to what Elsie was doing, and why, would eat deep into this precious time.

It was October, 1914, and the year was well on the turn. There was little enough time before the girls needed to scramble down the ladder staircase to the scullery, and start work. When Mary was gone, Elsie would have to do her work, too. She couldn't see Mrs A hiring another skivvy, not with this war started, Master Jack away to the Navy and Miss Sylvia over to nurse at Hackthorn, as a VAD. And Captain Weston wouldn't be coming home any time soon.

Mary was thrilled to be leaving. Kettlethorpe was a poky little house, she'd grumbled, with a servants' hall not much bigger than a cupboard. Mrs A was a tartar, and the parlour maid Eliza just as bad. But Elsie knew there were many worse places. And if Mrs A had a sharp tongue, doubtless she'd needed one — she'd been a widow for seventeen years, with a lot on her plate.

He'd been hunting-mad, the Major. And he'd died, aged only forty-three, on a day out with the Burton, over near Baumber, surviving his fall only long enough to say it was nobody's fault but his own. He'd died doing what he loved best, they said, but that, Elsie thought, could have been small comfort to his widow. Emily Grace Cracroft-Amcotts, at thirty-eight, was left with three children and the estate to run on her own.

That she'd done, with boundless energy. Nothing happened in Kettlethorpe, Fenton or Laughterton without Mrs Amcotts' say-so. The estate owned the schoolhouse, and most of the shops; she was President of the Women's Institute, kept an eye on the Sunday School, and above all was patron of the church, with of course the right to "present" the Rector; and if you wanted to rent one of her cottages, you'd get a quizzing as to your church-going habits.

She was a big supporter of the new Boy Scouts, and had found a piece of land at Laughterton for the Gainsborough Troop to camp on; and she'd always hand out the prizes to the winners in the annual produce show. Tartar she might be, but to Elsie's way of thinking, that was a lot better than dwindling into one of the fussy old ladies that abounded in some of the gentry's other houses hereabouts.

It was all the more remarkable in that she had been at the Hall for less than three years before Major Cracroft-Amcotts was killed. The family had owned Kettlethorpe, of course, for over a century, but until 1894 the house had been let to a family of farmers. A new farmhouse had been built for the Gourleys at the other end of the great elm avenue, when the Major — a younger son — had wanted to take the Hall back.

He had grown up at Hackthorn, the family's big Georgian house, north of Lincoln. Mary had yearned to work there, when there had been a young footman to simper at, and more maids to giggle with, not just Cook and Eliza — and then Elsie with her books. But

Hackthorn was a hospital now, and Mary had said she wasn't going there to empty bedpans and boil up bedsheets, even if it was full of handsome young soldiers. She was going farther south to a house where it sounded as if they didn't know there was a war on at all.

Elsie sighed. She was wasting time, brooding on Mary, and she wanted to finish this test. She was following bookkeeping and shorthand courses by correspondence. They absorbed much of her spare time, and her small earnings, but were her way to greater things.

She kept her books and pencils in an old pillowslip, which of course had aroused Mary's curiosity. She had shrieked with laughter when she had pulled them out. Shorthand, what was that? It looked daft! Hadn't Elsie done enough sums at school? And school, in Mary's view, was something you left as soon as your mother could find you a place.

Not Elsie. She had been glad to get to school, her refuge from a home life of violent father, ailing mother and failing farm. But her mother's death had threatened to put an end to her education. The day after the funeral, her father had barged his way into the schoolhouse, to demand that Elsie came home to mind the house, pigs and poultry. He had, however, been foolish enough to do so on one of Mrs Amcotts' days for a visit.

Kettlethorpe School, it was called, though it was a mile away in Laughterton, because it belonged to the Kettlethorpe estate. Mrs Amcotts took a keen interest. Any girl who did not bob a curtsy to her, any boy who did not tug his forelock, would receive a sharp rebuke, but she kept the school building in good order, even when the estate was short of money.

There were two classrooms, and two cloakrooms into which they had to squeeze at midday, on those days – so many days – when the playground was too wet or chilly to eat their pieces outside. There were two earth closets, and two bowls of water to wash in, which were thick brown soup by the end of the day. But the classrooms were dry, and warm from the stove that served both. So far as Elsie was concerned, it was a haven.

When her father had lurched through the schoolroom door, Elsie, just eleven years old, had been reciting *The Lady of Shalott*, in a high, clear voice. She stood next to Mr Stevenson's desk, facing the senior class – a thin stick of a child in black dress and grey pinafore, eyes as pale as a winter sky, white skin sprinkled with freckles.

Her curly, red-gold hair was tied back tightly with a rag: Mr Stevenson was a stickler for neatness. One day, Elsie had promised herself, she'd have blue hair ribbons. Just like Daisy, the baker's daughter, sitting there in the front row in her crisp white pinafore, with her yellow ringlets and milk-and-roses complexion, conscious of the boys' admiration and caring little for the words of England's greatest poet.

For that was what Lord Tennyson had been, Mr Stevenson had frequently assured his pupils. "And what's more," he would add – so predictably that the class would anticipate him under their breath – "he was a fine Lincolnshire gentleman, too. From over in the Wolds."

Mrs Amcotts was not a great one for poetry. *The Field* and *The Lady* were her preferred reading. But she loved to hear the Kettlethorpe pupils recite – and she approved of Tennyson, too. What's more, as Elsie had reminded Mary, whenever she called their mistress a tartar, Mrs A wasn't one who believed that servants knowing their place meant they shouldn't try to improve themselves. When Elsie's father had appeared to demand his daughter's return, Mrs Amcotts had told him to take off his cap and hold his tongue while she spoke to the schoolmaster. And before the whole class, she had asked whether Elsie was a good scholar.

Elsie had flushed to the roots of her hair when Mr Stevenson told his patron the girl was the best pupil he had. Daisy had tittered, the boys had muttered, and Elsie had avoided meeting their angry eyes. But Mrs Amcotts had smiled a tight little smile, and given her ruling.

Elsie would stay at school until she was fourteen, a year after the usual leaving-age, and as far as elementary school would take her. Her father must pay for an honest woman to care for his other children meanwhile. He had a good small farm-holding, and could easily afford it, Mrs Amcotts told him, if he'd give up strong drink and put his back into his work. And when Elsie reached fourteen, Mrs Amcotts herself would find the girl a place.

So now fifteen-year-old Elsie was working at the Hall. But for all she appreciated Mrs Amcotts' intervention, her gratitude had waned: she was longing to make better use of her schooling than scrubbing pans in the scullery. In the past four years Elsie's reading had gone well beyond Tennyson. She even had some suffragette pamphlets under her mattress that she certainly hadn't let Mary see, lent to her by Mr Stevenson's niece Coletta, who had come north from Battersea full of political fervour.

Coletta's uncle would have been horrified to see some of the stuff she had brought with her, on everything from Irish independence to the revolutionary stirrings in Russia. Since Coletta had taken Elsie under her wing, the girl's adolescent mind had been churning with new ideas. Encouraged to see her world in a different light, her instinctive loyalty was fractured by new and powerful resentments.

Some days she was fired into militancy, others it seemed a stupid distraction from real life. And now all that had been washed over by the patriotism that had swept the country into flag-waving excitement, and a war that was supposed to be over by Christmas. And where, Elsie wondered, did that leave her hopes?

The suffragette movement had been put on hold – by most of its leaders – for the duration of the war. It had, in any case, been treated with deep disapproval in the newspapers that came to the Hall, particularly since the occasion when suffragettes had tried to blow up a Grimsby train. Even Mrs Amcotts, who considered it ridiculous that a head of household like herself did not have the vote, had turned against the suffragettes after the events at the Derby last year. It was a pity the poor Davison gel had died, Elsie heard Mrs Amcotts tell her daughter Sylvia, but it had been her own stupid fault, rushing on to a racecourse – Mrs Amcotts' sympathies were with Anmer and his jockey.

Eliza and Cook took the same view. But in all of them, a robust conservatism was mixed with free thinking, a legacy perhaps of Lincolnshire's history of revolt and revolution, tempered into strong liberal sentiments. As for Mr Stevenson, he was old enough to remember the time before the Forster Education Act, and was inclined to remind his pupils how fortunate they were to have been born after it. But in his youth, he had (Coletta said) himself had advanced ideas.

He had once heard Miss Boucherett speak. And he had been greatly influenced by her. Unlike most schoolmasters, therefore, he put as much of his energy into teaching the girls in his school as he gave to the boys, and often compared them, to the boys' disfavour. Perhaps that was why he had spoken up for Elsie. Indeed, Mr Stevenson had wanted her to train as a teacher's assistant, like Coletta, and even perhaps become a teacher, like Alice Crawford, the miller's daughter. But Elsie longed for the wider world. And it was Miss Boucherett herself, or rather her organisation, that had given Elsie the idea of how to do it.

Jessie Boucherett, born into Lincolnshire county society, had become a writer and campaigner of national repute. Her attention, Mr Stevenson had told Elsie, had been caught by the debate about "superfluous women". Way back in mid-Victorian times, he said, it had become apparent that there were more women than were "needed" as wives and mothers. And that there was nothing for the rest of them to do.

Well: nothing for the middle-class ones to do, Elsie had thought. Skivvies, seamstresses, dairy maids – there was plenty of hard grind for her own class. But the efforts Miss Boucherett had made to open employment opportunities for the less fortunate of her social equals had opened chinks of possibility for working-class girls, too.

Elsie was determined to find her way through one of those chinks. Mr Stevenson had given her Miss Boucherett's *Hints on Self-Help for Young Women*. Way out of date, now, of course – quite laughable, in places – but her Society for Promoting the Employment of Women was still thriving, and it was through this organisation that Elsie had found her correspondence courses.

She had chosen bookkeeping partly because she liked numbers. Putting poetry aside – that was for pleasure – arithmetic had been her favourite school subject. But shorthand was the key, she felt, to getting a job in an office; unfortunately, she couldn't learn the new skill of typing. No one in Kettlethorpe – certainly not Mrs Amcotts, nor even her agent – had a typewriter. And she hadn't much hope of getting into a soliticitor's office, or a land agent's: secretaries there spoke nicely, coming from middle-class homes. She couldn't compete with those girls.

In any case, she didn't want to work in a lawyer's or agent's office, endlessly taking dictation from some desiccated old fossil, even if that was the best route to a middle-class life. Elsie wanted to work in a real business.

Lincolnshire was booming with engineering firms. Elsie kept hearing of more of them: Ruston's, Clarke's, Rose's and Foster's. Then there were Hornsby's, Cooke's, Robey's, Clayton and Shuttleworth. They made threshing machines and ploughs, engines and tractors, electric lights and road rollers, train and ship parts. And now, of course, they were making machines for war, for land, sea and even air, like the strange thing called a Sopwith Camel that had got the boys at school so excited, circling over the villages.

Now women were finding jobs in these works, since the men were being drawn away to the war. She had seen pictures in the paper of "munitionettes" – girls with rolled sleeves and caps tied over their hair, wielding drills – but that was not what she wanted. She'd known enough hard physical labour on the farm. And as Coletta had pointed out to her, come the end of the war, the men would take those drilling jobs back.

The picture she kept, cut secretly from the *Lincolnshire Echo* before she crumpled the rest up in the kitchen range, showed something else to aim for. Behind the foreground of stout seated factory managers, there was the blurred image of a statuesque young woman in shirt and tie, clutching a notebook. She was what Elsie wanted to be.

Her test was still not finished. But she could hear sounds of the milk churns being delivered, and whinnying from the stables. Most of the horses had been taken for the war, leaving only the pony that drew Mrs Amcotts' trap, and her daughter Sylvia's elderly hunter. But those spoilt pensioners could hear the boy who came to feed them and muck out, and they were making their impatience felt.

There was little for the coachman to do, now, especially since he couldn't be doing, so he told Mrs Amcotts, with anything that didn't eat hay. It had taken a young mechanic from Fenton to keep the Amcotts sons' motor car on the road. But that, too, had been put away when they left for the war.

The war! Not only was Mary going today, but John Amcotts, "young Jack", was coming home on leave. Embarkation leave, they called it – before he sailed for Lord knew where. His sister was coming home to see him: the pony trap would be busy, to and from the railway station at Torksey.

They would all be busy. Elsie sighed, and put her books away.

*

By evening, the excitement had faded, along with the light of the late autumn day. Mary had left, easy tears streaming down her cheeks, promising to come back and visit, and weighed down with goodies from Cook. Jack had arrived, all shipshape, Eliza said, in his sub-lieutenant's uniform. But after enjoying the flutter of female admiration, he had changed into his old flannel trousers and dived under the bonnet of the precious car. Sylvia had returned too, in her VAD uniform, to a warm but less excited welcome, and the two of them had sat down quietly to dinner with their mother.

The washing-up hadn't taken Elsie long, with only the three of them in the dining room. All she had to do now was put the dinner service away in Eliza's pantry. There'd be many more to cope with over the next few days. Not Captain Weston, though: he was already overseas, with the Royal Engineers, but Mr Edward and his wife from Hackthorn, and Mrs Amcotts' family from Rauceby and Wellingore.

Cook had been planning for weeks, muttering darkly about the rising prices at the butcher's and the shortages at the grocer's. Tonight, however, it was quiet enough for Elsie to think, as she carefully stacked the dinner plates, about what Miss Sylvia had said.

Elsie had taken up Miss Sylvia's hot water, and she had asked Elsie to help her to put her hair up. As the maid struggled to pin the slippery, fair mass into place, Sylvia had asked her whether she would miss Mary.

It was an idle inquiry, to make conversation, but Elsie couldn't help herself: to her horror she found herself pouring out her longing to leave, as well. Sylvia put down her hairbrush, and gazed at Elsie in the mirror.

"I thought you were happy here, Elsie. Happier than at home?"

"I am, Miss, honest, I am – and I know how good Madam's been, helping me to stay at school and then taking me in. But I want to use what I've learned, and what I'm learning now." And in a rush she told Sylvia about her correspondence course, her bookkeeping exam, and her shorthand.

Sylvia swung round from her dressing table, to look at Elsie properly. "Where do you want to go, Elsie? Maybe I could find you something to do in the hospital…"

Elsie shook her head, desperately. "I don't want that, Miss – I know it's wonderful work you're doing, but it'll be over when this war ends, and then where'd I be? I want to find a business that needs someone to keep the books, and will keep me on afterwards. A real business, one of those in Lincoln that makes things. Like tractors, or bicycles – things people'll still want, after the war. Engineering. That's where they say the future is."

Sylvia untangled one last wayward strand of hair, and turning back to the dressing table, began brushing again, thoughtfully.

"But Elsie, I don't know anyone who runs an engineering business. They're not… quite our sort of people."

In the mirror, her blue, puzzled eyes met Elsie's. She was all right, Miss Sylvia; not toffee-nosed, like most young ladies, just honest. What had Elsie expected, after all?

"I know, Miss. Thank you for listening. I'm sorry, it's not my place to have bothered you, I forgot myself. Please don't tell Madam." She took the thick blond strand from Sylvia's hand, and twisted it up on to the top of her head. "There, Miss Sylvia, it looks lovely." It did, too. They were a good-looking family; she often wondered why Miss Sylvia hadn't yet married.

"Of course I won't tell," Sylvia said absently. She had been thinking. "Captain Weston must know lots of the right people, surely – he's in the Sappers, after all. Royal Engineers, that means, Elsie! But I don't know when he'll get leave. Perhaps Jack knows some too, too – they have lots of engineers in the Navy, don't they?"

Their eyes met in the mirror again. And both giggled, joined suddenly across the gulf of class by bafflement about the world of men.

"Really," Sylvia said, "I am stupidly ignorant. I will ask Jack. I promise. I'll write to Captain Weston. And ask Mama. She knows everybody!"

Elsie reran the conversation in her mind as she finished wiping down the shelf. Don't get your hopes up, she told herself severely, most likely Miss Sylvia will forget, or young Jack won't pay any attention, and why should they bother Captain Weston, anyway, while he's away doing something hush-hush in France, or further afield? Not many letters found their way home from him, as she knew from the look on Madam's face when the postman came, bracing herself for disappointment. And true, he was in the Royal Engineers, but that didn't mean he'd know factory bosses in Lincoln.

As Elsie put the silver away, the quiet was broken by an insistent jangle. You could hear the row of bells on the wall of the back hall from the servants' hall, where Eliza and Cook were sitting, but you couldn't see them, as you could from the pantry. "Drawing room!" Elsie called.

The scrape of chair legs sounded resentful. Eliza came out, scowling at the bells suspiciously, as if Elsie could not be trusted to know one from the other, then pushed open the green baize door to the front hall. There was a clink of glasses. More washing up, Elsie thought.

*

Sylvia did not forget. On Jack Amcotts' last afternoon, when the weather was foul and he and his sister had asked for tea in the drawing room, Elsie was summoned. Eliza, stiff with disapproval, told her to take off her apron and go through, smartly now.

"What do they want?" Elsie asked, more to cover her embarrassment than in hope of information.

Eliza wasn't fooled. "I'm sure I don't know, and I hope you do, young Elsie. Here, you can make yourself useful and take this with you."

Grateful for something to do to hide her confusion, Elsie clutched the wooden handle of the silver teapot and scuttled to the drawing room. The fat, elderly Labrador lying at Jack's feet raised his head, hopeful of more biscuits, subsiding with a sigh of disappointment.

Jack glanced at Sylvia, who smiled encouragingly, taking the teapot. "Thank you, Elsie."

He leant forward, linking his hands around his knees. "M'sister tells me you want to go and work for an engineering firm."

Elsie nodded, eagerly. "Yes, Sir. I've done courses – in shorthand and bookkeeping."

"And Miss Sylvia tells me you were a good scholar."

"Not for me to say, Sir, but Mr Stevenson spoke well of me to the Mistress."

"Well: there are lots of those kind of firms in Lincoln, now. I'll see what I can find out. The Navy's using them to build all kinds of machines."

He turned back to Sylvia. "And they are employing women, too. Lots of them. But as munitions workers, mostly."

He hesitated, glanced at Sylvia again, and went on, looking at his hands, not at Elsie. "The problem is, Elsie…" He stopped, flushing.

Sylvia rescued him; she was always the blunt one. Kind, but blunt. "He's not sure they'd want a scullery maid, Elsie. Not in the office, anyway."

"Who wouldn't want a scullery maid?"

Mrs Amcotts stood in the doorway. She was, as even Coletta admitted, still a fine-looking woman: her children's blond hair, blue eyes and rosy complexions had come from her, to judge by the portrait of the Major. Her eyes were darting between Sylvia and Jack. Then they shifted to Elsie, standing silent, and mortified. "Run along, now, Elsie, and get on with your work."

She was glad to escape.

Eliza looked at her shrewdly. "Get what you wanted?" Elsie said nothing. Eliza grunted. "Well, no use fretting. You can help me clean the silver."

It was a full week after Jack and Sylvia had left before Elsie heard more. Mrs Amcotts was in the morning room, a small Victorian addition to the north of the house. She was sitting at the walnut bureau from which she ran her life.

It was a room that still spoke loudly of the Major: the inkstand made from a horse's hoof, shelves of books on hunting, and dark, heavy furniture impregnated with cigar smoke. But most of his trophies – the heads of ibex, moose, bear, even a crocodile – were in the hall, where they had frightened Elsie witless, the first time she was allowed into the front of the house.

When it came to the morning room, however, Mrs Amcotts had been firm. It needed pictures. Nothing too fancy – hunting prints, an old map of Lincolnshire, a small muddy oil painting of Kettlethorpe in its glory days. But pictures, not heads. Anyway, the moose stank. She swung round when Elsie came in, and looked at the girl over the top of her half-moon reading glasses. Elsie bobbed.

"You asked for me, m'um?"

Mrs Amcotts put her pen down. "Yes." She paused, and Elsie wondered if she was going to be told not to bother her betters with her nonsense. But that did her mistress an injustice.

"Master Jack tells me you want to go and work in Lincoln. At an engineering firm. In the office, not on the factory floor. That shows sense. But he's worried you don't have the right experience."

Elsie nodded, thinking: that was a polite way to put it.

"Well. He made a suggestion. I'm not sure I agree with it, but I'll give it a try."

She couldn't refuse him, Elsie thought, going away to the war. But what had he suggested? Please God, not something too daft. I'll have to do it, whatever it is.

"I've had a word with Tuxford. Master Jack thought you could give him some help, and learn from him at the same time. You'll have to fit it in with your work in the house, of course – I'll talk to Eliza and Cook. You can go over to Tuxford's office for a couple of hours in the afternoon."

She paused. There was a glint of humour in her eyes. "You can tidy things up a bit there, anyway. The office needs a good dusting."

*

Mr Tuxford's office certainly looked as if it could do with a clean. Black metal boxes of papers were stacked high; more papers, weighted down by whatever strange objects he had had to hand, were piled up on a big pine table. It had a wobbly leg – as Elsie found when she incautiously lent on it, and the papers slid ominously to the edge. Elsie had to spreadeagle herself across them to stop the avalanche: Mr Tuxford tut-tutted with annoyance.

There were great bundles of bills, each folded into a narrow strip, with a name scrawled on the top. A big Windsor chair sat behind the table; a padded stool, parted sometime from its piano, was placed in front. The small window had clearly never been opened, or cleaned.

Light forced its way through the grime, to sparkle the dust in the air and lick the peeling brown paint. A rose wallpaper had faded to a barely patterned khaki.

Mr Tuxford had been the agent at Kettlethorpe for longer than anyone could remember. He kept the rent roll, organised the estate's workmen, paid the wages and let the tenancies. It was to Mr Tuxford you went, if you were short on rent day, if your roof leaked, if you wanted to sow flax rather than barley, or if your neighbour had moved the boundary fence.

There was nothing he didn't know about the estate, and he was a shrewd judge of people, as new tenants learnt soon enough. As he was fond of telling Mrs Amcotts, he was getting on. But Elsie didn't look to him like the answer to his problems.

He was a small, spare man with a receding grey hairline, counterbalanced by a magnificent pepper-and-salt moustache. He wore a brown cotton working jacket, stained with ink, over his elderly tweed suit, and had an unlit pipe clenched between his teeth. "I wanted Master Jack to take an interest," he grumbled at Elsie, "since the Captain will have the Hackthorn estate. But I don't know what I'm going to do with you, girl. You can make me a cup of tea, I suppose. Put the kettle on the stove, there's a pot somewhere."

It was some time before Elsie was allowed to do anything more. But eventually she persuaded him to let her dust the shelves. No more than that, however: when she tried to rearrange the toppling stacks of black metal boxes, he complained crossly that she was muddling things. "Just dust them, girl, and leave them be." And he guarded his books of accounts jealously, refusing to let her see any of them.

She nearly went to Mrs Amcotts to own that the idea hadn't worked. Elsie was doing nothing, and learning less. Only pride held her back. But it was hard to keep on going, particularly when, back at the Hall, Eliza made clear her disapproval by finding Elsie endless, tedious tasks on her return.

Cook saved her: ten years younger than Eliza, she had more sympathy for the girl's ambitions, and finally spoke up. "Don't be so spiteful, Eliza, Elsie's only trying to make the best of herself. She should have her chance. The world's changing, you know," – a dig that Eliza didn't like. "I say what gets done in this kitchen, and if I say the pans don't need polishing, it's not for you to tell Elsie otherwise."

Eliza looked furious, but said nothing. It didn't do to cross Cook. She might be young, but cooks had ways of making you regret annoying them, when the plates were handed round – the dried-up chop, the shepherd's pie that was all potato, the steam pudding with unaccountably little jam.

And then Elsie's breakthrough came, one freezing afternoon in February, when she'd nearly given up and stayed at the Hall to nurse her cold rather than brave the snow. When she pushed open the office door, the blast of cold air lifted the piles of paper in a flurry, and Mr Tuxford swung round, angrily. Several of the black boxes were on the ground, and open, their contents exposed and disordered.

"Don't bother me now, girl, Mrs Amcotts wants the papers for Stow Park Farm, and quickly." His voice shook, and he looked wildly around, as if the papers might suddenly present themselves. Elsie realised he was in panic, and had been searching for a long time. "I told her how it would be if she let you come here, everything would get disorganised."

Elsie ignored him. He knew she'd moved nothing. But by some miracle she'd remembered seeing Stow on the lid of one of the smaller boxes – she'd been struck by it, having had no idea Mrs Amcotts owned land that far over the Fossdyke. Now she pulled the piano stool over, stood on it, and hauled the right box down. "Here you are, Mr Tuxford. See – Stow Park Farm."

He didn't, of course, thank her. Instead, he went on muttering: there you are, he knew she'd hidden it – he'd have to tell Mrs Amcotts, and goodness knows what she'd have to say about it. But by the following day his innate decency had overcome his shame and resentment, and he'd said that, well, maybe she could sort things out a bit. Just so long as she told him where she'd put everything.

Of course, she said. If he'd allow it, she'd label each box on the side, so you could know what was in it without lifting it down. And he grunted, saying it hadn't been necessary, since he knew where everything was, but now she'd muddled things up, maybe it wasn't such a bad idea. If she had the time to waste.

After that, everything got better. Each day, he grew less grudging, letting her do just a little bit more. One day, he allowed that – just occasionally – she made herself useful. In April, at the Quarter, he began to let her see the books: not to write in them, that would be going too far, but to see how he wrote up the entries.

In a sudden burst of honesty, he admitted that he never used to bother much with the contents of the black boxes. "It was all in my head, you see – I never needed to look up the terms of a tenancy. But now... I keep telling Mrs Amcotts, I'm not as young as I was."

She persuaded him to try dictating a few letters, so she could practise her shorthand. But this wasn't a great success, as he was slow, and embarrassed, and covered it up by complaining about her handwriting. When she suggested he ask Mrs Amcotts to buy a typewriter, he was horrified.

But in June he announced that he was going on a three-day holiday, taking his wife to visit their daughter and her new baby. And provided Elsie didn't actually do anything while he was away, she could be in charge.

It was a start, but it wasn't taking her anywhere. Elsie spent the three afternoons on her own thinking fruitlessly about how she could move on. It seemed, instead, that she was going backwards, for when Mr Tuxford came back, he found fault even with how she'd dealt with old Mrs Hardwick, when Elsie was foolish enough to let him see she thought she'd done rather well. He knew perfectly well there was no pleasing Mrs Hardwick, Elsie thought resentfully, and nearly lost heart again.

The war was changing so much. She'd heard of women taking all sorts of jobs, filling the places of the men who had gone to the front. The factories in Lincoln were full of them. She almost decided to give up on her office ambitions, and sign up for a munitions job. But Jim, her eldest brother, saved her from that mistake.

She went home to see them all most Sundays. Things were better there now. Jim and her second brother, Sammy, were old enough for farm work – and big enough to stop their father ill-treating the little ones. Susie, next in age to Elsie, and the loving heart of the family, was happy to stay home and mind them, and told her father to send home the old woman he'd so grudgingly hired.

But Jim was sixteen now, and longing to enlist. Walking home with them all after church, Elsie reminded him anxiously of his promise, not to go before he was seventeen. Surely, she thought, the war would be over by then? But Jim was tall, and strong, and said he wouldn't stay a day after his birthday, to be given white feathers by women who didn't know his age. Tom could look after the beasts, and the little ones would help.

He was a good brother, Elsie knew, even to think of them: and of Elsie, too. She mustn't give up, he said, and waste all that studying. If she wanted to go to Lincoln, he said, he'd take a day off the farm and escort her. She was touched, but the truth was she still didn't know where to go.

Until Captain Weston came home on leave. Elsie hadn't placed much faith in Sylvia's assurances that he'd help. He'd left home long before Elsie had come to the Hall; he was the eldest of Mrs Amcotts' children. And, so Eliza'd told her, he was the brains of the family. Jack had been sent to Osborne, to train for the Navy, when he was thirteen. But Weston had been to some grand school near Windsor, a "King's Scholar", Eliza had told Elsie, as if she should know what that meant, although Elsie was pretty sure Eliza didn't know, either.

Elsie was a bit scared of him, in a way no one could be scared of Jack. So when Eliza told her she was to go to see him in "the Major's den", images of angry lions came unbidden into her mind.

He was sitting at his mother's bureau, frowning slightly, a big, square-built man – in uniform today, for he'd just come back from a meeting in London. Maids' gossip had it he had been far away on the King's service over the past year, and certainly his fair skin had been burnt by a hotter sun than shone on Flanders. Lines of strain were etched on his young man's face. But his expression was reassuring.

"It's Elsie, isn't it?" She nodded, dumbly.

"My mother tells me you want to go to work in Lincoln."

She nodded again, trying to find the words to explain. He raised his hand, only a little impatiently. "I know, she's told me. You want to work in an office, not on the factory floor. In a business where there are prospects. And you've been studying, and working for Tuxford, to learn... modern office ways."

His voice was dry, and his mouth twitched. But Elsie thought it safest to say nothing.

"All right. My mother spoke to me about you. And as it just so happens, I have an idea."

Don't get excited, Elsie told herself: it's probably just something else on the estate, here or at Hackthorn.

"I have a friend, in the Navy, who might find you useful."

The *Navy?* Not in Lincoln, then...

"He's an engineering genius," Captain Weston went on. "I got to know him when he was at Cambridge. He left to design cars, but he's built boats too, and now he's joined up again – in the Royal Navy's Armoured Car Service."

A glint of humour, surely, again. "Why the Navy needs armoured cars, I have no idea. Anyway, now he's written to tell me he's been seconded to a firm in Lincoln to help design them. And he asked me if I can help to find him a secretary."

He looked at Elsie keenly, and now his expression was more severe. "Mark you, Elsie, this is important work. Top secret. He has to travel a lot, so he needs a secretary in Lincoln he can trust. Discreet. Careful. Are you trustworthy, Elsie?"

She forced herself to speak, not just nod again like a dummy. "Yes, Sir."

"He asked me if I knew a well-educated girl who could do the job."

Well-spoken, he means, Elsie thought: a lady. But perhaps young ladies won't want to work in an engineering factory…

"My mother tells me you were an excellent scholar. Good at sums," – he smiled again – "that's important to an engineer! I've spoken to Mr Stevenson, and he agrees. So I've written to Lieutenant Wilson suggesting that you might fit the bill."

She was almost too astonished to speak. "Thank you, Sir," she muttered, eventually. "But I'm not sure I…"

He went on, regardless. "Lieutenant Wilson will be working very closely with the General Manager at Foster's – Mr William Tritton. So Mr Tritton wants to interview you first. You're to go there this Sunday, and we'll see what they think of you."

Now he paused, and looked a little embarrassed. "Tritton doesn't suffer fools gladly, Wilson says, so it's up to you to impress him that you can do the job. You'll have to – er – smarten up a bit. I've asked m'mother to help. It's a great opportunity, Elsie. You'll need to put on a good show."

*

In the glass in Miss Sylvia's bedroom, it had all looked "a good show". A coat and skirt made for Miss Sylvia when she was fourteen was still too big for Elsie's slight frame, but she had taken it in with Cook's help. And Cook had been inspired to run her up a blouse from an old damask table cloth.

There was nothing that could be done about her boots, except polish them to their best – even as a girl, Sylvia's feet had been much bigger than Elsie's. But at least they could be discreetly hidden beneath her skirt.

Infected by the excitement, even Eliza had helped, condescending to do Elsie's hair, and pinning on Elsie's head the hat her sister Susie had found amongst their mother's things. She'd worn it mostly for funerals, Elsie remembered, and it was a little worse for wear, but better than the battered felt object Elsie had worn to school.

There was quite a little feeling of achievement when they'd finished. Mrs Amcotts, called upon to pronounce, expressed the opinion that Elsie looked quite respectable. The stable boy was co-opted to drive her to Torksey station, and looked satisfactorily impressed. Jim had stuck to his promise to come with her. And at the last minute, Susie had thrust her mother's old black leather handbag, well polished, into Elsie's hand. "You can put your certificates in there."

The train journey to Lincoln had been fine. But now, as Elsie walked down Waterloo Road on Sunday afternoon, her confidence slowly evaporated. The heavy bag banged against her thigh, making her wish she'd had the heart to refuse it. Her tweed coat and skirt were hot in this sultry weather, and out of the corner of her eye Elsie could see her nose was shining with sweat. Damp tendrils of hair were escaping from under her hat.

How she wished she had Susie's smooth, brown hair, which stayed where you put it. She brushed the stray red curls back, and saw how much of the boot blacking on the handbag had transferred itself to her gloves. By the time they arrived at Foster's, Elsie felt a mess.

The gatekeeper emerged from his hutch, and looked at her doubtfully. But after consulting his clipboard, he nodded her through, telling Jim curtly that he'd have to wait outside. She gave her brother one frightened glance. "You'll be fine," Jim said, patting her on the shoulder, as he would a nervous horse.

"Do I look all right?" Elsie asked, anxiously.

"Just the job." He didn't sound convinced.

Elsie crossed the yard, which was surrounded by large brick buildings. Following the gatekeeper's instructions, she headed for the one on which was painted "William Foster and Company Ltd". It seemed a long way. And it turned out she had gone to the wrong door. Through it she could see, and hear, the pulsating, busy vastness of engineering production, but no offices. Humiliatingly, the gatekeeper shouted after her, pointing angrily towards a smaller entrance to the left.

"Up the stairs. First on your left."

She pulled the door open, and saw an iron staircase, leading up a single flight to a narrow corridor. She stopped, breathless with anxiety, before the first door at the top. Peering through the glass panel in its frame, she saw this office was occupied by a middle-aged lady, of formidable appearance and obvious efficiency.

Elsie paused, drew breath, and beat a timorous little tattoo on the glass.

The lady inside rose, without hurry, and opened the door. She was well upholstered, much taller than Elsie, and knew how to use her height. She wore a high-collared blouse, like the woman in Elsie's newspaper cutting, but instead of a tie, an onyx brooch – a concession to vanity that somehow only made her look more severe.

"Yes?"

Nerves had deprived Elsie of the power of speech.

"Have you come to see Mr Tritton?"

Elsie nodded, dumbly.

"He's very busy." Elsie thought of saying she had an appointment, and thought better of it.

"I'll tell him you've arrived. Wait here."

Once Elsie was on her own, she became capable of taking in her surroundings. There were two desks in the office, placed at opposite ends. The nearest was ferociously neat: an in-tray (empty), an out-tray (full), reference books, an inkstand and spotless blotter, a pencil box and an elderly typing machine, looking slightly out of place.

A large object sat covered on the second, but otherwise there were no signs of occupation. The walls were stacked with box files, but on a corner cupboard there were domestic touches: a tea kettle on a spirit lamp, a biscuit tin covered with appliquéd cut-outs of girls and kittens, some rose-patterned tea cups.

The superior lady was soon back. "You're to go on in." She held the connecting door open. Elsie dropped her gloves, then her bag, picked them both up again, felt more strands of hair come loose, and tried not to hear the irritated sigh her clumsiness provoked. The door shut behind her, and she found herself in Mr Tritton's office.

This room had a curiously unused look, and its occupant looked restless, as if he'd rather be somewhere else. He was a plump, pugnacious-looking man, his shiny waistcoat and trousers tight across his barrel chest and thighs. He was reading something, through his round gold-rimmed spectacles, and pointed Elsie to a chair in front of him. She perched on its extreme edge.

His eyes still on his papers, he said: "So you're what Captain Amcotts has found for us," in the same tone that Eliza would say, "Look what the cat's brought in."

But then he looked up, and she saw that his eyes were shrewd and good-humoured.

"Yes, Sir."

"Mrs Amcotts gives you an excellent character." He tapped the letter. "Says you're trustworthy. Honest. Hard-working. And you've been helping out with estate business."

"Yes, Sir."

"Humph." He leant forward, unclasping his hands, and hammering his desk with his forefinger as he spoke.

"This isn't gentleman farming, you know. It's a real business. Hard graft, and war work. Round the clock." The words were fierce, but Elsie found she was much less frightened of him than of his paragon in the outer office.

"Yes, Sir. I know. That's why I want to work here."

He grunted, and switched his attention to the second sheet of paper. "This schoolmaster of yours, Mr..." – he picked up her reference, scowling at the signature – "Mr Stevenson, is it? He seems to think you're smart as paint." He looked up again, grinning. "At least, I think that's what he's trying to say. You've done a bookkeeping course?"

Elsie nodded, pulling the certificate from her bag. He waved it aside. "Give it to Aggie – Miss Twisterton. And shorthand?"

"Yes, Sir."

"Right. What do you know about Foster's?"

"Not much, Sir, only that you make big machines!"

"Well, then. Let's try your shorthand. Here." He handed her pencil and notebook, left ready, she felt sure, by Miss Twisterton.

"Take this down: William Foster was a mill-owner. Then he set this place up, as a foundry. A good decision. But he didn't make old bones. So when I came here ten years ago, I can tell you, this place was in trouble."

He paused, to see if she was keeping up. No problem, so far.

"I sorted that out, and we built up a good business, making tractors and threshing machines. Now it's all change again. This, young woman, is top secret, but if you're going to work here, you'll need to know. We're making a completely new kind of tractor. Working for the Admiralty."

He beamed at her.

"I know what you're thinking, girl. Why does the Admiralty want tractors?"

Fortunately, before a bemused Elsie could respond, Mr Tritton rattled on.

"Because they're the only people with the sense to be interested, that's why! That fellow Winston Churchill, when he was First Lord, he started it all. Gave it a good push. Set up a committee, under Mr D'Eyncourt. Told us we could have the contract if we came up with the goods. And sent Lieutenant Wilson to work with us."

He picked up the rest of Elsie's papers impatiently, tapping their edges on the desk to align them, then shoving them aside without a glance. "So that's why you're here. Wilson has to be all over the place. London, of course. Burton-on-Trent as well as Lincoln. That's why he needs a girl – to mind his papers, watch the books, take his messages. You'll have to travel a bit. All right with that?"

Before she could answer, he charged on. "Wilson's been seconded to us, though he's got to keep on with his work elsewhere too. But he's here more and more."

He looked at Elsie, very seriously. "That's because we're on to a big thing. We're making water carriers for Mesopotamia. Know where that is? Well, never mind. Water carriers. Hard to make. Know what the men call them? Bloody tanks!"

He stopped. "Got all that? Read it back to me."

She did, easily, though hesitating at the last couple of words. Mr Tritton grinned. "That's what I said: 'bloody tanks'. Aggie would give me a right talking-to if she heard me. Don't you tell. Here, give me your notes, they'd best be destroyed. Go and see her now, and say I said you're to start Monday week. She'll do the rest. I must get back to the drawing-office."

He bounced up, relishing action, relief obvious at a dull job done, talking as he went. "You're to share her office, and go wherever Lieutenant Wilson wants." As he reached the door, a knock came from the other side, and a very different kind of man looked in.

"Talk of the devil," Mr Tritton said. "Wilson, here's the girl your friend wrote you about. I've told her to start Monday week, but you'd better look at her first."

Lieutenant Wilson came fully in to the office. He too looked in his early forties, balding, with spectacles, but there the resemblance ended. Wilson was taller, quieter, less exuberant: Elsie thought he looked like a teacher, rather than a metal-basher. He was in uniform, but wore it as a doctor wore a white coat – as necessary working clothes, not for military show. He smiled at Elsie. "I'm sure she'll do very well." Elsie's spirits soared.

Wilson turned back to Tritton. "William, I've thought of a workaround I'd like you to see. Rigby's drawing it now." In his eagerness, Tritton almost pushed Wilson back out the door. "I knew you would." He glanced back at Elsie. "Run along to Aggie now, and tell her what I've said. She'll give you the drill." He chivvied Wilson ahead of him, talking as they went.

Miss Twisterton didn't seem the least surprised at how little he'd told Elsie. "Monday, then. We start at six in the morning – sharp, mind you – and you can leave at six in the evening, unless Lieutenant Wilson needs you later. That's the same as the shift on the shop floor. Every second Sunday off – and time for church on the other Sunday, of course. Eighteen shillings a week. Have you anywhere to live?"

"No, Miss – not close enough."

"You call me Miss Twisterton. I thought you'd need a lodging, so I've spoken to one of the charge hands who lives close. A respectable family, and his daughter Dot is just starting as a machinist. There are lots of girls working here now, though all the charge hands are still men, of course. You can share a room with Dot. You'll have most of your meals here, of course, but her mother will give you something after work, and do your washing. Seven shillings a week."

Miss Twisterton consulted her notes, though Elsie thought she probably had no need to. "Ah, yes. Dress. You must be neat, with your hair out of your way." She looked pointedly at the wisps curling down Elsie's forehead. Miss Twisterton's own hair looked as if it had been glued into place. "You don't wear a cap, or overall, like the girls on the shop floor. Your own clothes. They must be respectable – clean and tidy. And no foolish behaviour – particularly," – she paused, lowering her voice impressively – "with the men."

"No, Miss Twisterton."

She nodded, pleased. "Then…"

But Mr Tritton was back, breezing in from the corridor. "I nearly forgot. I bought something for the girl to use, Aggie. Bang up to date, not like the old thing you cling to. They should've put it on her desk. Take the cover off, and we'll show the girl."

But he didn't wait for Miss Twisterton, bounding over to the empty desk to whip off the cover himself.

"A brand new British model," he said, his voice softening with an engineer's love of machines. "Imperial. Made in Leicester. Saw it at an exhibition. Thought we should have one."

Elsie looked at it in horror. It looked nothing like the pictures of typewriters she'd studied. The letter keys bristled out from the machine like the spines on a hedgehog. Her fingers twitched, nervously, and she clutched her bag tightly to control them.

"They told me it's a 'Qwerty', Mr Tritton went on. "Made me laugh, till they said that's how the letters are placed, and I had a go m'self, for fun."

Miss Twisterton was rolling her eyes in disapproval, but Mr Tritton ignored her. "They said that's how you'll have been trained. Aggie's got one of the old ones. Can't get her to change. Maybe she'll change her mind when she sees you banging away on this one."

Well: she'd do her best, Elsie thought, but it was one thing to practise on a keypad traced on a piece of paper, quite another to stretch her fingers across the hedgehog's back, and try to hit the keys with the right strength.

Mr Tritton hadn't finished. "Look, they've designed it so if you sit up straight, you can even see what you're typing, as you go. That's new, I'm told! They've changed the way the keys strike, lifted up the platen. Clever. Big difference. It means you can spot any mistakes you make, right away."

There'll be plenty of those, Elsie thought.

"And look at this."

Would he never stop? She must concentrate, she told herself, it might be her only chance to learn about the infernal machine before she had to use it.

"Look, girl, here – they call it a tab key. Handy for figures – puts 'em in columns."

Elsie gazed at it, trying to commit to memory the way he'd used it to limit the movement of the carriage. Pray God she had some time on her own, to master the Imperial, before it mastered her.

Miss Twisterton cleared her throat in a minatory fashion, and Mr Tritton swung round – half annoyed, half apologetic. He was just in time to see a small man in a brown overall appear in the doorway, loaded with account books.

"Ah. Here's Broughton. He manages the books. You can help him when Lieutenant Wilson doesn't need you. He'll show you the ropes."

It was almost a relief, to face a problem Elsie had dealt with before. Mr Broughton wore the same expression as the agent at Kettlethorpe: a mixture of suspicion and resentment, though in Mr Broughton's case, also fear. Mr Tritton abandoned the typewriter.

"Afternoon, Broughton. All right, all right, Aggie, I'm off. Leave it to you."

Miss Twisterton took over.

"Mr Broughton's been with us ever since the early days of the Wellington foundry. Knows everything about Foster's."

Mr Broughton nodded, expressionless, not looking at any of them. Elsie caught sight of the thickness of his spectacle lenses: he must be extremely short-sighted.

"He's been wanting to retire for years," said Miss Twisterton, leaving Elsie in no doubt who wanted this most. "But we haven't been able to spare him, now both of his clerks have joined up. He's willing to teach you their job, now there's no man we can find to take it on." Mr Broughton sniffed. Yes: it was, Elsie thought, Mr Tuxford all over again. Oh well, she'd found her way to work with him, she could do it again at Foster's.

"His office is opposite, though we have to use the boardroom, too, now. Mr Pennell – he's our chairman – doesn't mind. He's not here that much. With all these new orders there's a lot of paperwork. We'll be getting new clerks as soon as we can."

Elsie was too young, and had had too much of a struggle herself, to have spare resources of pity. But even a girl in a hurry could not fail to see how pitiable Broughton was, how reluctant to acquiesce in the ending of what had evidently been, for sixty years, his whole life.

Once gone, he wouldn't live long, even with one of these new Old Age Pensions. Elsie'd seen it too often: men who retired, sat by the fire and stayed there, until chased out of doors for a "nice walk" by impatient women wanting to clean up their fathers' pathetic little messes. Pretty soon the old men turned their faces to the wall, and lost the will to go on.

She could not be sorry that the war had given him a reprieve. And to her own surprise she found herself saying, "It's very kind of Mr Broughton. I know there's so much he can teach me."

The thick lenses glinted. His small, rheumy eyes peered at her suspiciously, and seemed, against his will, to like what they saw. Grudgingly he said: "I'll do me best, duck."

A fleeting smile crossed his sad old monkey's face. "But I can't help with that newfangled thingy Mr Tritton's bought you – spider's breakfast, I call it. Ten pound the bill was, too. Shocking. I said to him, that young girl you've found, she'll break it in a week, and then where'll you be?"

Oh dear, Elsie thought, that's all too likely.

Miss Twisterton sniffed, though whether at Mr Broughton or Elsie it was hard to say. "You'll work up here, but you should get to know the whole place, in case Lieutenant Wilson or Mr Broughton want to send you with messages. And I'll get one of the girls to show you the, er, facilities."

She paused, waiting to be given the books Mr Broughton was clutching, but the old man just stood there, blinking behind his heavy lenses.

"Thank you, Mr Broughton, I'll take those for Mr Tritton to look at. You'll see Elsie Monday week." He pottered meekly off.

Miss Twisterton looked again at her notes. "I think that's all, if you give me your certificates – I don't suppose Mr Tritton asked you for them. Dot's mother is expecting you a week today. They live close to the back gate to Foster's. Here's the address. Coulson Road. Foster's owns the house."

She looked at Elsie, nodding dismissal. Elsie longed to see how good she was at typing, but she couldn't hang around to watch, especially as it didn't look as if Miss Twisterton's machine got much use. She did a little bob – like a schoolchild, she told herself crossly afterwards – and left.

Mr Broughton was still waiting in the corridor. "Thought I'd show you where my office is, afore ye go." He pottered down the corridor, not waiting to see if Elsie was following, to the last door on the right. It was very different from Mr Tuxford's – there was a row of modern metal filing cabinets, a shelf of neatly labelled account books, a table scrupulously clear of papers.

Mr Broughton began to tell her what was what, but in truth she took in only one word in ten. To stop him, she began to ask every question that came into her head, until exhaustion from the excitement of the day overcame her.

"I'm very sorry, Mr Broughton, but my brother's waiting. I have to get back – there aren't many trains on a Sunday. I'll see you next week."

*

It was kind of Susie to stay and help with Sunday school, kinder still to leave Jim and Elsie to walk home alone after church. A last chance for both of them, as Jim was leaving tomorrow. Elsie had made a last try to get him to stay – to come to work at Foster's instead.

She'd told him the men now had special badges, showing they were doing essential war work, so that no one could call them shirkers. The Admiralty, Mr Broughton had told her, had been reluctant to issue the badges, saying it would bring attention to highly secret work, but had finally relented, after learning from Lieutenant Wilson how many skilled workers they'd been losing to the trenches.

Jim, however, wasn't persuaded. Cal Grimes, who lived at Hall Farm in Newton, had wangled him into the posh Lincolnshire Yeomanry, by supplying horses for both of them. Jim was going to Lincoln with her again tonight, and the regiment was off to Southampton the same week.

There wasn't the heady excitement that had gripped the first recruits. The boys signing up in 1915 were burdened by scraps of knowledge about the reality of war. There'd been the telegrams to wives and mothers. There'd been news of brothers and friends who had been sent home, wounded, burnt, shell-shocked.

The lucky ones, home simply on leave, had said little, blotting out the past for fear of the future. But those who did speak told of mud-filled trenches where the troops huddled for days, before going "over the top" towards other trenches filled with the enemy. They told of a war of small distances gained at dreadful cost, only to be lost again in moments. The talked of the mud – endless mud, in which you lived, and which sucked you down to die. Yet still the boys like Jim were joining recruitment parades, coming home proud in their new uniforms to say goodbye, heading off full of a patriotic ardour that seemed to Elsie to make them younger even than they were.

"You will write?" she asked, for the tenth time, and for the tenth time was not reassured by Jim's answer; he had never been much for writing.

"And to Betsy?"

Elsie felt the burden of the girl, who had been walking out with Jim ever since they were fourteen, and still seemed to have no idea of what he was going to, or how long he might be away.

That last evening, she had chattered of small preoccupations, as if he were off with the Scouts to Mablethorpe again. Elsie had drawn breath to reproach her, caught Jim's eye and let it go again. A tearful, frightened Betsy would be more than he could bear. Best she went on in happy ignorance, fearing nothing.

As Mrs Amcotts could not. When Elsie went to the morning room before church on Sunday, to pay her parting respects, she was struck by how the mistress had aged. The harsh morning light found out the marks of stoicism, etched into her face over the years of widowhood, deepened now by worry over her sons. But she gave the girl her full attention.

"I wish you every good fortune, Elsie. And I shall expect full reports from Molly as to how you are getting on." Elsie's next-sister-after-Susie, twelve-year-old Molly, had come to work at the Hall. She was young for it, and painfully shy, so Elsie had been anxious about how Eliza would treat her – but she seemed to have taken the older woman's fancy, and Eliza was mothering Molly in a way she had never tried to do with her elder sister.

Elsie stopped at the servants' hall, to say her last goodbyes. Her hand already on the door, she heard Eliza telling Cook what a good girl that Molly was, careful and neat, not like the other one. Elsie hitched up her parcel of belongings, set her chin and walked resolutely out the back door, banging it behind her. Let them see if she cared. Good riddance to them all.

She could wait in the church for Jim. He would carry the parcel for her afterwards: they were going in to Lincoln together. But a call made her turn back: Eliza, to her surprise, was beckoning her, waving a brown canvas bag.

"That's a nice way to leave, without a word to us. And there I was waiting for you, with this thing of mine for you, so you don't shame us with that untidy parcel." She didn't meet Elsie's eye, embarrassment written on her own face.

She wasn't such a bad old thing. On impulse, Elsie gave her a hug. Eliza pushed her away, flustered, but Elsie saw the brief flush of pleasure.

"Don't you go messing me up, in me Sundays, and don't waste your thank-yous on me, mind you thank Cook, she suggested it. You go back and see her now, she's got something for you to take to these Lincoln folk giving you a bed. Can't have you arriving empty-handed, she says. And you can pack your bag in the servants' hall, can't have you doing that out here for the gentry to see."

*

It was a month before Elsie could make any sense of Foster's, and her work there. The days seemed to flash by, and to begin with she was always staying late to catch up. She was horribly homesick for

Kettlethorpe at night. Her supper was waiting when she dragged herself back to Coulson Road, but usually dried up by then, and everyone else abed: Dot was usually fast asleep. She missed Cook, and Eliza, even Mary.

Still, she got a hearty breakfast and dinner in the canteen. Cook wouldn't have thought much of the food, but Elsie was ravenous, and it was hot and welcome. At first she'd hesitated about going to join Dot and the other girls. They'd looked confident, proud to be doing a man's job, and she'd been afraid they might be contemptuous of her office work. Still, anything was worth risking to avoid taking every meal with Miss Twisterton. So one morning she'd walked over, and asked Dot if she could sit with her.

Dot had squeezed up to make a space, and made the girls on the other side – two sisters, Kathleen and Ivy – do the same. It was out of Miss Twisterton's line of sight, where Elsie could gossip happily, or still better nod off unseen through the duller of the talks Mr Tritton arranged to enliven the breakfast breaks.

But you had to watch out for the engine oil on the munitionettes' overalls: one smear on Elsie's sleeve, and Miss Twisterton would make her spend her next break running back to Dot's house for a clean blouse, and more of Elsie's small earnings would disappear into the washtub. Dot's mother was kind, but she counted the pennies.

Up in the office, Miss Twisterton told poor Elsie as little as possible. Lieutenant Wilson came and went, always in a hurry. Mr Tritton might give her a brisk good morning, if he remembered, but mostly she seemed to be invisible.

So Elsie took mystifying telephone messages, about something called the Landships Committee, and got them wrong; and she banged out reports on the new typewriter, using so much correction fluid that Miss Twisterton complained at the cost. Feeling a failure in her special job, Elsie recovered her self-esteem a little by displaying her skill at double-entry bookkeeping. Mr Broughton seemed grudgingly to welcome her help, but his was a world of numbers, not machines, and Elsie suspected he had little interest in what was being put together in such secrecy.

But gradually, she began to get some idea of what Mr Tritton, Lieutenant Wilson and the chief draughtsman, William Rigby, were trying to do. Mr Rigby was patient. The messages Elsie brought from Lieutenant Wilson were often for him, in the drawing office, and as he tried to disentangle them he saw that Elsie needed to understand a little more to be of much use. He rarely seemed to leave his drawing board, but he explained things to her, more clearly than anybody else seemed able to do.

Unlike Tritton and Wilson, he was a local man, and spoke in accents familiar to her, not with a sharp London voice. He'd had his schooling in Lincoln, and come to Foster's as an apprentice, so he told Elsie, in 1904. And he was younger than the other two, dark-haired, with strong, angular features. He'd made his way up the firm rapidly, drawing designs for all kinds of new agricultural vehicles. He became Elsie's hero; she dreamt about him before falling asleep, and was thrilled when he showed her his design for the latest "tank". So he took her down to see it.

A second iron staircase led from a platform at the end of the office corridor, straight into the works. It was like walking into a storm. A confusion of sounds – drilling, metal-cutting and hammering – assaulted Elsie's ears. The darkness was punctuated by the glow of tungsten filaments above the benches, the sparks from the metal work, the angry red glow of the furnace. It was a little time before Elsie could begin to work out what was going on.

Most of the drilling was being done by the girls she'd seen in the canteen, in their blue overalls, with their hair tucked into their caps. Some were even younger than Elsie. There were lots of them, at work on slabs and sheets of metal. The noise they made soon began to make her feel dizzy. She wondered how the girls could stand it; but at mealtimes they seemed cheerful enough.

Mr Rigby was moving fast through the works, and Elsie hastily started paying attention again. "Follow me, and keep close," he shouted, and Elsie did as she was told, shrinking from the noisy, frightening machinery being operated on either side of the narrow gangway. One day Dot had come home with the sleeve of her overall ripped off, through inattentiveness: she'd been lucky, her father had said, not to lose her arm. The floor was slippy with oil, and when Mr Rigby stopped, Elsie nearly slid into him.

He had halted only to open the door at the end of the building and head on into the construction shed. Two lines of landships, at various stages of development, stretched ahead of them. Mr Rigby finally came to a stop before one with a swarm of men working on it, under arc lights. It was like a giant coffin, Elsie thought, barely twice her height but three times as long as it was high. Above a long wheelbase covered by tracks on each side, pieces of flat boiler plate were being riveted together to make the hull. And for the first time, she understood why this might be a job for the navy.

The "tank" wasn't like any tractor, or threshing machine, she'd ever seen. Most of those resembled huge metal insects, with men perched on top, rather as her fingers perched on top of the typewriter. This was more like the cargo boats she'd seen steaming up the Trent. Its squat hull, with its caterpillar tracks beside, gave it a curiously amphibious look. Only small observation holes, like shark's eyes, punctured its sides. It was a primeval creature, taking an evolutionary rest on some muddy shore. The only thing that made it look at all like motor transport was a wheeled unit attached to the back.

The noise was even worse here. Elsie'd soon had enough. She tugged at Mr Rigby's sleeve, and pointed back to the door. He nodded briefly, distracted by a man who had just joined them. Elsie recognised him: Charlie Maughan, Foster's Chief Tester. Charlie was "a character", Miss Twisterton had told her, quite without respect for anybody, even Mr Tritton. But he was, she had added reprovingly, as if it had been Elsie who had passed comment on him, a man greatly respected for his skills.

Elsie left them to it. As she wove her way cautiously back along the line of vehicles, she thought of the men who would have to sit inside them. She remembered being told they'd been having trouble making the machines light enough to move at all; the engine was at the limit of its capacity. There'd been endless, unsatisfactory recalculations. But there wasn't a better engine to be had for love nor money, Mr Ribgy said, than the Daimler-Knight. It'd have to do.

"This war is reaching a stalemate. The side that's first to make a machine that can roll over the trenches, that's the side that will win. That fellow Churchill, he understood, for all he was a horse-soldier."

It was the first time Elsie had come up against the idea that the war was something England might lose. Our boys were dying in their thousands; everybody knew that. But nobody talked of losing the war, or of anything other than courage and good leadership being needed to win it. Mr Rigby, however, seemed to think it was all about machines.

Last year, he'd told her, they'd made something they'd called a Trench Crosser – a tractor with track links wrapped around each of its wheels, to roll over ground and trench both. The wheels were huge, and even then the Trench Crosser needed to lay its own bridge across the biggest trenches to get over them. So it was very slow, and easy to attack. Mr Rigby had driven it himself, down at the trials in Shoeburyness, and the bridge-laying had taken a full ten minutes. That, he'd said, was never going to win them the war. "It'd be blown to bits before the bridge was down."

So now, he said, they were working on a new idea – with a single stretch of track links wrapped round a row of wheels on each side of the machine. That made the track long enough to roll over a trench without laying down a bridge first. And the contract from the Landships Committee for the first one had just come through.

They called this new kind of armoured tractor the No. 1 Lincoln Machine – though the boss, Mr Rigby said grinning, liked to call it the Tritton. But whatever it was called, they were making slow progress. The big trouble was still the track.

"It's a tough one," Mr Rigby told Elsie, when they were back in the office. "The Admiralty says the darned thing's got to be able to climb a parapet four foot six high, and cross a trench five foot wide. And deal with barbed wire and mud in between, without getting stuck."

Over at Burton-on-Trent, he told her, Lieutenant Wilson had been using Bullock tracks from America. But Mr Tritton didn't like them. They might work fine on the open American prairies, he said, rolling over mile upon mile of dry, level ground. They didn't work on broken, war-torn ground, with mud-filled craters and tangles of barbed wire. The tracks sagged, and kept slipping off the wheels.

"What we need," Elsie heard Mr Tritton tell Lieutenant Wilson, "is a completely new kind of track. We'll not get anywhere without it."

"So there you are – we're burning the midnight oil on this one," Mr Rigby said. "Up at the White Hart."

Elsie knew that. She'd been backwards and forwards with papers, along Waterloo Road and the High Street, through Stonebow and up Steep Hill to Bailgate, which housed Lincoln's best hotel. Mr Tritton had commandeered the Yarborough Room. The three men worked late there every night, reducing rejected ideas to ashes in the small fireplace, sending Elsie back with others to be tested out at Foster's.

"Mr Tritton says we think better away from the office," Mr Rigby had told Elsie. "No distractions. I reckon you'll wear out a good deal of shoe leather afore we're done. Ah well, it's worse for poor Miss Ghillies."

Elsie looked blank. She knew Miss Isabella Ghillies was Mr Tritton's fiancée – Miss Twisterton had deigned to explain that, after a pleasant, well-dressed lady, with a slightly resigned manner, had turned up at the office one day. Not young, at least not to Elsie, though a good deal younger than Mr Tritton. But what had she to do with the No. 1 Lincoln Machine?

"Mr Tritton has said he won't agree a wedding day until this track problem is solved," Mr Rigby explained, "for all she's waited years for him. But she knows his work comes first."

As it did with Mr Rigby. At Foster's they said his drawing board folded out to make a bed, so he never had to leave it. He was as dedicated as the other two.

After dark, Elsie had an escort on her walk up to the White Hart. An apprentice was assigned to accompany her. At first he seemed to begrudge the time, taking him away from his mates and machines. Long-legged, and impatient, he walked faster than she could, sprinting ahead and waiting restlessly at the level crossing. After the first trip, she heard him asking the foreman if he couldn't take the pouch himself and leave that slowcoach girl in the office.

But by their third trip he had thawed. She learnt his name – Patrick – and he began to tell her something about himself. He was the eldest of ten, with an Irish mother and no father. None he'd ever known, anyway. His apprenticeship at Foster's, he said, was the family's biggest-ever piece of luck, and it was all down to William Rigby.

Patrick's mother had had a cleaning job at Foster's, and early one morning, she'd found Mr Rigby asleep over his drawings. He'd told her to make him a cup of tea, and when she brought it, made her have one too. She'd not wasted her opportunity to tell him about her wonderful son, having – so Patrick said, wryly – kissed the Blarney Stone. And Mr Rigby had listened, the Saints knew why. "So I got me apprenticeship, four years ago, it was. Four years this month."

In turn, Elsie told him about Jim, and how desperate he had been to join up. Patrick touched his badge, showing him to be on war work. "I wear it so I'll not get called a shirker by some old bitch, but I'll not fight unless I'm made to. Why should I fight for the English, after what they've done to Ireland?"

"But you're making 'tanks' for England! It's the same thing!"

Patrick shook his head. "That's for Mr Rigby, I'm doing it. And so I can be an engineer."

"What about Lieutenant Wilson? Didn't he come from Dublin? Isn't he Irish? And he's an officer in the Royal Navy!"

"'Ascendancy', they call themselves," Patrick said bitterly. "The cheek of it. Bastards who came over with Cromwell, and stole Ireland for the Proddies."

They'd reached Steep Hill now, which was lucky, because Elsie had an excuse to save her breath. Patrick was something new in her life, so much the same in age and ambition, so different in his loyalties. She'd put radicalism aside – for the war, or her own advancement – but Patrick awoke it again, along with other, simpler emotions. At night, he'd replaced Mr Rigby in her last waking thoughts.

Whatever Patrick felt about England, they were both caught up in the excitement of the challenge, watching the faces of the three – Rigby, Tritton and Wilson – when they scrutinised the latest results from Foster's. Wilson was impassive, Rigby always tense. But Mr Tritton was sun and storms, alternately delighted and exasperated, driving them all on with a massive exercise of will. Elsie wondered if Miss Ghillies knew what she was taking on, after another explosion of frustration greeted the test results brought from Foster's.

Sometimes Rigby came back with them to Foster's, to explain his notes, or to look at progress in the construction shed. Everything except the track seemed to be going well, although they knew the Daimler-Knight engine was still a worry. Nothing to be done about that; they'd lightened the hull as much as possible. Patrick muttered that the thin metal walls would never stop a bullet. "Pity the poor lads inside. It only goes about three miles an hour, they'll be a fine target, so they will."

But the track still worried them. Bullock tracks were complicated things, with suspension springs. When the Lincoln Machine had its first outing, they slipped off the guide rollers with monotonous regularity. The weight of the tank was also a problem: at sixteen tonnes, it was more than the tracks could cope with.

Mr Tritton insisted they needed something simpler and more robust, to be capable of carrying the machines across the rutted fields of Flanders. There were only storm clouds now, as time ticked on and the tension mounted in the Yarborough Room. The Admiralty, it seemed, was getting impatient. Every other firm seemed to think the Bullock tracks would do. The contract might be given to one of them.

And then, suddenly, the clouds parted. They started experimenting with an idea Mr Tritton had had, to rivet pressed steel plates along a simple chain link. And one evening in September, Elsie and Patrick arrived at the White Hart to find the three men in a kind of exhilarated exhaustion. Lieutenant Wilson read the notes she'd brought from Foster's, which seemed to make him even happier.

He shared them with Mr Tritton, who slapped his knees with satisfaction, then calmed down enough to scribble a note on a small piece of paper. "That's to go to the Admiralty, Elsie. Take it round to the telegraph office, at once. Wake 'em up if you have to! And on your way out, tell the waiter to bring us three whiskies. Large ones."

The note puzzled her.

New arrival by Tritton out of pressed plate STOP
Light in weight but very strong STOP
All doing well, Thank you STOP
Proud parents

"How can I send this?" she panted, as she and Patrick hurried to the telegraph office. "It's daft! Sounds as if he's had a baby!"

Patrick grinned. Caught up in the excitement of the moment, he grabbed her arm and pulled her up to him.

"Better than that. He's had an idea for the track that actually works. It's all we've been waiting for, don't you see?"

Elsie could see nothing, he was holding her so close. She protested, half-heartedly, and he laughed and let her go.

"Now we can finish the thing. You know what they're calling it?"

"Of course I do," she said. "It's the Lincoln Machine."

"No. It's Little Willie."

"After the Kaiser?"

"Well, that's one story. But I reckon it's after the boss. Mr William Tritton."

*

And that was, of course, only the start of it all. Early in 1916, Mr Rigby let Elsie come to the trials of the next tank model, Big Willie. They were conducted in the dawn – for "security" – on South Common. His Majesty's Landship No. 1, Centipede, the "Wilson", finally "Mother": this one was given no end of different names, but most importantly, the accolade of being the first true tank.

It had the rhomboid shape that would become so familiar. The new-style tracks ran all round the hull, not just around wheels on either side. That was Lieutenant Wilson's bright idea, and it gave Big Willie the look of the future.

Then the tank stopped being a boffin's bright idea, and Foster's went into full production. How many had they made? A few hundreds of Marks 1, 2, and 3, many more of the Mark 4, when even the army began to think them worth having. And that despite the false start of action in June 1916, when they had learnt that one of the first group of tanks to be driven in combat had trundled into the enemy-held village of Flers.

It was a Foster's tank, a Mark I, "Dinnaken", whose production number Elsie could still recall: 759. It was a big moment for the firm. But the engine failed, and the commander, Lieutenant Hastie, had to abandon Dinnaken in Flers – a landmark in every sense – and get his crew to safety in a hurry.

It was a setback, only slightly softened by learning the full story. It seemed that the tanks had gone farther than expected, and so had been unsupported. That was hardly their fault, Mr Tritton angrily pointed out to the team at Foster's, glossing over the fact that rather a lot of them had broken down and got nowhere at all.

Major Wilson (he'd switched to the new Tank Corps by then) did his best to cheer them all up. Everybody knew it had been too soon to have a go. He read them a letter from Mr Churchill to the Admiralty, complaining that "my poor land battleships have been let off prematurely and on a petty scale." But of course Churchill had been sidelined by then, and didn't count for much.

However, production continued, and the Tank Corps was expanded, bolstered by the recruitment campaign for men who had "a way with engines", and the tanks' reliability improved. The following year, when they were deployed at Cambrai in force, they made their mark. And Foster's was so important to the success of this new kind of warfare that King George himself, along with Queen Mary, came to visit. Another big day for Elsie to remember; you could just see her, she'd told Susie and Molly, in the corner of the pictures, on her toes in case Major Wilson needed anything for Their Majesties.

By the end of the war, there were nearly 2,000 men and women employed at Foster's. Elsie was given more and more responsibility, in charge of new clerks joining almost every week. They were keen as mustard, for by then the tank had become famous. The two Mark IVs kept in England for fundraising had only to rumble into a city for huge crowds to gather: the "tank banks", they called them. Elsie herself bought a war bond she could ill afford, for 12s 6d: she'd cashed it, in the early 1920s, for £1.

The tanks even had their own song, intoned to the tune of the National Anthem, written (of course) by Mr Tritton. How did it go?

The glorious Foster Tanks,
Have smashed the German ranks...

Postcards with the lyrics printed on them sold for a penny – Elsie still had one in a drawer at home, somewhere – and she was told to calculate the profit and pay it into a comforts fund for soldiers, sailors and "tank boys". The cards raised a tidy sum.

And then it was all over. The munitionettes lost their jobs, as the men came back, but Elsie kept hers, looking after the books at Foster's until she married. Mr Tritton had got his knighthood, and his promised prize, but unlike other munitions bosses he hadn't been greedy: he'd given his share of the £15,000 to the workers, saying he had enough. Major Wilson used his share of the tank prize to invest in new engineering projects, starting a business focused on transmission units. But William Rigby seemed happy to go on working at Foster's. In 1920, he was best man at Elsie and Arthur's wedding.

Patrick was long gone by then, back to Ireland. He'd been executed for his part in the East Rising, unlike his hero, Eamonn de Valera, who'd been brought over to Lincoln prison and staged a spectacular escape, which Patrick's family were suspected of aiding. At the time, Elsie was sure he had broken her heart, but it turned out to have been a greenstick fracture.

Young hearts, she now knew, heal fast. Arthur was another Foster's man, fifteen years older than Elsie. From farming stock, he was big, fair and ruddy-cheeked; perhaps that was why Elsie said yes, because he was as different from Patrick as she could imagine.

Arthur was her refuge and her strength at a bad time. In the influenza epidemic that scoured the villages at the end of the war, she lost two of her siblings, almost before she knew they were poorly. And one of the two, to her especial grief, was Susie.

There was only Molly to be Elsie's bridesmaid, at the Methodist church in Lincoln where Arthur wanted to be married. But she brought some Kettlethorpe flowers for Elsie to carry, and Cook and Eliza came too.

*

It was time to start paying proper attention, Elsie told herself: the funeral had started, and she could hear, if not see, that Sir Weston was reading the lesson. She wished Arthur was there with her, but of course Kettlethorpe meant nothing to him, and he was very busy. He'd become one of Foster's most senior engineers, and they'd bought a fine house, not all that far from Sir William and Lady Tritton's.

The labourers in the vineyard, Sir Weston was reading: very suitable for Mrs A, Elsie thought. But her mind kept drifting away.

She'd kept in touch with Foster's, with Arthur there, and followed the careers of the big Whitehall names once so familiar to her. The Chairman of the Landships Committee, Mr d'Eyncourt – Mr *Tennyson* d'Eyncourt, Mr Stevenson had reminded her, when he paid a visit to Eastcliffe Road – had also been knighted. No – Mr Stevenson had corrected her again – Sir Tennyson was made a *baronet*, as well as a big man in naval construction.

But the tank's godfather, Mr Churchill, hadn't fared so well. Up and down in government, and now out of it altogether. He was a Conservative again, which Elsie didn't like: she'd got the vote, at last, and regularly voted Liberal. Most people thought Churchill was daft, going on about another war. But Elsie still had a soft spot for him. Mind you, he was an old man now, in his sixties; his day was over. Mrs Amcotts had been a Tory, of course: Elsie wondered what she'd have thought of him, these days.

Elsie had gone back to the Hall to see Molly quite often after the war, and the mistress of the house seemed to like to hear her news. As Elsie grew up, she came to realise that this was how Mrs Amcotts staved off loneliness and ageing: by being interested in everything. "Old bitch, always poking her nose in," Elsie's father had grumbled, but Elsie, who had reason to be grateful for that, took a kindlier view.

She admired the way Mrs A always kept busy, and put on a brave show, even towards the end. Why, only two years ago, she'd hosted a huge rally of her beloved Women's Institute in the Hall gardens. Molly, awed, had told Elsie that 1,500 people came, and Mrs A invited all WI members to pick a bunch of flowers to take home.

But Elsie could see that the garden was not what it had been before the war, and she knew that the family had started to sell off bits of the estate. They didn't seem to know what to do with the Hall; the contents were now to be sold, but not the house. Sad to see it unwanted and unloved, after all Mrs Amcotts had done there.

And unlike most people, Mrs A had got more open-minded with age, not less. Elsie remembered talking to her about the vote, after the franchise was extended in 1918. For all she'd thought little of the suffragettes, Mrs Amcotts had been incensed that the new law still made a difference between men and women, who had to be at least thirty to vote. "As if gels didn't grow up quicker than boys. And have more sense." It had taken another ten years for Parliament to agree with her. But meanwhile, she had become the area's first woman Justice of the Peace.

The Rector was speaking now, but he wasn't really doing Mrs A justice. There'd been more to her than Lady of the Manor; maybe that was the Rector's problem. He was new, Mr Holme, and perhaps he'd had to learn who was really in charge of the parish, even when she was in her seventies.

The church was very much hers. Not that she'd thought much of getting women in general more involved; when the Bishop of Lincoln had shared his novel ideas with her, she'd told him briskly that women had much too much to do already. But the organ and lych-gate were hers, given in memory of the Major. Even the pulpit the Rector was preaching from had been installed by Mrs A. It was seventeenth-century: she had an eye for such things.

She'd found it in France, Eliza had told Elsie, smothered in white paint. They popped it in the river for her, and a week later it was back to its natural oak. And it seemed that Mrs A's influence extended even beyond death: electric light was to be installed in the church, the Rector was telling the congregation, by her friends, in her memory. He was, he told them, most grateful.

He finished his address, with obvious relief, and they were all rustling to their feet and clearing their throats. For *Jerusalem*, of course, for this green and pleasant land, followed briskly by a blessing. And then in the full, thankful voice with which congregations always sing the last hymn at a funeral, they vowed to thee, my country:

> *... all earthly things above,*
> *Secure and whole and perfect, the service of my love.*

The love that asks no question, the love that stands the test,
That lays upon the altar the dearest and the best…

Well, Mrs A had had to lay two dear sons on the altar of war, and had been lucky, for both had come back. With honours, too: Sir Weston with a Military Cross, young Jack a Lieutenant-Commander.

And dearer, of course, to Elsie, her brother Jim had come back whole too, with a Distinguished Service Medal and a sergeant's stripes on his sleeve. He'd been better off in the desert than the trenches, though he and Cal had had to give up their precious horses and learn to use the maxim gun. In one of his very few letters from the front, Jim wrote to say they'd buried their saddles and spurs in the sands. After the war (and a pint or two), he'd talk about how he'd like to go back and collect them. "And the horses, if we could find them."

Elsie glanced up at the marble war memorial plaque again, at the list of those who had not come back – too long a list, headed by young Major Wells-Cole. All the boys who, daunted or undaunted, had made "the final sacrifice" lauded in the hymn.

But now the congregation was on to its second verse. It took them into "another country," with its countless army, and its unseen King. A country of faithful hearts and righteous ways, whose:

… ways are ways of gentleness,
And all her paths are peace.

For how long more would there be a peace path for this country to follow? The clouds had broken while they were in the church, and they came out into a thin sunshine. The family clustered round the coffin, carried to the spot where they had buried the Major nearly forty years ago, looking southwards towards the Hall. Dear God, Elsie prayed, not a second world war, please. Anything rather than that, anything. But Arthur said men didn't build weapons not to use them, and those Nazis were building a lot. Good tanks, by all accounts.

Churchill was right, Arthur argued, to Elsie's distress: we needed to do the same. Because next time, it would be a war of machines, not trenches; a war of movement, not men holed up in tunnels of mud. Tanks on the ground, and more important still, Arthur insisted – "Mark my words, Elsie" – warplanes in the air. Hundreds of them. Fighters. And still more, bombers.

Which meant, he told her, that this time, war wouldn't be a far-off affair. Bombers would bring it here. To their factories and homes. To Lincolnshire.

1936–40

*L*ittle Willie survives, but Big Willie was cut up for scrap in the Second World War. A Mark IV – Foster's most successful version of the tank – is tucked away in the Museum of Lincolnshire Life. And on the centenary of the battle of Cambrai, a memorial to all those involved in building the tanks at Foster's was installed on the roundabout at the end of Lincoln's Tritton Road. In metal cut-outs, the inventor, the engineers, the munitionettes, are crawling all over the familiar rhomboid shape again.

But few of those stuck in the traffic jams on Tritton Road could tell you why that highway is so named. William Tritton, Walter Wilson and William Rigby received support from the Admiralty and encouragement from Winston Churchill as First Lord. But it was their drive and determination that created the "Mesopotamian water-carrier" which changed land-based warfare for ever.

They did not make a fortune from the tank, and Sir William Tritton did indeed share out his reward. Moreover, even before the "Landship" proved itself in war, it had earned its living as a fundraiser, trundling around the country to help flog war bonds. Lincoln itself raised an astonishing £150,000 from one successful outing.

At Kettlethorpe, Mrs Amcotts, her family and servants were also real people, who have their place in village memory. So were

Mr Stevenson and his niece, who did indeed work at Kettlethorpe School. But Elsie and her family, Patrick and Arthur, Miss Twisterton and Messrs Tuxford and Broughton sprang from my imagination, to illustrate the social changes that went hand in hand with both the technical advances and human suffering of the First World War.

Elsie was right to fear for Kettlethorpe's future: the contents of the Hall were sold after Mrs Amcotts' death. Most of the land went to auction in 1942, and, after various rentals, the house itself was sold in 1961. But before that would come the Second World War, when Elsie and the many who had thought like her would discover that Winston Churchill's days were not over. On September 3rd 1939, the Admiralty sent two signals to the Royal Navy. "Commence hostilities against Germany" was followed by "Winston's back".

Only a few years after Mrs Amcotts' quiet funeral, the county's great open skies were throbbing with engines. Lincolnshire became bomber county. More than half the country's entire complement of bomber airfields criss-crossed its flat fields, sending over 50,000 to die in their mission of destruction.

The farmland has gradually healed, the runways are broken up with grass and willowherb, but the scars of war are still visible to this day.

HOMECOMING

KETTLETHORPE: 1940–44

"Kettlethorpe? Never heard of it." The plump, thirty-something British subaltern plonked his beer glass on the bar, spilling quite a bit of it. "Damn," he said mildly, mopping it with a torn khaki handkerchief. "Why d'you want to know?"

"My folks always said they came from there, way back. Sounded quite a place." Jo smiled, disarmingly. He had a big man's mildness, and he'd been in England long enough not to take offence at the suspicion of strangers, stoked up by wartime paranoia.

"Where do your 'folks' live now?"

"Baltimore – Maryland," Jo added, knowing Britishers had rarely heard of any US cities beyond Washington, Chicago and New York.

"My mother came from Tennessee," the subaltern said, surprisingly. He had a puckish face, with slightly pointed ears, short tufts of hair like a naughty baby, and his grin suddenly made him look a lot younger. "She tried to teach me the Rebel yell. You haven't chosen a very good time for sightseeing."

The RAF officer who'd brought Jo interrupted. "At ease, old chap. He's not sightseeing – far from it. Mr Carroll wants to join up. And we'd be glad to have him."

"Indeed." The subaltern didn't look much abashed, Jo thought, but his tone changed. "Kettleton, did you say?"

"Kettle*thorpe,* I reckon. That's what Grandma called it. Said her husband's grandfather came from there."

"Kettle*thorpe.* Mmmm. Danish then, not Saxon. Somewhere along the Humber or the Trent, most like. You ever heard of it, Mike?" The RAF officer shook his head.

"Fat lot of use you Intelligence Officers are. You'd better get back to your Welsh bogs, Mike. Well, if the Air Force can't find it, it'll have to be the bloody army. We need a map." The subaltern bounced off his stool and shot out of the bar.

Jo recognised the easy familiarity with which the British upper classes abused each other. He'd probably find his escort and the subaltern had been at school together. Or in the same playpen. He looked helplessly at Mike. "Who the heck was that guy? Isn't he kind of old to be a Lieutenant?"

"He's a lawyer, like you. And a Member of Parliament. Didn't have to join up: could have sat on his arse in Westminster. Got elected on an appeasement ticket two years ago, so when that went wrong he felt he had to fight." Mike paused, looking reproachfully at his empty beer glass. "And he's no older than I am."

Jo waved hastily at the publican.

"So now he's a Second Lieutenant, camped out at Hainton, just down the road from here. Brilliant brain, King's scholar, All Souls, so what do those fatheads at the War Office do with him? Send him up here with a platoon of lads from the East End of London, to teach them how to ride motorbikes and drive Bren Gun carriers. Well, I'm not sure who's teaching who, to be frank. If he offers you a ride on his bloody BSA, for Christ's sake don't accept. He nearly killed himself on the way up here."

The beers arrived. "He's not at all a bad chap," Mike went on, happily refuelled. "Will argue the hind leg off a donkey, and browbeat you if he can, but doesn't puff off his genius. Decent fellow, really. I've known him for ever: and he's some kind of relation of my former wife's. Ghastly woman, but that's not his fault. From what he's told me, doesn't sound like his marriage is that hot, either."

Nice of you to pass that on, Jo thought, making a mental note not to share any of his personal secrets with Mike.

"Not a lot of company for him at Hainton, except old Lord Heneage to shout at him for cutting up the lawns. His platoon is supposed to be guarding a huge chunk of the county, too – God knows how – so we sometimes meet up for a drink. I've seen him quite a few times since I came to Kirton."

Kirton Lindsey was the airfield to which Jo had come in search of his chance to join this war. Back in 1938, beginning his last year at Harvard Law School, he found his room-mate was a Jewish refugee, whose parents were still trapped in Vienna. Jakob's stories, painfully and reluctantly shared late at night, were of humiliation and terror and guilt at having escaped. They had inflamed Jo's already passionate interest in the fate of Europe. The following year, the chance of an exchange studentship at King's College London had come his way. He'd grabbed it.

Come 1940, and the year at KCL over, he found himself deeply reluctant to return to the States without having done anything more than a bit of fire-watching to help the war. His resolve to stay had hardened after May, when Winston Churchill became prime minister. Now, at last, he could be sure. Whatever messages to the contrary that old devil Kennedy was sending back from the London embassy, Britain was going to fight on.

Jo wrote home trying to explain, suppressing emotions he knew his father wouldn't share. His mother would have understood; she had always taken fire from his tinder. But he had lost her six years ago, under the wheels of a truck, in a pile-up on the freeway.

His stepmother was narrower in mind and spirit: her life was limited to fussing about her husband's needs and wants. This self-imposed servitude of hers, at first balm for a widower's loneliness, turned into a poison for them both. Jo's father had become increasingly demanding and pernickety, his wife less and less content with her lot.

Carroll Senior had left the family farm for the city. He yearned for academia, at least in theory. In practice, the bookstore he had acquired provided an intellectual veneer over a reasonable underlying income. He did not take easily to fatherhood: his feelings for Jo were a corrosive combination of pride and jealousy. After Jo's mother died, and Jo left for college, distance alone saved his relationship with his father from grinding itself to dust.

They had had one brief day of mutual understanding before Jo had left, a cold spring day of 1939. He drove his father out to the eastern shore, and they had walked in the wind together, until their lungs were full of chill ocean air. Then Jo found them a little place to eat away from the beaten track, a place where the owners made their own clam chowder, and not much else, and father and son could relax in the warmth of a driftwood fire.

At the table, after they'd eaten, Jo's father had dug in his pocket, and brought out a small package – a piece of muslin, wrapped around an elaborate little gold cross. "If you're going to England – which I don't agree with – you can take this with you. See what you can find out about it. Your grandad said it came from this place, Kettlethorpe it's called, that his great-grandma came from."

He turned it over in his hands. "I took it to an antiquarian, once. Said it was mighty old – up to a thousand years old, maybe. Not worth much, all the same – that's a garnet, not a ruby, in the middle. It'd be good to know where it came from. See what you can find out from those Limeys."

Jo had thanked him, and taken it, and the moment of intimacy was over. His father had slapped his hands on the table, and said they'd better get moving. Joyce would be wondering where the heck they'd gotten to. He put on that look of irritable complacency Jo loathed. "She worries about me, you know."

They drove back to Baltimore almost in silence.

Jo hadn't decided what to do until he heard of plans for the formation of an American squadron in the RAF. This must be it. He'd gotten his pilot's licence back in the States, while he was in college. So he got himself an introduction to Charles Sweeny, the glossy American businessman who was helping to bankroll Eagle Squadron. When Jo learnt it was already fully subscribed, he wheedled an invitation to meet some of the RAF personnel involved – and found himself on a succession of slow wartime trains up to Kirton Lindsey.

The Station Commander had had a call from the War Office. "The first Yankee squadron's coming your way soon: the PM's keen for it to happen. Good for morale. There's Yankee money behind it, too. But we want a second, if we can, though we won't have the planes till next year. So the game is to keep them warm, tell them it's any minute, just got to clear it with the powers-that-be. Get someone to do that with this chap, will you? He looks useful. You've got Mike up there, haven't you? Just the man for the job."

The Station Commander had groaned. But he made space in his diary to see Jo Carroll – briefly. Then he had handed Jo over to Sir Michael Duff-Assheton-Smith, who combined the duties of Intelligence Officer, social secretary and PR director.

Ready to expend his aristocratic charm on a brash know-it-all cowboy, come to save the enfeebled old country, Mike had found himself charmed in turn by this soft-spoken lawyer, ready and willing for a war his government had declared to be none of their business. Faced with Jo's disappointment that he couldn't start tomorrow, Mike had decided to be franker than his superiors would like.

"Right now you're better out of it, old sport, we've few decent planes. Poor bloody Poles are having to put up with Defiants. Personally, I like to be able to fire forward rather than squirt it out the back like a skunk. But we're getting a lot quicker at knocking Spitfires and Hurricanes together, and meanwhile I'm sorry to say we're losing pilots faster than we can train them. This summer's been rough."

He had lent forward, earnestly. "So a chap like you, who actually knows how to fly something, that's awfully good news. And two squadrons of you: well, that would give the American press hounds something to write home about, what? Take my word for it, they'll form the second Eagle Squadron chop-chop, but it won't be operational for few months. My bet is, early next year. Stick with us. We bloody well need you."

He had jammed his cap on at a jaunty angle and jingled his car keys. "Come on. All quiet on the western front. I feel like going for a spin. There's a damn good pub in Tealby." To Jo's astonishment he'd been shepherded out to a gleaming Rolls-Royce.

*

The pub counter was now covered with dog-eared maps, proudly produced by the subaltern. He was leaning over them, stabbing with a stubby finger. "AA book's no use – too small-scale. Ordnance Survey should do it. I've got walking maps for some bits of the county, anyway. Let's see if we're in luck."

Jo discreetly moved the beer mugs out of range. The subaltern was shuffling maps around, muttering with irritation where he found the edges didn't quite meet. "Why are places you want to find always on the join? Right. Here's where we are now. And here's the Humber – even the RAF ought to be able to spot that."

He looked up at Jo, grinning again. "I learnt to map-read in the Corps. 'Bout the only useful thing I did learn. We were still forming fours when I was in College." He ran his finger along to the mouth of the Trent. "Let's start from here. Scunthorpe – Messingham – Blyton – Gainsborough. Back close to the river again. Torksey – Fenton – Laughterton – Newton. Now we're into Nottinghamshire. You're sure it was Lincolnshire? Danelaw was pretty big. It could be in Yorkshire?"

"Lincolnshire for sure," Jo insisted, with more confidence than he felt. It was only a family story, after all. But the map-reader was no longing listening. "Hang on – I've found it! Well, I've found *one* Kettlethorpe, anyway. Just on the Nottinghamshire border. In a cleft between the Trent and the old Fossdyke. Nearly missed it, it's so small." With his finger on the map, he looked up again, beaming with triumph.

It did say Kettlethorpe, Jo saw, in tiny lettering, with only the smallest of roads leading to it, a dead end between Fenton and Laughterton.

"There's a church," he was instructed. "No pub. A village hall. And see that little thingummy? That means a historic monument of some kind."

Jo looked doubtfully. "I recollect they told me it was a big place. Quite a district. And surely it would have got bigger since the old days?"

Mike laughed. "That's the Yankee in you talking. Lots of villages here got smaller, as people moved to the cities. My Welsh bogs are practically empty these days. No one to talk to but sheep."

He glanced at the map. "It probably is the place you're looking for, and it's not far, but I'm afraid I can't take you. I have to get back to the station. Maybe you can go and take a dekko next time you're up here."

The subaltern was still studying the map, but his head was cocked, listening to Mike. "I'm going down south this afternoon. Three days' leave, praise be. It's not much out of my way. I can drop you off, if you like. My bike's outside."

Jo caught Mike's eye, and opened his mouth to give a polite refusal. Instead he found himself saying: "That's mighty kind of you. I'd appreciate it."

They headed west, on a twisty wood-lined road until the Wolds flattened out and opened up, giving a view down into the Midlands plain. They turned left, on to the road that ran Roman-straight south to Lincoln. The Cathedral rose up before them. When they checked at a road junction, Jo dug the Englishman in the back, and pointed.

The subaltern swung round, nearly toppling the BSA. "Never seen the Minster before? I was going to cut through Scampton, but we'll go via Lincoln instead. Just as quick, I expect. Not much traffic." He jerked forward again, and Jo had to grab his pillion seat in a hurry.

They dropped into the top of the city, leaving the castle behind them as they turned through the arch into the Cathedral Close. The Englishman braked slap in front of the Minster's glorious west front. "I'm not a great admirer of Ruskin," he observed, "but he was right about Lincoln. Quite the best of our cathedrals."

"Of course," he went on, swinging the bike round again, "you've got its greatest treasure." He glanced at Jo, pleased to see he was mystified.

"And you a lawyer! Magna Carta, of course. The Cathedral owns the best of the four originals from bad King John. The Dean lent it to you, or should I say to the Library of Congress, last year. Damn awful timing – they now reckon it's too dangerous to try to send it back. I suspect the PM wants it to stay there, whatever the Dean thinks – hopes it will niggle Uncle Sam's conscience."

The bike hurtled down Steep Hill, scattering pedestrians. Jo began to regret not taking Mike's advice. Under the Stonebow, down again, and right, they emerged at – or very nearly in – Brayford Pool, where the Witham and Fossdyke met, and swans drifted sleepily along the rotting dockside. Then they turned right again, on to a road that took them along the dyke towards the Trent. Twenty minutes later, after a false turn near Drinsey Nook, they were entering a small, straggling village.

"This can't be right," Jo protested, as the lane narrowed to barely more than a track. "There's nothing here."

His companion, wise in the way of English villages, puttered on through the puddles and potholes. "Wait till we see the church. It'll be there, if it's anywhere."

As the road petered out, they found the church on their left, an open green in front, and beyond it, an old stone archway. It was attached to low brick walls, in turn connected to a steep-roofed barn, with a cottage alongside. The walls were punctuated by three gateways. And beyond them? A building, yes, but definitely not a stately home: an unpretentious brick house, which even Jo could see was probably less than a hundred years old.

It wasn't much to look at. A bit lopsided, with the roof to the left of the porch higher than to the right. Even the windows weren't symmetrical, with two of the four to the left of the porch bricked in. And it didn't look in very good repair – to the right of the house, a small yard was surrounded by tumbled-down brick sheds.

The Englishman looked at Jo. "Not what you expected? Sorry about that. These family legends. Always blow things up a bit. Disappointing for you. Never mind, I'll drop you off at Newark."

But what Jo felt wasn't disappointment. It was elation, feeding a powerful hunger. This wasn't a mausoleum, an anachronism, a husk of former grandeur. It was a house that had adapted to the times. The adaptation might have been a struggle, the results clumsy, but the essence of the house had survived. It was somewhere you could live. Even, he thought, with mounting excitement, somewhere he could live.

He wasn't in any doubt that it was the right place. As he began to take in the details, he saw that the stone above the porch bore the Amcotts' coat of arms, with its chirpy squirrel perched on top, and its motto – *Loyaul en Service.* His grandmother had shown it to him, on a page torn from some old reference journal, saying somehow – she wasn't quite sure how – his grandfather was related to the Amcotts. She loved that kind of thing.

The walls, as he looked more closely, weren't uniformly nineteenth-century: parts were built of the thin, softer-coloured bricks that he knew signified an earlier date. And the archway – when did that date from? There was a gargoyle sticking out, somewhat randomly, from one side, which must surely be medieval.

The house was quiet. In his pocket Jo had his letter from Mike, with his impressive long signature on official RAF paper. It might serve as an introduction, just give him a chance to look round, maybe find out who owned it. Might they want to sell it, after the war? Surely a lawyer could earn his living in one of the cities nearby. His imagination went racing ahead to a family running across the grass. He checked it, hastily. There was no way he could live here. But he had to try, at least, to see it properly.

"No: it's fine," he said. "I'd kind of like to look round, now I'm here. Do you think I could just pull the bell, and ask? Back home we're all keen on ancestors, they'd understand, but I don't know…"

The Englishman snorted. "Ancestors! We've got too many of the damn things. Don't expect southern hospitality over here. But look, I'll have a go for you. No skin off my arse. Can't be worse than canvassing." He tugged hard at the iron bell pull, and they heard a distant jangle.

A woman in her forties came, impeccably dressed in the uniform of the Women's Royal Voluntary Service. The lady of the house, Jo guessed, back from her war work, but the subaltern seemed to know better.

"Good afternoon. Is the master of the house at home?"

Before she could reply, a man in his fifties, with ruffled grey hair and a dirty old tweed jacket, trundled a wheelbarrow into view. An elderly spaniel grumbled along beside him. Jo guessed he was the gardener, but again his companion knew otherwise.

"Ah. I see he is. Good afternoon, Sir."

The man stopped, and frowned.

"Don't I know you? Have you appeared before me? I don't see any barristers at home, you should know that, young man."

The object of his displeasure wasn't at all put out. "No, Judge. I don't think I've had that pleasure. You are under a misapprehension. I'm merely here to make, er, a small contribution to the Special Relationship."

The man looked even crosser, but the subaltern ploughed on regardless. "My dear Sir, I'm not asking for your money! It's simply that my American friend here has a great desire to take a look at your house. His family used to live here, I believe. He's come over to join up. Perhaps, in the circumstances, you'd be good enough to let him have a quick walk around."

Jo found his voice. "The Lieutenant..." (He's a serving officer, you old devil, not a favour-seeking advocate!) "... the Lieutenant, he's been mighty kind, Your Honour." (Was that what they called a judge over here?) "I asked him where Kettlethorpe was, and he gave me a ride here. But if it's not convenient..."

"Heel," the judge said, snappishly. Jo jumped. The spaniel, which had been snaking forward on its belly, checked, but didn't stop growling. "Well. You look harmless, whatever Flossie thinks. Damn bitch. I'll put her in the kennel before she has your trousers." He looped a lead round the dog's neck.

"Take yourself round the garden. You can take your time, but you'll find there's not much to see. And if the Loo-tenant – subaltern, are ye? Bit old for that, what! – if he hasn't any business here, he can be on his way."

He gave Jo's companion another puzzled look, and stomped off, admonishing his dog. The off-duty parlourmaid had hurried back into the house, leaving his two visitors to themselves.

Jo blew out his cheeks. "Gee, I'm sorry you had to put up with that. I'm mighty grateful – I'll take a quick look around, and find my own way on."

"I told you, I'm used to canvassing. Didn't get a piss pot thrown at me, which makes a nice change. His bark's probably worse than his bite. Just a bit of 'judgitis'. They all get a touch pernickety, particularly if they don't make the High Court bench."

He was strapping up his helmet, ready to go, and not at all abashed. "It's not far to Torksey, and you should get a train there. If they're running."

They shook hands, formal strangers again on parting, after the fellowship of the past hour.

"Thank you again. I sure appreciate your kindness," Jo said. "Guess I've made you late."

"Not a bit of it. Good luck. Hope you get into your squadron."

Jo watched him putter off again past the church, a slightly comic but endearing figure. He suddenly realised he'd never learnt his good angel's name. Perhaps he thought Mike had already given it, or that Jo ought to know who he was, anyway. These folk are so strange, Jo thought. Then he turned eagerly back to the house.

The subaltern found the way back to the main road without difficulty. Funny chap, he thought: didn't look the sentimental type. Wonderfully courteous. Hope that blasted judge isn't rude to him. Damned good of him to come over and fight. We need a lot more like him. Don't think we'll win without.

He turned up the throttle, and headed for Oxford.

*

The first Eagle Squadron was formed of American volunteers in September 1940, 71 Squadron. It became operational the following year, and arrived at Kirton Lindsey in March. When it moved to Suffolk, in May, the second bunch of American volunteers took its place.

121 Squadron included Pilot Officer J.W. Carroll, fresh from Operational Training, and Mike was attached to nanny it along. Its Hurricanes were to be replaced with the promised Spitfires in November, and it, too, was then scheduled to be moved south. Jo went to see his Squadron Leader, Peter Kennard.

"Sir. I want to transfer to a bomber squadron."

He looked sourly at Jo. "You bloody well won't be any safer there."

Jo didn't take offence. If he told Kennard that, simply, he didn't want to leave Lincolnshire, he'd get a flat refusal. Superstition was rife among pilots, as among all fighting men. But if it amounted to anything more than the little rituals of preparation they all employed, it had to be stamped on.

"I guess I know that, Sir. But I think I'd make a better bomber pilot. I can fly a twin-engined plane, I'm a good navigator, but aerobatics aren't my strength."

Kennard sighed. "OK. You're a bloody nuisance. But I'll see what I can do. Dismissed."

"Sir."

Jo joined 103 Squadron, at Elsham Wolds, north-east of Kirton Lindsey. It was the month after Pearl Harbor, and his country's final declaration of war – a moment of intense relief. His father stopped writing him resentful, baffled letters about foreign wars, and the desertion of his only son, "the last of his line". Now, instead, his father was pressing him to switch to the USAAF. Jo ignored him.

Soon the Eagle Squadrons were moved wholesale to US command. And US fighter and transport squadrons began to be posted to Lincolnshire. But having just joined it, Jo stayed put in 103 Squadron.

He flew in Wellingtons, then for a brief – and extremely frightening – period, a Halifax. Then, after a break, in July 1942 Flying Officer Carroll flew his first Lancaster, the plane that would take the Squadron through the rest of the war.

The Lancaster was a big beast, with a big payload. A noisy beast: to stand by the runway, as a squadron prepared for take-off, was to subject oneself to a level of sound that amounted to a physical assault.

On the runway, the pilot sat three times a man's height from the ground, in a glasshouse above and behind the nose, with his second pilot or engineer beside him, the bomb aimer forward below, the rest of the crew – usually seven in all – in the fuselage or gun turrets behind.

In the case of the rear gunner, far behind, lonely, trapped and freezing: but it was he who kept them alive, not so much by his sharp-shooting as by his sharper warnings over the intercom: the noise inside the plane, suffered for ten hours at a time, was punishing, too. Even on the ground, the persistent noise of bomber squadrons passing overhead was the most vivid recollection of many who passed the war in Lincolnshire.

Jo had learnt soon enough that, contrary to what he had supposed, piloting a bomber didn't excuse you from aerobatics. The Lancaster was four-engined and strong, capable of flying at 20,000 feet and at over 200 miles an hour, life-saving attributes that earned it aircrews' affection. Its upper surfaces were painted earth colours, its belly black, to blend it with land and night sky when searched for by an enemy, from above or below. It was still under-gunned, and acutely vulnerable.

Some pilots flew dead level, high or low, others made constant changes of height and angle; but all, when the rear gunner spotted an enemy fighter, knew that their only hope lay in flinging the plane violently out of its sights.

Banking, falling a thousand feet, testing the plane to its limits and the pilot's own physical strength beyond endurance, pulling the monster up again, soaring as far as you had fallen, listening to the rear gunner and ignoring everything else, the screaming engines, spewing aircrew, agonies of men or machine. That was how a bomber crew survived.

The same when ground searchlights managed to "cone" you, bringing several at once into a single focus on one plane, outlining it perfectly for the gunners below. That, they all knew, was akin to a death sentence: only with the most extreme gyrations could they hope to escape. And with extreme luck.

Jo soon began to feel he was living on borrowed time. A tour was, usually, thirty sorties, but your chances of lasting the full tour were slim. Over half the aircrew would die, perhaps another fifth would be sick, or wounded, or have to bail out over enemy territory, leaving only one in four to complete the tour.

"Write your will," they told the "sprogs" – new, painfully young, aircrew – when they arrived. "You won't be here in six weeks." The brutal attrition numbed them all to the deaths of others, even friends. When familiar faces disappeared, survivors saw them as merely a step ahead on their common journey, to be joined soon enough.

But Jo, somehow, did not join the queue. He had to bail out once, after holding the plane level long enough for even the rear gunner to struggle out and grab his parachute. They all landed safely between Caistor and Market Rasen with nothing worse than a few sprained ankles, new members of the "Caterpillar Club", whose jokey little badges, supplied by the manufacturers of their silk parachutes, showed they'd been put to successful use. Another time his navigator was hit by flak, and died in agony before they could land, for all the rest of the crew could do with the morphia they now carried.

Some did not die, but could not go on. His flight engineer broke down, in the autumn, was demoted and humiliated, marked LMF for "Lack of Moral Fibre" and assigned to ground duties at a lower rank – a routine cruelty which sprang from the RAF's constant fear that bomber aircrews might resile from the terrible risks they were asked to take. He was a severe loss to the aircrew. But Jo himself struggled on.

Elsham village was bleak, up there close to the Humber. "Nothing between you and Siberia," they told the newcomers, as the north-east wind cut across the airfield. But they were fed better than anyone else in this tightly rationed country, to keep them fit to fly.

The equipment and techniques were becoming more sophisticated, with the introduction of better radio-navigation aids, and Pathfinders – special crews who marked targets with flares to improve bombing accuracy. But still the losses mounted. 103 Squadron flew more sorties than any other in 1 Group, which covered North Lincolnshire and East Yorkshire. In all, Elsham Wolds was to send over 1,000 young men to their deaths between 1941 and 1945, and the losses in 103 Squadron were the highest.

Almost the greatest strain, Jo found, was the constant crossing and recrossing of the bourn between peaceful rural life on the ground and living death in the air. Aircrews had different ways of coping, tame or wild: they tended to cling together, and by and large the local pubs were tolerant of young men so close to death, but sometimes strain spilt over into violence. Some piled into cars illicitly tanked up with aviation fuel and headed for city excitement;

others headed home, with unpredictable results – they were all like smouldering fuses, easily lit.

Jo's way of coping was to immerse himself in what he had come to see as his homeland. When better weather came, and his tour ended, he spent all his leave exploring the county, from the Humber to the Wash, beaten-up Grimsby to lush Stamford. Most of its great houses were boarded up or requisitioned, but its churches were open and busy.

He climbed into the roof of the Cathedral, gazed at Louth's spire and Boston's Stump; got to know, and love, Stow Minster, the oversized, pre-Conquest forerunner to Lincoln Cathedral. He sat by candlelight in little Coates, by the Trent in Knaith Church, found his way even into the little Saxon chapel at Aubourn. He had been brought up a Catholic, and heard Mass a few times with the Poles in Lincoln; but in the 1940s, the distinctions in Christianity that had convulsed past centuries seemed pointless to Jo.

He gulped down draughts of the county's history, learnt of the battles there that had changed the course of England's story – the defeat of King Stephen, the repulsion of French rule, the local skirmishes that had turned Oliver Cromwell into a military leader. And, whenever he could think of an excuse, he visited Kettlethorpe.

The Judge had unbent after Jo had wandered round the garden, and the parlourmaid, still in her WRVS uniform, had produced tea. Jo had confessed to being a lawyer himself, in Maryland, and his host had expanded happily on the English County Courts. When Jo had come back to Lincolnshire, he had tentatively written to tell the Judge, and was invited back.

His name was Harold Langman, and Jo soon learnt that he came from Devon, was lonely, far from stupid, and had a fundamental kindliness he tried hard to disguise. He knew about war, too: eventually Jo extracted from him the information that, although already in his thirties – "another elderly subaltern," he said, dismissively – Langman had fought his way right through the 1914–18 war.

"Your compatriots saved us then," he told Jo. "And they will again. But it'll take longer. Hitler's a tougher nut than the Kaiser. And we've not even got a foothold on the continent, this time."

He understood how hard Jo found normality. "When I came home from the trenches on leave, m'mother wanted to trail me round her sewing circle. Her wounded hero, drinking endless cups of tea. Couldn't stand it. It sounds crazy, but I was glad to go back to the front."

He pushed the port round to Jo. "You can stay here, any time you like. No one will fuss at you, I can promise you that."

Jo accepted with pleasure. He learnt everything he could about the house, and much else about his adopted country, from Langman, during long evenings lingering over the best of the Judge's pre-war cellar. On the excuse of saving his host's legs, Jo would go down for the second bottle, and to poke around.

He could see where runnels had been set into the ancient brickwork to carry away the winter water that had flooded there for centuries, and where the tunnel to the church had been blocked up, who knew when. Upstairs, he made sketches of the delicate stucco in the drawing room. Outside, he looked for other traces of history, and found, around the south side of the house, the remains of stone walls, and the lintel of a wicket door, built into the younger brickwork.

To thank his host, he spent some weekends doing small jobs around the house, and when knocking out some brickwork to re-lay it, found a clay pipe lodged within. Any time in the past three centuries, it could have been lost there, according to the Judge: working men made their own.

But Langman was not much interested in the house: he didn't own it, Jo learnt, he was just renting it. "The family didn't need it, after old Mrs Amcotts died. But they kept the land. Two thousand acres of it. All this village, and the next one. Not worth much now, of course."

Quite soon Jo learnt just how little. In May 1942, nearly 1,200 acres of the estate came up for auction, together with the houses, shops and cottages that made up most of the villages of Laughterton, Fenton and Kettlethorpe.

He got the particulars from Messrs John D. Wood and Co., and read about woods and paddocks, desirable smallholdings, a blacksmith's shop with two forges, the schoolhouse and school (leased to the governors rent-free). The dwellings ranged from "old-fashioned" cottages to "superior" farmhouses, one of which (the only house, apart from the Hall itself, boasting a bathroom) was said to be suitable for a "gentleman farmer". He noted with astonishment that the marshland along the Trent was still owned, if not farmed, in the narrow strips of medieval agriculture.

The land was going cheap – from £4 to £20 an acre, the top price only when there were buildings on the land. But even if Jo had been able to get a mortgage – and what bank would be crazy enough to lend money to an RAF pilot, in 1942? – it was the Hall he wanted, not the estate. After the war, when the Judge retired south, Jo wanted to live there. If he should live so long.

The air war was stepping up, several notches. After his tour on 103 Squadron, Jo had been "rested" with a posting to RAF Bawtry, the headquarters of 1 Group, to liaise with the US 8th Army Air Force, which was beginning its preparations for bombing operations from bases farther south. These began in August, and by the autumn Jo felt the urge to return to flying himself. December found him back at Elsham.

Lincolnshire was carpeted with airfields by now, almost all of them under Bomber Command. Hemswell Cliff, Scampton, Waddington, Swinderby, Coleby Grange, Wellingore, Fulbeck – those were just the ones strung south of Elsham and along the Ermine Street escarpment.

Jo could only guess how many airfields there were in all. (Forty-six, in fact, were operational in Lincolnshire at the peak of war, covering some 30,000 acres of agricultural land.) From them were flying the RAF's most famous airmen, the new heroes of this new kind of war.

Most famous, perhaps, was Douglas Bader, who had captured public imagination by, so it was said, turning disability into advantage. Fighter pilots often suffered blackouts during their extreme aerobatics, when the blood drained into their legs from the rest of the body; but Bader had of course lost both legs in the early 1930s. (Jo heard of him first from the Station Commander at Kirton Lindsey, not Bader's greatest admirer since Bader had left most of his undercarriage on his runway, returning from Dunkirk.)

Then there was David Halford, who became the RAF's youngest Wing Commander, and had joined 103 Squadron much the same time as Jo. And there was 50 Squadron at Swinderby, perhaps the most famous in 5 Group, which considered itself the elite of Bomber Command.

Danger became a drug to some, making aircrews shy away from them. There were countless stories of extraordinary self-sacrifice, as pilots stayed at the controls of burning aircraft to give their crews a chance to escape. But there were also reports of wild risk-taking in pursuit of higher "scores", without concern for others' lives. Commanding officers were supposed to look out for these, and ground them, but the aircrew knew first.

Friendships came easy, but without depth. Everything came second to the grim routine. For the bomber crews at Elsham, the pattern seldom varied. In the morning, meticulous aircraft checks, which few pilots cared to leave entirely to ground crew. The briefing at 3pm, when they learnt just how dangerous that night's mission would be. That was worst for any new, young airmen; there was a blind look about them, as they turned inwards to face the imminent prospect of death.

Back to "rest" and eat, then the construction of flimsy defences against mortality. For the luckiest, there was religious faith; for others, only stranger superstitions. All of them had the little rituals which up till now had brought them back safe, so surely must be followed again: the left boot before the right, the way you tied your scarf or filled your pockets.

They all had a talisman: a photo, a charm, a lucky penny, a St Christopher medal. Jo had his cross, on a chain around his neck. He'd never found out anything more about it, but if it were a thousand years old, that must count for something.

With the evening came the dark journey across the airfield, driven by a young WAAF. They were quiet now, beyond even gallows humour, the tips of their cigarettes glowing like fireflies in the back of the truck. The tumbril, Jo thought, wondering if those headed for Madame Guillotine had been as silent.

Then careful checks: survival was a matter of obsessive attention to detail, as well as courage and skill. The long night-time journey to the target, never letting discipline slip or concentration lapse. The weary return, when one slip of attention would expose the crew to a German intruder – a night fighter waiting to ambush aircraft preparing to land – or to the final irony of being shot down by your own anti-aircraft batteries.

In a foggy dawn, tired crews struggled to find their airfield; for Elsham, they usually used the Humber as a route marker, but sometimes, particularly if they had engine trouble, they would turn inland at the Wash, before turning north over dry land. It was then that Lincoln Cathedral, that unmistakable landmark on an unremarkable plain, earned the pilots' blessing. Restrictions had had to be imposed on flying over the building itself, for fear of collisions.

Even now there was danger. Drift below 14,000 feet, to get a better view, and to the batteries you were the enemy: no questions asked. German batteries at Essen, British on the Humber – it was a toss-up which were more of a threat to the bombers limping home.

Landing was always charged with fear as well as relief, as damage often went undetected until then. Finally, at the debrief, came the bloody reckoning of questionable success and unquestionable loss. Then, at last, came release, relaxation, eventually sleep.

Fire haunted their dreams more than death. Death they expected. But fire, dear God, not fire. They had all seen the flames

– or worse, heard the screams. Survival was not always to be wished for. Fit young men could survive an appalling degree of incineration, but the suffering was immense and the outcome not pretty. The medics did their best – plastic surgery came on in leaps and bounds – but membership of the Guinea Pig Club was not to be wished for.

Jo kept going, leaving for sortie after sortie in charge of a Lancaster with bombs in its belly, and man and machine both coming back empty. They went very heavily loaded in 1 Group, to which some attributed their greater losses.

After the destruction of Coventry, some station commanders had tried to whip up a desire for vengeance, to maintain aircrews' zeal. But in the bombing zone, there was no bloodlust among them – only fear of what the ground could throw back at them, a prayer that they'd come close enough to target to lay their eggs, take the required photographs, and head for home. Jo knew that he'd been numbed and brutalised by war, become indifferent to deaths, including his own. Nothing to be done about that, now.

*

In the spring of 1943, close to the end of his second tour, and struggling to suppress hope of completing it, Jo was sent for by the station commander. He was recommending Jo for transfer. Showing yet again why the aircrews at Elsham Wolds loved him, Hugh Constantine was generous but honest.

"A new squadron. Just down the road, at Scampton. Cochrane's asked all of 5 Group for their best, though I'll bet lots of stations are ignoring that. He's asked me too, as a personal favour, given our experience at Elsham. No question that you're our best, but you're coming to the end of this tour, and in all conscience I'd have to ground you this time, so if you want to go I can offer you without much loss to us. Can't tell you what the mission is – very secret. Don't know myself."

Jo felt sure it was the *Tirpitz*, and his heart sank. Tucked into a Norwegian fjord, a constant threat to the convoys, it was a death-wish target. "Guy Gibson is to be in command," the Station Commander went on. "Bit of a maverick. Huge courage. I've told Scampton that it must be your choice; and if you go, they must let us have you back. What do you say?"

What Jo didn't say was that it was easy enough for Scampton to agree to that: the chances of him surviving, led by Gibson on a suicide mission, were paper-thin.

"Of course, Sir. When do I leave?"

Scampton: already Bomber Command's most renowned station, even more than Swinderby, from where many of Gibson's aircrew were coming. Two VCs had already been won by aircrew operating from Scampton. But when he arrived, Jo found that Constantine had been right: the call for heroes had been treated by many other stations as an opportunity to offload their duds, who were furiously rejected by Gibson.

Entering his office, Jo found the twenty-four-year-old Wing Commander shouting down the phone. "And what's more, you can take back those bloody WAAFs you sent me, right now. Two of them are in the club. It's a squadron I'm trying to give birth to here, damn it."

He glared at Jo, and snatched the papers the new arrival held out, but a quick read seemed to appease him. Jo's record clearly passed muster. A black Labrador looked up from the rug by Gibson's desk, yawned, and thumped his tail. The Wing Commander grinned. "You'll do. And you've got a twin here – another Yankee who joined early in the war. Tell him I'm putting you in his flight."

Joe McCarthy wasn't his twin in any way except nationality and height – the physical attribute to which Gibson was most sensitive, given his own small stature (the story went that his short legs had originally led to his rejection by the RAF). McCarthy was from Brooklyn, but not a typical New Yorker, either – big, muscular, blond, before the war he'd earned his living as a lifeguard on Coney Island.

"Done much at low altitude?" Jo shook his head. "OK. That's what you'll be doing here. Flying low. And I mean real low. We started at 150 feet, now we fly as low as 50. Hedge-hopping. It needs teamwork. Try not to hit a church, there's a hell of a lot of them round here, as you know."

For the next fortnight, Jo flew a Lancaster lower and lower over the English countryside, dropping off the "cliff" on which Scampton was perched, skimming the crop-fields, scattering flocks of sheep and herds of cattle, hedge-hopping his way across country. He followed McCarthy up to the Lake District, learning to fly low over the water and pull up in time not to pile into the surrounding hills.

He used the excuse of training to fly low over Kettlethorpe on the way home, making out the line of the old moat and lifting the plane just in time to avoid clipping the top of the *Wellingtonia* by the gatehouse. But in truth, any hopes of a future life, at Kettlethorpe or anywhere, had faded: he did not know what 617's mission was, but there was a terror about it, in the voices of those planning it, beyond anything he had yet experienced.

Security was tight; and, Jo came to realise, not just because without it they might fail but because surprise was their only thin chance of survival. Anyone who breached it, however slightly or inadvertently, felt the violence of Gibson's anger.

Their Lancasters were adapted to fit the unknown mission, with cumbersome bomb-racks slung below, and lights on the undercarriage that solved the problem of estimating height at night, their focus converging when the plane was exactly 60 feet above the surface. Gradually the pilots discovered a little more about what they would be asked to do, and trained with their bizarre new weapon, but not till the day itself did they learn the targets.

The briefing room was thick with tobacco smoke and the sharp, sweet smell of fear. Jo gazed at the models of the three Ruhr dams into which their bombs were intended to "bounce", and felt a ridiculous sense of relief. He heard another man mutter his own thoughts out loud: "At least it isn't the *Tirpitz*."

Two of the twenty-one crews, including Jo's, were being cannibalised to fill gaps in the other nineteen. McCarthy was to fly one of five planes whose mission was to bomb the Sorpe dam, down in the hills south of Gibson's primary target, the Moehne. With no crew of his own, Jo persuaded his compatriot to take him along as a "second Dickie"; useful if McCarthy was hit.

When they left the briefing room, Jo went to see Flight-Sergeant Powell, the disciplinary NCO who was everyone's problem-solver. One of his ground crew was in trouble: he'd got into a nasty brawl in the pub, leaving a local lad with a cracked skull. Jo'd promised to try to talk Powell into leniency, and superstition told him he couldn't leave this until after the raid.

Powell was non-committal, but his expression wasn't encouraging. Jo tried again, but Powell checked him. "Leave it with me – Sir. You've done what you promised. It's not your problem, now."

A mound lay under sacking behind the door, and Jo nearly tripped over it on his way out. "Gibson's dog, Sir. Run over, would you believe it? This morning of all mornings. Bugger didn't even stop."

They nearly didn't take off at all. The hydraulics in McCarthy's Lancaster were found to be leaking, so they transferred to the spare plane. Jo found it was missing the little card giving the compass deviations, without which they had no hope of finding their way along the narrow "safe" route plotted to their destination. Just when McCarthy had decided, with insane courage, to go without it, to Jo's everlasting relief Flight Sergeant Powell rushed it to the truck.

They took off twenty minutes behind the rest of their formation, but by the time they reached the Sorpe dam theirs was the only one of the five bombers directed that way still in action. There was no flak, but a church spire on the run-in, and hills immediately beyond the release point. McCarthy made no fewer than nine attempts before he was satisfied. To the crew's desperate relief, he dropped the bomb on the tenth run. It exploded by the dam wall, and the crest crumbled. A couple of the reserve aircraft followed up, but they did not hang around to see the result. Limping home, they learnt that, for all their suicidal bravery, this part of the raid was only a partial success.

Back at Scampton, Jo learnt the reckoning. It had taken immense expenditure of courage and lives. To achieve the destruction of the Moehne dam, Gibson had not only made the first run himself, but had flown distraction runs, with his lights on, to draw the flak from others until their bombs burst the dam. At midnight, just when Gibson was over the Moehne, Powell had buried his beloved Labrador.

His VC was well-earned, along with the gallantry awards to thirty-two others, including McCarthy. Only eleven of the nineteen Lancasters involved got home.

No other single Bomber Command operation had as dramatic an impact as Operation Chastise. Films, music, hero-worship – all followed for the "Dambusters". At a time when even the biggest bombing raid seemed to have disappointingly little impact on the enemy's capabilities, the images of flooded valleys spoke triumphantly of destruction, in Germany's industrial heartland.

It wasn't till some months later that they learnt how quickly the damage from even this raid had been repaired, and how few of the lives destroyed by the torrents of water flooding the land below the dams were actually their enemies'. Russian PoWs made up most of the victims, together with forced labour from the occupied countries, brought there to feed the German industrial machine.

But meanwhile it was a huge morale boost back in Britain. 617 Squadron became world-famous. Gibson, still more so. He was soon travelling to North America in Winston Churchill's company, with a circuit of press conferences and celebrity appearances ahead of him, enough to destroy the equilibrium of any hero. The squadron was handed over to Wing-Commander George Holden, a safer pair of hands; even so, Jo requested a transfer back to Elsham Wolds.

Constantine looked at him, for a long time. "I gather Gibson's been grounded. Best thing to do with heroes. Danger to themselves. And others." He handed Jo a form. "I don't think you're one of those, but I'm grounding you, too. Take some leave: that's an order."

*

On leave, most of his fellow officers now headed for London, to see if its febrile wartime gaiety could break into their nightmares. But Jo needed a different therapy. It may have been his farming ancestry, but he hungered for physical work, open fields. Jo spent his time lending a hand at one local farm or other, open air an antidote to the claustrophobia of the cockpit.

Pulled back to a corner of the Trent by the magnet of Kettlethorpe, he found himself haymaking alongside prisoners of war housed at Drinsey Nook – Italians, mostly. He felt no hatred even for the Germans among them – like the Russian PoWs drowned below the Ruhr dams, indeed like Jo himself, they were simply cogs in the machine of war. Pity, even hate, was a waste of energy he could not afford, just as he could never afford to be paralysed by fear.

It was then, when the ice in his veins was slowly beginning to thaw, that he found the girl. There'd been plenty of girls, through the past three years, generous to the airmen who counted their life expectancy in hours. But this one was different.

She was part of his nightmare world, working in Ops at 5 Group HQ. She'd been on duty the night of the Dambusters raid, and told him of the triumph and despair with which they'd tracked the bombers' course. And then, with a giggle, she told him of the mortification suffered by her best friend, who was working on the switchboard that night. Told to contact Sir Charles Portal at the White House, she'd got straight on to the Grantham pub of that name, demanding the landlord. Who was, not surprisingly, bemused.

Jo met the girl not with the RAF, but at a Young Farmers' Club dance, after a gaggle of "land girls" at Fenton had wheedled him into using his last trickle of stolen fuel to take them. He was staying at Kettlethorpe again, and the Judge urged him to go.

"Take you out of yourself," he said gruffly. "Easy company."

She was with a lad who, she told Jo later, had been her brother's best friend. She came from a family that farmed north-west of Grantham, and her name was Becky Storer. She wasn't beautiful, but she had dark gold hair, bright blue eyes, an open, friendly face, and the dry humour he'd come to associate with Lincolnshire.

The land girls, good-humouredly, found someone else to take them back to their billet; her brother's friend equally good-naturedly conceded defeat. Life was like that, in wartime: too short to waste disputing love.

Becky had left school only months before, he learnt, having done her Highers, and told her crotchety Scots headmistress at the Kesteven and Grantham Girls' School that no, even so, she didn't want to go to Nottingham University. She wanted to join the WAAF. Her brother had died in the skies over the Channel, on only his second sortie in a Spitfire, caught in his first dogfight. Something in her, she told Jo later, made her want to do as much for the war as anyone would let her, to take over where her brother had left off.

Miss Gillies was having a bad year with insubordinate sixth-formers. Becky told her parents that the headmistress's other chosen candidate for Nottingham had also said no. She was determined to get to Oxford. Becky's father said Margaret was an uppity so-and-so, like her father the Alderman, but Becky's mother said – give the girl a chance. If she were a lad, you wouldn't try to put him down just because he tried to do the best for himself.

Becky's parents would both have preferred it if their daughter had gone nowhere – stayed home, helping with the farm. God knew they needed help. But neither of them tried to hold her back. When she came home on leave from the WAAFs, she mucked in, and slipped back into her old friendships. It was in her old world, not her new, that she and Jo met. That gave them reality, and even – hope.

For a month they spent every minute allowed to them by God and the Air Force – in 1943, was there any difference? – together. They talked about everything in the past and present; nothing in the future. He met her parents once. It was harvest time, and everyone was too busy to do more than shake hands, swallow a pint and a pie, and get back into the fields. That was a good way to meet people, he thought – no questions, no uncomfortable silences, just doing what you could to help with the job in hand.

They had little enough time to be alone together, but made the most of what they had. He hesitated, not out of uncertainty, but from fear she might think he took it all too lightly, that she might not understand how serious he was. If they did not talk of the future, it was growing in his mind.

When they finally made love, it was as natural and life-affirming as the sunlight. They found a hedge-sheltered corner of a thirty-acre field, shorn of its wheat but with a comfortable pile of straw where the baler had given up. And they spent the afternoon as timeless generations of young had done before them. She pulled off her flimsy summer dress, tousling her neatly rolled hair; he had only his shirt for her to lie on, and took her gently but with passion.

He was half-expecting the note he received next day. She'd been posted. She had told him with her body, if not with words. In her note she said no more than that she'd write properly, as soon as she could. When, after two unutterably bleak months, he had still heard nothing, he wrote, hesitantly, to her parents. It was a non-committal letter, just saying he'd be glad to hear she was well.

The reply came quickly, blotting out the sun. Her plane had dropped into the Mediterranean, before she even got to her posting. There was no room for hope: the pilot alongside had seen it plummet, nose first, and no one had bailed out.

It took Jo painful hours to compose a letter back to the Storers. They were suffering so much already. Two children dead, and for neither loss had they been permitted the healing rituals of mourning

– the comforting words of the funeral service, the grave by which flowers could be laid and prayers said.

They did not need the extra burden of his grief. Recently, at the funeral of a fellow pilot, whose girlfriend had sobbed uncontrollably throughout, he had heard the pilot's agonised mother suddenly and shockingly cry out: "You'll find someone else. But no one can replace my son."

So in the end he wrote a letter full of Becky's love for her parents, not for him: of what she'd said about them, how grateful she'd been for the life, love and care they had given her. He added only enough about himself for them to know that he too had cared. He did not expect them to write again, and was a little comforted when they did.

But he did not see them again.

*

Bomber Command was focused on German cities again, "dehousing" them with increasing intensity. Only with Judge Langman, on leave at Kettlethorpe, did he allow himself to surface questions about what aircrew were being asked to do.

It had been a good meal, by wartime standards: a boiling fowl, only a little overdue for the pot. But the port was better. Langman took up his glass, raising it to the light.

He spoke slowly and evenly, as if making allowance for a court stenographer.

"Well, now. I am not, myself, an admirer of those clerics who think wars can be prosecuted without suffering, or rather with suffering only by the guilty. I have more respect for appeasers who know that war is indiscriminate, and therefore do everything to avoid it – even if, on this occasion, they were in the wrong."

He took a judicious sip.

"I have also frequently wondered about the morality of those wars of the past, demanded by civilians happy to leave the killing

313

and dying to others. Cheering them when they marched to war, abandoning them afterwards. Good Queen Bess left her sailors to rot on the dockside. She wasn't the first, or the last."

The Judge's voice had sharpened. "Our Brave Boys. In the last war, civilians who slept safe in their own beds gave white feathers to young men slow to offer themselves up for slaughter. Have you read Kipling? *It's Tommy this, an' Tommy that, and 'Chuck 'im out, the brute!' But it's 'Saviour of 'is country' when the guns begin to shoot.*"

He took a bigger gulp of his port, and wiped his mouth angrily with a frayed napkin. "You can say this for total war: no one this time can count on being in the audience, rather the play. Do you know the Bishop of Norwich?"

Jo blinked, then remembered, and hastily gave the decanter a push. At their first dinner together, this hint had been explained by the Judge. Whether you replied that you did or didn't know the Bishop, the next remark would be that he was a wonderful fellow, but never passed the port.

It was January, and they were dining well after dark, in the little panelled tower room. Candle flames lit the oak table, like flares marking a bomber's target. Jo's eyes blurred. A voice spoke from somewhere inside his head.

"But then, there are the children." Had he even said it aloud?

Langman filled his glass, and passed the decanter on to Jo again like a benediction. Or a painkiller?

"Oh yes. There are the children."

A pause. An eternity. Then he spoke again, steadily and softly.

"There is no safety for children in this kind of war, and never will be again. Children died in Coventry and Southampton, and in London. Children are used and abused by Herr Hitler. Taught propaganda. Trained up as cannon fodder. They say the Hitler Youth is being called up, now. Boys of fifteen! And all those newsreels of children playing in the Jewish Labour Camps. Pray God I'm wrong, but I don't think we'll find it's that idyllic."

Jo said: "Yes. I know about all that. But what are we doing in this nightmare?"

Langman took a deep breath. "You came in 1940, didn't you? Then you know what a lonely, threatened country this was. We'd been chased out of France and Norway, we were losing at sea and struggling to hold off invasion. Isn't that why you joined up? Became a bomber pilot?"

Jo nodded, and Langman smiled, gently. "I won't insult you by asking if you believed in 'precision' bombing."

"Hell, no: if we came within three miles, that was bull's eye."

"Then there was Coventry. And we started bombing German civilians by intention, rather than by mistake."

Jo nodded again.

Langman leant forward. "Remember how it was. We desperately needed to take the war to the enemy. For a long time, bombing Germany was the only way we could do that. And at night, you couldn't find small targets like arms factories, so you were ordered to bomb whole towns. Payback for Coventry – all right, that took us off the moral high ground, but – it's what kept up morale here, for sure."

"And now?"

"Jo, I don't know if what's happening now is breaking morale in Germany or not. Bomber Harris clearly thinks it is, and will make the ground war easier. Saving Allied lives. Maybe he's right, maybe he's wrong. The historians will tell us, when they have the luxury of hindsight. But if I've got an issue with Harris right now, it's whether this is good use of brave young lives like yours."

Jo raised his hand, silently arresting the suggestion. The Judge nodded, and paused to snuff out a spluttering candle end. When he spoke again, it was with more deliberation in his voice than Jo had ever heard.

"Oh yes, my boy, I know. You mustn't talk about your station. But no one can live in this county without gaining some notion of what's happening to you chaps. Terrible losses. And you came, when your country didn't, and you've stayed, and done the job for us, whether it's clean or dirty. When you're up there, in your bomber, you're as close to death as anyone on the ground below you. And I, for one, am grateful to you."

*

Jo was sent south to instruct at one of the Operational Training Units. It was supposed to be a respite from night bombing, though the combination of old planes and new pilots led to frequent casualties. Through the OTU's transient population, rumours of an imminent land assault across the Channel spread like forest fire.

Before returning to Elsham, Jo had been to London, to collect his DFC. In a big, chilly, damaged building, he received his medal from a thin, upright, careworn man in naval uniform. He seemed the embodiment not so much of royalty as of the national stoicism of Jo's readopted homeland.

Jo took the opportunity to meet some old friends in the US forces, preparing for the landings. These meetings were not a success. The shock they tried to hide, when he turned up at bar or restaurant, made him, for the first time in three years, study himself properly in the mirror. A big man still, but hunched and gaunt, with deep grooves etched darkly below sunken eyes. His thick black hair was flecked with grey.

At twenty-eight, Jo had begun to wonder if he still had the resilience to recover, and lead a normal life when this was over. He could not re-enter normality now, at any rate, even on leave. An old, always rather foolish, schoolfriend felt obliged to talk about Jo's father, how he was ageing, and complaining his son never wrote, but Jo could feel nothing more than a mild irritation.

He was glad to go back north again.

Flicking idly through the paper on the train journey, cold and delayed, he spotted a face he knew. It was a wedding photograph of his old acquaintance with the motorbike. So one unhappy marriage had been brought to an end, and was hopefully being replaced by something better.

It was a curiously touching picture of a wartime wedding. The eager, pretty girl, in a plain dress and suitably frivolous hat, who didn't look as if she could make anyone unhappy. Her unglamorous spouse, in pinstriped double-breasted suit and Homburg hat – both a bit too tight – whose round face was split into the schoolboy grin by which Jo had recognised him.

Jo felt a surprised relief that he could still feel pleasure at others' happiness. And, not that it mattered, he finally learnt the Englishman's name.

When he came back to Elsham, only the ground crew were familiar. The aircrew were, yet again, almost all new. They had had a new Station Commander, too, in his absence, Jo was told: he had been involved in the early stages of planning the forthcoming invasion, but they still got no pukka gen. And only weeks after his arrival, he had been shot down flying co-pilot, Jo was told, but survived to be taken prisoner, to the War Office's intense alarm.

D-Day came, at last, and the Allies grabbed their finger-hold on the continent. But many of the old friends Jo had seen in London died on Omaha beach, leaving Jo full of complicated regrets.

Hopes of a quick end to the war were soon dashed, and the bombers' tasks were changing. One of three flight commanders, Squadron Leader Carroll and his crew were now regularly flying south, trying to help the Allies break out of Normandy and force the tenacious Germans back to the Rhine.

The USAAF was again demanding that Jo transferred. They needed war-hardened veterans, they said, to help run their stations. He thought they were getting a poor deal: the husk of a pilot. But this time he felt he had to agree. He owed that much to those friends dead in Normandy. Four of Lincolnshire's airfields now had American bases, and Jo was to go to Barkston Heath, as a Major in the USAAF 61st.

On his last day at Elsham Wolds, his commanding officer came to find him, packing in his room.

"Sorry to ask this, Jo, but would you do one last sortie with us? We're two crews down, and now Jim's gone sick. George Brown needs someone experienced alongside him, it's a new plane – flying fine, but still some glitches. Would you ride shotgun, as a favour? It's Fontenay-le-Marmion – tricky to pinpoint, but there shouldn't be any interference. Piece of cake, really."

They took off just after 9pm, on a fine summer evening, in the brand-new Lancaster that had only been at Elsham a week and still smelt strongly of paint. As the CO had promised, they met no enemy aircraft. But the target was obscured by fog and smoke, and they were ordered home, still loaded, as the dawn rose on the 8th of August.

Over the French coast, the port outer engine failed without warning. The navigator saw the results first: the engine was on fire. They had to shut it down, but even though the fire went out, the propeller refused to feather and and the plane became harder to manage. Even so, they got very close to home before the engine again burst into flames and this time it could not be extinguished. The plane plunged. "You get the others out, Sir," George Brown shouted.

Jo shook his head, furiously. It needed both of them to control the plane. He bellowed to the rest: "Get ready to jump, all of you, NOW." The flight engineer disregarded him, and came forward to help.

They managed to level out. Five members of the crew scrambled out of the back. The plane was very low, and the wing in flames. It was time for the rest of them to leave, now.

But there was no time.

The Lancaster ploughed into the marshy ground between Kettlethorpe and the Trent, the bombs still in its belly causing a massive explosion.

The five who had jumped all landed safely, just north of the Fossdyke. One of them had a second narrow escape, finding himself hanging by his parachute straps from the roof of a barn, above a bull pen. Its occupant did not look welcoming.

RCAF Flying Officer Brown's body was blown clear; he was buried with honour in the military cemetery at Harrogate. The engineer, RCAF Flight Sergeant Corless, was consumed in the explosion: but he is listed with gratitude on the memorial to Commonwealth dead at Runnymede.

And who knows where RAF Squadron Leader Carroll, DFC, lies, with his lucky gold cross?

Perhaps he was never there.

1944–2018

When one of the last surviving bomber pilots died in 2017, he left a million pounds to Lincoln Cathedral, in gratitude for the relief he had felt when the sight of its familiar outline told him he was safely home. And the following year, finally, the courage of the bomber aircrews was properly commemorated in the county.

On Canwick Hill, where the ground rises again south of Lincoln, a solitary spike, or obelisk, has been erected (www.internationalbcc.co.uk). English Heritage, in its wisdom, decreed that it should not stand higher than the nave of Lincoln Cathedral. So it is "only" the height of a Lancaster's wingspan – 31 metres. But it can be seen from miles around.

The names of the 57,861 who died serving in Bomber Command are engraved on the granite blocks around the spire. In contrast to past practice, this roll of honour includes ground casualties, women as well as men, including the poor young Wrens who were on parade at Fulbeck airfield when a damaged aircraft crashed into them.

The Avro-Lancaster was the most successful of the bombers created in this period of astonishing advance in aircraft design. But "success" is relative. Some 7,377 Lancasters were built, and their pilots flew 156,000 sorties. But over 4,254 were lost, mostly taking their aircrew with them.

A scattering of newly planted trees marks out, as if on a map, the locations of the airfields spread across the county. The Visitors' Centre displays, in rightly challenging conjunction to the celebration of heroism, images of the terrible effect of the bombing on German cities. But wherever blame may lie for that, it is not with the crews who showed courage beyond question, doing what they were asked to do, to prosecute the war.

The names show how far and wide the net of sacrifice was cast. The dead come from all over the world. There are refugees from occupied Europe among the dead – many Poles, in particular – and casualties from amongst a particularly brave group of German Jews, who flew on "Special Duties", using their native language to confuse the enemy over the airwaves. They flew under false, Gentile names, but were still terribly at risk if they had to bail out.

There were many aircrew from the Commonwealth, and I have used this story to tell the tale of the two Eagle Squadrons – those American heroes who joined the war ahead of the rest of their countrymen. A few stayed in the RAF even after the US entered the war: one such was on the Dambusters' raid, so I have allowed my fictitious Jo Carroll to shadow him.

Kettlethorpe was ahead of the county in its commemorations. Its own memorial, a modest Lancaster propeller blade on a stone cairn, was erected in 1994, just where the road to Kettlethorpe leaves Laughterton.

It stands in memory of the men who died in the two Stirling and Lancaster crashes that took place in the parish in 1944. I hope their souls will forgive me for allowing Jo to join them. The Canadian aircrew who survived the Lancaster crash came back for the day of dedication, to tell their stories and be honoured by the people for whom they had risked their lives.

They found much in the villages changed in fifty years. The estate long gone, the Hall had finally been sold by Mrs Amcotts' son in 1961. The baker, the butcher, the forge, grocer, carpenter and greengrocer were all gone from Fenton by the 1990s, but mains water, electricity, TV and phone lines had come. And since then, (doubtful) broadband and (patchy) mobile coverage have come as well, and new houses have been built in both Fenton and Laughterton.

Kettlethorpe school is gone, and finally Laughterton post office. But Newton still boasts both, and there Colin and Jill Kyme will find almost anything you could ask for in their cornucopia of a shop.

A bus still rattles through the villages, finding its way eventually, by some minor miracle, to either Gainsborough or Lincoln. And Kettlethorpe church survives; indeed, in the past twenty years, the parish has repaired the tower, the clock, the organ and the central heating, put in some proper plumbing, redecorated the interior and soon its bells will be pealing again.

Hard work for a congregation which has shrunk with time, but even here not all change is for the worse: gone are the days when the single, absent Papist in the parish had to be recorded in its returns. By 1999 the old religious prejudices had subsided to the point where the Anglican Rector, a Roman Catholic Chaplain and a Rabbi could happily collaborate to celebrate a wedding. And in the new millennium, gay couples have been able to enjoy the church's blessings – and, like every other pair wedded here, have their photos taken before Katherine's arch.

In that final story, there were only two wholly fictitious characters: Jo himself, and his girlfriend, Becky Storer, along with their families. (There is a wonderful farming family called Storer over near Allington, and I could not resist adding Becky to their pedigree.) All the other actors in my final play have at least roots in reality – even the eccentric motorcyclist. He had his own modest place in the footnotes to English post-war history, so I have left the puzzle of his identity to those sufficiently intrigued to unravel it.

AFTERWORD

The moon was huge. A supermoon, taking a closer look at earth. A blue moon, too: it'd be back to full again within the calendar month. The swollen disc reflected cold faery light on to the grass, illumined the stone remains of the gatehouse, and silhouetted the *Wellingtonia* that loomed over Charles Hall's brick garden walls.

Well over a century ago, when the craze for the *Sequoiadendron giganteum* from the Sierra Nevada was gripping the owners of British manors and rectories, one sapling had found its way to Kettlethorpe, and flourished. It was the temper tree, I'd told my children, and again my grandchildren: when you're cross, go punch it. You won't hurt the tree, it won't hurt you.

Perhaps one tree, however miraculous, couldn't quite make up for the loss of the famous avenue that had led from farm to house. Saved from Sir William Ingilby-Amcotts' axe, it had finally fallen victim to Dutch elm disease. But all the same, the *Wellingtonia* is a prize: a sentinel at the gate of history, a statement of the past's belief in the future.

Gazing at its dark outline against the night sky, I could hear the laden Lancasters, almost brushing past it, eastwards on their long weary journey to target. And into my imagination drifted older trees, cut down to enclose the hunting park that Katherine Swynford was permitted by Richard II. A little ghost passed through the dark shadow from a still older, wilder wood, light catching the golden cross in the hollow of her throat.

We started planting soon after we came to Kettlethorpe. Native trees first: five hundred "whips" to begin with, then bigger saplings, new sentinels for the future.

That was what places like Kettlethorpe did to you, or for you. They made you live for times you would not see. Trees are reminders that we are tenants of our home on earth, at most its guardians – never truly its owners. Which is a comfort, not a regret.

The moon clouded over again. Calling to the dogs, I went through the old gatehouse arch, and picked up a small pebble. The moonlight coated it in white gold. I went into the old house.

And slept.

Kettlethorpe, 2018

BIBLIOGRAPHY

Asbridge, Thomas: *The Greatest Knight*, HarperCollins UK

Bennett, Nicholas: *Lincolnshire's Great Exhibition – Treasures, Saints and Heroes*, Scala Arts

Brickhill, Patrick: *The Dam Busters*, Pan Books

Brooks, Richard: *The Knight Who Saved England*, Osprey

Carpenter, David: *The Struggle for Mastery, The Penguin History of Britain, 1066–1284*, Penguin Books

Cole, R.E.G. *The Manor and Rectory of Kettlethorpe, in the Parts of Lindsey, in the County of Lincoln*, Volume 36, Lincolnshire Archaeological Society and *The Royal Burgh of Torksey, its Churches, Monasteries and Castle*, The Architectural and Archaeological Society of the County of Lincoln

Cormack, Patrick: *English Cathedrals*, Artus Books

Cotter, Patrick: *Lincolnshire Airfields in the Second World War*, Countryside Books

de Lisle, Leanda: *White King*, Chatto and Windus

Foyle, Jonathan: *Lincoln Cathedral, The Biography of a Great Building*, Scala Arts and Heritage Publishing

Fraser, Antonia: *Cromwell: Our Chief of Men*, Orion Publishing Co.

Gurnham, Richard: *A History of Lincoln*, Phillimore & Co, The History Press

Hastings, Max: *Bomber Command*, Michael Joseph

Hill, Francis: *Medieval Lincoln*, Cambridge University Press

Hunt, Tristram: *The English Civil War at First Hand*, Penguin Books

Jenkins, Simon: *England's Cathedrals*, Little, Brown

Lucraft, Jeanette *Katherine Swynford, The History of a Medieval Mistress*, The History Press

Mackman, J.S.: *Lincolnshire Gentry and the Wars of the Roses*, etheses. whiterose.ac.uk

Moorhouse, Geoffrey: *The Pilgrimage of Grace*, Weidenfeld and Nicolson

Mortimer, Ian: *The Time Traveller's Guide to Medieval England, The Fears of Henry IV, The Time Traveller's Guide to Restoration England*, Vintage Books

Purkiss, Diane: *The English Civil War, A People's History*, Harper Perennial

Pullen, Richard: *The Landships of Lincoln*, Tucann Books

Rex, Peter: *1066, A New History of the Norman Conquest*, Amberley Books

Roberts, David L, *Lincolnshire Houses*, Shaun Tyas

Seton, Anya: *Katherine*, Hodder Paperbacks

Thurley, Simon: *The Building of England*, HarperCollins UK

Trentside Memories, Tucann Books

Uglow, Jenny: *In These Times, Living in Britain through Napoleon's Wars*, Faber & Faber

Vickery, Amanda: *Behind Closed Doors: At Home in Georgian England*, Yale University Press

Wedgwood, C.V.: *The King's War*, Folio Society

Weir, Alison: *Katherine Swynford, The Story of John of Gaunt and his Scandalous Duchess*, Jonathan Cape